CPSIA information can be obtained
at www.ICGtesting.com
Printed in the USA
BVOW03s1929220617
487620BV00001B/1/P

Dinosaur Lake III

Infestation

(Sequel to Dinosaur Lake & Dinosaur Lake II)

By Kathryn Meyer Griffith

*For my family, as always,
with all my love...*

Other books by Kathryn Meyer Griffith:

Evil Stalks the Night
The Heart of the Rose
Blood Forged
Vampire Blood
The Last Vampire (2012 Epic EBook Awards Finalist)
Witches
The Calling
Scraps of Paper (1st Spookie Town Murder Mystery)
All Things Slip Away (2nd Spookie Town Murder Mystery)
Ghosts Beneath Us (3rd Spookie Town Murder Mystery)
Egyptian Heart
Winter's Journey
The Ice Bridge
Don't Look Back, Agnes
A Time of Demons and Angels
The Woman in Crimson
Four Spooky Short Stories
Human No Longer
Night Carnival
Forever and Always
Dinosaur Lake (2014 Epic EBook Awards Finalist)
Dinosaur Lake II: Dinosaurs Arising
Dinosaur Lake III: Infestation
Dinosaur Lake IV: Dinosaur Wars ~ Coming 2017

Dinosaur Lake III: Infestation

Text copyright © 2015 by Kathryn Meyer Griffith
All rights reserved.
Printed in the United States of America.
Dinosaur Lake III:
Infestation

by Kathryn Meyer Griffith
(a thriller/horror novel)

Cover art by: Dawné Dominique
Copyright 2015 Kathryn Meyer Griffith
All rights reserved. No part of this book may be reproduced, scanned or distributed in any form, including digital and electronic or mechanical, including photocopying, recording, or by any information storage and retrieval system, without the prior written consent of the author, except for brief quotes for use in reviews.

This book is a work of fiction. Characters, names, places and incidents either are the product of the author's imagination or are used fictitiously, and any resemblance to any actual persons, living or dead, events, or locales is entirely coincidental.

* This book is not meant to be based on scientific facts of any kind…it is purely a fictional made up story about make-believe dinosaurs.

Chapter 1
Henry

"So Chief Ranger...have you seen any of those flying dinosaurs lately?" The person asking the question, hand shading his eyes from the blindingly bright August sun, was a healthy looking man perhaps in his mid-forties, dressed in one of those expensive sporty shirts and matching walking shorts. A pricey camera hung around his neck. His glance was astute and the glint in his eyes inquisitive. He had that air of self-assurance and wealth about him. Except the guy should have been wearing a hat and a pair of shades because his skin was already the hue of a ripe cherry.

Chief Park Ranger Henry Shore had turned away from studying the wall of dinosaur fossils, the amazing discovery he and his son-in-law paleontologist, Dr. Justin Maltin, had stumbled upon almost six years ago. The activity at the paleontological dig had slowed a great deal since those first days, most of the fossils had been unearthed and shipped to eager museums all over the country, but there was still a scientist or two hacking away at some part of the area most days. Not today. The site was abandoned. Silent.

"Not lately," Henry replied, feeling a sinking in his stomach. It'd only been a few months since he and his men had freed the park from the latest prehistoric threats, the winged monsters he'd satirically labeled gargoyles, and he was still a bit uneasy. His eyes on the skies more than normal. "How did you hear about that?"

The man snickered. "My aunt and uncle were here in May. You know, when you cleared everyone out of the park? But, they are getting up in years, so I don't always believe every whimsical tale they tell me of their travels. They like to embellish a lot. You know how old people can be? Always trying to get attention."

Great. A non-believer, Henry thought. *This should be easy.*

"We did have a problem here in the park back then, but we handled it. The park's safe now, if you're worried."

"No, I'm not worried." Another snicker. Man, was the guy's face sunburned. He'd feel it tonight for sure. "Flying dinosaurs don't frighten me. No matter what I read or see on the Internet. The stories, by the way, and the photos were sure scary. So real looking they were almost credible. Isn't Photoshop great? But I don't believe in monsters."

Henry wanted to deck the guy, but smiled instead. He had to be nice to the visitors. It was his job, after all. And after the tumultuous spring he'd had it was just nice to go back to normal. Visitors bugging him.

"This, on the other hand," the man waved at the wall of fossils, "is a wonderful discovery. Actually monumental. This is real. I've been reading about the specimens the scientists have been removing from this place for years. The paleontologists have dug out some quite unique remains of species never recognized or seen before. Especially in the lower levels of the rock.

"Absolutely astonishing."

Henry nodded. Yeah, he thought, the lower levels had proved to contain the most bizarre fossils of all. Except he wanted to tell the man, unfortunately, he'd seen some of them in the flesh and hadn't thought they were that amazing...when they were trying to maul or devour him, his rangers or his friends.

"It is." Henry's eyes beneath the brim of his park ranger cap returned to the wall. He and Justin were both proud of what had come out of the fossil site they'd stumbled on. Though he would have liked to tell the disbeliever with the expensive camera they were prouder of the way they'd dealt with the live creatures that had off and on haunted the park in the last half decade; prouder still of the real flesh-covered specimens they'd tracked down, captured and had been able to study and learn from or the lives they'd saved by killing them. But he knew it'd do no good to say any of that to the man in front of him. The man would think it was all a publicity grabbing joke.

"Well, thank you, Chief Ranger, for the informal chat about this place and all the interesting tidbits about the park. It was very informative."

"You're more than welcome." He hadn't meant to entertain the small crowd of six people he'd found at the fossil wall with a park lecture, but old habits died hard. He'd always enjoyed speaking on the park's history. Once the visitors hanging around had started asking him questions, he couldn't stop.

"I'm Doctor Richard Clements." The gentleman held out his hand for Henry to shake. "My family's been here visiting the last few days and we've really enjoyed the accommodations at the lodge, which is so rustic; the lake and the view. We love this place."

"Thank you. So do I." Henry finally smiled. "How long are you here for?"

"We leave tomorrow, but first thing in the morning we're taking one last boat ride to Wizard Island. We're going to spend a few hours exploring it."

"You and your family will enjoy that. Be sure to take snacks and water. Jackets, because sometimes the weather can change on a dime. You'll be there for a couple hours before the second boat picks you up."

"Thanks for the tips. We'll do that.

"Nice meeting you Chief Ranger. I'm sure I'll see you again. We only live about three hundred miles away in southern Oregon and my family has already begged me to bring them back here next summer."

"I hope you do that." Another ranger smile.

"Goodbye for now."

"Good bye."

Henry watched the man wander away with the rest of the crowd. His eyes went to the sky, then returned to the wall of dirt. He tried not to think about what had happened in May. Flying monsters attacking park trolleys and stalking visitors. A huge nest of the critters they had had to obliterate. Nightmares he didn't like returning to or dwelling on during the summer days. It was hard. It was still too fresh.

He was turning away, ready to hike down to ranger headquarters when a short, muscular fellow in blue work pants and a gray T-shirt appeared at his side.

"Hi Henry. You got a minute?" The man, someone Henry recognized as one of the tour boat captains, took off a dirty blue ball cap and wiped the sweat off his forehead with the back of his arm. His face was tanned a light brown and his longish gray hair was a halo of frizz around his head. He looked more like a mad professor than a boat captain.

"Captain Willie Sander. As I live and breathe." Henry shook the man's hand and his face broke into a welcoming grin. "I haven't seen you for a while. Where you been hiding yourself?" Willie and Henry went way back. Willie had been working at Crater Lake when Henry had accepted his chief ranger's job thirteen years past and he'd been the last one to see and hear from Sam Cutler, another boat captain who'd been one of the earliest fatalities of the first park dinosaur. Godzilla, as Henry had dubbed the original monster at the beginning of its terror reign, had smashed up Cutler's boat in Crater Lake and gobbled up the man.

"Not hiding, just been kind of busy puttering my boat all around the lake for the visitors. Got to make a living, you know?"

"Don't we all.

"So did we just happen to meet this fine morning by accident or were you looking for me?"

"I was looking for you. I spoke to Ranger Stanton down at your headquarters and she said you were up here gawking at the dead bones. I heard your lecture, too. I was lurking behind those bushes there eavesdropping. Ha, even learned a few things I'd forgotten."

Willie fell in stride beside Henry as he walked along the trail.

"Well, what's wrong?" Henry queried. "I assume there is or you wouldn't be off your precious boat in the middle of the morning on a working week day bothering me." He glanced at his wristwatch. "You should be casting off for your eleven o'clock trip in about ten minutes."

Willie came to a dead stop and looked directly at him. "There's something in the lake again. Like six years ago? I saw them this morning right after dawn. Near Wizard Island. They were swimming around, pretty as you please. Moving faster than sharks and *much* bigger."

Oh no, echoed in Henry's head. Not again. It'd only been three months since the last prehistoric assault. Was he and his park cursed or what? "Them?"

"Yep. I counted at least five of the beasties scooting right below the water line. I couldn't see them too clearly because they were moving lickety-split but they were...big...all right. Startled the bejesus out of me. I got off the lake as quick as I could. And, after our last couple of run-ins with monsters in this park, my boat and I won't be going on the lake again until I know those things are gone and it's safe. I haven't forgotten my poor friend Sam. I don't want that to happen to me."

"Did the creatures threaten or attack you in any way?"

Willie seemed to think about that for a moment. Scratching the side of his head, he replaced his ball cap, shoving it down over his wild hair. "Nah, can't say they did. Might have been a different story if they had; I wouldn't be here chatting with you. Most likely I'd be fish food. They swam alongside my boat for a bit, though, like they were playing with or were curious about me, but they never rammed me or nothing."

"And you can't describe them any better than 'they was big and they was fast'?"

"Sorry. They pretty much stayed below the surface. I only saw swells and scaly green skin breaking the water. Jagged fins. Whatever was below the waterline, though, had to be huge by the way the ripples seemed to go on forever. The fins were different sizes, too. All in all, the strangest thing I ever experienced. And frightening."

Oh, Henry knew well enough how scary being on the lake in a boat was when there were unidentified giant creatures swimming around you. Been there, done that.

"What are you going to do about this?" Willie demanded, planting his feet firmly on the sloped ground, his mouth a taut thin line. His eyes were an old man's eyes. They'd seen too much. His body, bent from arthritis and age, an old man's body. But it took a lot to scare the old guy and he was scared. If the situation kept him off the water and making a living, it was bad.

"I'll look into it. Don't worry, Willie, we'll take care of it." So those eerie animal calls he'd heard months ago in the rear fringes of his yard could have been those primeval leviathans. For Henry had no doubt that's what was plaguing his lake, his park, again. No, still. As he and Justin had feared, they'd never left. He, his rangers and Captain Sherman McDowell's soldiers hadn't killed all of them. The live monsters and the nest they'd destroyed hadn't been all there'd been. That was the dilemma.

There were more.

The two men walked along a little farther together, discussing the present and the past, and when Willie veered off towards Cleetwood Cove and his moored boat, Henry continued on to park headquarters. His thoughts as heavy as his footsteps.

Above him brilliant feathered birds reeled in the blue sky and the breeze had the sweetest of summer flavors wafting on it. The smell of summer heat, sun and leaves. Yet all his earlier optimism and happiness had ebbed away and worry had replaced it. He'd thought they were finally in the clear. The park was safe. All the rogue dinosaurs had been taken care of. No such luck.

Shoot. Now what was he going to do? The previous battles had exhausted him. He couldn't face the thought it wasn't really over.

He was still vexing over that question when he strode into park headquarters and made his way to his office. He needed a strong cup of coffee and a few minutes to himself to think. The office was quiet. It was in between shifts and his rangers were out in the park doing their jobs or at home off-duty. Only Ranger Kiley was at his desk in the far corner on the phone yakking to someone. Kiley waved at him as he passed by and Henry motioned with his hand that Kiley needed to end his phone call and follow him into his office. Now.

With a sigh Henry settled into the chair behind his desk and a minute later Ranger Matthew Kiley strolled through the door.

"What do you need Chief?"

All Henry had to say was, "They're back."

"Good Lord, not again?" Ranger Kiley didn't sit down, but stood before Henry, as his glum expression reflected his concern. "What's happened?"

Henry told him.

"We're going to close the lake again, aren't we?" Ranger Kiley, an older man with short white hair, a stocky build, and a calming way about him, was the only ranger who'd worked in the park longer than Henry. He'd been a ranger going on twenty years. And he'd been with Henry through all the dinosaur adventures of the last six.

Henry exhaled and leaned back against his chair, rubbed his eyes with his fingers. "I don't see a way out of it. We can't take the chance these new *Loch Nessies* are hostile. Just because they didn't ram Captain Sander's boat doesn't mean they're peace loving."

"What excuse do we use this time?"

Henry groaned. It hadn't been that long since the last forced closure. The tourists and visitors always needed a reason when their park was kept from them. "We'll just say we're doing purity tests on the lake's water. We don't want any boats on it; and, of course, divers and swimmers have been prohibited for a couple of years now. That's convenient."

Ranger Kiley shook his head. Unlike Henry, he still wore his Smokey-the-Bear style of hat all summer, while the other rangers, including Henry, preferred the ball cap style when it was hot. He took it off and, placing it in his lap, sat down across from his boss. "Seriously, shouldn't we shut down the whole park as well? I mean, until we're sure the creatures aren't roaming the land and woods, being all destructive and stuff?"

"Let me think about that and I'll let you know tomorrow." Henry trusted Kiley and valued his opinion so he'd have to seriously consider what he proposed. The ranger was smart, calm in a crisis, and had been a widower for a decade. His only daughter, Gabrielle or

Gabby for short, at twenty years of age, had spread her wings five years before and moved to Chicago to follow a modeling career. But Gabby had vanished four years ago and no one, including her father, had heard from her since. Her disappearance was Kiley's greatest sorrow. It was a good thing that finally after years of looking for her, grieving, he and Ranger Ellie Stanton were now a couple. It had stabilized him. Ranger Kiley, at last, had found some peace, some happiness. Henry was happy for him.

The men spoke a little longer about the lake closing, preparations, and what they could do about locating and containing the creatures in the lake. Henry, as the times before, still couldn't believe it was happening again. Then Kiley rose from his chair and headed out to start the process.

Henry mulled over calling his paleontologist son-in-law, Dr. Justin Maltin, and letting him know the bad news, but decided to make the call that night from home. It was only five hours away. In the meantime he needed to think about what they were going to do.

Unlike the first time an unwanted *American Nessie* had appeared in their lake and they'd gone after it in a submersible, that option was no longer available. They didn't have a friend who had a friend who could loan them a Deep Rover. And renting one was too expensive and too invasive to the lake's ecosystem. Since they'd done that the park's regulations had changed drastically. No submarines or divers were allowed in the lake. Ever.

He didn't feel like looking for the things on an exposed boat, as he'd done the times before, yet knew there was really no other alternative. Someone–and of course it'd have to be him–had to find the creatures. Assess the danger. He'd ask one of his rangers and Justin to accompany him in the morning. At dawn. They'd bring binoculars and a lot of high-powered weapons. The standard operating procedure.

Damn those dinosaurs. Because, of course, that's what the lake creatures were. That's what they always were.

*****

The sun was still bright above when he called it a day and drove his jeep into the driveway in front of his and Ann's cabin. He was tired and worried over the day's disclosures so he was happy to see Ann's car in the driveway. She was home early, too. Since she'd finished her first round of chemo a month ago, facing death the way she'd had to do with the cancer, she had made a decision to spend more time at home and with him. She'd spend more time taking better care of herself. Her doctor had informed them the lung cancer appeared to be gone. Remission. For now. But Ann hadn't believed it and was gradually changing her life accordingly.

"I'm not going to wait any longer to do what I want to do. To spend time with you. To smell the roses and lilacs. Play with my sweet Sasha."

Sasha was their new kitten. "Enjoy every minute of my time here. To be happy. Work isn't the end and be all for me anymore. The news was here before me and it'll be here after I'm gone. Like the world. But I only have one life, one piece of eternity to call my own and experience. I'm not going to work all my hours away anymore. I'm going to delegate my responsibilities."

And she'd been true to her word. Since the cancer diagnosis and treatment, she'd shortened her hours at the Klamath Falls Journal, the newspaper in town she owned, and spent more time just…living. Henry liked the change. Suddenly the thought of retiring, for him, didn't sound so bad. Which was strange because for years he'd dreaded the mandatory retirement the National Park Service levied on their rangers. Now he actually looked forward to it.

When they retired, he and Ann talked about getting a mid-sized camper and traveling around the country; seeing the sights. She'd always wanted to see Maine and he wanted to visit Yellow Stone. She could keep the newspaper, but leave it in the hands of a capable manager. They'd live a simple, inexpensive life. Together.

In about five years he could take early retirement and would. No longer was he afraid of it. In fact, since Ann's illness, he craved it. The sooner the better. He just prayed God would give them the time to enjoy it together. Even though Ann's cancer was in remission, that could change and he was aware of that. It was the one thing that scared him more than dinosaurs.

Getting out of the jeep and walking up to the partially rebuilt porch, it reminded him of the flying dinosaur, one of the *gargoyles* as he'd called them, that had attacked his home a few months before; the one that had almost killed Ann. She'd escaped, but the porch hadn't. The monster had destroyed it, ripping it from the front of the house and smashing it into the middle of the yard. Henry had been spending his days off the last three months rebuilding it. The basic foundation was done and he was planning to nail together the porch overhang that weekend.

He was making the new porch better than the old one. Bigger. Longer. Fancier. He and Ann loved sitting on the porch swing in the evenings and watching the night. He had to get it done soon. They missed their porch therapy, as Ann called it. And now, he had the sneaking suspicion, they were going to need it even more.

Once inside the cabin, he smelled the cooking ham and beans right off. Cornbread. It was one of his favorite meals and Ann hadn't made it in a long time. Chemotherapy had stolen her appetite and her desire to cook, but in the last few weeks it had returned with a vengeance. Lucky for him. He was oh so tired of frozen dinners.

Stirring the pot on the low flames, Ann was smiling when he moseyed into the kitchen. As he watched her before she knew he was there, he felt the love he had for her, the years of love he'd had for her. The image of her, pale and frightened, as she sat in that chair in the clinic with all those tubes and bags of poisonous liquid flowing into her veins haunted him suddenly…then was replaced with the smiling woman he beheld before him. The doctors thought she'd beaten the cancer. It was gone. Henry was so thankful to God for making her well. Of course she'd have to have check-ups every six months from now on and indefinitely but the prognosis was hopeful. She looked so healthy, so happy now. He smiled. The earlier reports of mysterious sightings of lake creatures forgotten.

Ann looked over her shoulder and her face broke into a welcoming grin. "Henry, you're home early. Good. Supper is about ready." She paused. "Why *are* you home so early?"

He tried not keep anything from her, so he told her what Captain Sander had claimed he'd seen in the lake.

"Oh, no, not again," she grumbled, turning off the flame beneath the pot, putting the spoon down on the counter and wiping her hands off on a kitchen towel. "Are we safe here?" Her gray eyes held unease, as she shoved a strand of blond hair away from her sweaty forehead. Her memory of the monster attacking the cabin and her was apparently still vivid.

"I think so. Sander has been the only one to say he's seen anything and it was in the lake. And it wasn't aggressive, according to him. I can't panic until I know more.

"Tomorrow I'm going out on the water and see for myself,"

Ann was placing bowls and silverware on the table. She looked up.

"If Sander is telling the truth couldn't that be dangerous?"

"Could be, but I'll be careful. I promise."

She gave him a sharp look. "You better be. I remember the last lake creature you went chasing after in the dark with Justin. Night after night. I was worried sick about both of you. And you know how that ended."

"I remember, too." Inwardly he shivered, recalling the foggy nights patrolling the lake years ago. The cold. The endless searching. The terror when what they were looking for found *them.*

Then he said, "It looks like we're about to eat?"

"We are."

"I'll go clean up and be right back. Smelling that ham and beans is making me hungry."

"Go ahead, but make it quick. No dawdling. I'll finish putting everything out."

Henry laughed softly. "No, mother, I won't dawdle."

When they were sitting at the table, enjoying their meal, they ran down what their days had been like. They did that every evening. Shared their experiences as much as they could. Henry often laid a hand over his wife's and gently stroked it. Like tonight.

Outside the day merged with shadows. The

temperature fell. The frogs and crickets began to sing. A normal summer evening.

"By the way, where's the little fur ball?" Henry asked as they were eating the chocolate cake Ann had brought from the bakery. He sipped his coffee, slid back in the chair, full and happy. The meal, as everything Ann cooked, had been delicious. "I haven't seen her yet. Usually she's all over me."

"Sasha? Last I saw, she was sitting in our bedroom window staring at the birds outside and making those weird funny little throat noises."

"Bird talk." Henry laughed.

"Yeah, translated she's probably saying, *Come inside, birdies, and let me tear out all your feathers and eat you.*" Ann got up from the table and started clearing it off.

Henry rose and helped her. "Probably. Though she is a little young, still a kitten really, to be doing that yet."

"You would think."

Sasha, the black-and-white kitten Ranger Ellie Stanton had gotten from a friend for them was four months old and a bouncing ball of energy, curiosity and affection. The animal had helped Ann get through her chemo, never failing to lift her spirits. Though she was Ann's cat, the feline had imprinted on Henry and followed him everywhere when he was home. Ann didn't mind. So what if the kitten loved Henry more, she also loved Ann. And both humans had grown very fond of the cat. It'd been a long time since they'd had a pet and they were both going overboard doting on the little thing. She already had more cat toys than was normal, was given special canned cat food, and had a fluffy cat bed.

"Speaking of the devil." Ann chuckled, looking down. "Here's the queen herself."

A tiny bit of black-and-white fluff ran up to Henry, meowing plaintively as if she were trying to talk. It climbed up his pants leg and planted itself on his shoulder.

"Whoa!" Henry yelped good-naturedly. "Take it easy, cat, those claws are sharp." He grabbed the kitten in his hands and cuddled her against his chest. Purring could be heard all over the kitchen. "This cat," Henry shook his head, sitting back down so the animal could snuggle in his lap, "has the loudest purr I've ever heard. Sounds like a motor or something."

"She does have an unusually loud purr, doesn't she?" Ann agreed. "And, you know what? I swear she tries to talk to us. Her meows are so strange. It's like she's trying to mimic our speech."

Henry smiled at the creature in his lap. Cute little thing. He stood up and put it into Ann's arms. "Here, you hold the baby. Don't let her follow me. I'm heading out to the porch to check some things. I need to measure, calculate how much wood I'm going to need this weekend to finish. I want to do it before it gets dark."

"Okay, honey." Ann took the cat and settling on the couch with it next to her, she switched on a side table lamp, grabbed her Kindle and clicked it on. "I'm just going to read while you're out doing that. Got a great ghost story I want to finish."

"After I get done measuring why don't you come out, I'll grab a couple of chairs, and we'll porch sit for a bit...watch the night come in like we used to?"

"Oh, you mean before that flying gargoyle snatched the porch and the porch swing away?"

"It is a beautiful evening," he coaxed. "It's cooled off."

"You talked me into it. Just holler when you're done."

"I will."

Henry pawed through their junk drawer and found a measuring tape, a scrap of paper and a pencil and headed towards the front of the house and the unfinished porch.

The sun was low on the horizon, sitting on top of the tree line; the sky was a rainbow of sunset colors, gold, pink, white and touches of amethyst. A cool breeze rustled his hair. It was going to be a beautiful night, he thought, as he shut the door behind him. He didn't realize he hadn't closed it all the way. He walked out onto the porch and the smell of fresh lumber hit him.

A little later, he'd finished measuring and just happened to glance up to see Sasha sitting in the front window watching him. She wasn't allowed outside. There were too many perils in the park for a tiny kitten. Too many larger predators. She'd be a nice quick appetizer.

He wobbled his fingers at her and behind the glass the cat opened her mouth and began meowing frantically. Jumping up against the window, her paws flailed at the glass as if she was trying to get out. Her eyes wide. Henry couldn't hear her, but thought it odd the cat was behaving so erratically. She never acted like that.

The night had hushed. Even the wind.

He heard something near the tree line of the surrounding woods. A click-click-snarl sound. Click-click-growl. Bushes and leaves were being thrashed aside. And his skin prickled. He didn't want to look, but he couldn't help himself.

He turned around slowly and three things happened at once. He saw he'd left the front door slightly open, the cat came bounding out onto the porch heading for the edge of it, and he caught something moving out of the corner of his eyes at the end of the yard. Something that shouldn't have been there.

He reached down to snatch up the escaped kitten, but it slipped through his grasp and raced across the yard towards the mistiness lurking among the trees.

Almost without thinking, Henry dashed into the house, grabbed his .40 caliber SigSauer from his gun belt where he'd left it on the couch, and ran back out in the direction the kitten had gone. Yelling, "Stay inside, Ann! Stay inside!"

"What's wrong?" She cried behind him as he slammed the door shut and took off after the cat down the yard. He didn't have time to answer. Not if he wanted Sasha to live. The feline was going after what he'd heard, glimpsed, at the edge of the woods. Whatever it was.

Dinosaur Lake III: Infestation

The kitten had entered the trees and Henry was right behind her, gun raised and ready. "Sasha! Sasha!" he called out. "Come back here, you little runaway! It's not safe out here for you."

He plunged through the perimeter of the forest and into instant night. The woods was like that at twilight. One step beneath the canopy of limbs and leaves and it was utter darkness.

"Sasha!" He yelled again when he saw her. Crouched against a tree base, back up, hissing like a big cat at something poised above her. Swooping her up with his hand, he swung around and stared at what she'd been hissing at. A shadowy form about twenty feet away hiding behind a tree.

"Gosh darn, I should have grabbed a flashlight, too." But he hadn't had time.

The shadow moved. Crept closer. It was about four feet tall, slender, erect on two thin, but lengthy, legs; with an overlong neck and a compact angular head. Large claws at the end of upper arms held out, curved, in front of it. It had triangular stripes across its back and up along its head. Huge eyes that glittered in the faint light when the creature tilted its head at him. It saw him. It saw the kitten crying in his grasp and its tongue flicked in and out in hungry anticipation. Henry knew if he would have been a child or if the creature would have been bigger, he might have been the intended target and not the feline.

It wasn't a natural park animal. Not the way it moved, stood, glared at him, with a stumpy tail snapping back and forth. Another low growl echoed in its skinny throat.

Good lord, another dinosaur. What the hell...was the park infested with them now? A whole Jurassic Park right where he lived? Well, why not? What had begun years ago could be finally reaching its full and frightening potential. Dinosaurs, of different species, roaming the woods. Good God.

Henry, clutching the struggling, crazed kitten tightly against his chest as it dug its claws into him, stared at the creature. It was hard to see it in detail but what he saw was bad enough. He knew what he was looking at. Trouble.

The miniature dinosaur released a shrill wail that reverberated into the night, a war cry, and lunged at the kitten in Henry's arms. The dinosaur butted up against Henry and its mouth, now all razor-sharp teeth, gaped open as it attempted to wrestle away and swallow the small cat. It almost got her.

Henry thrust the kitten above his head to keep it from the hungry maw and with his free hand he brought his duty weapon up and shot the little monster and somehow–as close as he was– missed it. The explosion of the gunshot seemed to aggravate it.

Really pissed off now, instead of scuttling away in fright, the monster hissed at Henry, barred its wicked-looking fangs and slashed at him with its claws. Its saucer eyes flashing with malevolent intent.

Henry jumped back just in time and the claws

barely ripped through his shirt and raked across his flesh. Pain made him realize they'd gotten some skin, but the wounds weren't deep. They'd skimmed flesh, not dug in. Still hurt like hell, though.

This time when he shot at the creature, at least one of his bullets hit dinosaur flesh. *Got it!* The little monster shrieked in pain, knocked Henry and the kitten to the ground, and scuttled away into the woods.

Sprawled in the grass and stunned, clutching the meowing kitten with one hand and his gun with the other, Henry watched the dark forest close around the fleeing dinosaur.

Only when it was gone did Sasha cease meowing, squirming, and digging her claws into him. Between the dinosaur and the cat, man, was he going to be scratched up.

He shuddered and came to his feet. "Let's go home, Sasha, before that thing returns and maybe…brings a bunch of its little monster friends with it. Wouldn't put it past it, either. It looks like the type of vermin that runs in packs. I know. I've seen Jurassic Park. All three of them."

Sending quick looks behind him every second or so in case he was being followed, he wasted no time reentering the cabin and getting inside. Nothing followed, or nothing he could see. *That creature hadn't been afraid of him.* Ha, what was next, invisible dinosaurs? Wouldn't put it past them. Talk about adapting.

"What happened!" Ann, with anxious eyes,

was at the door waiting for them, and her hands eagerly gathered in the kitten. She snuggled her, soothing the animal with gentle caresses. Danger and its close call already forgotten, it began purring. Though not as loud as usual.

Breathless from his getaway, Henry blurted out, "Dinosaur...little body, big teeth and claws...mean little sucker...out at the edge of the tree line. It wanted Sasha for an hors d'oeuvre. The cat slipped out the front door somehow and ran into the woods and practically into the creature's jaws. I almost didn't get to her in time."

"Poor little kitty," Ann was murmuring endearments, nuzzling the feline. "Poor Sasha. You've had quite a scare, little one, haven't you? That mean old monster tried to *eat* you. Bad monster! But daddy saved you." Ann looked up at Henry and bestowed on him a hero's smile. "Daddy's so brave."

"Daddy was so lucky, is what daddy was," Henry huffed, peeking out the front window through a slit in the curtains. But it was too dark outside and he couldn't see anything. A sudden blade of black, night had descended. If the creature had returned and brought friends, he couldn't see them. But the thought made him uncomfortable.

There could be more of them out there. Oh boy.

"So there's another one, huh?" Ann said.

"There's another one." Henry slumped down on the couch and laid his gun carefully on the nearby coffee table.

"This changes everything again, doesn't it?"

Henry nodded, rubbing his eyes and reclining against the couch cushions. After a second or two he added, "None of us can go outside any longer without keeping our eyes open and having protection. Weapons."

"You going to shut down the park again now?"

"I don't see where I have a choice. There are possible Nessies in the lake and now a dinosaur kangaroo with big teeth and a nasty attitude bopping around in the woods looking for snacks. Oh crap," he muttered, shaking his head. "I can't believe the nightmare continues."

It was at that moment Henry's cell phone, attached to his belt, rang. He put it to his ear and answered. It was his son-in-law Justin.

"Wow, you must be psychic, son. I was just about to call you." Henry glanced up at Ann, whose expression alerted him she knew who he was talking to.

She sat down beside him and the kitten jumped from her arms to his lap. Settled there, promptly curled up and fell asleep. The cat had already forgotten her recent close call or was too exhausted to keep her eyes open. Oh, the blithe sleep of innocent tiny animals.

"I beat you to it," Justin responded and plugged onwards without taking a breath or giving Henry a chance to say anything else. "We've got another dinosaur problem. A big one, too. You won't believe what I've recently discovered. I waited to call you until I was absolutely sure. Now I am. I know you're sick to death of dinosaurs encroaching in your life but this is going to blow your mind. I know it did mine."

Henry's expression became distressed and his eyelids lowered. He sighed. "Well, you give me your bad news and then I'll give you mine."

"Oh, you have news, as well?"

"Yep. But you go first."

"Remember when we smashed their eggs and exterminated all those dinosaurs in the nest a couple of months ago and I thought some or all of them were sick?"

"Yes?"

"Well, remember when I said that, ill or not, diseased or not, I suspected there *might* be more…infestations…of the creatures in other national parks similar to ours–in the future if not already? You know, parks along the volcanic ridge that travels up the western North American coast all the way to Washington state? Areas and wilderness reserves with the same environmental conditions as we've had? Locations, like us, that have been experiencing deep subterranean earthquakes which could be regurgitating eggs, of various unknown species, that could be birthing more prehistoric creatures?" A heavy pause.

"Yes?" Now Henry was getting nervous. Ann, sensing his disquiet, was watching him. Waiting. Outside the night was silent. No kangaroo dinosaur noises. No noises of any kind.

Eerie quiet highlighting the moment.

"Unfortunately, I'm afraid I might have been correct."

Oh no. No, no, no.

Justin was forging on. "I've made contact, telephone inquiries and emails, with a number of chief park rangers or superintendents in Redwood, Yosemite, Death Valley, Sequoia National Park in California, Great Basin, Spring Mountain Ranch State and Horseman's Park in Nevada and grilled them on any strange animal sightings they might have been having recently. They've all had recent powerful earthquakes or a history of them in the last decade."

"And they actually told you if they had seen something suspicious?" Henry was surprised.

"Well, not all of them and not in so many words exactly...."

"What do you mean?" Henry only wanted Justin to spit it out now and stop drawing out the suspense.

"Some of them got really odd sounding when they were answering my questions. One or two cut me off quickly accusing me of being a crackpot or an out-and-out nut. Some hung up on me the minute I mentioned prehistoric beasts or dinosaurs.

"But two of them I somehow got through to and they admitted, yes, some strange creatures were prowling their forests.

"One, Chief Ranger Witter from Redwood National Park, finally broke down after I'd talked to him three times, sent him digital pictures of our Hugo, and other irrefutable proof of our dinosaur experiences, and admitted he and his men had hunted and actually bagged two bizarre looking specimens in the last six months that *could* have been young dinosaurs. Two. When he described them to me one of them sounded an awful lot like a young Hugo before his wings had grown out but the other one didn't sound like anything we've come across yet. It was larger, had spines on its back and liked the water. They disposed of the corpses but he took a couple of photos first. He's emailing me them later tonight.

"So...more species of dinosaurs are sprouting up. In more locations. Just what I had hypothesized and feared. Sorry."

Henry was in shock and had to remind himself to breathe. This was his worst nightmare. A plague of dinosaurs all along the American western seaboard. Birthing, breeding, growing. Spreading destruction. Gobbling up all other creatures in sight. Damn, damn, damn.

"Henry, you still there? Henry?" Justin was insisting on the other end, his voice sounding worried.

"I'm still here. Justin, what's the worst case scenario that we're looking at? Be truthful."

"I hate sounding like Chicken Little but the worst consequence is that these creatures keep multiplying in many places and keep spreading. Heaven knows where it would stop."

"Heaven knows. A dinosaur apocalypse?" Henry was now looking at Ann. Her face was wan, her eyes locked on his. She'd figured out what he and Justin were talking about. Her reporter's sixth sense. She picked up the kitten and hugged her closer as if to protect her.

Henry knew dinosaurs brought back horrifying and haunting memories to his wife. She'd lost friends in the dinosaur encounters. They both had. And now there were more, suddenly appearing in different places. Not a good thing at all.

"I wouldn't dare say that, Henry. I don't want to jinx the peaceful world we have now."

"Best to not think about it or speak of the worst results," Henry said to Justin. "Only how to fix it, right?"

"Right. For now. And so far it's only been a couple sightings. Small numbers. We have time. I think. I have more people and places to call and more information to collect." Justin's weariness was obvious in the way he spoke his words. Hesitant. Slowly. "Okay, we can discuss what we can or will do when I see you next. Let's make it soon. But I'm just too tired tonight to discuss it or even think about it anymore. It hurts my brain.

"Well, that's what I essentially had to tell you. Sorry I've monopolized the conversation so far. So...what news did you have for me, Chief Ranger?" Justin used the term he sometimes still affectionately called his father-in-law. "I hope it's better news than what I gave you."

"It's not." And Henry told him about the unidentified creatures spied in the lake and the feisty kangaroo dinosaur in the woods.

"Oh, my, then it's already begun."

"Or something has begun. I already closed the lake down to visitors earlier today. Going to shut down the whole park again as well. Can't take any chances this time. But I'm going out on the lake first thing tomorrow morning to see what I can see and I thought you might want to come with me?"

"Going to take a boat tour for yourself? See if any unidentified aquatic beasties show up, huh? See if there's really something there?"

"Something like that. You want to come?"

"I'll be there," Justin said. "Ah, here we go again. Lake maneuvers."

"Meet you at Crater Lake Lodge's dining room at seven a.m. then? We'll have breakfast first and take a little time to discuss our strategy." Henry finished and after saying goodbye hung up.

He didn't need to tell Ann much. She already had guessed most of it by his end of the phone conversation and he quickly filled her in on the rest.

Twice, during his explanation, Henry stole looks out the window into the night searching for movement or glittering ruby eyes among the trees and leaves. But he saw no signs their earlier visitor had returned–or, if he had any, his friends.

Soon after, he and Ann retired to bed. He made sure the windows and doors were securely locked and he kept his duty weapon nearby. He gave Ann a weapon, a large caliber revolver, of her own and insisted she take it with her everywhere she went. Promising to also provide her with a rifle when he could get to headquarters and retrieve one.

Henry had accepted, as Ann had, that from that night on living in the park was going to be a little different. Just like those poor human survivor wretches in The Walking Dead television show...they would have to be forever vigilant, armed and prepared. Always. Because, if Justin was right, a new age had just begun.

Chapter 2
Henry

When Henry left his house the following morning, the sun still hadn't lifted from the horizon and it was that glowing dark right before sunrise, but already warm. It was supposed to be an extremely hot day and he'd dressed for it. His summer uniform and ball cap. A water bottle attached to his belt and plenty in his jeep. His duty weapon snug in the holster at his waist.

His eyes were peeled for any of the little cat-hungry critters like the one he'd run into the night before. His nerves were on edge, watching for them, but none showed up. He didn't know if he should be relieved or suspicious. If the one that had attacked him wasn't lurking around their cabin, it had to be somewhere else and he didn't want to think about where. He hoped any cats in the vicinity were safely tucked away in their homes. Or dogs. Or small people.

After a stop at headquarters, he stashed a couple high-powered rifles and extra ammunition in the jeep's rear seat. Best to be prepared, no matter what they came across in the water, or on the land. On the way to joining up with Justin, he phoned Ranger Kiley and Ranger Stanton to inform them the entire park was also being shut down. Again. He filled them in and gave instructions, then hung up, satisfied they'd take care of everything. They were his best rangers. Besides they'd been through all this dinosaur craziness before and not so long ago. The visitors would be escorted from the park and any new ones turned away at the entrances; the businesses within would be closed until he was sure the park was safe. He'd learned his lesson the first two times and would never put unsuspecting people in danger again if he could help it. And he could help it.

He'd notify the National Park Services and Superintendent Sorrelson of the developments as soon as it was late enough. There usually wasn't anyone in the offices this early and Sorrelson didn't like being disturbed before nine in the morning. Then he'd put in a call to the man in charge at the National Forest Service because the park also had forests within its boundaries and came under their jurisdiction as well. He had to alert both of them. They'd need to know.

He pulled into the parking lot at Crater Lake Lodge. The sun was inching up over the lake and the light was permeating the murkiness around him. He loved this time of day in the park. The mists that eddied around his boots gave everything an eerie ambience and he imagined the land, the woods, must have looked just this way hundreds of years past. Perhaps thousands. More.

No wonder the primeval beasts returned over and over to reclaim it. It was their home and always would be.

He strode into the lodge's dining room. At this hour it was practically empty though it opened at the crack of dawn. Many visitors liked getting an early start on their hikes or park tours, but there weren't many up at this hour yet. And as they came down today they'd be politely asked to leave the park. The windows lining one wall and overlooking the lake framed a beautiful dawn. The view, as always, was inspiring. It made a person love and appreciate the raw beauty of nature and everything in it. The lake with the new sun shining across the water, the birds dipping their wings in flight across the sky, and the trees a circle of emerald around the blue oval of water created a panorama Henry never got tired of looking at, even after all these years.

He spied Justin as soon as he entered. But the young paleontologist wasn't alone. There was another man sitting at the table with him, nursing a cup of coffee and speaking animatedly, his hands and arms gesturing. The guy was about Justin's age, Henry guessed, with shaggy black hair not as long as Justin's, and a neatly trimmed beard. The two men appeared to know each other. Just Henry's first casual observation.

Justin stopped talking, glanced up at Henry, and greeted him. "Hi Chief. I already ordered you coffee. It should be here in a minute. We've already eaten. Sorry, I couldn't wait. You know me and food. If I don't eat every few hours my mind freezes up and I can't think." He grinned as his eyes went to the man beside him. "I want you to meet an old friend of mine, since childhood really, Steven James. We go way back. Fifteen years at least. He plays here at the lodge on weekends sometimes. He's a musician/songwriter and in my humble opinion a truly gifted one." Justin's smile was genuine as he looked at his friend and then back to Henry. "I've been his biggest fan for years. I guess you could call me a Steven James' groupie. Sometimes Laura and I even travel to his other gigs, some out of state, to hear him. We both love his voice and his amazing guitar playing. He's the best I know."

Henry plunked down in a chair across from them, reached out and shook the other man's hand. "Nice to meet you, Steven James. Musician extraordinaire."

"Good to meet you, too, Chief Park Ranger. Justin's told me so much about you and about all your adventures together." The young man's handshake was firm. His gaze direct. First impression Henry thought, *here's a man who knows what he wants, who he is and likes himself. Self-sufficient.* Henry could always tell.

"I hope all good stuff?" Henry's expression was amiable.

"Every bit of it. Justin thinks the world of you and your wife, Ann."

The musician paused, and leveled his eyes at Henry. "I hope you don't mind me barging in on your breakfast meeting? I sang this weekend at the lounge here–scheduled for next weekend, too–and for some reason decided to stay over another night. Got up early to see the stunning sunrise over the lake. It's such a spectacular sight from here." His eyes shifted to the vista on the other side of the windows and then returned to Justin. "And I just happened, luckily, to bump into Justin. So serendipitous. I had no idea he was going to be here. What a nice accident."

"It's a small world, Mr. James. The older I get the more I know it. Coincidences abound."

"Call me Steven."

"All right. You know I hate to be the bearer of bad news but since you mentioned you're supposed to perform here again next weekend, I should tell you. The park's closing indefinitely beginning immediately. We have an emergency. I'm sorry but you probably won't be singing here next week. The lodge, with the rest of the park, will be closed."

Disappointment flashed in the man's eyes. "That's too bad. But I can understand why, under the circumstances I mean, you have to shut the park." His regret had been swiftly replaced with a curious eagerness Henry couldn't misconstrue and he was pretty sure he knew what the two young men had been discussing when he'd first approached the table. Henry recognized that look. Dinosaur madness.

"Ah, so Justin told you about our little water outing we're going on today, did he? About the rare creatures in the lake we're looking for?" Henry sighed. Well, here it comes, he thought.

"Yes," Steven confessed. His eyes were shining brighter now. His long fingers made a graceful arc in the air as if to introduce his next words. "And I was hoping–"

Henry's coffee arrived, cutting the man off in mid-sentence. One of the younger waitresses, a college girl, named Delores, just there for the summer, placed the cup in front of him. "You know what you want, Chief Ranger?" she requested, ready with her order pad; not realizing she'd interrupted a conversation.

"The usual. Three eggs, over easy, three pieces of toast and burnt bacon. About another five cups of coffee whenever you see my cup is empty."

"It'll be right out. And I'll keep the coffee coming like an endless faucet." The waitress scribbled on her tablet, amusement on her face, and scurried away.

Henry's attention went back to the musician, waiting for the man to finish what he'd begun.

Instead it was Justin who spoke up. "I told Steven he could come along with us on the boat today on our little...voyage. Boating is second nature to him. We've been on many a boat ride together and he can handle himself like a pro. And he's a true dinosaur fanatic and has been following our exploits here in the park for years. He's grilled me endlessly for every detail of every dinosaur odyssey we've ever been on."

"Mr. James–" Henry began, not looking at Justin but his friend.

"Again, please call me Steven."

"Okay, Steven...why in heavens name would you want to come along? It could be touchy if we run into any of the creatures we think we might. Sometimes they tend to react violently to intrusions in their territory. I can't vouch for your safety."

"Because," Steven admitted, ignoring the thing about his safety, "I'm not only a musician. I also write fiction novels under an alias and I self-publish them on Amazon Kindle. EBooks, you know? They make me a tidy second income I've come to depend on. And I've been toying around with the idea for years, ever since Justin regaled me with the story of your first dinosaur incident here, of writing a dinosaur tale.

"Accompanying you and Justin today on the lake, searching for a school of possible American Loch Ness Monsters...wow, what a story that would make! Firsthand experience can't hurt my writing, either. It'd give it that genuine touch which makes the narrative so believable." He clenched his fist and dramatically shook it a few inches above the table. There was the fever of a zealot in his eyes and voice.

"I don't care if there's danger. Our lives are tottering on the precipice of danger every moment we're alive. Anything can happen at any time. Sitting at this table...a stray scrap of meteor could come crashing through the roof and squash me dead. Outside in the parking lot, a sink hole could open up under my feet and suck me in. Riding in a car could be dangerous. Walking across a street. Taking a trolley ride."

Henry caught that reference. For a moment in his mind he saw the rim trolley being snatched up by a flying monster and tossed into the lake. It made him cringe inside. The man had quite an imagination, but he was right. There was danger everywhere, every second.

"So what's the difference? So can I come along?"

Henry stared at the man. Was he nuts? Putting himself in harm's way for what...an eBook? He had to stop himself from laughing out loud. Instead he tried one last time. "It could not only be dangerous, it could be *extremely* dangerous, based on past experiences. I don't know what we'll come across, or if we'll come across anything at all. See anything at all. But whatever we find could be hostile. Do you know how to handle yourself in such an emergency, protect yourself? Can you even shoot a weapon?"

The man's expression was serious. "I joined the army when I was nineteen and logged in four years. Not in a war zone, mind you, but I know how to defend myself. Shoot a gun. Hit the side of a small barn."

Henry met eyes with Justin, who was nodding his head. "I've known him for a long time and he knows how to handle himself, Henry. He won't get in our way. Let him come along. He is, besides a fantastic singer/songwriter, a pretty good writer. Don't tell Ann this, but even better than she is."

"Don't ever say that to Ann."

"What, do I look stupid?"

Henry mulled it over for a second. "Oh, what the heck. Okay. Steven, you're on board. As long as you do what I tell you and accept the risks, you're welcome." What could it hurt? Chances are they wouldn't see anything, not on the first junket anyway. The lake was large. The creatures, whatever they were, might be napping at the bottom somewhere.

"I accept the risks and I will follow your orders, Chief, to the note." Steven promised with a straight face.

"All right then. We're leaving as soon as I gulp down the breakfast coming my way." The waitress was close to their table with a tray of food. "Can you be ready?"

"Fantastic!" The music man grinned as if he'd won a million dollar lottery and stood up so quickly he nearly knocked his cup of coffee over when the corner edge of the tablecloth went with him. "And I'm almost ready now. I'll just pay up my room bill and be right back with you. I was already packed, bags in my car, just in case." Then he rushed off.

"Eager, isn't he?" Henry said to Justin as he watched Steven run across the room.

"He's the excitable kind, I will say that. But he's a good guy. Smart. And he has a heart as big as that horizon out there. I couldn't ask for a better friend."

Henry's breakfast arrived and after thanking the waitress, he dug in. Time was a wasting. "So...I can read between the lines, what's

Steven's real story?" he queried of Justin between bites, eying his son-in-law.

Justin laughed. "Exactly what I told you. He's a thrill seeking old friend of mine who wants to write a dinosaur best-seller. That and he wants to see a real live dinosaur if there's one to see…and, well, he's at loose ends since his wife died two summers ago. He's been taking on more singing gigs and traveling as much as he can. Trying to outrun the grief, is what I think. He loved his wife dearly. A remarkable woman, she was a musician like he is and sometimes even sang with him. A sweetheart. She loved life so."

The husband in Henry empathized with Justin's friend but the ex-cop in him had to ask, "If I'm not being too nosy, what did she die of?"

"No, you're not. It's no secret. A car accident involving a drunk driver. She died immediately. That was the only thing that gave Steven any peace of mind. But he's taken her death so hard. They'd been married for seven years and were trying to have a baby. Happiest couple I've ever seen. It was all so tragic. I feel for him."

"I'm sorry to hear this. Do you think he'll be all right coming along with us? He's not suicidal or anything, is he? You trust him?"

"No," Justin stated emphatically. "And I'd trust him with my life. He's resourceful and a quick thinker. I knew you wouldn't like the idea of a stranger tagging along, but he won't impede us in any way, I assure you.

"In fact, I think this little undertaking might

be good for him. He's been unhappy for far too long. Unexcited with life. This will get his mind off his loss. At least for a while."

Henry nodded his head. "Okay. When he gets back, we'll leave. Ranger Gillian is meeting us at Cleetwood Dock in," he checked his wristwatch, "about twenty minutes. We'll take off from there. This time I have procured us the fastest boat on the lake with the biggest motor. Don't say I don't learn from past experiences. If there's something in the lake we'll be able to outrun it for sure. Or try to anyway."

"So it'll be just the three of us, huh?" Justin drank the last of his coffee.

"Yeah, just the three of us and Ranger Gillian. The other rangers are busy closing up the park and shooing out the visitors. Notifying the business owners they have to shut down and leave. That can't wait. I should be helping them and not going on a wild goose chase after unidentified swimming water monsters, but I need to know if there really is something in the lake again."

"You mentioned last night you'd already closed the lake, though?"

"Yep. All boat and trolley tours were canceled yesterday. We can't take the risk. Especially after what happened to me last night."

"You were lucky you saved your cat. Ann loves that cat."

"Don't I know it," Henry replied. "I was hero for the night in her eyes. Not to mention the kitten was real appreciative, too. It wouldn't stop rubbing against me."

"I wonder if we'll get to see the lake creatures today?" Justin mused out loud.

"As long as that's all we do. See them. I still recollect the last time we were on the water with a prehistoric leviathan and what happened. I don't want a repeat performance of that debacle. We were lucky to have escaped with our lives and I never like to stretch my luck."

Justin had a funny look on his face. "Neither do I. But I sure would like to see what's out there. See if it's like that first one years ago."

"And heaven help us if it is. Six years of multiplying and growing would make them real giants." Paleontologists, Henry thought. Always wanting to see, chase and catalog dinosaurs. All he wanted to do was exterminate them. And now he also had another dinosaur fanatic sailing with them…this one wanting to write a book about them. So be it.

Henry finished his breakfast and coffee, pushed his plate away. Left a ten dollar bill for the meal which included a generous tip. In the meantime, a grinning Steven was making his way back to them through the empty tables. "Time to go. But I have to make a quick stop at the front desk first. I need to inform the lodge's owner, who I see has returned from the supply room, he has to close up again and batten down the hatches until we know what we're dealing with. He's not going to be happy at all so I feel the least I can do is give him the bad news in person."

They came to their feet as Steven joined them. On their way out Henry spoke briefly to the lodge owner, who, as he'd surmised, wasn't thrilled with what he had to tell him, and then they left.

Ranger Gillian would be waiting for them at the dock with the boat. The sooner they got out on the lake and found out what was in it, and got off the water, the better, because Henry had the gut feeling things were going to get worse quickly. And he always listened to his gut. It was usually right.

*****

The day was a calm one but as hot as a small sun. The heat a palpable presence crowding in around them like the inside of an oven. It was better when they got out on the lake. The water cooled things off a bit, but it was the warmest August in the park Henry could recall. It was strange to think about their last dinosaur hunt, the one done in the freezing weather and snow on Mount Scott just months before. It seemed like a lifetime ago.

As they roared onto the lake Justin declared loudly so to be heard over the motor, "Does this all somehow seem familiar to you, Henry?" His eyes behind the gold wire-rimmed glasses swept the lake around them searching for anything unusual in the water.

"What? You mean us out on a boat trolling for Crater Lake monsters? Maybe in danger of being capsized any second and eaten alive by them? Yep."

Justin, hand shading his eyes from the glare and water spray so he could see better, answered, "Yeah, that. We've already done this way too many times. It's starting to feel almost normal." He stumbled and righted himself as the boat hit against a wave or something and bounced slightly. They were moving fast.

"Not normal to me. Never will be." Henry snorted. "I was way over it after that first time…you know where we were out on the lake in the middle of the night and first bumped into Godzilla?"

"I remember. It was dark and cold and I had never been more frightened in my whole life…until the next time and the next."

"Ah, memories."

There were no other boats on the lake. No people. Henry's rangers had done their jobs and cleared everyone out. The park, too, would soon be empty of visitors. He'd kept in communication with his men and everything was progressing as planned. It was a relief there'd been no further reports of strange animal sightings or attacks from tourists because he couldn't get that creature he'd fought off the night before out of his mind. Were there more? And, if so, where were they and what were they up to? He almost didn't want to think about it.

He knew he'd have to ask the Governor to bring in the National Guard again at some point and dreaded it. The troops had occupied the park so often in the last few years they might as well build permanent barracks and keep a base there. Oh, that'd be fun. Better yet he could turn the whole park over to them and coast until his retirement.

But at that moment he was more concerned with the water creatures that Captain Sander had claimed to have seen. He studied the water as it streamed past them. Beautifully blue. Deep. Mysterious as always. And this time the home to...what?

Ranger Gillian was steering the craft and Justin's friend, Steven, was braced against the railing by them, eavesdropping on every word they uttered–and Henry tried to sound as intelligent as he could–and probably filing them away in his head for his book; a big grin on his face as he regarded the lake and the boat moved across it. They'd already made three circuits and were speeding by Wizard Island yet again.

They'd seen nothing in the water but a couple of fish jumping and some floating flotsam. So far.

"Hey, there's the *Old Man* of Crater Lake. See that log sticking out of the water?" Justin pointed downwards and to his right. "You see it Steven?"

"I see it," Steven answered. "But it's just a log, huh?"

"Not just any log. It's a mountain hemlock trunk that has been floating upright in the water for more than a hundred years. Wind currents enable it to travel to different locations around the lake. It never stays in the same place."

"Interesting but weird. A traveling tree. The roots must make it bottom heavy and that's why it stays upright. Any Indian or lake folklore connected to it? Any neat stories?" Steven had directed the last part of his inquiry to Henry.

Henry gave the young man a sideways glance. That was a question he'd never asked and he found himself wanting to know the answer, too. But he didn't have it. "Not that I'm aware of. But I could ask around for you. Maybe one of the rangers who have been here longer than me, or one more seeped in the Indian legends of the park, would have an answer." Like Ranger Stanton. "Come to think of it, Ranger Stanton would be the one to ask. If there's a native legend or story attached to the *Old Man*, she'd know it."

"Thanks. Throwing in local color and tidbits help add to the word count and make a book more believable."

"I bet," Henry remarked, his attention still on the scenery around them.

They circled the lake for hours, slowly losing faith they'd see anything that day, then Justin voiced a suggestion. "Do you remember what drew the water dinosaur to us that first night on the lake all those years ago?"

Henry went back in his memory. "Ah, ha!" he snapped his fingers. "We made noise? The motors made lots of noise and it heard us?"

"You do remember."

"So, we've had the motor clanking away as

loud as a trash truck, but no creatures have popped up their heads. But what if we make more noise, blow the horns and yell a lot, perhaps they'll come to see what's making the ruckus?"

"That's a possibility."

Henry nodded at Ranger Gillian and the man gave him the okay sign with his fingers.

The boat's air horn began to sound. Again and again. The noise vibrated over the air and across the water and spread out for miles. With no other boats or people anywhere on the lake, it was ear-shatteringly loud.

"That should do it. They probably hear it all over the park," Henry shouted. "Let's see what happens now."

The men on the boat waited, listening, and studied the flowing waters around them.

After a while Steven, his hands clamped over his ears from the horn's din, yelled, "Maybe they're hard of hearing?"

"Maybe they're leery of us?" Justin offered another explanation. "The gargoyles were really smart; maybe these are, too."

"Captain Sander claimed they didn't appear to be. They swarmed around his boat like dolphins. Chased him. He just didn't know what their ultimate intent was."

"Maybe–" Steven started to say something else when suddenly Justin cried out beside him.

"Look! There! By the bow...there's something coming up from the water!"

Ranger Gillian silenced the boat's horn and

slowed their speed.

The four men were staring as the something rose up into the air next to the boat, shoving itself three, four feet out of the water, and then lowering back in. All Henry could see of it was greenish scaly skin as it slithered through the waves. It looked like a giant snake. No eyes or mouth. Making it hard to tell how large it was. Was what he was seeing the neck or back? He couldn't tell. It swam along easily keeping up with them, and they were moving over the water at a good clip. So it was flying in the water, whatever it was.

"Look! There's another one!" Justin's fingers gestured a ways behind where the first one had breached.

"And another!" Steven cried out, excited, pointing to the other side of the boat. "And another!" His eyes were reflecting awe. He clapped his hands over his mouth for a moment, then exclaimed, "Oh, my God! Look at them! They're amazing! I don't believe I'm seeing what I'm seeing. But I am. I mean I didn't actually think we'd see anything out here. To be absolutely truthful, I didn't really believe in your dinosaurs, Justin...but now...." He seemed to run out of words. The shocked expression on his face saying what he couldn't.

Henry's mouth tightened as he examined the water around them. *They're here. They are right here.* They were surrounded by a school of the aquatic creatures. On all sides. Four, five, six or more of them. And from what he could see, they weren't anything like the first lake dinosaur. They didn't appear as large, unless the rest of their bodies below the water were.

Something bumped against the underside of the boat. Not hard. A gentle nudge. Just saying *hi there*. But it could have been a branch or a piece of floating wood. Probably was.

Then the old fear reawakened and Henry's inner voice warned. *There's too many. Too close.* They should speed the boat up, get away and return to land where they'd be safe. They had no idea what the creatures would do.

"Wow! What a rockin' picture this is going to make!" Steven cried, aiming his smart phone towards the water as one of the Nessies broke above the surface again. This time they could see more of it. A column of reptilian skin shot seven feet out of the water.

Steven and Justin clicked away with their phones, getting the best photos of the creatures they could because they were moving so swiftly. Once and a while a portion of a body would come up and the camera phones would snap-snap-snap.

"They aren't behaving aggressively," Steven commented as if he'd read Henry's mind, peering over the rails as one rushed by. None of them had brushed against the boat. Yet.

Then on their left another one of the creatures lunged up through the water and high into the air in a graceful jump. Up, up, up. Eight human eyes followed its arc.

"God, look at that thing! Wow," Steven

muttered, picture taking forgotten for the first time.

Justin and Gillian didn't say a word.

It didn't resemble the first dinosaur, but it wasn't like any of the more recent flying ones, either. It was long, sleek, with a lengthy neck and a small head. Twenty, thirty feet from head to tail tip. As the creature slid by, it turned its head towards them and, opening a mouth full of sharp fangs, snarled. Its eyes were black orbs full of sly intelligence.

It was checking them out.

Henry stared at the airborne leviathan with undisguised horror. "I think it's time to leave." But no one was listening to him.

Almost in choreographed succession the other leviathans followed its actions and lunged into the air, one by one, then returned to the water around the boat, splashing water everywhere. There were smaller ones among the larger ones. One, on the other side of the boat from where the men were hunched down to their knees, holding onto the rails with clenched hands, was huge. It had to be over forty feet long. That one not only growled at them, but spit. Henry saw where its spittle landed and smoke sizzled up from the boat's deck in the same spot. *Acid?*

"I don't like this," Henry squeezed between clenched lips. "We need to get away from them. Now."

"You don't think they're all that friendly, do you?" Steven's gaze was riveted to the now calm waters around them. There wasn't anything moving anywhere. The lake was eerily tranquil.

"No, based on past experience, I don't."

Henry made a shooting hand signal to Ranger Gillian and the other man brought out an armful of high-powered weapons from the boat's cabin and handed them to all three men, leaving one for himself. Henry had learned long ago never to go anywhere in the park without the special firearms his ex-FBI friend, Scott Patterson, had had doctored up for them. The weapons could kill almost anything and had.

Steven held his gun, a MP7, familiarly, as if he'd used one before, but his lips were frowning. It was easy to see he didn't like guns, but knew their value when they were needed. Henry was glad he did.

"Ranger Gillian, get us out of here. Move this boat. Let's see how fast she can go without exploding the engine, huh?" Henry's tone dead serious.

Ranger Gillian did as he was asked but before they could rev up and begin moving, something beneath them reared up and the boat was violently jolted. The craft hopped in the water.

Steven nearly dropped his smart phone. Justin fell, sprawling, his Steyr SPP rocketed from his grip and skittered across the deck. Performing an adept salvaging act, he barely recaptured it before it slid off into the lake. "Got it!"

Henry didn't yell, stumble or fall. He'd

already braced himself against the railing. Lifting his MP7, he shot into the water where the disturbance had come from. What occurred next happened so rapidly that later Henry would have a hard time believing he'd seen what he'd seen.

"Gillian, get us out of here NOW!" Henry ordered. "Top speed."

The lake behind them was cresting into a towering frothy wave and another creature, not like the ones they'd just seen, or unbelievably, like any other dinosaur Henry had ever seen in the park, emerged to lift its head above the water. A deeper brown in color, and bigger than the others, its malevolently hungry eyes were focused on the humans on the boat. It had a bumpy head with rope-like flesh and a shorter neck. Its body was below the water, so no idea what the rest of the beast looked like. The head was all they saw and that was enough. It opened its jaws and the teeth were as big as a man's arm. It glared at them and the boat for a few breath-catching seconds and then it slid below the water.

"Oh, my," Justin blurted out, now on his knees, struggling to come to his feet. He shoved his glasses back up his nose. The look in his eyes full out alarm. "That's not good."

"You think?" Henry quipped.

Steven snapped a few more pictures of the men around him, their guns in hand. The guy was creating a whole photo album.

"Gillian!" Henry shouted again.

"I'm trying, Chief!" Gillian shouted back.

"The engine's stalled. It's flooded. Give me a second."

Yet, again, something either below or next to them forcefully rammed the craft and this time the boat jumped so high in the water, Steven, phone, gun and all, was propelled from the deck and tossed, screaming, into the lake. His phone fell from the sky and skidded across the planks, stopping at Henry's feet and Justin grabbed it.

The musician was thrashing around in the water, trying to get back to the boat. He wasn't wasting his energy on screaming or cursing and, incredibly, he hadn't let go of his weapon, which he'd thrust up over his head. "Help! Help!" he wailed as he bobbed, struggling to keep his head and his gun above water.

Justin climbed up from his knees as Henry scrambled for a life preserver and threw it out to the man in the water.

"Steven, behind you!" Justin screamed. One of the snake-like Nessies was coming after the man, its head lifted above the surface and eyes glowering down at him.

Steven was the one screaming now. He was trying to shoot the thing with his weapon, but the roiling water wouldn't let him take a steady shot. Henry tried to put bullets in the Nessie's head, but it was moving too quickly. The thing was just about to strike, swoop Steven up in its mouth when something else in the water interrupted its meal.

The newest monster, the beast with the monstrous teeth, attacked the Nessie. Taking its slender neck into its strong jaws, it yanked it down into the water before the other creature could swallow Steven.

It wasn't going after the human in the lake, it was going after one of the other dinosaurs. Probably because it made a bigger meal. Within seconds, the beast came up rolling in the water and it had the other, smaller, creature in its jaws, ripping it apart like it was a minnow. The water was turning crimson and the bellows and snarls of the two dinosaur combatants filled the caldera so completely Henry couldn't hear anything else; not the boat's restarted motor–Gillian having finally gotten the engine to catch–nor Steven's cries.

In the meantime, Steven had grabbed the life preserver and Henry and Justin had pulled him back up into the boat. He was still holding on to his gun. There was gratefulness in the rescued man's eyes and relief in Justin's.

"I thought I was a goner!" Steven sputtered, spitting up water and shivering from the cold dunking and the fear. Then a smile stole out. "But, hell, along with the pictures I took, what a heck of a scene this will make in my book! Almost devoured by a mighty lake Nessie! Wow!"

Writers, Henry thought, and not amused. Just like his wife, anything for a story. But he was happy the guy was alive and not in pieces. It'd been a close call and practically a miracle it'd ended as well as it had. Steven had been extremely lucky.

The boat roared off, putting distance between it and the raging battle between the bigger dinosaur and the pack of smaller ones. Now it was Justin who was taking pictures.

The water was a churning mess of dinosaur flesh, whipping tails, and snapping teeth. Blood. The shrieks and roars of the fighting monsters echoed high into the air and swirled around above them. A bloodletting free-for-all. Survivor of the fittest. Just like it'd been millions of years ago when the dinosaurs ruled the earth. A shiver crept through Henry's bones. Please don't let some of them get distracted and come after the boat full of fleeing humans instead, especially that gigantic monster. The boat would be a single gulp for that behemoth.

As they raced away, the men on the boat gawked at the battling monsters behind them and Henry couldn't help but wonder: How many more of these creatures were in the lake? In the park? How many more different species?

And how many liked to eat people?

If Justin's theories were right, then this kind of event–the rising of ancient and long thought dead dinosaurs–was happening all along the western coast of America in who knew how many lakes, wild park lands and forests. The results of deep earth volcanic eruptions. The whole concept was so horrible he couldn't bear to dwell on it. Please, this one time, let Justin be wrong.

And what the hell was he going to do about his problem here *this time*? How was he going to get rid of these new intruders? He'd about run out of ideas. Too many crazy, hungry dinosaurs to deal with in too short a time.

Heck, he could blow up the caldera and the park...that might work. A nuclear bomb or two dropped in Crater Lake would accomplish the task. Nah, then where would he and Ann live, where would he work? He'd have to find a different solution. But what?

Truth was, he was so very, very sick of the whole dinosaur conundrum. Especially now when they, the humans, were running for their lives. Again.

He'd think about it after they were safe. Maybe tomorrow.

Chapter 3
Ann

Ann was sitting at the table eating breakfast when her cell phone rang. Outside the sun was shining and she could see the heat waves dancing across the backyard. Henry had left before dawn for his *secret* lake expedition. She knew what he and Justin were really up to; they were searching the lake for more swimming dinosaurs. She hadn't wanted him to go, she never did when it came to the dinosaurs, but, as always, did he listen? Nope. *Call the army in again. The Feds. Park or Forest services. The government. Let them handle it,* she'd pleaded with him. *This is getting too big, too perilous, for you and your staff to keep tackling.* But what had happened the night before with that potential cat-snatching dino out in the woods had primed him right and proper. He was going to see how bad the situation was himself. Like always. Her husband the hero. Ha, he was going to get himself killed if he wasn't careful.

She swallowed the toast in her mouth and, wiping her buttery fingers off on a napkin, she answered the call. It was Zeke, a dear friend and the old man who'd once published the newspaper she now owned.

"Morning Ann," Zeke's gravelly voice greeted her. "So what's the latest?"

It wasn't like Zeke to just call up and pass the time chatting. There was something wrong and she was tipped off right away by the weariness, the tiniest touch of apprehension, between his words.

"Ah, you know the usual...cunning dinosaurs running amuck in the park. Henry and Justin off on another hair-brained lake cruise to throw themselves right into their starved mouths. Cat-hungry dinosaurs in the night forest trying to eat my Sasha. Same, same. How about you?"

"Oh, no, not dinosaurs again." Zeke actually chuckled. "Well, at least, you haven't lost your sense of humor, my girl."

"How can I? I need it living in this prehistoric park with that husband of mine–oh, and the dinosaurs, of course. Can't forget them."

"So the dinosaur problem has reared its ugly head up again, huh?"

"Regrettably, yes it has. There's been Nessie sightings in the lake and these small irritating striped dinosaurs in the woods around our house. You wouldn't believe what's going on. Ah, never mind that. What can I do for you?" He wouldn't have called if he didn't need something. Usually it was her calling him.

"Were you planning on coming into town to the newspaper today? I know some days you work from home, and was wondering if today was one of those?"

Ann knew then he needed something and she didn't waste any more time before she asked. "What's wrong, Zeke?"

He hesitated and she could almost see the frown on his wrinkled face, she knew him that well. They'd been friends for years, worked together and understood each other. He'd been the closest thing to a grandfather she'd ever had. He'd taught her everything he knew about the newspaper business and that had been a great deal. He'd always been there for her, but hated asking for help for himself even when he needed it. Stubborn old cuss.

"Are you driving into town this morning?" he repeated.

A step ahead of him, she replied, "I could be, if you need me to. Zeke?"

"Okay, okay. It seems I might have done something weird to my, er...back."

"You hurt your back?"

"Sort of. I mean it's not life threatening or anything, I wrenched it out somehow, but it's sore and I can't quite bring myself to do my weekly shopping. Bags of groceries are heavy, you know. And I really need bread, milk, and a sprinkling of other necessities. My cupboards are bare." An embarrassed chuckle.

"*Ok-kay*. And how long has your back been out?"

The old man wouldn't answer right away, then, "Not long. And it's getting better every day, but I was hoping–if you were going to be in town anyway—if you'd pick up a couple things from the market for me and drop them off? I'd pay you for them, of course. No rush."

Ann didn't let her friend hear her sigh. His back had probably been out longer than he'd admit to, which would explain why she hadn't seen him at the newspaper the last week or so. And he was always there underfoot, giving advice, helping, even though he no longer, officially anyway, worked there.

She did some quick thinking. Henry had asked her not to leave the cabin unless it was a dire emergency, and positively not unarmed, because of the dinosaurs he suspected might be in the woods. And she'd promised not to. Except...Zeke was alone, old, and needed her. In the refrigerator there was that container of stew she'd had in the freezer, she could take that to Zeke. It'd make him at least three dinners, maybe more. She often took him frozen homemade meals. His retirement check only went so far.

Henry had left her his extra duty weapon, a .40 caliber semi-automatic SigSauer, for protection because it had the larger, heavier bullets. She would take that. Keep her eyes sharp and her ears open for any strange creatures lurking in the park. Wear drab colors so as not to attract them. She'd be very, very careful. Look around before she ran from the front door to her car, which was parked next to the house. Once in her car, which was an olive green and merged easily into the woodsy background, she'd be safe. She'd drive fast. Get into town, stop by the grocery store and Zeke's house and drive back before dark. No problem. Henry didn't really expect her to be a prisoner in her own house, did he? Because heaven knew how long *this* dinosaur crisis would last.

"You're in luck, old man," she chatted in a cheery voice. "I was planning on driving into town this morning anyway. Give me a list and I'll pick up those supplies you need. Got some homemade stew and biscuits for you, too."

"Oh, that'd be great. I love your stew, Ann. What a treat. Thank you." Zeke gave her a list of things, wasn't many, then she hung up after telling him she'd see him soon.

Henry was going to be angry with her, but it couldn't be helped. Zeke needed her. And besides, Henry had only seen that one specimen–and he'd said it had been *small*–in the woods by their house. Didn't mean there were more. Right? Not any worse than a bear or a moose, which the park was full of.

She showered, dressed and bagged up a food package for her friend, then looking around outside, being ever so careful, the SigSauer secure in her purse and easy to get at if she'd need it, she ran out to the car. No dinosaurs showed up or attacked her so all was well. It was so hot. She'd worn shorts and a sleeveless top, but she was already sweating.

Inside the car, she switched on the air conditioning, and pulled out of the driveway. The rangers had been emptying the park of visitors, and the campgrounds were vacant and so were the roads. She drove through the park cautiously, her eyes on the surrounding woods, remembering the warnings Henry had given her, but her mind wandered as the bright sun dazzled above. It was too beautiful a day. It was easy to forget about the new dinosaur quandary and everything else bad in the world. Dealing with cancer the last year had taught her to cherish the minutes and days, just to be happy she was alive, and not to waste the time.

A smile took over her lips at the thought of her daughter's coming baby. Laura was five months along, due in November around Thanksgiving, and she and Justin had found out they were having a boy. Henry was so excited. Finally a grandson he could also teach to fish, hunt and love the land. Ann was excited, too. Another grandchild. She wouldn't care if it were a boy or a girl, it would be a baby, a child, she could shower love on and be loved by in return. She'd already begun buying little infant toys and clothes for him and trying to guess what her daughter and son-in-law were going to name him. Laura liked the name Matthew, while Justin was leaning towards Sam. Ann didn't care about that, either. She'd love the baby no matter what he was called. She couldn't wait. There was nothing like the feel of a baby in your arms.

Then her smile faded away. A lot was going to happen, be decided, settled by the time Laura had her child. Four months from now.

The newspaper being one of them. Ann

hadn't said anything yet to Henry, she'd been going to the night before...until the episode with the cat-hungry dino. The newspaper was losing money like a severed vein loses blood. Newspapers all over the country were dying and small town papers were the most terminal. Her newspaper's revenues were decreasing each month because of the Internet, well, and because people just didn't care about reading a real newspaper any longer, especially the young ones. People wanted the easy news fed to them in quick, condensed bytes like what they saw on the nightly news or read on the Web. Twitter appetizers. Newspapers were going out of style. Their days were numbered, or so she believed.

So Ann had fretted over her options long and hard and, truth was, she was seriously considering selling the newspaper; getting the best price she could for it in a weak market, and taking early retirement. Another casualty of her cancer. She didn't want to waste her time writing folksy narratives, selling ad space or sending green reporters out on stories no one would remember a week later. None of it made any sense to her lately. Not since her illness. The greater world no longer seemed as important as her own tiny world.

When she'd had cancer she'd taken stock of her life and asked herself what she really wanted. The answer? She wanted to spend whatever time she had left in her life with Henry, her family, nature and, maybe, write a book or something. Something that might live after her. Disposable newsprint wouldn't. A novel would.

And now? Her frown had grown and a familiar ache began to throb inside her somewhere. Now there was a chance, slim, but still a chance, that her cancer had returned. Oh, it wasn't for sure yet. She hadn't gone back to the doctor for tests. It was just a hunch, a twinge of a suspicion that had begun to haunt her. She wasn't feeling quite herself lately. Unexplained weariness again, and pain. She knew she had to go see her doctor, but kept putting it off. She, of all people, knew if the disease had returned there was a good chance this time she wouldn't beat it. Two of her uncles had died of cancer, and one of her sisters. They'd all followed the same downward spiral. Found it once, beat it once; got it again and, eventually, even after endless treatments, that was the end. She wasn't even sure if she'd try to fight it a second or third time. If. If. If.

The doctor. She needed to go to the doctor. She was afraid to go to the doctor.

Maybe she'd think about it tomorrow.

She'd let her mind wander too much and abruptly the world she was driving through tugged her back to reality. Outside the vehicle, it was strangely silent. No hikers or visitors. No other cars, RVs or campers. That made sense. But there weren't any animals scurrying about in the tree limbs or from bush to bush. Not a bird, a bunny or a squirrel. That wasn't normal.

She slowed the car down as she drew near the park's exit. She'd picked a little used one because she knew there'd be no check point, no barricade, with rangers to stop her.

That's when she saw it.

Planted in the middle of the road on its stringy haunches, it was just sitting there watching her car approach. It stared at her with large shining eyes. Unafraid. Unmoving.

She slowed the car down a few feet away from it because the creature wouldn't budge. And she looked at it. It was about three feet or so tall, maybe a little more and a burnt reddish color in the sun, scaly, with a thin bumpy torso, a small head and long neck. Stripes crisscrossing its back. Actually quite graceful looking. A stunted tail kept thumping back and forth as if the creature was irritated. Or hyper. Definitely of a prehistoric genus. Definitely a dinosaur.

Oh, crap.

Could it be the one Henry had come up against the night before, the one that had tried to eat Sasha? Its appearance looked to be similar. But she was over ten miles away from the cabin. What was it doing so far from their house? *If* it was the same one.

But she wasn't afraid. It was one little dinosaur and she was in a big car. Protected. For a moment, she thought of pulling out her phone and taking a picture of the creature. But she couldn't find her phone in her purse. She knew it was in there somewhere, but her hand couldn't locate it. Darn. And she couldn't take her eyes away from the thing in the road to look for it, so she kept searching with her fingers. Still no phone. *Oops, I hope I didn't leave it at home.*

She inched the car forward but the animal still refused to move. She was on a stretch of the road very close to the exit itself and there were small trees and bushes lining each side so tightly she really needed to drive on the road itself up to the exit. If she attempted to go around the little monster she'd be driving through the bushes. It'd scratch up her car. Maybe she'd get stuck in a ditch.

"Move, you little devil," she grumbled at it, her foot lightly tapping down on the accelerator pedal. Now she was only about five feet away.

It scowled at her, lifted its angular head; opened its mouth and made a noise like she'd never heard before. A kind of hissing snarl loud enough for her to hear through the closed car windows. The dinosaur might be small, but it had rows and rows of really sharp teeth. Like a piranha.

Then, in one swift movement it jumped onto the car's hood, hopped up to the windshield and throwing itself at it, tried to get at her, claws raking and teeth biting at the glass. The look on its wizened face one of frustration when it encountered the clear barrier. Cheeky little bastard.

"What the–!" was all she could get out before her eyes caught more movement on the sides of the vehicle. "Oh God...more?" By then she'd stopped rummaging in her purse for her phone.

A herd of the things were swarming around her car, jumping on it and trying to get to her like she was some sardine morsel tucked into a can. But they were small and so were their claws and mouths and they couldn't break through. There were so many, though, so quickly, the car began to rock. The suddenness of the attack took her off guard and she screamed. That seemed to make them even more belligerent, hearing and seeing her fear. Their claws scratched, gouged, and ripped at the hood and roof.

And, turning to glance over her shoulder she thought she saw more of the monsters rushing out at her from the woods. An army of them. Oh, my.

Time to get out of here, her inner voice yelled. *Now!*

"Get off my car, you vicious gremlins," she cried. "I'm leaving."

She rammed down the accelerator, the car lurched and sped down the road. She purposely jerked the wheel violently to the left and then to the right. Stopped as quickly as she could and then stomped down on the accelerator again and again. The car jumped and bucked. From the squealing and scratching sounds above her she could tell she'd lost most of her primeval parasites. In the rear view mirror she saw a bunch of them falling to the ground behind her. Instead of chasing her, though, they fled off into the trees. Cowards. Good riddance.

She didn't stop. She drove right through the unbarred exit at the highest speed she could manage, turned off on and headed down the highway. She was pretty sure she'd lost all her unwanted passengers, but she wasn't taking any chances. After about five miles, she pulled over and, saying a quick prayer, opened a window and stuck her head out to see if she was alone. She was. No little gremlins anywhere. She closed the window.

She laid her head on the steering wheel and took deep breaths. That'd been close. Close to what, she wasn't sure. Would they have bitten, mauled or eaten her if they'd somehow gotten inside? She was so glad she hadn't found out. They hadn't been large, as dinosaurs go, but, whoa, those teeth had been needle sharp. Those eyes, voracious.

She finally located her cell phone in her purse, it has slid into a side pocket, and called Henry, but on the other end all it did was ring and ring. If they were on the lake, as they were supposed to be, they might be in a dead spot where the phones wouldn't work. She left an urgent message telling him what had occurred and warning him that, yes, as he'd feared, his cat-eating dinosaurs ran in packs. And attacked humans. In cars. But, yes, she was okay. She didn't dare tell him why she was out in a car after he'd asked her to stay in the cabin. She'd explain that to him later, face to face. And perhaps he wouldn't get mad at her. Well, except for the scratches her car must have on the roof and hood.

Her inner voice told her to turn around and return to the cabin, but then she'd run into that pack of little terrors again. Something inside her cringed. She decided it was safer to go on. Get out of the park for now. Hopefully by the time she returned, the agitated horde would be gone, moved on to another site. To be sure, on her return trip, she'd drive through a different entrance.

She started the car and got back on the highway, praying her scratching hissing hitchhikers would remain somewhere behind her. Her hands on the wheel were still shaking.

She couldn't get the thought out of her head how close her attackers had been to the exit. On the fringe of the park's lands. Had they already left it? Were they bopping down the roadways and highways exploring the territory? Gone into the neighboring towns yet? Trying to eat domesticated pets and…people? Should she call the police or something? No, the creatures were still contained in the park and Henry was taking care of that. And what could the police do anyway? Not much.

As Henry would say, *damn dinosaurs*.

A short while later she was pulling up in front of the Klamath Fall's IGA. She dashed into the store and got the stuff on Zeke's list and dashed back out. She checked her car. There were scratches and puncture marks across the hood and roof. Darn. She'd need some body work and a new paint job done. What would that cost?

Nothing seemed any different as she traveled through the town. It was an ordinary summer's day. Heat waves churned across the asphalt and over the brown grass of the front yards and the hum of air conditioners were everywhere. People were walking and driving here and there, going about their daily tasks as if nothing was wrong in the world. Lucky them for believing that.

She didn't see one dinosaur, of any size or variety, anywhere, thank goodness. Miles away from danger, Klamath Falls was still untouched.

Then she was parking in front of Zeke's house. Before she lugged in the groceries she tried Henry's cell again. No luck. No answer. She even tried Justin's phone. Again no one answered and she felt a jab of concern. She hoped they were okay. After what she'd gone through, she had an uneasy feeling perhaps they, too, had had a run in with something dinosaur. Dropping the cell into her purse, she'd try to reach them again later. Her nerves were still jangled, her stomach upset from the hostile encounter.

Zeke didn't answer the door right away and, worried, she was about to get out the extra key he'd given her and let herself in, when he opened the door.

"Zeke," she said, balancing the bags of stuff in her arms, "you look dreadful."

"Thanks, nice to see you, too," the old man griped as he stood out of the way to let her in.

Inside, he followed her, stumbling slightly, to the kitchen where she put the groceries away. "Sit down," she told him. "Before you fall down."

Zeke slumped in a chair and watched her

stuffing items in his cabinets. She noticed the kitchen needed a good cleaning. There was dust over everything. Dirty dishes in the sink. Overflowing trash can in the corner. She'd tidy things up before she left. She knew she'd be telling Zeke about the random dinosaur ambush but wasn't sure when to broach the subject or how. Zeke, slow moving and thinking, didn't seem himself.

She couldn't get over how frail her friend looked. Like a twig could knock him over. His eyes tired and his face slack. He'd lost more weight and his clothes hung on him. His expression bland. Life, she thought. He was tired of life. She could almost sympathize.

"How's your back?" she asked.

"Same as usual. Old. It creaks and groans when I make it carry my body from one place to another. Lately," his voice as feeble as he looked, "it doesn't always want to carry me anywhere. Spend half my time lounging around in bed like some lazy lay-about or something. Since I let you in, it's been behaving." His brave smile was heartbreaking.

"Have you been to the doctor yet?" It felt odd asking him something she'd been asking herself so often lately. Kind of ironic.

"Sure. Many times. He says I'm decrepitly old and not to take out a long term loan on anything."

"Is there something you should be telling me?'

"No." He sighed. "Nothing I want to tell

you."

"Zeke–" Frustrating man. Of course, most men were.

"Ann, mind your elders now and stop pestering me about things I don't want to talk about. Not now anyway. I'll let you know when.

"So," he pried, changing the subject, "you going to let me in on what's going on now in the park? You said you would. I've been dying of curiosity. Don't make an old man wait like this. Bad for my heart."

"Your heart is the strongest thing about you, old man."

"Well?"

Here goes. And, without preamble, she disclosed everything. The dinosaurs spotted in the lake, the cat-craving dinosaur in the woods behind their house and the herd of them that had attacked her as she exited the park. What it might all mean.

"I couldn't believe it when they jumped on the car, tried to get at me like that. And there were so many of them," she murmured softly after she'd made them cups of coffee, and settled in a chair next to him. "Vicious little boogers.

"For a while there I was terrified they'd get in. Get me. Or follow me from the park."

"But they didn't."

"No," she said, "as far as I could see, they didn't."

"You say Henry's shut down the lake area and now the park again?"

"He had to."

"Where's all this going to end," Zeke brooded out loud. His eyes went to the window above the sink. A tiny gray squirrel was sitting there peering in at them. Tiny paws hugged close to its chest. Cute petite face with begging eyes. Big fat fluffy tail, bigger than the squirrel itself. Probably one of Zeke's little yard squirrels. So tame, he'd told her, they ate out of his hand sometimes. Some even came to the window to beg. This must be one of them.

"Don't know. But, where ever it's going won't be good."

"Henry calling the army in again?"

"He's thinking about it. Him and Justin are out on the lake right now dinosaur hunting. Seeing what they're up against, if anything. I imagine I'll know more tonight when he gets home."

"Hmm. You'll let me know what's happening, won't you?"

"Of course. Don't I always?"

He was just looking at her in an attentive way, the hand picking up his coffee cup trembled. He must suspect she had something else on her mind.

Well, no time like the present to drop the bomb, she thought. "Zeke, I do have something else I wanted to talk to you about. You got some time?"

"Oh, I always have time for you. What's bothering you, Ann?"

In as calm a voice as she could muster, she spoke of her desire to sell the newspaper and retire. And her old boss, and previous owner of the Klamath Falls Journal, surprised her. With a supportive smile when she was finished, he said, "If that's what you want. If you're sure. I say go for it. Life is too short to not do what you really want to do. Take it from an old codger who now reflects on his life and wishes–desperately–he would have taken off more time from work to…live. Enjoy life more. Ha, I waited too long. Worked too hard. My family suffered and now I'm suffering. I retired too late and now, look at me, I'm a sick old man no good for nothing. Can't travel or enjoy the time I have left because my mind and body's plumb worn out. No, girlie, you retire now and do what you want. Have some fun. Spend time with your husband and kids, that new grandbaby when it arrives, while you can.

"I'd do anything to time travel twenty years back and do the same. Work should never be a person's whole life. Now it's too late." He stared out the window at the sunny day. The squirrel had scampered off. Probably looking for nuts somewhere. "And after that scare last year with your cancer, I don't blame you one iota for wanting to retire. So go for it, I say."

"Oh, Zeke, I'm relieved you feel this way. I was afraid to tell you of my decision about selling the paper. I know it's been your baby all these years."

"Babies grow up, Ann, and sometimes they're not what you were expecting them to become. It's time. The day of the print papers are about over. The Internet is making them extinct. Sell while you can; get what you can. Go off and do what you want to do. Be happy."

She gave him a hug. He was so dear to her. If she retired she'd have more time for him, as well.

"You know, I might be able to help you sell the old place," he declared. "Over the years I had an offer or two for it. The owners of the other major newspapers in town approached me right before I handed it over to you. One of them would gladly take it off your hands for a fair price. I'll give them a call for you and let you know."

"Thank you, Zeke, that would be so good of you. Sooner the better. Now I've decided to retire I can't wait to start my new life. I can't even bear to go into the newspaper today. So I'm not. Suddenly, none of it seems to matter anymore."

Zeke's glance was intense. "Anything else you want to tell me?"

She hesitated and she knew he caught it. "No," she lied.

"You sure? I can keep a secret if a secret is what you want it to be."

She shook her head. "Still no. You were right, though, the cancer scare last year is why I'm reassessing my life. That and all these new dinosaurs in the park." She met his gaze. "I'm going to write about them and sell the stories to any newspaper that wants to run them. Might make some more money with it. That and whatever I get from the newspaper's sale, and our savings, will tide us over until I can collect social security."

"Henry know about this idea of yours to retire and write dinosaur articles?" Zeke smiled at her over his coffee cup.

"Not yet. He's been busy. But I'll be telling him tonight, if I see him.

"Would you like a bowl of that stew I brought over before I go? I can warm it up, along with some biscuits, for you?" She couldn't stay long. She needed to get back home. The park was dangerous enough when the sun was shining and Henry was going to be irritated enough at her for leaving in the first place. Best to get home quick. In the daylight.

"Stew sounds good. I am kind of hungry now that you mention it. Thanks, Ann, you're an angel."

Yeah, and she'd be an angel for real if Henry caught her out gallivanting around like this.

She heated the stew and biscuits in the microwave, served it to Zeke, told him to call her if he needed her again, then saying goodbye, she left.

Not looking forward to reentering the park, but there was no other way to get home. She'd just drive through fast. Not slow down or stop for anything. If one of those little monsters were in the middle of the road, this time she'd run the thing down before she'd stop. Make dinosaur jam of it. See if she cared. Maybe she'd make it to the cabin without any more incidents.

She could hope, couldn't she?

*****

Zeke was sad when Ann drove away. He felt better when she was around. The loneliness that had taken hold of him the last year was always assuaged when she was with him. He looked up when he heard the chattering outside the kitchen window. One of his squirrels, the baby one, was sitting outside, talking to him.

Oh, he knew what it wanted. The peanuts he threw out to them every morning in the back yard. He had a family of the critters that had taken to showing up every day and he'd feed them peanuts or pieces of fruit. The baby one at the window was the friendliest of the lot. It didn't seem to be afraid of him at all. He moved to the window and tapped the glass on his side. The squirrel kept chattering at him and put its paws up against the glass. *Come out. Come out. Feed me.*

Imagine, he thought to himself as he took the bag of peanuts from the lower cabinet and hobbled towards the rear porch, if someone would have told him even five years ago that someday he'd be so desperate for entertainment or companionship, of any kind, he'd befriend a bunch of fluffy-tailed rats, he would have laughed his head off. Now here he was. Squirrel daddy. And tickled pink to be. At least it gave him something to do. Something to care about. Something to love.

Dinosaur Lake III: Infestation

He took the bag and shuffled out to the porch, then out into the yard. His back wasn't hurting too much so he carefully made his way down the lawn to the spot, beneath a towering oak tree at the end of his property, where the squirrels gathered and liked to eat the treats he gave them each day. The tree was on the perimeter of the modest woodlands that encircled Klamath Falls. It was one of the reasons he'd bought the house years before. It had trees behind it. Made him feel as if he were out in the country somewhere instead of in the heart of town.

Sure hot today, he fussed, as he tossed the peanuts on the ground below and around the oak tree. Sweat was already trickling down his neck and under his shirt. It made him itch.

"Ah, there you are, little buddy." He chortled, spying the baby squirrel bouncing across the grass towards him. "I knew if I put out the bait, you'd be here to collect it." The squirrel darted up to Zeke and let him hand feed him the peanuts. He even grabbed up with his paws to grasp them and stuff them into his mouth. Tame little beggar.

By then there was a mess of the fluffy-tailed rats cautiously emerging from among the trees and bushes to snatch the peanuts. Most of them stayed far away from him, but some ventured nearer, unafraid of the human they'd become accustomed to.

Zeke looked up at the sweltering sun and the blue sky, breathed in the warm air full of the scents of summer. Freshly mowed grass and dirt. Memories of when he was a child and used to run the paths barefoot in the forest, exploring. He smiled. He always felt better when he was outside near the woods, felt better when he was outside period. The sweet aroma of baking bread drifted on the breeze. There was a bakery down the street he often walked to. Maybe he'd go get some cheese Danish later if his back would let him. Someone in the neighborhood was frying bacon and eggs. He could smell it. These things, too, made him feel better. Alive. Like he was part of something and not merely a lonely old man. He often thought lately he should sell his house and move into one of those retirement homes. At least he'd have company. Yep, he needed to think about that. He loved his home but he sure was tired of being alone.

The baby squirrel began to behave strangely. Tittering loudly and running in circles. It seemed to be scared of the trees behind them. It raised its head and its eyes were so big.

"Hey, little fellow, what's wrong?"

Still making a racket and acting like it was on speed it ran up Zeke's pants leg and perched itself on his shoulder, holding on to his collar with its claws. A raving maniac. Something was scaring the wildness out of it.

By then the other squirrels had scattered. They were running in all directions and hiding. Some made it, some didn't.

That's when Zeke saw the first interloper rushing out of the woods towards him. It wasn't very big, about thirty-six inches from foot to top of its head or so. It looked like a skinned kangaroo, but reddish hued. Scaly. Long neck. Not a very big head. Faster than he could believe the creature could move, in a flash it had pounced on one of the larger squirrels he'd been feeding and popped it into its mouth like a tic-tac. It had lots of sharp teeth. Curved claws at the end of short arms. Dinosaurs. They had to be. Like the ones Ann had told him had attacked her earlier coming out of the park. But what were they doing here? In his back yard? In his town?

He didn't have time to think about it.

Because the woods were alive with the squirrel-eaters. All chasing, catching and devouring squirrels not speedy enough to escape. The cries and shrieks of the squirrels and the weird noises the predators were making created bedlam.

"What the heck! What–" Zeke hollered, but didn't finish because he'd turned and was limping as fast as he could back to the house. He was no dummy, he knew when to retreat. His tiny squirrel baby clinging for dear life to his shirt collar and chattering franticly in his ear. Probably giving orders in squirrel language.

As he grabbed the handle of the porch's screen door, he stole a glance behind him. There were at least six or seven of the ugly little dinosaurs chasing him and they were right on his tail.

He barely made it onto the porch and then into the house before he heard them slamming their bodies up against the screens. He had no doubt they'd tear open the metal mesh and be on the porch in seconds flat. With those claws and teeth of theirs, they'd have no trouble at all. Better than screen cutters. So he threw himself through the second door and locked it behind him.

His pet squirrel jumped from his shoulder and scurried away into the house somewhere, probably to hide—or find another exit.

Only then did Zeke allow himself to peek out the windows. His whole lawn seemed to be filled with the disgusting creatures. Bouncing around everywhere with their ugly bodies and snarling mouths. They were on his porch and trying to get in at him.

Fat chance! His house was strongly built. Or he hoped it was.

One even glared in through the glass on the other side of the kitchen window where the baby squirrel had been just minutes before. Its eyes sentient and scary as hell. Zeke closed the curtains and started praying the thing didn't smash through the glass. Maybe it was thinking about it.

If those monsters wanted in, it was possible they'd find a way.

Zeke ran to the wall phone and called Ann. It was the first thing he could think of. Before the police. Before Animal Control. She'd know what to do because his mind was fuzzy, his reactions muted. Maybe he was having a stroke or something. After he got through to her, he staggered off to get his shotgun out of the hall closet. For good measure, he also grabbed the wooden bat. At least his thoughts were still clear enough to do that.

If those things broke in he'd shoot or beat them to kingdom come or back to the geological period where they belonged. Didn't matter which. No way were they having him for lunch. Or having any more of his squirrel buddies, either. Freakin' dinosaurs.

Chapter 4
Henry

They'd made it to Cleetwood Cove and docked their boat without a lake monster swallowing them up. Henry considered them extremely lucky. The monsters had been too busy fighting among themselves to care about the small boat full of humans.

He was standing on the dock waiting for the others to disembark when he finally checked his cell phone for messages. He'd begun doing that more often since Ann's bout with cancer. He had to stay in touch in case anything happened. But when he'd been out on the lake reception had been spotty or dead.

Ann had left him five messages since that morning. Now that was unusual. Something must be wrong.

He hit Ann's speed dial button and she picked up after the first ring. She must have been holding the phone, waiting for his call.

"Thank God you finally got back to me, Henry," her voice sounded panicky. "Zeke's being attacked by some creatures out in the woods behind his house. He just called me and

I've turned around and am heading back there now."

"You're in your car when I asked you not to go anywhere? Ann! Where are you?"

"Ooh, about that. I didn't stay home like you told me to. Sorry. I'm roughly ten minutes outside of Klamath Falls, parked on the side of the road, and getting ready to turn around and return to Zeke's. I'll tell you quickly–and don't get mad at me because I had no choice–but Zeke phoned early this morning and I had to go take him some groceries. He was all out of food, some necessities, and I had to help him out some. He isn't feeling well. His back's acting up again. He can hardly walk.

"Anyway, I was heading home from his house when he calls me again, all upset because he says he was attacked in his own back yard by these…big lizards, as he called them. By his description they sound like they might be similar to the one you encountered last night outside our cabin. But he says there's a horde of them, like the ones that attacked me as I was leaving the park this morning. He's gotten back safely inside his house but is afraid they'll get inside–"

"Whoa, honey! You can fill in the rest of the story when I see you. But for right now, you *stay where you are!* I'm on my way and we'll go to Zeke's together. Don't you dare go back there by yourself. It's too dangerous. You hear me? *Stay*."

"But Zeke needs me now! I have to go back. I have a gun and–"

"We're on our way this very second," Henry

gestured to Justin and Ranger Gillian to get to his car, made them understand they were leaving, "and we'll catch up with you. Be there in minutes, I promise. Where exactly are you?"

She gave him her location.

"I know exactly where that is. Now…wait for us."

"Who's us?" Ann asked, her voice still unsteady.

Steven had planted himself in front of Henry. "Let me come, too?" he whispered, his eyes pleading. "Please?"

"Justin, Ranger Gillian, and a friend of Justin's, Steven."

"All right. But hurry, Henry. Hurry! I will call Zeke back now. Tell him we're on our way." She abruptly broke the connection.

And Henry hurried. He broke the speed limit the entire way, but didn't care. Ann was unprotected outside the park and he needed to get to her. Zeke was in trouble. Zeke, their old friend, needed help. He cared for the elderly man as much as Ann did and didn't want anything to happen to him. Then behind all his worry over Zeke, there was the new concern for the town and neighboring towns. If Zeke was being assailed by prehistoric beasts as far away as Klamath Falls…then the dinosaur epidemic had spread far beyond Henry's worst fears. They were in town now. Oh hell.

As he drove, his thoughts counted off the things he must do immediately. Alert the Park and Forest Services–darn, he should have done that already–the FBI, the National Guard as well as the local police. They'd need all the assistance they could raise as quickly as they could raise it. There were thousands of people living in and around Klamath Falls and now they might all be in danger if what Ann said was true. And of course it was. Ann or Zeke wouldn't lie about anything to do with dinosaurs.

When they screeched to a halt, wheels throwing gravel, beside Ann's car, Henry jumped out and got behind its wheel and had Ranger Gillian drive his car behind them to Zeke's. The two vehicles raced down the highway breaking more laws. Ann hadn't been able to get Zeke on the phone again and she was frantic.

Sitting beside him as he drove Ann caught him up on what had happened since he'd left that morning. Everything.

After she'd told him the story of how she'd been waylaid herself by a gang of the same creatures, Henry snapped, "You could have been hurt or killed! I asked you *not* to leave the cabin for any reason, didn't I?" But his eyes as he slid them to glance at her face, were more relieved than angry. He only wanted her to be safe, remain safe. Why did she always have to do the right thing even when it put herself at risk? But that was his Ann. She was nothing if not quick to act courageously if someone else was in trouble, regardless of her own personal well-being.

"But Zeke needed me, I had to go. I hadn't planned on being away long. Like I said, I was returning home when he called me. I couldn't have been gone over an hour or so."

"So you didn't see those creatures at his house?"

"No, it must have happened right after I'd left. I only saw the ones that accosted me as I was leaving the park on the way *to* his house. But as Zeke describes his dinosaurs, they sound a lot like the ones I encountered."

"Why didn't you just turn around and scoot back home when that happened to you?"

"Because I was already at the park exit on the highway and Zeke *still* needed me. I tried calling you, Henry." She shot his an accusatory look. "Many times. You never answered."

"I told you I was sorry." Henry met her eyes for a second before his returned to the road. Her face was flushed, her expression pinched. Her hands were held tightly in her lap. She was worried about Zeke. He pushed the pedal down harder. The car speeded up. "I must have been in a dead spot on the lake. Then we were in the middle of a leviathan lake battle…and running for our lives. I never got any of your calls when you originally made them. But as soon as we were docked, I noticed your messages on my phone and answered them."

"What are you talking about? What leviathan lake battle? What happened?" By the way she was looking at him he could tell she was shocked. It was in her eyes.

He told her about the dinosaurs in the lake, Steven falling in, the two different species' water battle, and their close call. He explained who Steven was.

When he was done, she laid her head against the headrest and moaned. "Oh, my, so dinosaurs are in the lake; the park is infested with them and it sounds as if they're migrating into town. What are we going to do?"

"Go help Zeke first and make sure he's okay. See what he has to say. After that I'll alert the proper authorities. I was only waiting until I had first-hand proof of what was in the lake, so I would know exactly what to say to the army and Park and Forest Services. Then I'll go from there. I'm trying to absorb what's happened. It's all been too much, too fast."

"I know what you mean. I still can't believe what happened to me this morning leaving the park. Those little monsters were organized. They behaved as if they knew what they were doing, what they wanted. Me. Remembering it now, it feels unreal. But I know it happened." Ann was watching the scenery as it flew past them. They had entered the town's limits. They'd be at Zeke's soon.

When they got there the old man let them in.

"I see you brought reinforcements, hey?" he commented to Ann. "It won't matter. The culprits have all skedaddled into the woods, the little cowards. There's nothing left to chase off or fight. Ann, I told you I was okay. You didn't have to come all the way back here."

"I had to be sure you were, Zeke," Ann refuted. "And you never know, those devils are crafty. They could still be out there watching and waiting."

"Ha, waiting for what? For me to put a load of buckshot in their butts?" He waved the shotgun in their faces. "Let me tell you, I'm ready for them. So just let them try."

Henry and Ann, with Justin, Steven and Ranger Gillian coming in after them, trailed Zeke into the kitchen. The old man led them out on the damaged porch. Outside the sun was low in the sky and purple shadows were dappling the woods at the end of the yard.

"See, those dinosaur devils did this to my porch. Trashed it into splintered wood. It's gonna cost me a pretty penny to fix it. Screened windows and wood aren't cheap these days; not to mention the labor to have it done. When I was a younger man I'd have done the work myself. Now days I have to hire someone to do it." Zeke shook his head. "Destructive monsters. They were all over my property trying to snatch and devour my squirrel friends—or me. But I showed them, I wouldn't let them!"

"I don't see anything moving out there right now." Justin was examining the yard and the trees beyond as he stood in the middle of the destroyed porch. He was right, nothing was moving anywhere in the descending twilight. The monsters had all gone home. Wherever home was.

The rest of them were gawking at the porch damage. "Wow, they did this much damage that quickly?" Steven was speaking excitedly. "Tell me, exactly what did they look like? How tall were they? How many were there? Did they make any distinctive noises–"

Zeke turned to Steven. "And who precisely are you, young man?"

"Just a musician friend of Justin's. I entertain at the Crater Lake Lodge some weekends. I was there this last one. Just my luck I hadn't left the lodge yet this morning and Chief Ranger Shore was nice enough to let me come on their lake adventure today. I'm thinking of writing a book on all these dinosaur happenings around here so Ranger Shore has let me tag along so I can get some firsthand observations."

"Good grief," Zeke expelled the words satirically, rolling his eyes. "Another book writer. Just what we need."

Henry reclaimed Zeke's attention. "Can you describe the creatures who attacked you and did this damage?"

"Sure. You all accompany me into the kitchen. I'll brew us a pot of coffee and we can discuss it."

"Go on inside, Zeke, and take Ann with you and we'll be in in a bit. I want to check out the woods first before it gets any darker. I have to be sure those creatures are really gone."

"Come on Ann, help me make the java," Zeke said, his voice raspy, his shoulders slumped with weariness, and Ann didn't resist; after a backwards glance at Henry she went with Zeke.

Henry signaled Ranger Gillian to follow him. And Justin, with Steven at his heels, fell in behind, and they moved towards the fringe of the woods at the yard's end. Both rangers and Justin had their weapons cradled in their arms, prepared for whatever they found. Only Steven had no weapon, but he stuck close to the other men as they entered the thicket of trees.

It was murky under the canopy. But after thrashing through the brush and exploring around the tree trunks the men discovered they were alone in the forest. There was no signs of anything living anywhere around them. No wildlife of any variety. No dinosaurs. The woods was eerily silent.

The men returned to Zeke's kitchen after an additional sweep around the house to be sure there weren't any dinosaurs lurking anywhere else. There weren't.

When Henry and the other men were seated at the kitchen table Zeke gave them his account of the events that occurred after Ann had left him.

It was quite a story.

Henry watched Steven scribble in a small notebook as Ann handed him a mug of coffee. The others got their own mugs and helped themselves. Everyone was listening.

Zeke finished with, "And I've been looking…there isn't one live squirrel left out in the yard. I think those dinosaurs got each and every last one of them. Ate them up like appetizers." His expression was sad. "I liked those squirrels. They were fine friends to me. I used to feed them scraps every day. Good thing I saved the littlest one, at least. He came in on my shoulder."

Henry's confused expression must have tipped Zeke off.

"Oh, my little squirrel buddy? He's around inside here somewhere." Zeke's eyes scanned the room. "Hiding somewhere under something, I suppose. He's not used to so many people, you know."

"Oh," Henry muttered. "You have a pet baby squirrel? And it's loose somewhere in the house?"

Zeke flashed him a grumpy look. "They make good pets. Mine is a smart one."

"Okay." Henry turned his head so Zeke wouldn't see his smile. Henry was just happy Zeke and Ann were all right. That they'd all made it through the day…unharmed and alive.

When Zeke was done, Henry came to his feet. "Zeke, we'll be leaving now. I want us home and safe behind solid walls before total darkness. And I want you to promise you'll stay inside once we leave. Promise. Or I'll never get Ann to leave here."

"I'm no fool. I'll stay inside," the older man responded. "Besides, I have to protect my little squirrel buddy. When I find him, that is."

"Justin," Henry turned to his son-in-law, "would you and your friend please drive Ann's car and take her home for me? You have weapons if they're needed. But be careful anyway. Don't stop the vehicle for anything. I'll take my car and meet you back at the cabin. I won't be long. We can talk about what we're going to do next when I get there."

"Where are you going?" Ann wanted to know.

"Ranger Gillian and I have to make a stop at the Klamath Falls Police Department. They need to know what's going on here in town. They need to be warned so they can prepare. I won't be long, Ann. I'll apprise them of the situation and be home fast as I can."

"They won't want to believe you, Henry," Zeke mumbled. "Dinosaurs running amuck in Klamath Falls. Ha. Just be careful they don't lock you up for a crazy person, son."

"Then I'll have them phone Captain McDowell or Agent Patterson for confirmation that dinosaurs do exist even in this day and age. Let the army or the FBI persuade the police I'm telling the truth."

"You won't be long?" Ann grabbed Henry's hand, edged up closer to him. She was frightened, he knew the signs. Frightened for him as well as herself.

"No, not long."

They said their goodbyes to Zeke, who was almost too busy searching for his lost squirrel under tables and sofas to be bothered and the four split up. Ann, Justin and Steven driving to the park and Henry and Gillian making a detour to the police department a few miles away from Zeke's.

As Ann's car drove away Henry hoped they'd end up at the cabin safely and he'd make it back in one piece as well. The night was coming and what else would it bring beside the darkness?

*****

Henry wasn't surprised when the Klamath Falls police chief, a stout fellow who went by the name Lester Chapman, didn't take him seriously about there being dangerous lizard-like creatures loose in the woods around the town. Henry knew better than to out-and-out call them dinosaurs. Most people tended to laugh at the very thought of them running loose anywhere in the real world. It didn't matter what had occurred in the park six years or a few months ago. If a person hadn't actually been there and seen the prehistoric creatures with their own eyes, they couldn't believe in them. It was only human nature to be a cynic about the implausible.

So Henry's visit with the police chief was short and not sweet. The man, eyes lowered and mouth a tight line throughout the conversation as he pretended to shuffle papers around on his desk, didn't actually laugh, but Henry could hear it behind his words.

"Where exactly did you say this, ah...confrontation took place, Ranger Shore?" The police officer was a small man with very short hair and bored eyes. He had this way of blinking a lot and looking elsewhere when he was talking. It was distracting.

"It's Chief Ranger Shore. And the

confrontation took place at Zeke Johnson's house on Main Street, not far from here. At the rear of his yard where the woods start. Zeke used to be the publisher of the Klamath Falls Journal until my wife, Ann, took it over from him."

"Oh Zeke, I know Zeke." Then the officer gave Henry a meaningful smile. "But he's getting up there in years, isn't he? Got to be in his eighties now. Not doing too well, I've heard. Physical ailments associated with age. A tiny bit senile. And sometimes older people, especially those who live alone, think they hear and see things that aren't really there. You know, to get attention, company?"

"Zeke isn't anywhere near senile. And he doesn't need to make up stories of monsters in his back yard to get attention. He has plenty of friends."

"I believe you, Ranger." He spread pudgy hands across the papers on his desk. There were other officers milling around outside the office, some listening to them through the open door, curious. "But he is an old man who spent his life publishing stories. I remember that series of articles some years back about the dinosaurs in your park. Very entertaining. Those photos were so real looking, too. Almost had me believing in them myself. Almost." Another condescending grin. Henry felt like punching his ignorant smug face.

"Just go take a look at the damage they did to his porch."

"Okey-dokey, I just might do that. Soon as I

have a little free time."

Oh well, Henry thought, he'd tried. He did warn the police chief. Just wait. Let him learn the hard way. What Henry was concerned about was the town and the people in the town. They needed to be warned, as well. Maybe Ann, who was friends with a lot of the owners, could call a couple of the local radio stations and have them put out a warning. She could run a front page story in her newspaper or post something on the Internet. Facebook or something. She knew more about social media than he did.

As Henry left the police station he told himself he'd have to have a few higher-ups drop in on the Chief to back up his story. Like Justin or Captain McDowell. Or perhaps someone from the FBI like Patterson. But he had no idea where Patterson was these days. Traveling, last he heard. Maybe the doubting police chief would believe one of them. Or maybe not. Henry had done what he could. Now he had his own problems to tend to.

*****

When he arrived at the cabin after dropping Ranger Gillian off at headquarters, Steven, Justin and Ann were gathered around the kitchen table eating cold meatloaf sandwiches and swilling down coffee. Ann had even scrounged up a cake for dessert. When he walked in, she rose from her chair and slipped into his arms. The day had unsettled her and she needed reassurance.

Needed her husband to hold her. He needed the same.

"Did you run into any more of those little monsters on your way back?" Henry asked her as Justin and Steven looked on.

"No, not a one. We drove here from town and nothing jumped out in front of the car or tried to hitch a ride. In fact, the park is strangely quiet tonight."

As if all the indigenous animals were hiding. Henry didn't blame them. If he could he'd hide, too.

Tugging away from his embrace, his wife smiled and sat down. She looked unusually tired. Probably from what she'd gone through. The scare she'd had. Zeke's incident. Any number of other things.

"And you...see anything suspicious on your way home?" She picked up her sandwich and took another bite. The kitten appeared from the other room and scrambled into her lap. With a yawn, it curled up and went to sleep there. Henry reached down and stroked the feline as he walked past. It meowed and went back to sleep.

"I saw no dinosaurs of any sort anywhere." He grabbed a cup of coffee and slid into the chair next to her. "But I, too, noticed how silent the park's land is. I didn't see one animal, furred or feathered, of any sort anywhere. Of course it's dark outside now and hard to see much of anything."

Steven, munching on a sandwich, between bites, spoke up, "Chief Ranger Shore, your wife's been kind enough to shelter, feed me and answer a whole mess of questions about all your earlier dinosaur exploits. Amazing stories she and Justin have been regaling me with." The young man grinned at him and for a moment it was like having two Justin's in the room. In so many ways, the men were alike. Even their excitement over the circumstances. Only difference, he was Justin years past. Overly eager. Innocent. Unaware of what was to come and how destructive and deadly the dinosaurs could be.

"Steven and Justin are both our guests for the night," Ann announced. "I don't think it's safe in the park in the dark. They shouldn't be out there. None of us should."

"I concur," Henry said. "Good idea, wife. It's not safe out there. Best to be cautious." They had two guest rooms so there was space for everyone. Henry got up and made himself a sandwich so Ann wouldn't have to. He was sure she'd waited on the men and she didn't need to be waiting on him, too.

"So what have I missed?" Henry asked when he was reseated, though it was easy to guess. Ann's laptop was open and humming away beside her on the table and its screen had on it a full color picture of the water dinosaurs from the lake that morning that either Justin or Steven had taken. Henry recognized the cast of characters. It was the big leviathan wrestling one of the smaller ones.

Justin had his iPad out, as well, and its screen

was filled with another version of the larger monster.

"These photos are incredibly disturbing," Ann murmured as she clicked through them, eyes glued to the screen, her sandwich on the plate in front of her, and which she hadn't eaten much of. There was a smudge of ketchup on her lower lip.

Steven launched into a recounting of the morning's adventure, complete with sound effects and embellishments, and Henry mused over what an intuitive guy he was. Witty. No wonder he was an entertainer. By the way he spun out his story Henry could see how he'd make a good novelist. His vivid descriptions made you feel you were right there with him on the boat seeing the monsters tussling, or him splashing helplessly around in the water trying to avoid being eaten. Henry had been there but listening to Steve's version had him reliving it over again. So much so it made him uneasy. The boat could have been wrecked and they could have died. Been dinosaur snacks. They'd been lucky. Again. Henry wondered when that luck would run out.

Ann seemed impressed with the musician. Her interest was genuine when she looked at or conversed with him. So he must meet her stamp of approval, which made Henry like the young troubadour even more.

The four of them studied the photos they'd taken and talked among themselves for a while, their eyes taking turns going to the windows, their ears alert for any suspicious noises beyond the glass. They'd brought the danger home with them.

"I think I'm going to go to bed. It's been a heck of a day and I'm tired," Ann told Henry and the others after they'd taken in the nightly news on the kitchen television set. There was nothing on it about dinosaurs in the park or in the town. No alerts, no alarms. No massacres. Not a thing. No reported attacks. No sightings. Nor anywhere else. Henry was relieved, yet he imagined they were only in the calm before the storm. The worst was coming, as it always did when dinosaurs were involved.

"Goodnight, honey," he told his wife. "Sleep in tomorrow. We'll be leaving early, I suspect. We have things to see to. But, please, this time, don't go anywhere. Stay here in the cabin. Keep your gun close. If Zeke needs you, call me or the police chief in town. Don't go out there alone."

"I won't," Ann sighed, "leave the house, Henry. I promise. I learned my lesson." Her smile was firm, but there were faint circles under her eyes.

She kissed him goodnight, took leave of her guests and exited the kitchen. Henry watched her go, a slight frown on his face. With all that was going on, most of the time Ann would want to be in the thick of it. Taking notes and scheming how she could use the developing story to boost the newspaper's declining circulation. It wasn't like her to slip out early on the action. Wasn't like her at all. But he'd observed her odd behavior lately. She'd been distracted, slow to react to anything and exhausted a lot. He pushed what that might be attributed to from his mind. He couldn't go there, not tonight.

Justin had been comparing Henry's description of the dinosaur that had assaulted him and their cat the evening before to perhaps a *Coelophysis*. "But that meat eater lived, oh, at least, thirty-five million years ago. I can't believe our species smorgasbord could reach back that far. But then, again, anything's possible with what we've already seen. Though *Coelophysis* does sound a lot like the creature you met in the woods. They were pack hunters and had small, birdlike heads with sharp teeth. The name means 'hollow form' because some of their bones were hollow making them lightweight like a bird. Their front limbs were like arms with three strong sharp claws to grab their prey. Yet the *Coelophysis* had a long tail, not a short one. Hmm." The scientist went back to scanning through dinosaur pictures on the website. "I'll keep looking."

Steven had been busy most of the evening, when he wasn't gaping at the photos or keying in things on his iPad. Notes, he maintained, for his book. He couldn't wait until the next morning when their adventure, as he was putting it, would continue. After what he'd been through already, Henry had to give it to him, the man had courage. Or he was just a thrill junkie.

"But on another matter," Justin questioned Henry after Ann had retired to bed, "I assume you've called in the troops and the appropriate authorities and they'll soon be inundating the park? Which means it's going to get crowded here again."

"Worse, I'm afraid this could mean the end of Crater Lake National Park as we've always known and loved it. My job. Everything. I could be retiring even earlier than I had anticipated. The park service could decide it's entirely too dangerous to remain open, this dinosaur problem has occurred far too often, and shut us down for good. I wouldn't blame them. Station the army here to keep people out until they can eradicate the creatures once and for all, if they can. I have my doubts. This situation has been building for years, six as far as we know of; probably more.

"I'd pack Ann off to Zeke's house as I did during some of our previous dinosaur crises, but if our prehistoric friends are already outside the park and in the town, I'd have to send her a lot further away than that to keep her safe. And there's nowhere else I could stash her. All our family and friends live nearby, except for you Justin. And I know my wife, she won't agree to being five hours away from her precious newspaper and Zeke. So for the moment she's as safe here in our sturdy cabin, stocked with high-powered weapons, as she'd be anywhere else. So far we've only encountered those small monsters and those living in the lake. Besides, I don't think she'd leave anyway. And she can be a stubborn woman when she wants to be.

"The way it's going, could be someday," Henry's eyes had returned to the dark windows, "they might have to wall in the whole place, make it off limits. Too many rogue dinosaurs prowling around. Too hazardous for human beings to be here." There was regret, but resignation, in his voice. "At least none of my men have reported seeing any of those giant flying gargoyles yet. We can be thankful for that." He paused, thinking.

"Someday," Justin echoed in a pensive tone, "if what I fear comes to pass and dinosaurs are being birthed along the entire western coast beneath other active volcanos, we'll have more to worry about than just this caldera and particular section of forest land being invaded with ancient human-devouring species."

"Wow," Steven had been listening and interrupted, "if there are other locations having the identical difficulties we are, we're in for a real fight. A dinosaur war. That'd be something." He was shaking his head, his eyes glinting with excitement. Oh, the ignorance of the young, Henry mulled. A dinosaur war would not be anything to desire.

"Yeah, that would be something all right," Henry groused, weary and fed up. Of all the times they'd been plagued with prehistorics, this could be the worst. It could mean the end of his and Ann's idyllic life and everything they loved. They might have to vacate the park for good and that depressed him.

The men didn't stay up much later, knowing dawn would arrive all too soon, but headed off to their bedrooms before twelve.

Dinosaur Lake III: Infestation

But Henry's sleep was restless. Strange night noises kept rousing him. Was that a bear or was that a dinosaur crying out? Was that a mountain lion or a prehistoric *velociraptor?* He had to be vigilant because they were out there and who knew when or where they'd strike next.

He dreamed of that reddish cat-snatching dinosaur. In his dream it grabbed Sasha between its sharp claws and bounded off into the darkening woods with her. He could hear her terrified meows as he chased them through the trees, swearing and stumbling. He had one chance to get the cat back, but when he caught up to them he raised his arms only to discover he had lost his gun somewhere along the way. And as he stood there the dinosaur ripped his little Sasha into bloody fur bits and stuffed them down its gullet; defiantly glaring at him the whole time. Licked its lips. Smiled. Honestly. Smiled.

Worse, there came a multitude of the creatures slipping out from behind the trees and around bushes, surrounding him. Larger ones. Licking their lips. Staring. At. Him.

In the dream he turned and ran for his life.

But he never knew if they caught him because he kept waking up.

Finally, he fell into an uneasy sleep and the dream didn't return. He was grateful for that because he was sick of witnessing his cat's bloody demise over and over. Sick of running for his life.

Chapter 5
Steven

The next morning Steven, Justin and Chief Ranger Shore, or Henry as he'd asked to be called, were up early, in the kitchen drinking coffee and eating a coffee cake Henry's wife, Ann, had taken out of the freezer the night before. Strategizing. Getting ready to leave. Ann was still sleeping and Henry let her.

Steven looked out the windows, hoping to see a live dinosaur. No luck. Darn.

Henry wanted to send him away. Out of the park. Steven didn't want to go, but his host insisted. "You'll be safer far away from here. Farther the better. So going is what you're doing."

His friend Justin, hoping to gather more facts and learn more, was driving down to the California coast to interview Chief Ranger Witter from Redwood National Park. Witter had come across what he feared were signs of dinosaurs in his park as well and Justin wanted to talk to him and the other rangers. So Justin was heading out, too. But not content to end his adventure yet, Steven had convinced his friend to let him tag along again. More fodder for the book he was writing. He'd leave his car at the lodge and they'd take off from there, with a ranger escort through the park for protection, of course.

Earlier Henry had suggested, "Since you're leaving this morning, I'd propose, Steven, you leave your car at the lodge if you're going to ride to California with Justin. Jimmy, the lodge's owner, won't mind. He has a large parking lot. I'll have one of my armed rangers escort the both of you onto the main highway and get you on your way. In case you cross paths with any more of those pack dinosaurs. That way it'd be three against a bunch of those little monsters, as Ann calls them. That should keep you from becoming their breakfast.

He and Justin didn't protest. A well-armed escort was welcome under the circumstances. He kept seeing the ferocious blood-lust of those lake Nessies in his mind and, as much as he'd love to come across some of the land dinosaurs, so he could say he'd seen them, he didn't want to end up in their stomachs, either.

"Don't be afraid, Steven. I'll help protect you. I, of course, have my own weapon," Justin disclosed with an amiable grin. "And I know how to use it."

"That he does," Henry had agreed. "You'd be as safe with Justin as you'd be with me or any of my men."

So Steven and Justin took leave of the ranger after they'd had their coffee cake. Steven had enjoyed the feeling of having a family, if just for one night and morning. He was alone way too much since his wife, Julie, had died. Staying overnight with the ranger, his wife, and Justin had reminded him of what he'd lost and still missed. He almost hated to leave, but the promise of a new adventure was a powerful lure. He was happy to travel to California and hear what the ranger there had to say. See the dead dinosaur Justin supposed they had in their possession. That would be so neat.

"I wish I could say goodbye to Ann before I leave," he informed Henry. "It was so kind of both of you to let me stay here last night. You have such a beautiful home. Well, except for the people-hungry dinosaurs lurking outside in the woods."

"I'll tell her you said our home was beautiful. She'll appreciate that. We've worked hard to make it this way. We love our home. I'll skip the stuff about *except for the dinosaurs.*" And the ranger looked miserable as he'd said it, his eyes roaming over the kitchen as if it might be the last time he saw it. Steven felt bad for him.

Then Steven and Justin got in Justin's Land Rover, leaving his Chevy station wagon at the lodge to be picked up later, and drove through and out of the park with a ranger escort tailing them. They saw or encountered no prehistoric beasts of any size or kind.

Ann had asked Justin the night before if on their way he could go through town and drop off a container of homemade chili for Zeke and also to kind of check up on the old man. Make sure he was okay. Justin had agreed. So they stopped at Zeke's house and had a visit. Once they got there, though, Zeke didn't seem to want them to go. He must be a lonely old guy. Steven looked at the man and, frighteningly, saw himself in forty years if he never found any one else to love and need him. It was a sobering realization. He wasn't getting any younger and he knew it. He couldn't be a lone traveling troubadour forever.

"Seen any more of those squirrel-eating forest critters since we left here yesterday?" Steven had quizzed Zeke before he and Justin had driven away.

"Not a one. But haven't seen one solitary squirrel or rabbit, either. I just pray those monsters aren't down the street somewhere snacking on one of my neighbors' pets or one of my neighbors. Wolfing down the Johnson's poodle or the Polk's golden retriever. I do believe if those monsters would have caught me, they would have thought I was just an extra big hairless squirrel and ate me, too." The old man gave him a rascally grin. "Let 'em try it now, I'm armed to the teeth. I bought a new rifle this morning. Just got back from the gun store. I'll shoot their stupid heads off. And I'm a crack shot."

"Colorful old guy," Steven told Justin as the man dwindled in the car's back window, then he turned his head to look around as they drove through town. He didn't want to miss any wandering dinosaurs if there were any to see.

But everything looked normal. A normal small town on a normal summer's day. Darn.

"You going to miss any singing gigs by coming with me?" Justin was swatting at a mosquito that had been trapped in the car, while he was trying to drive. It was flying around the inside of the windshield and his hand kept missing it. "I have no idea how long this trip will take, other than Redwood National Park is about six or seven hours away and we'll most likely be spending a night or two, at least, in Crescent City where park headquarters is located. It depends on what we find at Redwood and how cooperative their Chief Ranger is."

"Nah, it's providence, I had an eight day break between the lodge engagements and my next booking at the Red Carpet Nightclub in Tulelake. Now that this weekend's gig at the lodge is canceled, I have two weeks free. You think we'll be gone longer than that?"

Justin finally squashed the pesky mosquito, turned the wheel and they were on the highway leading out of Klamath Falls. Destination California. Not a dinosaur anywhere in sight. "I better not be. As you know Laura's five month's pregnant and she didn't like the idea of me going in the first place. Her anxiety level is already at an all-time high. She's worried about having the baby and now worried about me. With dinosaurs loose again and all." Justin seemed to remember something and abruptly stopped speaking.

Steven knew what his friend was thinking. He always knew. They were alike in so many

Dinosaur Lake III: Infestation

ways. Which was why they'd become instant friends that night so years ago when Justin had been in the audience at one of his very first gigs–gosh he'd been young, all of sixteen then–and asked him to play a tune he'd always liked. They'd began talking and had just hit it off. "It's all right. You can gush about your lovely nurse wife, the baby coming and your happy life. I can handle it. Now. Julie's been gone long enough that the pain's gotten better, bearable." He smiled sideways at his friend. "I'm happy for you and Laura. I know you've wanted a second child since you married her, even though you love her Phoebe.

"So, when we get to Crescent City where will we be bunking for the night?"

Justin's eyes were scanning the trees along the highway, inspecting the sky. "An inexpensive, but comfy motel called Quality Inn & Suites in downtown Crescent City. It's barely three miles away from park headquarters. So it'll be convenient." He looked at the dash clock. "If we make good time, we should have enough to check in before we meet Chief Ranger Witter at headquarters around six this evening, as he's getting off duty. I figure we can talk to him tonight, maybe over supper, and, if he has something to show us out in the park as he claims he does, tomorrow morning bright and early we'll take a hike out there with him to see for ourselves."

"Sounds like a plan. What's the weather like on the California coast anyway? I've always meant to go, see the majestic Redwoods, walk the beach, but somehow have never made it."

"It's strange you've never had a singing gig there."

"It is. Never have, though."

"Well, weather along the coast? I hear it's always between forty and sixty degrees Fahrenheit all year round. So I hope you brought a jacket."

"I always have one with me and, yes, I grabbed it from my car. I come prepared. I also have munchies in my suitcase for the motel tonight. A bottle of Jack Daniels. I recall you like that brand.

"You know, this is like a vacation to me." He was grinning again as the scenery swept by. The sun was out. It was a beautiful day and he was glad to be alive. After two years of grieving for his dead wife, it felt good to feel happiness again. It was still new to him. Being with his friend, Justin, helped. Though he'd met many people on the job, out in the nightclubs and bars, very few could he say were his friends. Fans, possibly, or hangers on, but seldom did he become close to them as he had with Justin and Laura. Justin was smart, ambitious and, scientist or not, he had the soul of a poet. No wonder they got along so well. And Laura was an interesting woman. Kind, as her mother was. Her daughter Phoebe was a spitfire.

Truth was, Steven liked their whole family. Ann was a sweetheart, also a kindred spirit being a journalist and all, and Justin's father-in-law,

Dinosaur Lake III: Infestation

the chief park ranger, was a hoot. A protector of the forest lands, a real adventurer and a dinosaur hunter. Kind of like Indiana Jones. The older Indiana Jones. The ranger told a good story, too. Talk about interesting people, they all were. In the middle of interesting lives.

"What do you think we'll find when we get there?" he questioned Justin, as he leaned against the seat, got comfortable. They had a long ride ahead of them.

"I don't know. Witter wouldn't talk about it on the phone. But he sounded a tad perplexed, scared, to me. So I figure he has something to show us. We'll find out when we get there."

"I've been wondering about some things," Steven broached after some minutes of thinking to himself and observing the town they were going through. One of those touristy quaint villages with historical buildings, shops and souvenir stores on every corner. An old-fashioned square in the heart of it, complete with band gazebo and ice cream stand. Looked like it was ready for the summer crowds to fill it up; for the music, an old polka band or something, to begin. Over the years, he'd played a couple places like it. He could almost smell funnel cakes and fried chicken on the air through his open window. He'd opened it because it had cooled down as they'd drawn closer to the coast.

"Like what?" Hunkered over the steering wheel, Justin appeared preoccupied with his thoughts but sent a quick look towards him, his expression patient.

"I know you've told me the stories many times about the dinosaurs you and your father-in-law have dealt with in the park already, but, you know, I have to confess something. I never truly *believed* everything you said to me about those escapades. Until I saw those Nessies for myself yesterday in the lake. I mean I believed you *believed* what you were telling me, but I couldn't *actually believe* a hundred percent. With the initial exhilaration of the paleontological dig and the wall of fossils you'd first discovered in the park, I thought you'd embellished the tales to impress me." He shrugged and was surprised when Justin laughed out loud.

"That's nice to know. That you thought I was a liar. I'm hurt to the quick." Justin took his right hand from the wheel and placed it over his heart, his expression a mocking wounded face. "But I bet you're a believer now, aren't you?" His laugh this time was softer.

"I guess I am, but it's still really hard. I've been a skeptic all my life when it came to anything fantastical, supernatural or previously...extinct."

"I get it. Besides live dinosaurs you didn't believe in vampires, witches or ghosts either, did you? I know exactly how you're feeling. Now seeing real dinosaurs makes you question everything you never believed in before, right?"

"Of course not! I still don't think those other fictional creatures exist. Do you believe in them?"

Justin shook his head and a flicker of light

bounced along the surface of his gold-rimmed glasses. He was still chuckling. "Not until I *see* them."

"No, wait a minute," Steven again plunged in, "I'm sure vampires and real witches don't exist, but I'm not so sure about ghosts not existing, though. Because you know, saying that reminds me of a story this crotchety codger laid on me one night last year when I was doing a gig in Klamath Falls. I'll never forget it. I was taking a break, having a drink someone bought for me. It was getting late and half the bar was empty. Outside it was storming. A perfect night for a ghost story.

"This elderly man was perched on a nearby bar stool, nursing a whiskey and soda. He leaned over and told me this wild tale. Like he had the need to tell someone. He talked, I listened. You know me, I have a weakness for stories. But the old guy really spooked me with his. You want to hear it?"

"Sure, entertain me with one of your fictional yarns, buddy. I love them. It'll help pass the time."

They were driving through another town, a larger one than the last, bright in the sunshine. Modern. Shiny windows and steel plated buildings. Lots of people and polluting cars. The traffic was terrible. It made Steven remember why he lived out in the country.

"All right. This old fellow said when he was a young man he spent many years wandering around doing odd jobs. You know, looking to find himself as many of us do. Anyway, for some years he'd worked as a companion/nurse to this elderly, retired gentleman name of Russell Graham. Now this old man he'd worked for had come from a sizeable, loving family and he'd outlived them all. There'd been three or four brothers and brother-in-laws he'd cared deeply for and dearly missed. And all of them, for many years, used to camp out in this wilderness spot. On one of his brother-in-law's land. They'd kiss their womenfolk goodbye for a long weekend once a year or more and all camp out at this place by the river. Under a huge Willow tree. They'd sit around a stone fire ring they'd built out in the woods the first year and when they came home they'd bring a large rock with the year's date and all their names scratched on it. They started out as nine of them.

"It was a treasured ritual. The nine of them traveling to that spot. Deep in the forest. Every year. Building and sitting around the fire ring beneath the tree, spinning tales and talking about how they would change the world, when they were young, and then as the years went by, speaking instead of their treasured memories and their hopes for their golden years. They were family, they were friends of the best sort. Always there for one another."

Justin was listening, his eyes on the road. They came to a stop and then speeded up.

"The years went by. Life went on for the family. Good things happened and bad. They grew old, retired from the working world, all had their medical issues now and again. Still the men all went on the annual camping trip every year and remained close. Twenty, thirty years. Now they had a fine collection of the signed rocks. All of the brothers and brother-in-laws, one by one, got sick, had heart attacks or something as deadly, and passed away, except for this old gentleman my friend on the bar stool was taking care of in the winter of the man's life and the spring of his.

"By the time the old codger I met in the bar that night came on the scene, all but the old gentleman had died. His client was the last one left. Feeling poorly, too. Age and chronic illness having finally caught up to him. The old gentleman would regale him with grand stories of their camping trips and mourn over their loss.

"Then the time of the annual camping trip came around. A crisp fall afternoon with the promise of winter in the air.

"The last remaining old gentleman wanted to travel to their special spot in the woods beneath the Willow and toast all his dead comrades one last time, even though the weather was forecasted to turn frigid later that night and a storm was coming in. So he asked his companion/nurse, a much younger version of the man on the stool beside me, to take him. Oh, not for the whole weekend. Just for the evening. Let him sit around the fire ring, build a fire. Remember those friends of his now gone. One last time."

When Steven paused too long, Justin asked,

"Well, did he do it? Take the old man to the woods to sit around the fire ring one last time?"

"Yes," his voice had fallen to a whisper, "he did. He bundled up the old gentleman in heavy clothes, his special camping cap that had seen better days, and took him out there, found the tree, the cold fire ring and plunked him on a lawn chair before it. He even built him a small fire because it had gotten so cold. Poured them glasses of whiskey and they toasted the ones no longer there. It started to rain and the wind to howl through the leaves. They knew they couldn't stay long. The old gentleman wasn't well.

"He began to shiver and cough, so the companion decided enough was enough and was about ready to take him home. First he had to run out among the trees and take care of some bodily business, if you know what I mean. When he returned he was shocked to see what he saw."

"What did he see?"

Still whispering, Steven finished. "As he came up on where he'd left his charge, he saw a blazing fire with a group of men around it laughing, drinking and talking. One had a guitar and was singing a haunting song he'd never heard before. But it was as if they were all in a smoky dream. He could see and hear them, but they were pale and see-through, as if they weren't really there. Just apparitions from another time. They were young, vibrant. Men he'd only seen in dog-eared pictures his employer had showed him many times. The brothers and brother-in-laws. His old gentleman was there, but real young. He recognized him by his beard, the shape of his face, the camping cap he always wore, and his silly grin. He even waved at him and smiled.

"And as he stared at the eerie gathering the men and their voices, the music, began to drift away on the wind, their forms dissolved, and suddenly there was no one there but his old gentleman, unmoving, in his lawn chair before a dying fire. Dead as stone. He'd gone to join his lifelong friends."

"Whoa...they'd all been ghosts, huh?" Justin's voice was restrained. "And they'd come to fetch him?"

"Well, yes I guess they did, if you believe in such things. Maybe the elderly gentleman's companion had had too much of that whiskey to drink and hallucinated the whole thing. Who knows.

"The old codger on the bar stool ended his story, winked at me, got up and left the bar. I never saw him again. It makes you wonder, though, doesn't it? If there are such things as spirits and if they come back for the right reasons?"

"Uh, huh, it makes you wonder. Interesting tale."

The rest of the drive they conversed about less spooky subjects such as their lives, their families and jobs. Catching up. Steven never getting tired of asking questions now and then about Justin's experiences with the earlier dinosaurs. He thought perhaps somehow he could use the stories in his book. He took lots of notes on his iPad.

"As strange as it sounds, because Oregon is so near to the coast, but I've never seen the Redwood trees either," Justin remarked as they were passing over the border into California. "I heard they're spectacular. Towering giants. I imagine I'll be seeing them now. You know some of them are over two thousand years old? They're some of the oldest trees in the world."

"Some of the oldest but not the oldest. I read about this one tree," Steven said, "I think it's called The Hatch Tree. It's a Great Basin bristlecone pine that grows in the California White Mountains. That tree they estimate is at least five thousand and sixty-three years old; which makes it the oldest tree in the world. Single tree, I mean. I think there are cluster groups of trees, clonal colonies they call them, that are probably older. One of them is almost nine thousand years old. And a colony of Huon pine trees covering two and a half acres on Mount Read, Tasmania, is estimated to be around, ooh, ten thousand years old, though there are even older tree colonies other places in the world, I just can't recollect them now."

"How do you know these things?" Justin slowed the car down for a stop sign and then increased his speed. "You're like a walking Wikipedia."

"I read…a lot. When you're on the road from one motel to another, singing for your supper, you have to do something to pass the down time and there's a great deal of that. I surf the web a lot, as well. I like knowing things other people don't. It makes for good over or after dinner talk."

"I bet. Okay, where's the biggest mountain in the world? The largest lake?"

Steven laughed. "Mount Everest, if you count total elevation above sea level. The largest lake is the Caspian Sea which is completely enclosed by Russia, Iran, Kazakhstan, Turkmenistan and Azerbaijan. And...the world's deepest lake, I believe, is Lake Baikal in Siberia, Russia, at around one thousand six hundred and thirty-eight meters deep."

"Photographic memory, huh?" With his right hand Justin opened the glove compartment and fished around until he came out with a bag of chips. Tore it open with his teeth, offered some to Steven who declined, and dug in.

"Most of the time. The older I get, though, the more faded the photograph."

"I guess that comes in mighty handy with memorizing all those song lyrics, right?"

"You know it. I have this older musician friend of mine, Colin Anders, in his seventies now. He began playing with bands in the nineteen sixties, what now is considered classic rock, and his memory is shot. Poor sod. He can't remember song lyrics for nothing any longer. Guitar playing is still real sharp, but not words. He had to stop playing because of it. Shame, he had such an amazing voice and could he pick that guitar. Hope that doesn't happen to me."

"I don't think it happens to every musician. How about The Rolling Stones, The Eagles and Paul McCartney? Countless others? They're still out there doing their thing well into their seventies or further. And doing it well, too."

Steven threw his friend a cynical look. "Those are the rare exceptions. Most traveling troubadours like me just grow old and fade away. End up broke and eating dog food in a rat-infested motel room. Die alone."

"Whoa, aren't you a pessimist. I guess you could say the same about most of us humans. None of us know how our old age will be," Justin concluded.

Then, as if he wanted to get off the gloomy subject, he offered, "Hey, there are Three Musketeers and Milky Ways in the glove compartment, too, if you want some."

"Thanks. You know the way to my heart. Chocolate and more chocolate."

"You and Ann have that in common, too, you know. She's also a terrible chocoholic."

"Nothing wrong with that." Steven was unwrapping a Milky Way. "Chocolate is one of the purest joys of life, for me, along with a well-played song. I eat it, I'm instantly happy. You can't say that about most other things in life."

Justin chuckled. "I wholly agree."

Steven blurted out in the carefree spirit of the moment, "Give me chocolate every day or give me death!"

The two friends exchanged an uncomfortable

look. Under the circumstances, it was a silly thing for Steven to have said. But, as he was discovering, it was difficult to be frightened every minute of the day or to remember that the world might now become more dangerous than it had been a few days ago. For him anyway. But he was more than aware that Justin had been dealing with the dinosaur problem far longer than he had, and had lost friends to the monsters, so he decided to go easier on the dying stuff from then on.

They made it to the motel long before six o'clock and Justin telephoned Chief Ranger Witter and arranged for them to meet at a local Applebee's where they could discuss everything over steaks. Besides, he and Justin really liked steaks. Rare. With heaps of onions on top. Yummy.

***

"No, I didn't want you to come down here and tell me what I already know. What I don't want to know, if you expect me to be truthful about it, Dr. Maltin. I'd really like to just forget what's happened and go back to the way things used to be. Normal. But I can't. The evidence won't allow me. Yet in many ways I still can't believe I've seen what I've seen. Don't want to believe it." Witter shook his head as he regarded Justin. Once and a while he glanced at Steven, to acknowledge there was a third person at the table, but most of his attention since the conversation had begun was on the paleontologist.

"You say there's been a couple of bad earthquakes in the park in the last five or six years?" Justin pressed, digging for more information. He had to pry it out of the ranger as the man wasn't at all forth coming with it.

"We always have a lot of earthquakes here in California," the ranger said with a somber expression. "So many that there are signs all over the park warning the visitors if we have one, especially if it originates out along the Pacific Ocean coast beneath the water, to be aware there could be a following tsunami close behind it...and to get to higher ground immediately."

"Have many of them lately?" Steven, suddenly uneasy, couldn't help but jump in and ask. "Earthquakes and tsunamis, I mean? Bad ones?"

"Seven or eight, maybe nine, in the last three years. But we've been very fortunate not to have had any tsunamis from them."

"What magnitude on the Richter scale, and where, were the earthquakes?" Justin asked.

"One we had in the park, oh, I'd say, about five years ago was a high six pointer. Another one two years later was almost seven. That one did a lot of damage. We're still finding destruction in the backcountry from it. Places we don't usually get into."

The Chief Ranger of Redwood National Park, Steven thought observing the man as he finished

Dinosaur Lake III: Infestation

his steak, couldn't have been more different from Chief Ranger Henry Shore if he'd been from another planet. Having come from work, he was in his ranger uniform. It was too tight, a little wrinkled. The man was short, sturdily-built and his brownish hair was shaved tight to his head making him practically bald. His eyes were a flat shade of coffee with heavy bushy eyebrows above them. Kind of reminded Steven of a short, chubby brown bear with a bad attitude. When the ranger spoke his voice was low, barely a gruff whisper, and you had to strain to hear him. But he was a no-nonsense kind of guy who rarely smiled, only stared at you as if he expected you to break park law any second. But then, he didn't have much to smile about at the moment, did he?

But there was something else odd about the ranger. He wasn't telling them everything he knew. Steven could feel it. There were unspoken words floating in the air between them.

"Will you take us to where the remains are?" Justin had barely eaten half his supper and was concentrating on what the ranger was saying and what he said back to him. The two men seemed to be sizing each other up, jockeying for control, and Steven was getting a kick out of it. Seeing Justin in his element, strong in his conviction of what needed to be done, was a new experience for him. His friend could sure hold his own all right.

Witter sighed, pushed himself away from the table and stood up. He'd told them when he first arrived he had something else work related he had to attend to and after a quick bite to eat he'd be returning to the office. "I'll do that. No trouble. I'll take you to where one of my rangers, Ranger Stricklin, was led to the dead creature last week. As I told you on the phone before you came, it isn't easy to get to. Way out in the back woods in a hard to find cave. The carcass is at the bottom of a pit in that cave. It'd be hell to retrieve so that's why we haven't pulled it up and gotten a closer look at it. I'll leave that to you and your team of scientists, Dr. Maltin, if you'd want to claim it for research. We only discovered it because some crazy spelunker decided to explore the cave and stumbled upon it. Came running to us to blab about it. He wanted to know if he could take away souvenirs if he could get down to it. I told him no.

"Now, excuse me you two, I have to get back to the office. I'll meet you at seven a.m. tomorrow morning at park headquarters and take you out to the cave. Come dressed warmly, prepared for deep woods and a wet, chilly cave climb. You can use our climbing equipment if you like. We'll share. Expect to be gone most of the day.

"See you both in the morning." And the ranger was out the door and into the faint light of a dying day, one much cooler than the one they'd left that morning in Oregon. But night was coming. Along the coast it would get much chillier when the sun went down.

"What a friendly fellow," Steven huffed sarcastically, taking another sip of coffee and making a grouchy face above its rim.

"About what I expected. Henry warned me he was a difficult man to get to know. A loner. He has trust issues. So I wasn't disappointed. But we don't have to be great friends to accomplish what has to be done."

"If you say so.

"What do we do now? The evening is young and we are in California. Just miles away from the coast and the ocean. And I've never been here before." Steven grinned at his friend across the table. "Let's go see it."

"Why not? We can drive along the coast and see the sights until the light is gone."

And after paying their dinner tab, that's just what they did.

Chapter 6
Steven

Steven woke before Justin, eager for their trek into the Redwood's deep forests to see what was waiting for them at the bottom of that cave pit. He'd charged his Smart Phone, dug out his new camera, and was dressed in warmer clothes as Justin was just dragging himself from bed. The room they'd shared to save cost for the night wasn't luxurious, no frills, but it'd been quiet and the beds had been comfortable.

"Up already, I see," Justin grumbled as he drifted past him towards the bathroom. "Impatient aren't you?"

"I can't help it. I want to see what's in the cave. Don't you?" He was sitting on the end of his bed. Tapping his foot on the floor. Fiddling with his camera. His eyes smiling.

"Oh, I can wait. Whatever it is, it's probably trouble." Justin closed the bathroom door. "I'll be ready in a few," his words came through the closed door. "Don't leave without me." Chuckles.

"I won't," Steven bantered back. Strolling to the windows, he pushed the curtain away to reveal the outside world. "Going to be a nice day. Sun's shining. No clouds in the sky except those wispy white ones. Great day for exploring caves."

Justin didn't answer, probably couldn't hear him.

They left the motel, drove through a McDonald's for a speedy breakfast and met Witter in his office at five minutes to seven.

"You can ride with us," Witter announced and strode past them outside to where a four-wheel drive park truck waited. "This is Ranger Stricklin–who the spelunker led to the cave–and Ranger Jefferies." On the way, he did introductions with a flick of his hand as he mentioned each ranger. Stricklin grinned from his tall height, his mustache partially hiding his smile, and tapped the brim of his hat that held down his long blond hair. Jefferies, much shorter than the other ranger, nodded, and his keen brown eyes matched the color of his skin.

As he and Justin hurried to catch up with the rangers Steven thought again how different Witter was from Ranger Shore. Shore inspired confidence whereas Witter didn't seem to care if he did or not. Wasn't very friendly, either. All business.

It was cool in the deep woods as the five men, with Ranger Stricklin at the wheel, drove the roads through the Redwood forest. Steven had to admit the trees were magnificent. Set amongst spruce, hemlock, Douglas-fir, berry bushes, and sword ferns which created a multiple canopied understory, they were a sight to behold. They rose to the sky around them. Wooden titans. It was good to know they were now protected from being harmed or logged. In 1850 old-growth redwood forest had covered over two million acres of the California coast, then after a minor gold rush brought miners to the area and the gold ran out, the gold diggers became lumberman and, uncontrolled, harvested the trees until there hadn't been many left. So in 1920 conservationists, seeing the urgent need, established a collection of California parklands to preserve and protect the ancient towering trees. Good thing. Looking up at their height, he thought what a shame it would have been if there'd been no more. If the lumberjacks had cut them all down for wooden tables and wardrobes. They were amazing. Ha, people. They needed to learn to cherish the planet, not plunder its natural resources until its surface resembled the moon. After all, nothing was infinite. Certainly not the earth and the gifts it gave humanity. When its treasures were gone, they were gone forever.

They drove for hours, he and Justin talking between themselves or with Ranger Jefferies or Stricklin. Justin wanted to know everything Stricklin had seen when he'd entered the cave the week before because he wanted to know what to expect.

"The cave's a huge mother," Ranger Stricklin revealed when Justin asked him about it. "To be truthful, I never knew it was there. Of course, the park's lands are vast. The man who stumbled upon the cave said he only explored a short stretch before he found the, er, remains. He didn't know what the carcass was because he didn't actually go deep enough into the pit he discovered it in to find out. All he said was it was massive. Stunk to high heaven, too. So he thought it might have been dead for a while."

"Are any of you coming into the cave with us?" Justin asked their companions.

All eyes went to Witter. He nodded. "Stricklin and I are. Jefferies will stay with the truck. Keep an eye out."

For what, Steven wondered to himself but didn't ask.

But Witter answered it for him. "Bears. There's loads of black bears in these parts. Big ones. They can be really mean if they stumble on you."

Okay. Bears.

By the time they got to the cave around noon Steven decided he liked both Stricklin and Jefferies. They'd been helpful and sociable. Talkative once they'd gotten them started.

Witter eventually thawed out, answering their questions and joining in the conversations. Once he'd seen they weren't crackpots or fame-seekers he questioned Justin about his dinosaur experiences and listened thoughtfully to what the scientist had to say. "These creatures have been extinct for millions of years so why is this happening now?"

"I wish I had the definitive answer to that, Chief Ranger, but I don't. I can only speculate what, in my opinion, is happening. I think it's the earthquakes. Crater Lake has been having a series of extremely destructive subterranean earthquakes the last decade, as has your California coastal region. And combined with the effects of the *ring of fire*, which includes seventy-five percent of the world's volcanic activity, that travels up through and into Canada and the heating up of the underlying magma meeting with long-buried dinosaur eggs…voila, live dinosaurs. I know it sounds unbelievable, but there you have it. That's why I've been making contact with all the National Parks along or close to the *ring of fire's* path. I want to know if other parks are infested like Crater Lake.

"If we find what I think we will in the cave, then my theories the dinosaur unearthing and birthing isn't entirely contained to Crater Lake National Park will be confirmed. And that it could be a nationwide event."

Witter studied the woods as if he'd never seen it before. "I hope you're not correct in that particular hypothesis, Dr. Maltin. I truly do. This forest is dangerous enough with its native wildlife so we don't need breathing dinosaurs skulking around also eating the visitors. And I wouldn't relish hunting the anachronisms down, either. I'm not much of a big-game hunter of any kind. I wouldn't want to have to hunt real dinosaurs."

"You wouldn't like it, no, if your park was overrun with the creatures. I've lived through that numerous times and, trust me, it's no fun. Some of this new breed is quite clever and they have species adaptations that are sometimes hard to believe."

Dinosaur Lake III: Infestation

"Species adaptations?"

"Oh, you know...mutants...bigger than the average known dinosaurs. Bigger teeth. Bigger bodies. Bigger brains. Wings."

Witter flashed Justin a strange look after that and fell silent. Probably still didn't believe in Justin's prehistoric beasts, yet Steven had to give the guy credit, he didn't look one bit scared. Ha, if he only would have seen what he'd seen, gone through what he'd gone through, two days before on Crater Lake with those battling Nessies. He wouldn't be so complacent, so sure he and Justin were the crazy ones.

Well, perhaps they were crazy and had hallucinated the whole Crater Lake water battle. Hmm. Uh, uh, he had an imagination, but not that much of an imagination.

The forest around them was thick with undergrowth beneath the tall trees and it felt more claustrophobic than Crater Lake's lands. Like a giant leafy hand closing down on them. The sun was pulsating above but the layers of branches and leaves transformed its light into dappled lace. Shadows rippled everywhere and Steven could almost imagine primeval phantoms skittering around and behind them in the vegetation. Shivering, he wondered if Justin was thinking the same thing. Were they really alone?

"We're about there," Witter announced, as Stricklin brought the truck to a halt. "We have to walk in the rest of the way. Hope you're wearing your hiking boots and have plenty of water bottles."

"We did and we have," Justin assured him. "We brought our own climbing equipment, as well, that we can use to descend into the pit and examine the dead creature. Whatever it is."

Steven caught the approving look Witter tossed Justin's way. "Good. You came prepared. Though, as I said yesterday we have climbing ropes and stuff with us, too."

Getting out of the vehicle, Steven accepted coils of rope and a backpack of supplies like what Justin had taken and their hike began.

They spent the next hour trudging through dense forest over compressed leaves, decimated limbs, brambles and rocks so closely packed together a car couldn't have gotten through. Steven was glad he exercised most mornings by walking or hiking wherever he was and that he kept in shape. Even then, with all the stuff he was carrying and how heavy it was proving to be, he was hard pressed to keep up with the rangers. Justin seemed to have no difficulty. Of course in his line of work he was always wandering or climbing around somewhere rocky, steep or wet and getting strenuous exercise. A couple minutes into their journey, Rangers Witter and Stricklin offered to carry some of the equipment and Justin and he gratefully agreed.

"Wow, now that's a cave. It's huge," he muttered as they stood before a jagged hillside hole surrounded by trees which partially hid it. The entrance was at least twenty feet in diameter. He made his way to the black hole opening and gazed in. "Looks really, er, dark in there. Smells awful, though. *Whoo-ie*. Something has definably went feet up down there. It stinks. What we should have brought along was gas masks." He covered his nose with his fingers.

Witter actually let out a chuckle.

"Well, no time like now. Stink or no stink, I'm going in." Justin had pulled a flashlight from his jacket, and a handkerchief he tied over his nose and mouth, and entered the cave. Ranger Witter and Stricklin fell into line behind him. Flashlight also out and on, Steven was last. He'd had to pull out his handkerchief and cover his face as well or he would have been gagging the minute he entered the cave. The rangers had nothing over their faces. Apparently they were used to the stench of dead things. Good for them. Show offs.

Steven had never cared much for caves and he knew Justin felt the same way. Any place dark, confining, slippery and wet, or full of wild animals like bears, snakes and bats, had never appealed to him. Justin also hated being on large bodies of water and he was afraid of heights. Those two things didn't bother him, just slimy caves. So he was impressed his friend was so brave about exploring it. But then if there was dinosaur at the end, or bottom, of anywhere, Justin would be gun ho to get there. That's one thing Steven admired about him, he was devoted to his profession. Loved it and everything to do with it. Just as he was about his. Music had always been and always would be his life, his obsession and greatest love. His calling. They had those passions in common. Probably why the two were such good friends. They were alike in that way, among others.

A short distance into the cave, Ranger Stricklin took the lead and within minutes the four men were entering a great cavern. Steven couldn't believe the cave was so big inside. "You have a lot of these humongous caves in your park?" he asked Witter as they stared around, sweeping their flashlight beams over the high walls and ceilings.

The stench was stronger now, just about unbearable. Steven hoped he wouldn't throw up and make a fool of himself. Something in his throat was trying to make him gag. God, what a disgusting smell. His hand was now clasped over the handkerchief tied around his face. Even that didn't help much. The odor was seeping in through his pores.

"I didn't know we had this one. Smaller caves, sure. The park is riddled with them. But I'm as surprised as you at the size of this mother."

Steven's flashlight beam found and tracked a tunnel that branched off from the main cavern, then another and another one. "Wonder where those lead?"

"They probably burrow for miles under and through the park," Justin said.

"And you'd be right," Witter answered.

Justin posed a question to Stricklin, "Where's the pit?"

"This way. Not far in." Ranger Stricklin led them across the open cavern towards one of the tunnel off shoots.

"I'm not a true cave expert, but this cave seems unusually large. Even the entrance." Justin directed light into corners and along walls as they struggled through the cave. His eyes roamed. Probably looking for cave dinosaurs. Afraid he'd see one.

"You're right, it is unusually roomy," Witter agreed evasively, yet offered nothing more.

Stricklin stopped and directed his flashlight into a deep hole. "The guy who showed me this said when he found it, a week ago, he thought he heard strange noises–from below. Growling or something. But real faint. That's what made him think it was some kind of animal. He wasn't sure what it was so he played it safe and didn't investigate up close. Said he looked down as best he could, saw something, something huge that wasn't supposed to be there, got spooked, and got the hell out of there. Reported his finding to us."

"Smart guy," Steven whispered. As the rest of them, he was staring into the pit. He thought he could see a lump of something, not rock or cave floor because its texture was different, far below. It wasn't moving. It looked like the left behinds of some animal. A really big animal.

Justin was slowly moving his flashlight's beam down into and around the pit. "Chief Ranger Witter, what makes you think the animal down there might be what I'm looking for? Might be prehistoric? Why am I really here?"

"Because *you* called me and asked the right

questions. Let's take a little side trip, Dr. Maltin. I have something else to show you. Follow me." The ranger swung away, led them to the other side of the cavern and sent his flashlight's glow to the wall in front of them. "This is one of the reasons why."

Steven closely scrutinized the surface, surprised at what he was seeing. Bones. Everywhere. The wall was embedded with hundreds of bones and fragments of something he couldn't identify right off. Egg shells, perhaps? There were loose bones on the cave floor, too. He followed Justin to the wall, and near enough to touch what was protruding from it. Even he recognized what he was looking at now. "Fossils? Dinosaur fossils?"

"Looks like it," Justin replied, skimming his fingers reverently across the wall, his face unable to mask his awe. "Just like the fossil wall my father-in-law discovered at Crater Lake. I'd bet it's full of previously unknown species of dinosaurs as well."

"Stricklin thought so, too," Witter interjected, "so when he was in the cave last week he collected a few of these loose bones and brought them back to me. I sent some of them to a paleontologist I know and he confirmed it. They're dinosaur bones all right...but there's another mystery...some, he believes, haven't been dead that long. Years maybe."

"Years?" Steven echoed, confused. "Not millions of years?"

"Not millions, no. Years."

Dinosaur Lake III: Infestation

"So that's why you think what might be down in the pit is what I'm looking for?" Justin had abandoned the wall and returned to the pit's opening.

"That's why.

"Well, what are you going to do now, Dr. Maltin?" Witter pivoted towards the scientist, his face darkened by the cave's shadows. "That's a dangerous drop. And you don't know what that thing at the bottom is. It may still be alive."

"I'm going to go down there and check it out. See what it is. But I'll be careful. I'm armed." Justin patted the pistol on his belt. Then he began uncoiling the rope, putting on his harness, and attaching the line to it.

"How far down do you think it is?" Steven wasn't sure he wanted to be lowered into the hole, but what a great scene it would make in his book if he experienced it firsthand, alongside his friend. If Justin, who was afraid of caves and heights, could do it, he should be able to. He wasn't a coward, though the thought of going into the inky abyss did give him a stomach ache.

It was so dark down there.

Behind the handkerchief, his mouth operated before his brain. "I'm going with you, Justin."

Justin didn't argue with him. "So I won't be alone. Anyone else want to descend into the hole with us?" He looked at the two rangers expectantly.

Both shook their heads no. No explanations, no excuses.

"We'll lower you two down and wait up here

for you," Witter said. "I need another man for that anyway."

"Thanks." After Justin helped Steven get harnessed, he handed the end of the ropes to the rangers, who used a sizeable boulder some feet behind them to wrap the ropes around.

"Ready?" Justin asked him and Steven nodded. *Maybe this isn't such a good idea*, he thought, but before he could voice his apprehensions Justin and he were over the edge and being lowered deeper into the cave...towards he had no idea what.

The drop was swift, though, and flashlight in hand, Steven was soon standing on the floor of the pit beside Justin. The two skimmed the black interior cautiously with their lights.

A minute later Steven breathed, "I don't see anything down here, buddy. Just a hole in a cave. Some rocks. That's about it. No dead creatures of any kind."

"Neither do I." Justin walked away from him and explored the rest of the area, his flashlight in one hand and his other hand on the butt of the pistol in his belt holster. It wasn't that large of a pit. Like the cavern above it was honeycombed with tunnels going in all directions. For some reason Justin didn't voice the desire to scramble down any of them. He barely looked at them. "You're right, there's nothing down here."

But Steven had the eerie sensation they weren't alone. There were eyes on him, he could *feel* them. His skin grew bumps. "Let's get out of here then."

"I'm with you."

Justin called to the rangers above to pull them up.

"We found nothing down there," Justin admitted to Witter when they were on top again. "Whatever was there isn't there any longer. If it ever was." There was disappointment in the scientist's voice.

"I did see something down there when I was here," Ranger Stricklin insisted, shaking his head. "I'm sure of it. And what about that smell, like something's been dead for weeks? The cave is permeated with it."

"It's another mystery then." Justin smiled nervously, his eyes moving around the cave as if he expected what might have been below to now be up there with them. Alive again, watching them with ravenous eyes from one of the tunnels.

"If you would allow us, I want to explore more of the cave, Ranger Witter, before we leave." Justin had undone his harness and coiled up the ropes, replacing everything in the backpacks.

"You don't need my permission doctor. We have a few hours before we have to start back, so use them up."

"You and your men can accompany us or wait for us here or outside. I want to see if there's any other signs of living creatures or more fossils."

"We'll stick with you," Witter said. "Just give me a minute to let Ranger Jefferies know what we're up to and we'll be with you." The ranger flipped open his cell phone and let the ranger outside know what was going on. Good thing they were close enough to the entrance for the phones to still work.

The four of them spent the next hour and a half exploring the tunnels rambling off from the main cavern.

They found nothing. But, many times, Steven could have sworn he heard strange animal noises, scratching and clicking, in the distance. He could never tell from what direction, never tell if what he was hearing was real or just his imagination. The exploration was filled with anxiety. He and Justin jumped at every unknown sound. He was sweating even though the cave was cold.

But they saw no dinosaurs of any kind. Dead or breathing. And they never found the cause of the revolting smell.

Steven was relieved. He hadn't wanted to be caught in the narrow tunnels with a live monster scuttling after him anyway. But as frightened as he was, if Justin forged on, so could he. In fact, it made him feel better about himself than he had in a long time, bravely following his friend through the tunnels. Looking for dinosaurs.

After they'd gone as far as they could, seen as much of the cave as feasible, with the time restraints, and found themselves in the main cavern again, Witter made the decision to leave for them. "Well, if there's nothing else to see or do, let's get out of this place. It gives me the creeps. Too far below ground for my liking. And the smell, I swear, has seeped into my bones. My nose can't take any more."

Yeah, Steven thought, my clothes probably stink like dead things. I'll have to either wash them right away or burn them. Most likely burn them. Which would be a shame. He really liked the shirt he had on. He'd worn it down to comfortable.

On the way out they stopped at the wall of bones one last time. Justin took samples from the wall itself he gently pried loose with his knife, picked up more from the cave floor and used his cell phone to snap photos. Steven brought out his phone and camera and took a full detailed series of shots. The find, at least, would be somewhat documented until local paleontologists could be sent out to further examine it.

They finally exited the cave.

Yanking off his handkerchief, blinking at the glare of the sun, Steven stepped in beside Justin. He didn't have time to utter a word before Stricklin joined them.

"Dr. Maltin, you asked me to tell you if I recalled anything else about what I saw in the bottom of the pit that day last week?"

Justin, after removing the cloth from his face, canted his head at the ranger. "You remembered something else?"

The ranger's voice was intentionally low as he continued, "Maybe. I think the creature I saw in the pit had…wings."

"Wings?"

Stricklin sent a furtive glance at his Chief who was walking ahead of them. It was warmer than when they'd hiked out and there were beads of sweat on Stricklin's face. "Yeah, I didn't mention it before because, well, it made it sound as if I'd seen a dragon or something. You know, the mythical beast from fantasy tales?" His grin was apologetic. "My boss already thinks I'm off the track a bit with what I say I saw in the first place. But, yeah, I think the thing might have had wings. They were folded against its body and they weren't that large. I just thought I should mention it to you."

Steven noticed how Justin's face changed to one of instant concern. "Thank you for telling me that, Ranger. And I don't think you're off your track, not one bit. Someday I'll tell you a couple of true accounts that'll make your really doubt your sanity, but not now. You're still one of the uninitiated.

"And," Justin murmured, "I hope you stay that way."

Ranger Stricklin gave the paleontologist an odd look. "What are your plans now, Dr. Maltin?"

"My friend and I will spend the night in town and tomorrow will head back to Crater Lake. I'll notify my job–I work for John Day Fossil Beds National Monument–of what we found in the cave. The wall of bones. The possible sighting. And I'm sure they'll be in touch with your local paleontologists and Chief Ranger about all of it.

"And, you never know, you might see us here again in the near future. I'm not done with that cave yet, or this park."

"You believe I saw something down there and you want to find it?" Stricklin concluded.

"You got it." Then Justin stopped walking and looked directly at the ranger. "But I have the feeling this isn't the last you'll see of the creature from the pit. My guess is it'll show itself soon enough to someone. If it does, could you please give me a call? Your Chief has my telephone numbers."

The ranger tipped his head affirmatively. "If I see another one of those *dragons*, I'll be sure to ring you."

The trek to the truck was mostly without conversation. Everyone was exhausted and the sun was inching lower every minute. Steven understood Justin, and the rangers, wanted to be out of the woods by the time night came.

So did he.

But all for different reasons.

The three rangers wanted to get back to their office and then home. Justin wanted to get back to Crater Lake and then home to his wife and child.

Steven wanted to see what came next.

*****

He and Justin were in the car driving to the motel when he asked him, "You believe there was a dinosaur in that pit, don't you? And that, if it didn't drag itself away some place to die, it's still there loose somewhere in the cave's tunnels or out running–or flying–wild in the park?"

Justin didn't take his eyes off the road as they parked in the motel's parking lot. "I'm sure of it. I saw too many signs something's been living in those caves. Good guess is it's prehistoric, as well. There's those cave bones and fossils. That smell. Very distinctive. I've smelled that particular odor before. Dead dinosaur. Dead Hugo, in fact."

"Hugo?"

And Justin explained about the specimen he'd called Hugo they'd found at Crater Lake the last dinosaur go-round. "Hugo had wings, too. So did his many brothers and sisters. And, man, did he have a shit load of them."

"So you think what that ranger saw in the pit was another, er, Hugo?"

"I'm pretty sure it was. Which is both a good and bad sign. That species could fly great distances so it's possible it flew all the way here from Crater Lake, drawn by the giant Redwood trees. That would be the lesser of two evils."

"What's the greater?"

"That it was born in that cave we just explored, in Redwood National Park, and there's…more of them. Which would prop up my theory the dinosaurs are an epidemic and it's spreading. Oregon and now California. And no telling how many other locations as well. I'm going to continue my inquiries with other park lands, especially those in the vicinity of volcanoes, in California, like Yosemite, Death Valley and Sequoia; and other national parks in Nevada and Arizona, and see if any of them have glimpsed any strange creatures roaming or flying around in their woods."

Steven didn't have anything to say to that. All he could think about was that if Justin was correct, then dinosaurs could soon be popping up all over the place across the United States.

Not a good thing.

He thought if that was what was happening then Justin might be right. They could be on the verge of a different life…where they'd have to learn to live with, evade or fight a new generation of dinosaurs.

For the first time he truly understood what it might mean. He got it. And it frightened the hell out of him. Everything would be so different. He couldn't imagine traveling from one singing engagement to another and having to always be on guard for dinosaur attacks, no matter how many books he could write and sell about them. Yikes, he'd have to carry guns, ammunition, and keep his eyes peeled for dinosaurs. Wear body armor. Get physically fit and stay that way. No more chocolate bars and donuts. Stay out of the woods. Avoid empty buildings and desolate places. Just like that crazy Walking Dead series, except with dinosaurs instead of zombies. It'd be a real inconvenience all right.

And suddenly he grasped it was not one he'd want to deal with twenty-four seven. Forever. Who would? So he sure hoped Justin was wrong about all of it.

Chapter 7
Ann

Ann left the doctor's office trying not to let her possible diagnosis bring her down. Doctor Williams had reported what she'd already known. The cancer might have returned and she could be facing another round of chemo and perhaps, this time, surgery. Further tests were to be scheduled along with a CT Scan and they'd know for sure. She was depressed over the very thought she might have to get back on the cancer merry-go-round and have more treatments when she'd just finished the last ones. Then, sitting in that chair in the doctor's office listening to her prognosis, in a heart-stopping instant, after months of believing she was cancer free, the fear returned. *It wasn't really gone.* She might still be sick. She wanted to scream at the sky, stomp her feet, throw up her clenched hands and run in mindless circles–she wanted the cancer to be gone. For good and forever. No such luck. How was she going to tell Henry? Tell her daughter? Wiping tears from her eyes, it was almost too much to bear.

As if she didn't have enough problems in her life at the moment with deciding to sell the newspaper, Zeke's worsening health and dinosaurs loose again in the park and in town. She didn't need another complication.

Like today. Henry didn't want her traveling back and forth to town for any reason since she'd been attacked but she'd slipped out this morning for her doctor's appointment because she hadn't wanted Henry to know she was going. She had to go alone. Why worry him further if there was no reason to and the cancer hadn't returned? If he knew she'd driven to Klamath Falls by herself he'd been really upset with her. But she figured she'd drive straight there and back, be extra vigilant, and he'd never be the wiser. She couldn't stay locked in their cabin forever like some prisoner, especially when there'd been no more dinosaurs seen for days. Besides, as far as she was concerned, those little reddish striped buggers weren't much of a threat. She could handle them easily enough. They weren't any worse than the park's wolves or bears. She had a gun and the protection of her car. She'd be fine. The big monsters were in the lake and she'd be sure to stay far away from it.

Getting in her car she reached across to the passenger side and retrieved the SigSauer holstered on a gun belt and slipped the belt around her waist. After her and Zeke's incidents Henry insisted she carry a weapon with her, so she'd be able to protect herself if she came across any more dinosaurs. Which was funny when she thought on it because, even though the park was shut down indefinitely, no one else–the media, the town or townspeople–seemed to believe there was a threat. Warnings had been given to the local news media, warnings they ignored even though verbal stories, and in some cases videos, of people encountering strange creatures were suddenly everywhere, and she'd run articles on the dinosaur outbreaks in her paper...but most people still thought it was a hoax. They laughed and joked about it. The local police didn't take it seriously, either. There was not much else she and Henry could do than what they'd already done. Now it was up to the dinosaurs. People would find out soon enough what they were up against. And when they did, they wouldn't be laughing.

Her thoughts returned to her home. It was strange living in the locked-down park in the heart of the summer season, knowing it might not ever open again unless her husband, his rangers, and soldier friends could rid the park once and for all of their prehistoric guests. Henry and Justin were out every day hunting for them in the woods. Henry had called in the army again, though she knew he didn't have much hope the soldiers could do the job. They never had before. The dinosaurs, Henry swore, were too clever to be caught if they didn't want to be. They knew how to hide. Not one sighting or encounter had occurred since the day he and Justin had been on the lake, that little run-in Zeke had had in his backyard and her own experience. The dinosaurs seemed to have vanished. Just like that.

Henry kept asking, where have they gone? Where could they be hiding? What are they waiting for? No one knew. So everything was in limbo as he and his men waited for the dinosaurs to make their next move. It had been so long now Ann could almost believe the park was safe and there were no anachronisms lurking anywhere. False security. Wishful thinking.

Another thing that was bothering her was what would she and Henry do if they officially closed the park for good? Would he lose his job; the insurance she so desperately needed now? Would they have to move? She kept telling herself even if the park never reopened they'd need someone to patrol it and keep an eye on the situation. Could be they'd still need some rangers for that. Ann wasn't sure how she felt about it, though. Living in the park with no visitors and maybe multiplying herds of dinosaurs? At what point would the scale tip and the park be completely claimed by them? At what point would humans be exiled forever?

She was aware of Justin's dinosaur search, his ongoing investigations of the other national parks in surrounding states. He feared the infestation was spreading. So did Henry.

Yet for right now, she had to keep living, doing her everyday tasks, errands, tending to her responsibilities, dinosaurs or no dinosaurs. What else could she do?

Since she was already in town and close by, she should stop by the newspaper and show her face. Make sure the weekly edition was on schedule. She'd been spending less and less time there lately and her employees must be curious as to why. But her decision to sell the newspaper was still pretty much a secret from everyone and she still hadn't discussed it with Henry. He had enough to deal with. Staring out the windshield at the storefronts and sidewalks full of busy people, she knew she'd have to talk to him soon. If the cancer had returned, she'd be selling the newspaper as quick as she could. *If she didn't have a lot of time left she didn't want to waste even one minute of it. She wanted to be free. She wanted....*

Someone she knew waved at her and plastering a smile on her face she waved back. Observing the unsuspecting townspeople going about their usual business, she knew most of them had no clue as to what was happening. They wouldn't be clueless for long.

Oh, well, something else I can do nothing about. Something else I can't control. Let it go, let it go.

Suddenly she just wanted everything to be the way it had been. Looking around, she thought, *it all looks so normal*. What are we all so afraid of? We're just being silly. If there's a problem, Henry and the army will take care of it like the last two times. Simple.

Heck, she should stop by Zeke's before leaving town and see how he's doing. She hadn't checked on him in days and she was worried about him. If he was eating properly, if he was feeling better...if a herd of dinos hadn't carried him away and devoured him. She was about to start the car and drive over there when she saw Ellie Stanton, in street clothes, her long brown hair flowing down her back, exiting from the Klamath Falls Market. The woman's eyes were on her. She'd seen her.

Ellie wasn't only one of Henry's rangers, she'd become a friend. They often had lunch together or would trade visits at each other's houses and gossip about what was going on in the world, brag about their children or their cats. Ellie had been the one to find Sasha for her. Ann hadn't had a true friend in years and it was nice having someone to girl talk with.

She leaned out of the open car window and shouted, "Ellie! Ellie! Over here."

The other woman had recognized her and, arms loaded with groceries, ambled over. "Well, hello Ann." She smiled, shifting the bag in her arms. "Ah, I see you escaped the park too? I'm surprised Henry let you out."

"Hey, he's not the boss of me! I can take care of myself. And I have a big gun," she smiled, "for protection."

"Hmm, don't we all these days." The ranger patted her waist. She had a gun, too. "Strange times. Even though there's been no dangerous *creatures* spotted in over a week, your husband still wants us to be cautious. Keep an eye out and be ready to defend ourselves."

"I'm surprised he let you come into town," Ann said. "What with all that's happening."

The ranger hesitated, looking a little guilty. "Like you, he doesn't know I'm here. I snuck out. I needed groceries and Miss Kitty Cat was completely out of food, too. I had to come into town to shop. You know your husband, my boss, hasn't actually forbidden us to leave the park. Not yet anyway. So, Ann, how about you? Are you in town working or just goofing off?"

It made Ann feel better knowing if Henry hadn't forbidden his rangers to leave the park, then her leaving it couldn't be viewed as a high crime, either. He was just being overly protective of her since her illness. "Neither. I had a doctor's appointment." Something in her eyes must have given her inner turmoil away because the other woman's expression immediately changed to a sympathetic one. But then Ellie was an usually perceptive woman. It was hard to hide anything from her.

"Okay. Something's wrong. I can see it on your face."

"No, no, nothing's wrong," she fibbed. "You know how I feel about doctors and hospitals lately. Just going for a check-up revives unpleasant memories."

Ellie didn't answer but went around to the passenger side, slid in and put her bag of groceries between her feet on the floor board. Leaning against the seat, her brown eyes met Ann's. "Don't lie to a friend. I know you too well and I can see you're troubled about something–besides the dinosaurs showing their ugly selves again, I mean."

"There is that," Ann replied.

"You've been to the doctor. Something's wrong. Spill it."

Ann resigned herself to blabbing everything. Ellie Stanton wasn't someone she could keep lying to. Besides, Ann didn't like lying. It was so much easier telling the truth. Easier to keep her stories straight.

Sitting there in the car's shadows, Ann let the words come. Most of them, not all. What the doctor thought might be going on, but not what Ann already feared was going on.

Dinosaur Lake III: Infestation

"Ann, I know everything's going to be all right. Doctors tend to play it safe these days. Tell you the worse scenario so it's not such a shock if it comes true. That's why she wants more tests. She isn't sure. Have faith."

"I always do."

"So, what are your plans for the rest of the afternoon? Have you had lunch yet?"

"I'm not real hungry right now. It's a little early. And I need to get back home before Henry finds out I'm gone. But I was planning on making a quick stop by Zeke's, to see how he's doing. I have to keep an eye on him these days because of his failing health. Not to mention he had a run-in with some small dinosaurs himself last week."

Ellie knew Zeke well. She'd met him at Ann and Henry's summer barbeque, knew him from around town. "Zeke was attacked by dinosaurs? When?"

Ann told her the story as they sat there in the car.

"But he's okay, huh?"

"He's okay. Just not feeling well these days. Old age, you know. Would you like to come along and say hi? He'd be happy for more company. He took a shine to you the few times he's met you." Her eyes went to the grocery bag. "Unless you have ice cream or something just as perishable in there."

"No ice cream, merely a steak that needs refrigeration. The rest of the stuff can sit in the car and be perfectly fine, even in this awful heat."

"You can put the steak in Zeke's refrigerator while we're there. He won't mind."

"Ha, the old coot might just keep it for his own supper."

"He might. He loves steaks. But he'd burn it to a slab of charcoal, that's how he likes them. Black. What a waste."

The women laughed.

Ellie started to ease out of the car. "I'll follow you over there then. I'm familiar with where he lives. You know the steak is big enough for all of us. We could grill Zeke a nice lunch while we're there. I have potatoes and ears of corn in the bag, as well."

"Well, I hadn't intended to stay that long…but I guess Henry couldn't get mad at me for being in town if you're with me."

Ann caught the funny look Ellie gave her and wondered what that was all about. But she didn't ask.

"You being one of his armed-to-the-teeth rangers and all. It's like I have a built-in body guard. And lately I stop by and make meals for my old friend because he hasn't been well. You sure you want to give up your steak for us? That's so sweet of you."

"That's me. Sweet and generous. But I like Zeke. He reminds me of my Yahooskin grandfather. He even looks like him some. Same eccentric character, too."

Ann laughed again. "Yeah, he's a character all right. See you at Zeke's then."

Ellie slid out of the car and hurried over to her vehicle. A few minutes later Ann, with Ellie's car practically on her bumper, parked in front of Zeke's house.

Dinosaur Lake III: Infestation

*****

"Zeke, where are you? Zeke!" Ann moved through the living room and entered the kitchen. She found him there speaking on the wall phone. She thought he must be one of the last people left in the country who still had one.

He glanced over, smiled, gestured a hello and for her to sit, and continued talking. Ann lowered herself into a chair. The kitchen was a mess. Dirty dishes in the sink, the table stacked with papers, plates and things that hadn't been put away. The floors didn't appear too clean, either. When Zeke got off the phone, Ann reasoned she'd guilt him into letting her clean up some. Wash the dishes. Sweep the floor. Put things away. He was usually such a stickler for cleanliness but she'd noticed his high standards had fallen drastically since he'd begun feeling bad.

Zeke's pet baby squirrel was curled up in a box by the stove, sleeping. A tiny ball of gray fur. It must be unafraid of people or a heavy sleeper because it didn't stir or wake.

Ellie had trailed her into the house and Zeke, also acknowledging the other woman's presence, signaled her to sit as well. This time a smile covered more of his face before a frown replaced it. Zeke, no matter how sick he was, loved company.

"Now, Wilma, take it easy." Zeke was in animated conversation, shaking his head, shutting his eyes for a breath or two as if he were overwhelmed by what he was being told. He looked tired. Thinner. Weaker than the last time Ann had been there. She wondered when was the last time he'd seen his doctor.

Zeke's eyes popped open and his voice rose. His wrinkled hand touched the side of his cheek. "Are you sure? Outside your house...your window...*now*?"

Ann's reporter sense kicked in and she sat up straighter. Oh, oh, trouble. She could hear, feel and smell it.

Zeke cried out, "Wilma, don't! You stay in the house, lock the doors and I'll call the police, ya hear! They'll be there in minutes. Wilma–".

Ann heard the screech through the line and abruptly cut off. A woman's cry for help.

The old man dropped the phone so it dangled from its cord. As he dashed past her and Ellie into the living room, he yelled, "Going to get my shotgun out of the hall closet and head down to Wilma's. There's something–some nightmare monster as she calls it–outside her back door, peeking in the windows and giving her the evil eye, and she's so scared she's escaped the house coming this way. I have to get to her before that thing, whatever it is, gets to her." He didn't wait for their reactions, he was already in the next room at the closet grabbing his gun.

Some nightmare *monster*? Oh, no.

"Zeke! Wait!" Ann shouted as she met Ellie's eyes. The off-duty ranger, too, had come to her feet and they chased Zeke who, shotgun in his arms, was already out the door and stumbling down the sidewalk in front of the house.

Ann and her friend rushed out behind him. She

was glad to have the SigSauer on her hip. Glad Ellie was carrying a weapon, too. They might need them.

She knew who Wilma was, everyone in town did, and she knew where the old woman lived. Wilma Stuart, a retired grade school teacher, resided in a rambling derelict of a house a block down from Zeke's. She and Zeke had lived near each other for decades and had been friends since childhood. Years ago Wilma had worked as a secretary at the newspaper. A widow, as Zeke was a widower, she was alone in the world; her children long grown and gone, scattered to distant states. Lately, Ann suspected there was more between the two old folks than merely friendship. There was nothing Zeke wouldn't have done for Wilma.

"Zeke! Zeke! Wait for us. Don't go over there by yourself." Ellie, faster than Ann on her feet, caught up with him, grabbed an arm and swung him around. "You'll need help. It could be more of those dinosaurs you faced. You can't go charging over there by yourself. It could be too dangerous."

But that poor old woman, Ann thought meeting Ellie's gaze, how terrified she must be.

"Okay," Zeke spat out. "But we have to hurry!"

As they ran down the sidewalk Ann was aware of how hot it was. The heat took her breath away. Sultry waves shimmered above the concrete and made the trees and buildings they passed look like mirages. The sun was a round oven above them radiating out its heat. Sweat was trickling down over her shoulder blades, covering her face and arms with a thin glistening film.

Ellie was communicating frantically on her cell

phone and by the tone and content of her dialogue Ann assumed it was the local police on the other end. Good luck, she thought, getting any of the cops to help them. The police chief still thought they were a bunch of loonies with their dinosaur stories.

They were nearly to Wilma's place.

And there was Wilma hobbling towards them. She was crying and carrying on hysterically. Her elderly face a mask of terror as her arms flailed around as if she was trying to fly or something. She was moving as fast as her seventy-something legs could move her. A tiny woman, barely over five foot tall, she had close cropped hair a silvery gray and pale blue eyes. She had a kind, generous soul and usually had a big smile for anyone she met. She wasn't smiling now.

"It's chasing me! It's…right behind me." The old woman collapsed into Zeke's arms. "We have to get out of here! I think it wants to eat me!"

Then Ann heard the creature. Its roar shattered the hot day. The buildings around them shook. She looked up and there it was. The monster. It was framed by the houses and businesses of the town's main street and completely, unbelievably, out of place. Barreling down the sidewalk, it was as vicious as a rabid bear, but a hell of a lot bigger. An otherworldly nightmare plopped into their mundane everyday existence. She almost couldn't believe her eyes until it roared again. A louder, angrier bawl of rancor.

It wasn't the same as the beasts that had swarmed over her in the park or, by his description, had assaulted Zeke. This was a genuine monster,

Dinosaur Lake III: Infestation

gigantic, rising at least thirty feet above them. Godzilla-like in so many frightful ways, but not the same as the first dinosaur that had terrorized the park years ago and Henry had called by that name. This one had scaly skin the color of dirty water, ran on four powerful legs, had a short, bulging neck with a ruff of fins, small beady eyes and a mouth, full of jagged teeth, that took up most of its small head. No wings.

Whoa, but the brute was big. And mad. Probably hungry. How in the world had it gotten all the way into town without anyone else seeing and reporting it? Now that was a mystery. It couldn't be missed as big as it was.

Ellie stopped and looked upwards and Zeke's mouth dropped open. Wilma was panicked as she peered over her shoulder at what was tracking her.

People around them had noticed the creature as well. Suddenly there was screaming and yelling, people tripping over themselves to run away. Cars whizzing by with wide-eyed people at the wheels. Staring at the monster in the middle of town.

All of it was so…unreal.

But the monster was real enough and Ann knew, in a heartbeat, there was no way of fighting the thing, just fleeing–as quickly as their human legs could carry them away. If she pulled her pistol and fired at the behemoth the act would only anger it more than it was already angered. She'd been here before and knew, with a dinosaur this big, regular guns rarely did the job.

Ellie drew her weapon and fired at their pursuer.

Zeke raised his shotgun and did the same. Ann

couldn't be sure if their bullets hit their target because the monster kept on coming. Ha, she knew tiny bits of metal wouldn't faze it.

"We have to find a place to hide!" Ellie shouted above the sounds of pandemonium as townsfolk scurried around and past them. Probably also searching for a place to hide, or get a stiff drink, somewhere. "Follow me!"

No one argued. They staggered behind the park ranger between two large houses and across the next street.

Ann heard, but didn't see because she was too busy helping the old ones whose legs weren't as spry as hers, a house being smashed to smithereens behind them–had people been in that house? A board embedded with nails zipped by her head, barely missing her.

A human scream and a series of guttural ranting curses erupted somewhere in their wake. Someone was being hurt; someone was dying. Ann's stomach heaved at the memories it revived. This, too, had happened before. People injured and slaughtered. Too many times. She couldn't believe it was happening again.

The stampeding nightmare bellowed. So close. Too close.

Someone, a man, was shrieking for help and it made Ann sick they couldn't backtrack and help him, they had the old ones to get to safety. His cries ceased abruptly.

Where to go. *Where to go!* They had to find somewhere to burrow into until the danger was past.

Ann took a chance and looked behind her at the

commotion. The creature was looming above them, not more than a house's yard or two behind them. It was busy. It had grabbed a woman from a front porch–thank God no one she knew–and was EATING her! Ann almost lost her stomach then and there, but Ellie yanked her on.

"Don't look!" Ellie cried. "Keep moving or you'll be next!"

"There's a cellar in Skeeter Lockwood's backyard here." Zeke was breathing hard, his useless shotgun still in his grasp. He pointed at a dirty red rectangle of ribbed wood hidden in the grass about twenty feet from them. "The old coot never locks it, says there's nothing worth stealing in it. He won't mind if we use it for a bit."

Ellie didn't falter, she ran over and pulled up the cellar door and ushered all of them down the stone steps into the gray hole, slamming the door over them. None too soon. The ruckus above let them know the beast was very near.

Wilma stumbled on the steps but Zeke caught her. She was weeping with exhaustion and fear and Zeke consoled her. "It's all right, my dear. We won't let it get you. You're safe. It won't find us down here."

The humans huddled together in the murky space beneath the door among the dirt and spider webs and listened. The noise, roars, cries and thuds of destruction, rose and then dwindled away. The creature had moved on, or so Ann prayed.

Outside there was silence.

"You think it's really *gone?*" Ellie asked, crawling towards the door in the dark.

Ann pushed past her, and lifting the cellar door, peeked out. The sunny day, the heat, was still outside. But now a destroyed neighborhood was out there, too. At first she could see no sign of the monster. Slowly she came out from the shadows of the cellar and stood staring around, blinking in the bright sunlight.

From the lower steps of the cellar, she heard Zeke say, "I got to get home to my baby squirrel, Ann. He's probably shivering from fright under a dresser or something. He needs me. I got to go."

"We'll go as soon as we make sure it's safe," Ellie said. "Give us a minute."

In the distance Ann heard the echoes of something crashing around and her eyes located the cause.

The rear of Skeeter Lockwood's house, as Zeke's, was bordered by woods and as Ann inspected the scenery she saw the monster poised at the edge of the wood line, its head raised to the skies as it screeched its annoyance. Apparently, it'd gotten tired of wrecking human habitats and businesses; tired of chasing and devouring screaming humanoids, and was leaving the vicinity. But as the creature merged into the woods Ann spied the other one. Not as large as the one that had been chasing them, but large enough.

There were two of them. At least. And for an awful moment she could have sworn she'd seen a third tail whip through the branches before the creatures disappeared, growling and spitting so she heard them clearly as they thrashed away.

She rubbed her eyes. Perhaps she'd been

mistaken? No, there couldn't be more than one, could there? What the hell had been happening…were the dinosaurs now multiplying like termites? If they were, then humans were in deep trouble.

Her fellow refugees had crept from the cellar and were gawking around. She looked, too. There was a wide track of destruction scarring the yards surrounding them. Ruined buildings and debris strewn everywhere. Just one of the creatures had totally annihilated a considerable section of the neighborhood. Just one.

"I need to call Henry. Right away," she told Ellie. "He needs to know the town's been infested, too. Something's going to have to be done. Soon. If those monsters are lurking nearby in the woods it'll only be a matter of time before they decide to rampage out here again."

Ellie nodded. "We'll get back to Zeke's house and our cars. I can't wait to talk to the police chief again. I wonder if he'll believe me this time when I say the town's in grave danger."

"Well, if he doesn't, all we'll have to do is bring him out here, have him take a look around, or speak to some of the other witnesses who ran from that monster like we did. Tally the missing people or left behind body parts. The smashed houses. I bet he'll believe then."

"Maybe yes, maybe no. Chief Chapman is one of those men that don't believe in the unbelievable until he's actually face to face with it. He'll probably invent some sort of crazy cover story to explain this destruction. You wait and see."

"Pity him then," Ann said. "He'll end up as a dinosaur meal."

The four of them returned to Zeke's, but Ann couldn't stopped watching the woods around them. Couldn't stop listening for suspicious noises.

She kept expecting the monsters to return and finish what they'd started.

Chapter 8
Henry

Henry hated seeing his park empty of visitors and thinking it might never open again. It depressed him to no end and it'd been one of his greatest fears since the first dinosaur had been discovered years before. He didn't want it to become a haven and breeding ground for prehistoric throwbacks instead of a tranquil vacation spot for people. But, for him and Ann, the ramifications went even deeper than that. He might be losing the job he loved. His home. His very way of life. He'd had a sobering phone conversation with Superintendent Sorrelson and had been advised if the park didn't reopen his job would either be changing drastically or could be eliminated completely. It was still too early to know what the army or government would decide to do with a dinosaur infested national park.

"We need to know the scope of the calamity before we jump to conclusions, Shore. See what the Park and Forest Services want us to do," Sorrelson had imparted in his usual gruff manner. "Could be you'll be needed as a sort of dinosaur guard, hunter, wrangler or some such thing. You do have experience with the creatures and intimate knowledge of the park lands. The army might have to put up fences to keep them contained. There could be a job in it for you and some of the other rangers. Let me talk to the powers that be and see what they say. I'll get back to you as soon as I can. Until then I advise you keep your eyes and ears open, weapons close by. You might think about moving you and your wife out of the park, for now anyway. It'd be safer."

"I'd prefer to stay, at least until I can gauge the level of infiltration we have. So far the infestation, as I am aware of it, in the park itself is mainly these smaller herd dinosaurs. They're easily controlled with the weapons I have available. The larger dinosaurs are the ones in the lake and so far they haven't left it. Not that I know of anyway. And there's been no fatalities as far as I'm aware of, either. It's not like last winter when our adversaries were those flying gargoyle types who actively came after us. The intruders plaguing the park are entirely manageable. So far. Ann and I want to remain in our home for now if you'll allow it."

"Up to you, Shore. Go or stay. Nothing's official as of yet. I'll let you know things as I learn them."

"Thank you, Sir."

"Shore?"

"Yes, Sir?"

"You be careful down there, you hear me? Don't take any chances. If things get worse you vamoose out of there pronto. Don't be a hero."

"I won't. You know me, I'm a realist, Sir. If the circumstances become too hazardous for me, my family or my men, we'll leave," he out and out lied.

No way he was ever leaving his park. The dinosaurs would leave, not him. "I'll keep you updated."

"You do that." And their connection had been broken.

He left the cabin and slid into his car, his hand resting lightly on the pistol at his waist and his eyes searching for any movement in the woods around the house. He had a high-powered rifle in the passenger's seat, easy to get to. The day was well on its way with the sun blazing its warmth across the land, not much of a breeze, which made it worse. Going to be another scorcher. So unusual for Crater Lake.

Ann had driven off to town earlier. She didn't know that he knew. Truth was, with Zeke being so infirm lately and the attack in his back yard, he'd expected her to eventually drive into town to check on him, no matter he'd asked her not to. He knew his wife so well. So he'd left one of his rangers to keep an eye on her, from a distance of course, and follow her if she left the house. He knew he could trust Ranger Stanton to protect Ann. And because the women were friends, accidently running into her in town wouldn't raise Ann's suspicions. Or that's how he saw it.

As he drove, he kept turning things over in his mind. Perhaps Sorrelson was right. He and Ann should vacate their home and the park. Move away. But where would they go? Town? Nah. Not there. The creatures were already invading that territory as well. He and Ann could move in with Laura and Justin, it was a few hours away and perhaps, safer. Or not. But he'd be too far from the park. Ann from her newspaper. And Zeke. No, they couldn't leave, not just yet. He was well aware, though, that in a short while, if the problem kept escalating, they might have no choice but to go.

He wished he'd hear from Justin. The paleontologist and his friend Steven had traveled to Redwood National Park and had promised to stay in touch and let him know what they discovered. Yet Henry hadn't heard from him in days. For some reason that made him nervous. He'd left messages on Justin's cell phone. Still no response. The man must be exceptionally busy, or his phone's battery was dead, or he hoped one of those were the explanation and not something else more ominous.

He drove out of the driveway and set a course for park headquarters. For the last week his rangers had been helping empty the park. The businesses had been shut down and boarded up and most of the park residents ushered to an entrance and sent on their way. Poor souls. It hadn't been easy. Some of the longtime residents and business owners had refused to leave and had to be convinced it was too dangerous to remain. Most of them had complied; some, Henry suspected, had gone into hiding and would have to be flushed out eventually. He didn't look forward to that. He knew these people, knew them well, and he was shoving them out of their homes and livelihoods. But if he didn't get them out of the park they'd end up dinosaur appetizers sooner or later. No job or business was worth a person's life. Well, that's what he told them anyway. Some agreed, some didn't.

So here they were–he was–and the hunt was on.

Dinosaur Lake III: Infestation

He'd called his rangers in for an emergency meeting at eleven. He wasn't sure exactly what he was going to tell them but he had to tell them something. This time the park was closed, as far as he knew, permanently and the National Guard would be marching in soon and perhaps would never leave. His men were cognizant of the new dinosaur threats and were awaiting his orders for what came next.

What was coming next? Hell if he knew. Part of him thought the best thing they could do was abandon the park and leave it to the blood-thirsty dinosaurs. Fence it in with electric thirty-foot walls, station guard buildings equipped with soldiers and weapons every few miles or so along it, and post EXTREME DANGER! DINOSAURS ON THE LOOSE! NO TRESPASSING signs everywhere. Give up. Walk away.

He could get another job somewhere else. Another park. He'd heard they were looking for rangers up in the Alaskan Denali National Park. Yeah, sure. Ann would kill him. The winters here were bad enough, but Alaska? Worse. And it was too far away from their daughter and granddaughter. If farther away would even be far enough. Well, perhaps, some other national park closer?

Who was he fooling? He'd never been a quitter; never run away from a trouble–and this growing infestation was an earth-changing serious one. He remembered what Justin had said about how this could be the beginning of humanity's extinction and the rise of a new dominant species. Dinosaurs versus humans. And this time the dinosaurs might prevail because they'd mutated and were cunningly learning to adapt. He had to see the drama through. If this, his park, was ground zero, it was where the human race needed to begin the fight and he needed to be one of the warriors. Stand up for humanity and all that crap. He sighed as he got out of his car and walked into the building, the sun pulsing above and the heat glimmering around him like falling glitter. Everyone was waiting for him.

The twenty or so uniformed men and women gathered around him in the conference room at headquarters. It was a tight fit. They took the news about the park closing, perhaps for good, fairly well, considering.

"Okay, boss," Ranger Kiley commented after Henry's short-but-not-so-sweet speech about what they were facing, "for now we're being turned into dinosaur trackers. Our objective is to search for and destroy as many of the creatures as we can flush out, right?"

"That's right. And if you come across any other humans anywhere in the park, protect them and escort them to the exits. The army will be moving in here any minute to help. We know the park's lands better than they do so they'll be working with us."

"What happens when we find and kill them all? The dinosaurs, I mean?"

Henry felt suddenly weary. He guessed he'd been fighting dinosaurs too long and too often. "That could take a while, Kiley. At this point, we have no idea how many dinosaurs or even species are loose in the woods, not to mention the lake and backcountry or how long it will take to deal with them." If we even can, Henry brooded. In the past the dinosaurs had proved unpredictable and unusually crafty, especially the flying varieties.

"At least," Kiley grumbled, "we still have jobs."

"That's a good way to look at it," young Ranger Eddie Cutters spoke up. At thirty years old, an ex-firefighter and paramedic, he'd been a ranger for only a few weeks and had never seen a dinosaur. Yet. "Except I can't believe what we're searching for are long extinct animals from another time. I mean, are we really labeling them…prehistoric dinosaurs?"

Ranger Kiley and Gillian laughed at the same time. Henry didn't. He kind of felt sorry for the man.

"Cutters, you're new. You weren't here the last two times we were faced with this situation," Kiley said. "You're not a believer. Yet. But the first time one of those monsters swims by you in the lake, or pops up in front of you and spits in your eye or attacks you with big fangs and a spiked tail, you will be."

"They are real. Dinosaurs. Believe it," Gillian seconded in a flat tone.

"If you say so." Cutter didn't seem convinced. At six foot-four and a sturdy build, he had long, thick reddish hair, a broad face and was a friendly sort. Took things easy and gave them just the same way. People liked and trusted him from the minute he first smiled at them. A newlywed, his wife, Marla, was a dental assistant in Klamath Falls. He was an amateur nature photographer and had shown Henry some of his work. He was good. It was one of the reasons he liked being a ranger in a park–so many photo opportunities. Henry would have to show him some of the pictures Steven and Justin had taken of the aquatic dinosaurs and see what he thought of them.

"What do we do now, Chief?" Ranger Gillian posed the question.

"I'm sending you out in pairs to patrol and search the park land and woods, day shifts only from now on. I don't want anyone out at night, too dangerous, looking for the creatures or any human stragglers. The army is bringing in more effective weapons but I'll give out what we have on hand so you can protect yourselves. Well, unless you come up against one that's too big to fight, then I strongly suggest you run. Like hell. As fast as you can." His swift grin was humorless.

Henry only hoped his men would be allowed to kill the dinosaurs. He was worried about what the government's final orders on that would be. He hadn't forgotten Dr. Albert Harris, who'd initially fought him to capture and protect the very first live dinosaur in the lake six years ago, not kill it. And how well he remembered that had turned out. What would the army and the government say about a whole park full of the damn things?

Well, he'd know soon enough.

After his men dispersed and began their patrols, Ranger Kiley, who'd lagged behind, strode up to him. Henry was at the gun case checking what weapons he had left after handing out most of them to his men.

"Chief, I wanted to tell you that Ranger Stanton

wasn't here this morning for the meeting and she was supposed to be. I mean, I texted her notice of it hours ago. She should have been here."

Henry turned around. "I noticed that, too. That she wasn't here, I mean. Have you tried calling her again lately?" Kiley and Stanton had been seeing each other for months and Henry knew how close they'd become. Practically inseparable. Ann swore she could hear wedding bells for them, but Henry wasn't so sure. Ranger Ellie Stanton was an independent woman who cherished her freedom. Since she'd been widowed and her two sons had gone off to college she'd reveled in it. Kiley would have a hard time getting that woman to the altar. Well, maybe that wasn't what he was after. Kiley was a modern man and he liked strong women. The two seemed content with their relationship the way it was. They were happy and that was all that counted.

"I have tried. A couple of times. No answer. I'm a little concerned. That's not like her to avoid my calls."

Henry eyed the other man and nodded. "No, it isn't. But since I don't want you to worry, I've had her tailing Ann the last week or so. Making sure she doesn't run off to town again, or by herself anyway. Ranger Stanton could be with Ann somewhere.

"Stanton wasn't at home, huh?"

"No, not at home. I think last night she mentioned she might have to go into town, do a little shopping or something. But she should have been back for the meeting."

"Hmm, then I suspect Ann's in town this

morning, too. Probably to check up on her friend Zeke. Or something. Ranger Stanton is with her in Klamath Falls if I had to take a wild guess." Henry had a sudden uneasy feeling. Ann hadn't called him all morning and that wasn't like her. Since the dinosaurs had taken to haunting the park and the town, they were keeping in closer touch.

"I thought you asked Ann not to go to town?" Kiley was grinning, hands casually on his gun belt.

Henry tossed him a dirty look. "Yeah, like she listens to me. If Zeke needed her, off she'd go."

Henry wrestled his cell phone from his pocket and keyed in Ann's number. "I think I'll give my wandering wife a quick call and make sure everything's okay." When his call wasn't picked up he said, "She's not answering, either."

"You're going into town now, aren't you?" Ranger Kiley's grin was gone. "You're worried something's happened like what occurred last week at Zeke's, and Ann, maybe Ellie, are involved?"

"Well, if something's going on, those two women will be in the thick of it, I have no doubt. A reporter and an ex-soldier, now ranger, always seem to find trouble."

Kiley smiled softly, his caring for both women evident. "You got that right. Ellie and Ann are two of a kind. Nosy, but competent women ready to help someone in need no matter the danger to themselves." The ranger had known his boss and his boss's wife long enough to be able to say such a thing. They were, after all, all friends. "Do you want me to come with you?"

"That'd be a good idea. You know the new rules.

No ranger travels in the park or to town alone. Let's go find our women and bring them home."

The men left headquarters and drove off in Henry's jeep. Henry keeping his eyes and ears open for any sights or rustling noises, suspicious or otherwise, out among the underbrush, between the trees or off in the distance. No one had seen or run into any dinosaurs of any kind for days and he was beginning to wonder where they'd all gone and what they were up to. He had this eerie mental image of all the dinosaurs, both small and large, like characters in a bizarre horror movie, gathered around in a clearing somewhere plotting the demise of the human race. Chattering, or roaring, and conversing in an intelligent newly created dinosaur language only they could understand. Ridiculous.

Oddly enough, there weren't any animals anywhere around at all. None. Not a squirrel or a rabbit or a deer or a moose or a bear or…any of the natural park animal inhabitants. Even the birds seemed to be in hiding. No birdsong. Utter silence. What was that about?

Of course, neither he or any of his rangers had been out on the lake recently because the water was off limits since he, Justin, and Steven had witnessed the fierce battle between the leviathans. If the park was perilous, the lake was a mine field. Henry prayed those water monsters couldn't or wouldn't come out onto land. Talk about a potential slaughter. For the first time ever, he wished the army would hurry up and arrive. Let them be dinosaur fodder, not his men.

They were near the outskirts of Klamath Falls

when Henry received a phone call from Ranger Gillian.

"Chief, just a heads up. The National Guard has arrived. In force. Obnoxious as ever and dragging in their big guns, Humvees, and–I swear–tanks. They're like a plague of gray camouflaged locusts. They're everywhere. Noisy. Pesky."

Tanks. Henry almost laughed, but didn't. The sinking feeling inside his gut wouldn't allow it. The arrival of the army was the final lid closing on his previously peaceful life and the park's future. He had the feeling this time the soldiers wouldn't be leaving for a long time. Maybe never.

"Give them anything they need, Ranger Gillian, and let their CO know I'll be reporting in to him or her as soon as I get back."

"Er, if I can ask, where are you, Boss?"

"Ranger Kiley and I are on a mission to Klamath Falls to investigate something."

"Oh, you mean Ann's run off to town again and you're worried about her?"

Gillian, as Kiley, was a friend as well as a coworker. This time Henry did chuckle. "You know me too well. We won't be too long, I imagine. We'll find Ann and her accomplice Ranger Stanton and return to the park long before dark."

"I'll cover for you, Chief. No worries. See you when you return."

When Henry tapped off the phone he said to Kiley, "The army has landed…and taken over." His voice was not happy, but deep inside he was relieved. He and his men needed the help no matter how he felt about the invading force. At least, they'd have massive and efficient weapons with which to detect and obliterate the primeval enemy, whatever and wherever it was. That made him happy.

"What's new?" Ranger Kiley made a sound in his throat that could have been a snort. Kiley wasn't a great admirer of the men in camouflage, either. Too many weekend warriors for his liking.

"More and more dinosaurs," Henry uttered in a monotone. "Heaven help us. We need to find Ann and your Ranger Stanton and get our butts back to the park. With all the reinforcements now there, it's about the safest place I can think of."

"Sure, Boss. We'll get in and out, fast as a bunny."

Henry chuckled and sped the car up. He didn't mention to Gillian that his small red dino friends probably loved bunnies…to eat.

****

The remainder of the drive into town was uneventful until they were within its boundaries. First came the sounds of ambulance sirens screeching and filling the hot day; then as they got closer, streams of people running in one direction as if there was a fire or a riot going on somewhere.

And the final jolt.

The unimaginable destruction started on Main Street and veered off in a wide swath across the yards, through the houses–what were left of them in the neighborhood–and into the distant woods. It looked as if a giant sickle had descended from the sky and just begun churning up the earth and everything on it.

"*What happened here?*" Ranger Kiley's eyes were taking in the chaos. But, as Henry, he knew what had happened. Along the first few blocks of the street there were more people staggering around, some bloody or weeping, and local police officers, most likely looking for survivors and taking notes, mingled with them. Squad cars and ambulances were everywhere. The local cops were there. What a surprise.

"*Dinosaur*," Henry spat out disgustedly. "And by the looks of it it was a big one and left a massive path of wreckage in its wake." He fretted over how many people had been injured or died. What the hell kind of dinosaur could have done this? And he was suddenly angry. He'd tried to warn the town authorities that this might happen. They should have believed him and should have been prepared. By the looks of it, they hadn't been.

"Another Godzilla, huh? Oh God help us." He used the sarcastic name Henry himself had used years before. "Now *they* have spread to town, as well. All those miles away from the park. Creepy lizards." Kiley was staring at the demolished buildings and yards with shock altering his face.

"Isn't the first time." And Henry told him about Zeke's close call the week before with the smaller breed. He should have told him when it happened, but he hadn't and he didn't really know why. Perhaps because speaking about it aloud would have made the whole incident, the unpleasant truth that some of the creatures had already migrated into the heart of town, too real. Now by the look on his ranger's face, he realized he should have said something. They were friends after all.

"God, it is the end of the world. Death by dinosaurs."

"That's what my son-in-law says, too."

"We need to find Ellie and Ann," Kiley stated, "if they're here."

And Henry remembered. Ann. She might have been in town when this melee occurred and fear bit him with sharp teeth. It'd be just like her, if she saw a dinosaur charging down Main Street, to go after it with her camera for the photo opportunity. Damn the danger. "You're right, we need to find them. First I need to have a chat with someone." He spun the wheel to the left, squealing tires, and parked his jeep at the curb behind a squad car. He'd seen the police chief conferring with one of his officers in the middle of someone's destroyed yard. He'd know something and possibly even where Ann or Ranger Stanton were.

His discussion with the police chief was brief.

"If you're looking for your wife and that female ranger of yours, Chief Ranger," Lester Chapman said the minute he spotted Henry, "they're both okay, but pretty shaken up, and they've taken Zeke Johnson and Wilma Stuart to Zeke's house to recover some."

"Is my wife and the others unhurt?" Henry asked.

"As far as I could tell. They fled from the, er, disturbance and hid in Skeeter Lockwood's cellar until the trouble was over."

"Dinosaur, Chief Chapman, not disturbance. *Dinosaur.*" Henry glared at the man. He'd have to accept that dinosaurs were roaming the earth again now. Or not. The disdainful expression on the Chief's face was clearly one of unrelenting denial.

"Nonsense. This destruction was caused by some sort of straight line winds or a tornado or something."

"What do the witnesses, the people who went through it, say? They say it was high winds or a tornado?"

"Well," the man appeared to falter, then regained his bluster, "they're all pretty upset. They've been through a horrible experience. They don't know what they saw, what they're talking about right now. It'll be clearer for them later."

Henry gave up. He hoped the creature showed up at the Chief's house and tried to eat him. That'd show him. Let him deny the existence of dinosaurs then. Idiot.

"I'll give you some advice, Chief Chapman, and if you're a smart man, you'll take it. Evacuate the town. Get all the people out of here *now*. It's only going to get worse. These prehistoric creatures have already taken over my park and the town is next on their list. And it looks like they've already moved in. Get the citizens out while you still can."

"You've got to be kidding. Abandon the town because of a little catastrophe? Make all the people leave?" His chubby arms spread out to include the scene around them. "That's impossible. These are peoples' homes and some have no place else to go to. There're old folks that can't quit their houses, too sick. How about the hospitals and the nursing homes? Where are they all going to go?"

"I don't know that answer, Chief Chapman. I'm just telling you that this," he also waved his hands around, "is going to keep happening and the damage, injuries, and the death toll will keep rising. The townsfolk need to get out. The farther away the better."

The police chief scowled at him but had nothing else to say about the subject.

Henry posed a couple more quick questions about the devastation and after barely getting the answers he wanted because the police chief was so evasive, he pivoted on his heels, with Kiley still with him, and darted to his car, got in and drove to Zeke's. He was more than relieved to see Ann's and Stanton's cars parked out front.

First thing he did after he burst into the house, seeing his wife comforting an old woman, Wilma, whom he recognized from town, was gather his wife into his arms. "Thank God you're not hurt! All of you. Tell me what happened." He would have kissed her but two rangers and two civilians were watching him. A hug had to do. Ann would understand.

"Henry, Ranger Kiley, sit on down and have some coffee. I just made a pot." Zeke motioned at some empty chairs. He and the rest of them looked beaten and exhausted; their clothes torn and their faces dirty. As if they'd been through that tornado or another natural disaster Chief Chapman had spoken of. Remnants of what they'd gone through still lingering in their expressions. Zeke's thin frame swayed as he stood by the sink and Ann moved over to prop him up.

"Sit down," she ordered. "You're ready to collapse." And she gently pushed him down into the chair she'd recently vacated.

Henry and Ranger Kiley found chairs and settled down as Ann poured coffee into cups for them and brought them to the table. "Help yourself to cream and sugar, you know the drill." Then she sat down beside him. He could feel her thigh against his and took a breath of relief. Ann, all of them, seemed bruised but otherwise all right.

Yet as he listened to their harrowing account of escape and survival his sense of relief dissipated and was replaced with growing apprehension. The creature that had chased them and demolished a section of the town was still out there…and perhaps more than one. They could make another appearance any minute. Anywhere.

"It's not safe around here any longer, Zeke. Wilma." Henry's eyes went to the two people who lived in town. "You both need to leave Klamath Falls for a while until this situation is rectified. Right now those things are still out there in the woods around the town."

He pressed the older woman, "You have family out of the area?"

Zeke, an arm around Wilma's shoulders, acted as if he truly cared for her. He was being so protective.

Wilma's head moved side to side in a negative motion. "No family. Zeke's all I have. Around here anyway." She sent a glance his way and her face broke into a faint smile. "But I have a very dear

Dinosaur Lake III: Infestation

friend, Rosie, who lives across the state border in Idaho. Not far from here. It's not a long drive and most of it is easy highway. I sometimes go to visit and stay with her. We were girls together and have kept in touch. More so since her husband died three years ago. She gets lonely, you know."

"Can you go visit her now? Get out of town for a while until we know it's safe?"

Wilma directed a questioning look at Zeke. Her smile faded. "I could. And Zeke, you could go with me. She knows all about you and has been wanting to meet you for ages. I'm sure she'd love to have you visit, too. She has a big house near a lake. Beautiful place. Her town is quaint and has endless things to do, places to go and visit. She has a garage she renovated into a nice apartment just for visitors like me. It has two bedrooms and is extra roomy. We could both stay there. I could call her?"

Henry nodded at Zeke. "That sounds like the perfect solution. Ann says you've been wanting to go on a vacation anyway. Here's your chance."

Zeke hesitated, and patting Wilma's hand, his lips returned her a stiff smile. "You know that sounds like a real fine idea. It might do me good to get out of this old house, this town, for a while. Meet your friend. Have a vacation. Broaden my horizons."

"And get away from the dinosaurs loose in the woods behind your house," Ann muttered, "and running crazy all over town."

"But," Zeke seemed to remember something and added, "Wilma, I have to take *little boy* there with me." He crooked a thumb at the sleeping squirrel.

"He's too young to leave by himself. I'm all he has since those other dinosaurs ate his family. I have a cage and everything for him. He won't be any trouble."

"He can come, too," Wilma said. "My friend adores animals. She's got a house full of them. Mainly cats, but other animals as well. I think she even has a ferret and a parrot. It chatters all the time, has quite a vocabulary."

"Good. I wouldn't go anywhere without *little boy*...I'm his family now," Zeke mumbled.

"You call him *little boy*?" Ann eyes were tinged with amusement. She was staring at the sleeping squirrel. The critter has slept through the whole dinosaur catastrophe and commotion. He hadn't woken up once. When they'd run from the house the squirrel had been curled up napping and still was when they'd come back. Something was definitely wrong with that squirrel.

Kiley watched the squirrel and said nothing. He was holding Ranger Stanton's hand beneath the table but Henry could see what they were doing. The two of them had been extremely quiet since they'd arrived.

"For now. He needs just the right name and I haven't come up with one yet." Zeke was looking fondly at his pet with a gentleness on his features Henry rarely saw. The guy really did love squirrels and this one in particular. Well, to each his own. Henry's late friend, George Redcrow used to like squirrels, too...to hunt, cook and eat that is. But he had to admit, glancing at the critter in the box, he was a cute little cuss. So furry and all. And small.

Really small. Nothing like the dinosaur monsters that were threatening them and their world. For a moment, in his mind, the tiny squirrel rapidly grew to a fifty-foot rodent with spiky teeth, a greasy tail, and red fiery eyes. Yikes! He shook his head and the terrible image sped away. He *was* losing it.

"Well, that's settled then." Henry slapped his hands on his legs and stood up. He'd drank his coffee and the day was going. He knew they had to go as well. Get to a safer place. For now. Out of town.

Wilma and Zeke telephoned her out-of-state friend and let her know they were coming to visit. On their way actually. Soon as they both could pack some clothes and get themselves into Wilma's Chrysler. Wilma still drove while Zeke no longer did. So it was a perfect friendship.

Henry's cell phone rang, and his eyes going to Ann, he put it to his ear. He was motioning to Ann, Kiley and Stanton they should go towards the front door. It made him nervous to still be in a town where giant dinosaurs could reappear any moment and the only weapons he had wouldn't do the job. Ann had whispered to him she'd spied more of the town-stomping monsters out in the woods. There was a gang of them. So as far as he was concerned they couldn't get out of there fast enough.

"Justin. Well, it's nice to hear from you, kid. I was getting worried."

"I'm fine. So is Steven. He's still with me by the way. Sorry I didn't answer your earlier messages, but we've been unimaginably busy down here. You won't believe what I have to tell you, what we've discovered. It's going to blow your mind. We made extra stops after leaving California to compare rumors, sightings and certain details that had caught my attention after some investigating. But right now we're traveling back to the park. I have to talk to you." Justin's voice was serious.

Henry's stomach did a roll over. Whatever his son-in-law had to say to him, he suddenly didn't want to hear it.

Boy, this day just keeps on getting better and better.

"And I have to talk to you." Henry brought Justin up to date as to what was happening in the park and what had occurred in Klamath Falls.

"Good lord. Now they're in the town. By your description they sound like another new species. When do you expect to be back home?" Justin asked.

"We're leaving Zeke's house as we speak, but we're going to park headquarters. I'll tell you all about it when you get there." Henry hung up. He'd grabbed Ann's hand and was leading her to the front door. Ranger Kiley and Stanton shadowed them. It was time to get on the road.

"We're following you two out of town to make sure you get far enough away safely," Henry informed Zeke and Wilma. "I'll give you five minutes, Zeke, to grab some clothes, anything else you'll need to take…and *little boy,* of course." He turned to Wilma. "Then we'll all drive to your house and you can pack as well. Five minutes. Afterwards we will convoy out of here and get you both on your way."

Dinosaur Lake III: Infestation

Zeke packed in seven minutes, including stuffing a resistant *little boy* into a cat carrier with his toys, and Wilma took less than five. Then they were in their cars, Henry and Ann in the lead, Wilma's Chrysler in the middle and Ranger Stanton in her car with Ranger Kiley, and rushing out of town. They took the main roads as far away from the surrounding woods as they could find. Their eyes nervously raked across the spaces around, above and behind them. No monsters stormed out after them or attempted to block their way.

Once Henry was sure they were far enough from town he pulled over on the shoulder, and giving Wilma and Zeke final instructions and goodbyes, he sent them on their way towards Idaho. As the two old people drove off he prayed they'd make it to Wilma's friend's house. He prayed the dinosaurs hadn't migrated as far as Idaho and he wasn't sending them straight into a mess worse than the one they left behind.

With Kiley and Stanton's car in front, Henry turned his jeep around and with them went in the direction of Crater Lake, taking a different route which circled around Klamath Falls and its woods. No sense in taking any chances.

*****

"Do you think we'll be safe at home, Henry? In the park?" Ann's eyes followed Ranger Stanton's car up ahead as he stuck close to it.

"With the National Guard in residence, ironically, it's the safest place in the state right now.

They have missiles, bombs and tanks." He grinned at her. "And to think I never liked them much before. *Tsk, tsk, tsk.*" He shook his head.

Ann didn't say anything else as the countryside passed and they drew nearer to the park. The day was waning but the heat was still floating in thick waves above the roads, settling in the sun lit spots like hibernating animals.

The forests on either side of them were laced in shadows and filled with dark drifting shapes, and an uneasy intuition took root and grew inside Henry. They were coming up to the park's south entrance. He could see the barricades across the road blocking access, but no guards, rangers or soldiers. Where was the sentries? They wouldn't abandon their post without a good reason.

Was that something moving among the trees to his right?

He detached his cell phone from his belt and called Ranger Kiley in the front car.

"Ranger, are you seeing anything strange around the trees on our right?"

"Like what?" Kiley's voice was guarded.

"I don't know. I think I keep seeing…forms bounding along between the trees keeping pace with us. I have this feeling…."

"Nah, Chief. I don't see anything."

They'd pulled up to the fence at the entrance. They'd have to move it to get through. Henry turned to Ann. "Stay in the car. Get behind the wheel and be ready to drive off if I tell you to. Kiley and I will see what's going on. Lift the gate so we can drive in."

He nodded at Ranger Stanton through her car's windshield, her hands on the wheel, waiting, and met Kiley at the obstruction in the road. Around them the skies were darkening. Clouds were racing in and misting away what light remained. In moments the day had descended into twilight. Lightning crackled along the distant horizon. The extreme heat of the day had attracted a storm. There was rain in the air. A strong, wet smell.

"Let's get this gate up, get the cars through here, and on the road again towards headquarters. This place is giving me bad vibes."

"Me, too."

Kiley helped Henry lift the wooden arm and open the road. Henry looked into and around the guard booth. "It's empty. No sign of any of our men. There should be someone, soldier or ranger, here. I gave orders. Where are they?"

Kiley was peering into the woods. "Don't know. But it's suspicious all right."

Henry knelt down at the corner of the small wooden building. "There's something on the ground here." His fingers went to the dirt and came up covered in red. "Blood. Lots of it." *Oh, oh*. His head came up and he motioned at the ranger to listen. "You hear that?"

"I don't hear anything. Not a thing," Ranger Kiley replied, standing ramrod straight, and still gazing at the bloodied grass.

Henry said in a low voice, "That's what I mean. Suddenly there's too much silence. I don't like it. It's unnatural. Let's return to the cars and get out of here."

Thunder ripped through the air and eked away in a series of diminishing echoes.

The men drove the cars through the check point, jumped out and dropped the gate back down. Henry's jeep took the lead this time, slowing as they traveled the road deeper into the park. They weren't that far from headquarters and he was beginning to breathe easier. Once they arrived, they'd be safe.

It was still disturbingly quiet. Still no sounds or animals. His skin itched with the oddness of it all. It was creepy.

He glanced in his rear view mirror. Stanton's car was still behind them. Though a little farther back than he would have liked.

Another streak of lightning snaked across the purple sky. There was a tension in the air, taut and portentous, as the wind picked up and the sun dimmed behind the shifting clouds. Storm coming. Not much longer. They should be within shelter before it hit, he thought.

The first growl shattered the stillness and was rapidly echoed by a chorus of them. All around. Everywhere.

And then they were ambushed.

The first dinosaur sprang from the murkiness on their left and leapt onto the hood of the jeep. Henry, quick to stop the car and react, grabbed the rifle between him and Ann, opened the window and shot at the thing. But instead of stopping it, the beast skittered up and along the top of the jeep and hurled itself onto Stanton's hood as a herd of the monsters launched themselves from the trees and bushes around them, while a smaller group encircled

Ranger Stanton and Kiley.

Henry rolled the window almost all the way up. The beasts, seeking ways to get in to the humans, were scrambling all over and there were lots of them. Thirty, forty or more coming from the woods. A shrieking, hissing, wailing river of them.

There were gunshots somewhere behind them.

Ann cried out, "Henry, they're trying to get in!" Then, lowering her window just enough to put the barrel out, she used the SigSauer Henry had given her.

Henry recognized their attackers as the same species that had tried to eat their cat Sasha outside the cabin and most likely the same ones that had waylaid Ann on her journey to town the week before. Except this time there was more of them.

And they were larger than the ones Henry had confronted or Ann had described. Much larger. And some of them had morphed into more hideous and deadly creatures than the ones before. Sure, some were three or four feet, but others were closer to fifteen; probably more mature specimens. Perhaps they weren't adults, but he couldn't tell. Heaven help them if they weren't–if they could and did get taller. Their angular heads and necks were thicker, their malicious eyes bigger, their mouths larger with more prominent rows of razor teeth that snapped at anything in their way. They hopped long distances on two powerful hind legs, short tails whipping wildly, and behaved as if they were crazed. With hunger? Ha, now he knew where all the animals had gone…into their stomachs. They were trying to eat the cars; tearing at them with wicked looking claws as they fought to get to the yummy humans tucked inside.

A rock hit the windshield in front of Henry's face. Then another and another. THEY WERE THROWING THINGS AT THEM. MAKESHIFT WEAPONS! It took innate intelligence, at least on a certain level, to do that. He kept shooting through the open window, fending off the advance as best he could. They kept coming.

Someone was screaming. Ann.

Henry stole a glance behind him and saw Ranger Stanton and Kiley firing their weapons through shattered windows into the mob.

The bullets weren't stopping the dinosaurs. There were too many of them. They kept coming. More and more swarming in from the woods, from under the foliage and behind the trees. Henry looked up. There was one beast at least twenty feet tall loping towards them, death in its eyes. Claws outstretched.

That's it! *We have to get the hell out of here.*

Henry pushed down harder on the gas pedal and the car surged forward, covered in a mass of clinging, clawing dinosaurs. Dinosaurs grabbing and biting at them as they were dragged along the road. He heard Stanton's car engine reeving up. They were following.

"We have to make it to headquarters!" he yelled at Ann. "Hold on!" He gunned the gas harder, rocketed ahead for a while, until the car hit something in the road, a limb or a dinosaur body, and flew into the air.

Oh, God! They were going to crash!

The jeep rose into the air and spun around,

coming down precariously on its wheels, off the road, and ramming into a dirt rut alongside. A tree stopped it dead. Crushed its hood like an accordion.

For a time, he had no idea how long, Henry slumped against the wheel, stunned by the collision. Then, shaking his head to clear it, he sat up and took Ann's arm. "Are you okay?" His eyes searching her face, her body. There was a bleeding cut on the side of her forehead.

She turned to face him. "Shaken but otherwise okay, I think."

Henry swung his head around. Stanton and Kiley's car was nowhere to be seen. But the dinosaur pack was close and coming on fast. They were emitting the shrill wails he remembered from the one who'd tried to take Sasha. A cacophony of high-pitched cries like a flood behind them. So loud he wanted to cover his ears and scream at them to SHUT UP! But he had no hands free to do that and it wouldn't have done any good anyway. Good lord, there had to be hundreds of them. As far as his eyes could see. They were a moving, chattering blanket razing the undergrowth as they bounced, stomped and bounded over the ground. Hissing, spitting and…throwing sticks, clumps of dirt and rocks. *Where did they learn that?* He didn't want to know, didn't want to think about it. It was too freaking scary.

"Where's Ellie and Ranger Kiley?" Ann's eyes were locked on the beasts closing in on them. Something, a clump of dried mud possibly, whizzed by in front of her face on the other side of the passenger window.

"I don't know. We lost them back there somewhere. But we can't stop to search or wait. They'll make it to headquarters. They can take care of themselves."

A large rock hit the windshield and shattered it. Then in succession the other windows went, too. The throng was getting closer.

"But right now we have to get out of here before those monsters catch up with us! Get your gun and come on!" Henry dragged her across the seat and they exited the car from his side, rifle in his other hand. They ran through the woods towards where he thought headquarters would be. The crash had disoriented him, but he was sure they were going in the right direction. Well, he was pretty sure.

He still couldn't get the thought out of his head that the monsters were smart enough to utilize anything at hand as a weapon. How many steps up the evolutionary ladder was that? And alarming as all get out.

Run faster, *faster*.

A segment of a tree trunk, a huge hunk of wood, went flying by Henry and the edge caught his arm and twirled him around like a top. He went down to his knees and Ann had to help get him to his feet again. They kept going, breathing heavy and sweating from the intense heat. Henry thought for a moment he was going to pass out. His arm hurt something terrible. Ignore it. *Keep running*.

"They're gaining on us!" Ann scooted around a formidable outcropping of rock and Henry slid on his feet, nearly falling. He righted himself and they kept going.

In the distance somewhere they heard gunshots. His rangers? He prayed they were all right. More gunshots. An eerie wail filled the afternoon that sounded as if it'd come from a colossus of some kind, it was so ear-shattering. How big did this variety of mutant get? Godzilla sized?

In front of them, blocking their path, there was one of them. Huge. Twenty feet up, or more. Oh, crap.

"Is this the same one," he asked, "who terrorized you in town?"

"No. Different. Smaller. Ones in town were much bigger."

Oh great.

"Henry, watch out!" She screamed as the monster started crashing towards them. Henry captured her free hand and they jumped into a dry gully and stumbled along its rocky bed until they came to a ledge jutting out from the wall. They could hear the dinosaur's cries closing in. Henry shoved Ann beneath the ledge and crammed himself in beside her. "*Shhh*," he said and for once she did as he asked. He held his breath, holding Ann and his rifle close. They waited. Listening.

He didn't think the thing could fit in the narrow creek, but he wasn't counting on it. It sounded angry, determined to find the snacks that had gotten away.

Above they could hear it searching, roaring and wailing to the blackening sky as the rain began to fall. The light show had passed and the night, aided by the storm, was settling in. The light was nearly gone.

Good, please let the rain cover their scent. The dark help hide them.

But Henry was worried. He could hear other things moving through the woods above and around them, searching, too. Other hungry things. God, how had they gotten into this mess? Hadn't he been careful? Hadn't he known this could happen? They should have high-tailed it for Idaho with Zeke and Wilma. All of them. The hell with the park and his duty. He hadn't. They hadn't. Now he just had to face the consequences and find a way to save Ann and himself.

More gunshots. Farther away this time.

"God, I hope Ellie and Matthew are all right." There was fear in Ann's voice. She was holding on to him real tight. Shivering now as the rain flew in and drenched them. A trickle of water was forming in the gully feet below them. He could see it glimmering in the going light and hear the water rushing past. *Better not rain too long or it'll flush us out of here like two leaves in a flood.* It began to rain harder. *Just what we don't need. How are we going to get out of this?*

"You think we fooled it?" Ann finally asked. "Think we're safe?" It was now so dark in their hiding place he could barely see her face. An oval of paleness.

"I don't know. I still hear it up there bumbling around somewhere but I can't tell where. Too much background noise." *Like dinosaurs growling and things thrashing about.*

"How long will we have to stay down here like bugs in the mud?"

Henry, as scared as he was almost laughed. "Yeah, we are like bugs…hiding in a creek bed as it turns to muck. Let's just hope this stream here doesn't turn into a river. I don't have a boat, either."

"Bugs in the muck. I like that." Ann made a muffled sound something similar to a chuckle. That was Ann, seeing the humor in any situation, if there was any to be seen, that is.

"We'll wait a little longer and try to make it to headquarters. I wish we would have had time to grab one of those flashlights I had in the glove compartment."

"You and me both, husband. It's awfully dark out here in the night woods. In a storm. In the rain. I can't see even a foot ahead of me."

"Neither can I. The only good side to our predicament is we should be fairly close to headquarters. If I remember correctly this creek bed winds around behind it. We might climb up to ground level again and follow it right to where we want to go. Dark or no dark."

"That's encouraging."

"Yeah, it is. Don't worry, Ann. We'll make it. I promise."

The rain had slackened, a lull, but the night had grown darker. No moon. Minutes went by.

"At least we're together, Henry. I feel safer with you at my side. I always do." She squeezed his arm and murmured, "I love you, you know that, don't you? I have since the first night I met you at that dance so many years ago. No matter what happens to us tonight I will always love you. You're the best thing that ever happened to me." She was shaking again and he didn't know if it was from the rain's chill or fright. For some reason, instead of reassuring him, her words made him uneasy. It wasn't like Ann to talk all lovey-dovey for no reason and definitely not during an emergency.

"And I've always loved you. I knew I'd marry you the first time I danced with you that night and held you in my arms, saw that smile of yours and that mischief in your eyes. I knew. Just knew."

For a moment their lips touched. A gentle kiss. Hers were very cold.

Henry froze. "You hear that?" A whisper.

"No, what did—"

They'd been found. The giant dinosaur they'd run from was hulking above them. Roaring and wailing, calling its little buddies to the feast. A huge shadow towering against the sky. Its claws raking at the mud and dirt shelf just feet above their heads. How had it found them in the rainy dark? How did it know they were down there? *Damn, damn, damn!*

Henry knew he had to shut it up. Chase it off or kill it or it would bring the others down on them. He didn't think, only acted. He pushed Ann deeper into the crevice. "Stay here. Don't move. Not one sound, not even a whimper."

And he was splashing out into the stream. Taking aim upwards he shot at the dinosaur's silhouette over him or where he thought the head, the eyes, would be. Knowing it would be pure dumb luck if his bullets hit his target where he wanted them to. He fired and kept firing. He emptied his rifle as the creature screeched and screamed so loud it about broke his ear drums. He heard a crash as if trees were falling or being yanked out by the roots and almost too late, realizing what was happening, he scrambled away from the sounds above and watched in shock as a massive blob of reptilian flesh fell into the creek not twenty feet from him and slid into the water. Unmoving.

Silence held reign again.

He couldn't help himself and a cheer escaped from his lips. He'd gotten rid of the thing. *He'd killed it!* He staggered backwards and his body shuddered with the adrenaline of it all. He felt dizzy and plopped down in the water, which is where his wife found him, dazed by his victory and how close he'd come to being squashed like a…bug in the mud.

"You showed that monster who the boss was!" Ann helped him up and back to their hole in the mud wall. "I'm so proud of you. My hero."

Not long after, he said, "I don't hear any more of those overgrown gremlins up there rummaging around. Maybe they didn't hear that creature dying or falling. Don't know it's dead yet. Yet with their keen sense of smell it won't be long before they find it. And when one of them discovers dinner over there in the creek bed we'll be overrun with the supper crowd–and they'll be hungry. Two courses will seem better than one. Time to go.

"Let's get out of this gully and be on our way. Be careful, footing will be slippery and we're going to get wet." The water rushing by them was deeper now. A couple feet.

"You're already wet," she reminded him. "And so am I. Good thing it isn't winter. The water actually feels good now."

"It does, doesn't it? After the heat. Let's go."

"Okay," Ann said. "You lead, I'll follow."

They splashed out into the creek bed. Good thing they were going in the other direction of the carcass blocking the channel. They would have had a difficult time getting around it. Henry stopped after ten yards or so. He was looking upwards. "I think we can get up here. There are trees we can grab onto to help us climb."

It'd be tricky with their guns, but Ann had an idea. "Tuck my pistol in your belt holster and give me your rifle to carry. It'll free your hands to help pull us up."

"Good idea."

He did what she'd asked and moved through the water, careful to make as little noise as possible so any dinosaur prowling above wouldn't hear them, and grabbing the thin trunk of a tree he began to climb; his other hand pulling Ann up behind him. Good thing she was a small woman and didn't weight much.

His feet slipped once or twice and it was difficult climbing when he could barely see where he was going, but they tediously made their way up the steep slope. The tree handholds helped.

At the top, breathing heavily, he turned and drew Ann into his arms. "We made it," he moaned in her ear and kissed her. They were both soaked and caked in mud, but they didn't care. They were alive. He reclaimed his rifle and taking her hand they walked into the woods following the path along the creek.

"I don't like it," he mumbled. "It's too quiet again." The thunder and lightning was a memory and the rain had ceased. The wind had died to an anemic breeze. The heat had returned.

They kept walking, treading hesitantly between the trees and rocks of the forest because it was hard to see. Henry had excellent night vision but, moonless, the forest was a shadowy place.

"Wish I had a flashlight," his voice a grumble.

All in all, he'd begun to feel optimistic about their survival–he knew they were close to headquarters by the landmarks they were passing– when the forest came alive with sounds again. Things careening around in the night. Dinosaurs. Looking for them. Somewhere behind them.

"Good grief! They've found us again," he hissed. *"Run, Ann, run!"*

They ran, or ran as fast as they could in the dark. Until breathless and stumbling like two drunks, they came out into a clearing.

Headquarters, the most welcome sight Henry could have seen, was rising up in front of them. It was lit up like Christmas, soldiers and their vehicles everywhere. He counted at least six of his rangers outside the building, rifles slung over their shoulders, on guard as if they'd been waiting for him and Ann.

As they sprinted to the door, his men rushing to meet them, he heard the increasing brouhaha in the night woods. The dinosaurs were coming.

Enclosed and shepherded into the sturdy building Henry welcomed the cheers of his rangers.

On the other side of the metal door Henry heard

repeated gunfire and shouting as the National Guard repelled the invaders. He hoped they had enough big guns, they'd need them. The squeals and squawks of the attacking monsters were deafening. He and Ann had led them straight to the human smorgasbord.

Inside, blinking like bats in the light, they were slapped on the back, hugged, and handed coffee and sandwiches. It felt so good to be safe. Ann's eyes were filled with tears and he held her as he told their story to his men. How they ran from and escaped the dinosaurs now residing in the park; hid in the creek and killed a huge one.

Everyone was tossing questions at them and they did their best to answer. Not easy because he was so exhausted, as he was sure Ann was, he could of fallen asleep in his chair right there. And almost did.

Ranger Gillian was standing above him. "Thank God you two made it. We'd about given up on you after Zeke called hours ago from Idaho, of all places, and asked if you'd gotten here in one piece. There's men out looking for you. They haven't come back. Yet."

"How many men and how long have they been gone?" Henry grilled his ranger.

"Three soldiers and Ranger Lauder and Duley. Too long."

Henry was looking around for Ranger Stanton and Kiley. He didn't see them. "Has Ranger Stanton and Kiley made it in yet? They were behind us but we lost them after our car crashed."

Gillian shook his head. "They haven't made it

back yet. But, Chief, don't worry, I'm sure they will. They can take care of themselves. Ranger Kiley knows these woods better than anyone else here and Stanton, well, Stanton is a superwoman, as we all know. I bet they'll be here soon. I'll radio the search team and let them know you and Ann are safe but they should keep looking for Stanton and Kiley."

"Thanks Gillian."

Henry glared at the door, listening to the battle going on beyond it. *We should have gone back for them.* But there'd been no time. He and Ann had been running; fighting for their lives. And it had been dark. Rainy. The guilt stung anyway, though, piercing deep. The two rangers were more than his employees, they were friends. *We should have looked for them.*

Too late now.

"Chief, I'm sure they're fine. They can take care of themselves. Probably hiding out somewhere until dawn. You'll see."

Henry wanted to believe him. The two would show up any minute. He took Ann's hand. At least he and his wife were alive. That was something to be thankful for, wasn't it?

Then a woman soldier came up and threw her arms around him.

"Well, I'll be, if it isn't Captain Sherman McDowell!" Henry was glad to see her. The woman soldier had proven herself to him the last time, when they'd fought the flying dinosaurs. She'd handled herself and her men with level-headed courage.

"Chief Ranger Shore," the woman declared. "About time. You had us worried sick." She hugged Ann too. "Ann. I knew you'd both make it here. I had faith in you."

Then she turned back to Henry and answered the question in his eyes. "Yes, I've been given command of this little band of soldiers here. Since I've dealt with your, er, problem before, the army, in its infinite wisdom, thought it would be more efficient if they dumped the whole kit-and-caboodle in my lap again." Her smile was warm. "I was tickled to have the honor. After out last adventure, dinosaurs are in my blood, I'm afraid. I'm ready to continue the hunt. Rid your park of these monsters once and for all."

"And I'm pleased the army sent you. I feel safer already. Is Patterson here, too?" Patterson, a freelance ex-FBI operative, was her fiancée and also a very good friend of Henry's. Another friend who knew how to fight, from past experiences, prehistoric interlopers.

"Not this time, Chief. He's consulting on some top secret case for some bureau or other…zombies, I think." And her grin let Henry know she was teasing. Or maybe she wasn't.

"Zombies?"

"Well, it's so secret no one knows what it's about. He can't even talk to me about the case. What's new? It's a wonder I love that man, always running off to places he can't tell me about; to do things he can't speak about. Could be we'll see him later. You never know. He checks in with me periodically just to let me know he's still alive."

Henry nodded. With Patterson you never did know. "I thought he was retired?"

"Supposed to be. But you know Scott, always ready to help on a difficult case. Your fault. Ever since his first dinosaur adventure here he's become another Mulder to them. He's in high demand."

Henry laughed. The thought of Patterson being a Mulder from the X-Files was funny. Mulder had been so much better looking.

Outside the sounds of fighting had stopped. Optimistically the soldiers and his men had either killed off or repulsed the horde. He was sure he'd find out soon enough.

He sent Ann to sleep on the couch in his office, she was so worn-out, and he sat down around the table in the conference room with Captain McDowell, her people and his rangers. They had much to talk about. To plan. Things had changed so quickly and they had to decide what to do about it.

The whole time his mind was on Ranger Stanton and Kiley, wondering if they were all right. And his eyes returned to the door often but his two lost rangers never came through it. There was no way he would accept their deaths. They had to be alive. They just had to be. Somewhere.

Chapter 9
Stanton and Kiley

Ellie Stanton whispered, "Is it gone yet, Matthew?"

"I don't know. I don't hear any dinosaurs skulking around out there but that doesn't mean anything. Those freaks are clever. They know when to be quiet. Stealthy. I swear they're out there in a huddle, scaly heads down, arms intertwined like a football team before kick-off, scheming how best to ambush us again. How to get in here and gobble us up."

Kiley's body relaxed and he lowered his rifle, laying it across his lap. He was breathing heavily, his body and clothes sodden from the raging storm outside as he slumped to the floor under the window. His back was against the wood, feet splayed out before him. When the lightning flashed and momentarily lit up the room, there was a steely expression on his face she'd seen many times before. No way lousy scurrying dinosaurs were going to get the best of him. He'd show them.

Well, that was until the big one showed up.

Dinosaur Lake III: Infestation

It'd been doggedly tracking them now for over an hour. The thing never gave up.

Ellie sighed, put her rifle on the floor beside her, and also leaned her backside against the inner wall of the cabin they'd taken refuge in. A rental now empty because the park visitors were gone. She'd known the cabin well and how to get into it, and it hadn't been far from where they'd left her car. They just hadn't made it to headquarters. The creatures had been too close behind. Running and hiding from the big guy and the rest of his pack, they'd been lucky to come across the cabin and scramble into it before the dinosaurs had caught up to them. But it was a small cabin meant for one or two people. So the building was an eight by ten square with two modest windows. Not a whole lot of protection, but better than nothing.

Now they were trapped inside, unable to get where they'd been going. And she knew they were near. Headquarters couldn't be but a few miles away. So close.

"I lost my cell phone somewhere out there in the mud...I think when we slogged through that creek in the dark," he said. "It must have fallen off my belt. Damn."

"I never had a chance to grab mine out of the glove compartment before we began the wild flight for our lives." Strange how something as simple as the loss of a cell phone could doom their rescue, when they were so near to safety. In this modern age, they took way too much for granted. Life was too easy. Too cushy. She was tired, wet and hungry. A little more than frightened. And there was nothing she could do about any of that. At least they were out of the rain, the night, safe and in one piece. Together. For the moment.

At first, inside the park, they'd been following Chief Shore and his wife as they'd fled from the dinosaurs, finally losing them. Matthew thought the Chief's car had gone over a precipice somewhere and crashed. They'd searched for them, but the storm had come and in the rainy gloom they hadn't been able to find anything. Not the jeep or their friends.

They could both be dead for all she knew.

Then their enemy had caught up to them. A mob of snarling, narrow-eyed, fast-moving, nasty looking little bastards with one collective thought in their brains. Catch the humans. Eat the humans.

She and Matthew had abandoned their car when the dinosaurs cornered them up against a rock cliff and started jumping and tearing at it. The creatures had dented the roof and torn off one of the doors. Strong little buggers.

Somehow they'd gotten out and fled on foot. It was easier to travel that way. Weaving between the trees and splashing through ditches and creeks, hiding behind and under things. Once, her suggestion, they'd laid on the ground in a ditch and burrowing into the leaves and mud as deep as they could manage using only their hands, had kept as still as they could. Some of the creatures didn't seem to have a decent sense of smell, but a handful of them did, like some had keener eyesight and others could throw like baseball's pitcher Walter Johnson. Smart devils. So their respite hadn't lasted long.

Three ugly little suckers about four feet in height and teeth sharper than pointed nails located them and one jumped on her and tried to bite her leg. She shot the miniature creep between the eyes and Matthew shot the other two. But their cover had been blown. Within seconds the call had gone out and the woods was full of hungry dinosaurs hot on their trail.

Hounded by the animals, they'd had to run on or be overrun. Ellie felt guilty about that. They should have kept looking for their friends, but the monsters kept finding them and they had to keep moving.

When, at long last, they'd seemed to be free and clear, a huge brute had broken away from the others and come after them with a vengeance. They finally lost the other smaller ones in the murky woods but nothing they did, not shooting at and sometimes hitting, trying to evade or hiding from the largest one stopped its determination. It always found them. Must be starving.

For a time they'd continued to dodge it. Once it'd found and had almost gotten them; taking erratic flight again, they'd practically bumped into the empty cabin in the dark when they needed sanctuary the most. A place to hide and rest. Thank goodness.

Now here they were. Hearts beating wildly,

run to ground like horrified deer before an unstoppable and voracious predator.

She couldn't help but brood: *You've escaped these monsters four times now...three times you've escaped death at their claws and teeth. You faced, shot that one out in the woods that day and saved that visitor's life. It almost killed you. On Phantom Ship Island one attacked you and knocked you down into the rocks and almost got you. Another close call. You've been carried away by one and dropped into its nest. You survived by hiding and waiting; being smarter, more patient, than they were. Matthew, Ranger Shore and the others rescued you. Now this. How long will your luck last? How many times can a person cheat death if it's their time?*

A shiver crawled up her spine. Why was she thinking of these things? She didn't know. But, suddenly, the world was so much darker and it wasn't because it was night. She had a premonition this time would be different. She'd had premonitions all her life and she'd learned to trust them. The spirit world was always near to her. And it wasn't just her Indian ancestry, she'd been born slightly...psychic. Knowing things from beyond the grave she didn't want to know. Seeing and hearing other unearthly things she didn't want to see or hear. How she hated her *gift*. Lucky her.

"We're *so* close to headquarters," Kiley groaned. "I can't believe we can't get to it because of some freakin' dinosaur blocking our way."

She took his hand. "We'll make it out of this, don't worry, or the other rangers will find us. I know. They're looking for us now, I sense it. It's only a matter of time."

"Yeah, time." He inched his body up from the floor and peered out the window. One quick glance. "I don't see anything moving out there. This time I think we really lost it."

"What can you see out there in the murk and rain?" she spoke, careful not to talk too loud. She felt grimy, covered in mud, sweat and rain as she was. But, if she forced herself, she could almost believe they were safe. Almost.

"I see with night eyes."

"You have night eyes? What, exactly, are night eyes?" For the first time since they'd began running from the dinosaurs she felt herself relaxing, just a bit. Her muscles and legs hurt. Her head was pounding. It was a relief to rest. She was in good shape but fear along with prolonged physical activity and dinosaurs attempting to devour them at every turn could deflate anyone.

"I see better in the dark than most people, is what it means. That and I have extra sensitive hearing, too. I'm just lucky like that."

A snicker slipped from between her lips. "I have the same sharp senses. We are a good match."

What she didn't say was that her psychic ability, or her Indian blood or both, also sometimes gave her secret messages, warnings, she'd come to think of them as that, and suddenly she was receiving a very strange one.

Time is short. Pray. But do not be afraid.

Sometimes she wondered if the messages were from her Yahooskin grandfather or some other of her Indian ancestors. Or some other ghost.

Remember nothing ever dies.

Now she was scared. Why was a spirit–and what spirit–talking to her? Now of all times. What was happening?

She studied the shadows collected in a corner. A tall pale wraithlike shape formed and stepped forward from them and smiled at her. Her dead husband. Charlie.

Hi Charlie, it's been a long time since you visited me...why are you here? her thoughts asked him.

Been a long time. Yes. His ghost hand reached out to her. She could almost see the love in his dead soldier's eyes. It'd been years since he'd died in Afghanistan but he was young now as he appeared to her, twenty-something, as when they'd first been married. So long ago.

She couldn't help herself and smiled in the dark at him. So many good and bad memories. He'd been her first love and the father of her two sons. She still missed him.

She kept calm, so as not to upset Matthew or let him know what was going on, and listened to the ghost whispers in her head. Her *ghost talking* only freaked him out so the less he knew the better.

You've raised our sons well, Ellie, her

husband told her. *They're good men. I'm proud of them and you. I wanted you to know that. Thank you.*

Are you angry because I love someone else now? She wordlessly spoke to the ghost. Are you disappointed in me? I waited a long time....

Charlie waved a spectral hand at her. A smile on his white lips, he said, *No. I'm happy you found love again. Especially now.*

Especially now? *So why are you here?* She was getting more uneasy by the moment.

I just wanted to see you, be with you....

Why? But the ghost didn't answer because he had vanished, fading back into the shadows and time.

What had all that been about? As warm as she was, she shivered.

Matthew, as if guessing her inner turmoil, scooted against her and put an arm around her. They'd been seeing each other for months and she already suspected she loved him and he loved her. It'd been that way from the first time she'd met him at headquarters. He'd never been just another co-worker or ranger to her. They'd had a strong bond from the beginning. They thought alike. Had the same goals and outlook on life. Were fighters. He was an excellent ranger, a strong man and she trusted him. He'd come looking for her in the summer when she'd been carried away to the flying dinosaur's nest and had saved her life. And she hadn't felt this way about any man since Charlie.

She knew she loved Matthew Kiley.

Outside she could hear the wind and rain, nothing else. They had truly escaped those blood hungry monsters and when the light came they'd leave the cabin and make it to headquarters where they'd be home free. Where they'd join up with the rest of their fellow rangers. Henry and Ann would be there, too. Everything would be all right.

Ellie kept seeing Charlie in her mind, even though his ghost had left. Why had he appeared to her? What had he wanted? As hard as she looked, though, she couldn't see him in the corner any longer. Couldn't see him anywhere. Poignant memories of their marriage, their boys, their life together, his death and her overwhelming grief that had lasted far too long haunted her. They'd been so happy. Long, long ago.

Matthew brought her thoughts to the present by saying, "Ellie, I know this isn't really the best time to ask but, if we get out of this alive…will you marry me?"

She didn't know what to say, she was speechless and not much could do that to her. Well, except rioting dinosaurs and ghosts. Oh, she knew the question he'd asked might have been coming but still it was a surprise.

"Well?" Now his voice was unsure.

"Yes."

"Yes?"

"Yes…yes."

He leaned over and kissed her. "I don't want a lengthy engagement, either. We're not getting any younger."

And the dinosaur problem wasn't getting any better.

"How about we run off as soon as we get out of this mess and go before a Justice of the Peace in Klamath Falls at City Hall? Next Friday at noon? I have a few days off. We could have a mini-honeymoon somewhere, your choice."

She smiled at him in the dark and she thought he was smiling in return. There was no lightning to show his face. She just had to imagine it.

"No sense in wasting any of our precious time," he continued. "No use in waiting until this problem is resolved, either. According to Chief Shore's son-in-law, Justin, it might never be."

She didn't like hearing that, but kept her mind on what they were talking about at the moment. Almost dying a couple of times that day had made her more than aware life was short. For some shorter than for others. She loved this man and didn't want to waste another week living without him.

"Next Friday? You mean it? What will all our family and friends say?"

"We won't tell them until after we're hitched." He squeezed her hand. "Then we'll give a big party and invite them all. But I would like to request Chief Shore and his wife to be our witnesses. I'm sure they'll keep our secret."

"They would. All right. Next Friday at noon," she said. "It's a date."

They kissed again to seal their promise, but suddenly her skin was prickling and her heart began to race...she'd heard something outside in the wet woods. Something not good. Something big was crashing through the night trees...coming straight at them.

"Do you hear that?" her voice shaky.

Matthew inhaled a sharp breath and his body froze beside hers. He'd heard it, too.

In the corner the shadows were again churning and shifting and there was Charlie. Smiling, holding his hands out to her; to both of them. Something inside her began to weep because she'd figured out what was going on.

He was welcoming them to the world of the dead.

The howling of the big brute outside the walls merged with the world collapsing in around and down on top of them. The sound of screaming and splintering, cracking wood was the last thing Ellie heard and then the world ended. Just like that.

And there was Matthew floating beside her, haloed in white, and smiling as he took her hand and they joined Charlie, and her grandfather, and endless people she'd known in her life who'd already crossed over. Matthew's deceased family, his daughter, and his friends, as well, were there. They all came to meet them. Her thoughts touched on her two sons for a heartbeat, an eternity, and poignant vignettes of them as babies, young boys, teenagers and college age swirled around in her thoughts. Leaving them made her sad. But she knew they'd be fine without her. They were grown men with their whole lives ahead of them. And she'd see them again one day. They all came to the same place.

So this, she thought, was how life ended? This was what death was like?

Not so bad...not so bad...as she rushed towards the light with those she loved around her and left the world of humanity, its problems and the dinosaurs far behind.

*****

The dinosaur, at least thirty feet from stumpy tail to spiky head crest, hunkered in the middle of the destroyed cabin after its hissy fit and roared to the rain-laden skies. It wondered where the tiny beings it had been chasing had gone and then, not seeing them anywhere, turned and stomped into the night woods. Searching for food. Always searching. Lately it didn't seem to get enough since the animals were disappearing from the forest. It had to go farther and look longer to fill its belly. That made it angry.

The woods swallowed the monster but its roars could be heard for a long time afterwards dwindling into the distance. Other smaller dinosaurs scampered behind it, teeth snapping and eyes starving, and tried to keep up. But the big one was faster and soon it had left them behind.

Chapter 10
Justin

"How are things at the park?" Steven asked Justin after the paleontologist got off the cell phone with his father-in-law. "Is it still shut up as tight as a president's compound?"

"Still shut down tight with soldiers and rangers guarding its borders. Henry and Ann just had a close call, though. Coming in from Klamath Falls–where he says dinosaurs are showing up as well and wrecking the town–they were barely inside the park before they were attacked by another assorted collection of the creatures.

"They're unharmed but Ranger Kiley and Stanton, who were with them but in another car, haven't returned to headquarters yet. That's where the rangers and army's command center has been set up and where we're headed now– after a detour through Klamath Falls. I want to see what the destruction looks like and speak to the Chief of Police about what happened. See if he has anything to add to what Henry said."

"So, things are worse in the park than when

we left and, on top of that, the town's been infected, too?"

"I'm afraid so." Justin, behind the Land Rover's wheel, was scrutinizing the road and the woods running on each side of it. They were approaching the town of Klamath Falls and after what Henry had told him he was being careful. If the town was overrun he'd better be. The spread of the creatures hadn't surprised him. Not after what he and Steven had discovered on their fact finding mission. After leaving Redwood National Park and getting more cryptic emails, one from the Chief Ranger at Yosemite National and one from a paleontologist friend of his associated with Death Valley National Park, he'd spur-of-the moment decided to take a couple detours before driving back to Crater Lake. And because Steven had the time and craved the adventure, he'd accompanied him.

The Chief Park Ranger at Yosemite National's email had been short:

Dr. Maltin

I read your earlier email over and over and finally had to respond. Usually, I'd have a difficult time believing in boogie men or, for that matter, living dinosaurs as I am the sort of person who doesn't accept anything inexplicable unless I see it in the flesh, myself. And I never have. But I am answering your request to talk because for the last few weeks my men and I have been bombarded by visitors in our park who claim to be hearing odd noises, especially at night, and seeing strange animals in the deep woods. Unusually large animals they can't identify. There's been enough of these reports that I can no longer deny something unusual, perhaps unexplainable, is occurring. You said you were on a fact-finding mission down this way and would be in the area. Drop in to see me if you'd like. You can generally catch me in my office each weekday between eight and nine a.m. if you'd like to discuss this. Respectfully yours, Chief Ranger Sallings of Yosemite National Park.

So their first detour had been down around San Francisco where they'd met with Chief Ranger Sallings at his office early one warm morning. He'd been polite, if a little stand-offish, but had confirmed Justin's fears. There was definitely something unidentified and possibly dangerous prowling the heavier forested regions of his park. There had been a growing number of missing hikers and deep wood campers. Three men and two women in the last fourteen days. And not a sign of them.

Justin feared Yosemite had the same problem as Crater Lake and Redwood and informed Ranger Sallings of that. "I'd be prepared. You might consider closing your park until you can be sure it isn't prehistoric animals prowling around. These creatures being reported to you could be dinosaurs. If so, you're putting people in danger if you do nothing. Your visitors, rangers and you included." Justin could tell the chief ranger hadn't actually accepted all he'd divulged but, at least, he'd warned him. If

Dinosaur Lake III: Infestation

Sallings preferred to not believe, that was his problem. If dinosaurs had invaded his park, he'd know the full truth soon enough.

After their appointment at Yosemite they'd driven towards the Nevada border and Death Valley National Park, and meeting up with his friend and fellow paleontologist, Curt Nostrom, they'd taken a strenuous hike into a desert wilderness zone to inspect a number of curious tracks. Nostrom had been exploring on his day off and been surprised at what he'd come across. Dinosaur footprints. Fresh ones. "I know they're dinosaur prints, but I've never seen any like them anywhere in my research or at any of the digs I've been on and I've been all over the world cataloging tracks."

"So let's," Justin drawled, "have a look at them."

He and Nostrom had attended college together and once they'd learned how much they had in common, beer, throwing darts in bars as well as dinosaurs, had become good friends. They'd kept in touch over the years and sometimes collaborated on anything of interest either found. Justin had kept Nostrom in the loop through the earlier dinosaur troubles because he trusted his friend's advice and often sought it. Nostrom had an uncanny way with solving tricky problems.

The heat was intense, Death Valley being the largest, hottest and driest of the national parks in the lower forty-eight states. The park fringed the northwestern corner of the Mojave Desert and contained a varied environment of salt-flats, sand dunes, valleys, canyons and mountains. Home to scorpions, snakes and coyotes and not much else. Until now. It was half a day's trek under the blistering sun which led the three of them to a gorge with the recent footprints of some extremely heavy and huge park inhabitants' feet. Basically unidentifiable to Nostrom's and a layman's eyes. But not to Justin.

One look at the tracks and Justin knew the dinosaur pestilence had spread even into the desert wasteland. "These look like a Hugo's footprints," he'd disclosed to Nostrom, who knew what and who Hugo had been.

"That's not good then, hey, to find them way out here amidst the sand and creosote bush? Adaptable little buggers, aren't they? It's got to be at least a hundred degrees in the shade. And not only that...but what are they eating out here? There's not much on the menu." Nostrom was as short as a Hobbit, but his shrewd blue eyes and friendly smile made him instantly likable. He was an ethical man; not one of those who'd knife a colleague in the back for the recognition he could steal. When Justin needed another paleontologist he could trust emphatically, it was usually Nostrom.

"Whatever they can find. By these impressions, they're not exactly little buggers. Whatever made these prints could be as tall as me, most likely taller." Justin, eyes shaded under the wide brim of a Stetson styled hat, had gazed up at the blazing ball of fire above. "And no, finding these footprints here is not a good sign. So far that makes four areas of natural wilderness, four national parks in this case, that the creatures have invaded—or been hatched into. Exactly what I was afraid of. They're spreading. Multiplying across state lines and across the country." He took photographs with his smart phone so he'd have proof and could examine them closer back in the lab.

Nostrom had grunted. "Well, that's what I wanted to show you. Pretty alarming if you ask me. If the size of those tracks are any indication of the size of the creature that made them...we have a monumental problem. What now?"

"We bug out of here fast as we can bug. It's getting late. I don't want to be anywhere near here when the sun sets. Don't want to bump into one of these creatures in the dark. I say we head back to our cars. Pronto."

"I'm with you, buddy."

Justin glanced at Steven. The musician's eyes were glued to the impressions in the dirt and his upper lip, beaded in sweat, kept twitching. Probably didn't want to be there after dark, either.

"Suddenly," Steven murmured, "this theory of yours, Justin, is becoming a little too real. Dinosaurs all over the place like Christmas candy at Christmas."

"Oh, it's real all right." Justin turned and the men dragged their sweating, exhausted bodies to the car. He'd found himself listening to every noise that floated on the sweltering air around them. Waiting to hear the cries he was familiar with.

He'd been relieved, hours later, for he and his friend to be in his air-conditioned car, driving down the evening highway. Finally and at long last on their way home.

*****

Now, a day later and in bright sunshine, Justin and Steven were coming into Klamath Falls down the middle of Main Street.

Around them cars and trucks packed with people and their belongings zoomed by. Since coming into the town's outskirts there had been a steady stream of them. Fleeing Klamath. Fleeing whatever had rampaged through it and might return.

"Whoa...look at the destruction." Steven's eyes were taking in the shattered buildings and debris everywhere through the car's windows. "Whatever went through here must have been gigantic. And mad as hell." He was shaking his head. "I don't blame people for leaving. I feel like leaving myself."

"We are," Justin said. "Right after we have a discussion with Police Chief Chapman. I want to know what happened here. The whole story. Maybe someone gave a detailed description of what did this, though I'm betting a thousand bucks it's dinosaurs. It might be he knows something more now than when Henry last spoke to him."

Pulling up in front of the police station and heading towards the door, Justin and Steven caught Chief Chapman rushing out. He didn't look like a happy man. He looked like a man in a hurry. His blood-shot eyes nervously darting here and there. His hands shaking.

Justin stopped him and introduced himself. Then asked, "Chief Chapman, I heard from Ranger Shore about what happened here. Can you give me any more specific information? How large were the dinosaurs, how many? How have people described them?"

The police officer glared at him. "There were NO dinosaurs in my town, Dr. Maltin. I told your father-in-law the same thing. It was straight line winds, a tornado or something. An earthquake. Some people have way too much imagination, that's all. Or they're trying to create anarchy where there is none. So reports of giant beasts running amok and destroying our little township have been *greatly* exaggerated. A bunch of malarkey, if you ask me."

"They why are you evacuating the town?"

"I'm not. It's only that some misguided, misinformed citizens are too frightened to remain. They believe the outrageous tales of a few demented yahoos who claim to have had monstrous creatures chasing them, seen them flattening houses and businesses. Whatever." The officer was defensive, his face flushed, his manner brusque. The guy was positively not a believer.

"It seems like more than a few townsfolk are vamoosing," Justin pointed out. And as he said it, a truck towing an RV drove by them going a little faster than the speed limit. Five other cars followed, so stuffed full of personal belongings and clothes the windows were blocked. "Looks like half the town is vamoosing."

"Well, yah. The destruction and the stories have scared a lot of people. But then, some people will believe anything."

"I take it you never saw any of these creatures?"

"No, I did not."

"And there really isn't anything else you can tell me about the attack? Did anyone get hurt?"

"Not that I know of. Doesn't that prove there wasn't any so-called monsters loose in town? Wouldn't *dinosaurs* eat people or at least leave body parts scattered all over the place?"

The thought came to Justin and the words followed. "Well, then, any missing people?"

The officer refused to answer, a scowl reshaping his face.

"Any people missing?" Justin repeated firmly.

The police chief hesitated. "Some. But I'm sure they'll turn up when everything settles down. Or, perhaps, they're some of the early deserters and they've already left town."

Justin knew he wasn't going to get anywhere with the man so he thanked him and he and Steven strode back to his car.

Driving slowly through town he couldn't get

over the amount of damage there was. At least Zeke's house was still standing. And Ann's newspaper. But for blocks around a lot of things weren't. This was what he'd feared all along. His ultimate nightmare. The dinosaurs stomping into a highly populated area. Smashing residential buildings and squashing people like toe jam.

"Oh, dinosaurs were definitely here all right. And more than one. Really big ones, too," Justin summarized, looking at someone's once beautiful house which was now a pile of rubble. "I recognize the signs." There was grimness in his smile.

"You think they're still lurking around here somewhere?" Steven looked around and then up into the sky as if he expected one of them to suddenly appear and drop on their heads. Midday. A strong sun beat down on them, but the heat wasn't anything like what they'd endured days before in the desert.

"I wouldn't rule that out. They're territorial, which means they'll most likely return. I think the townspeople who are leaving are the smart ones."

"Are you saying we shouldn't stick around?" Steven was surveying the businesses as they went past. Some were still open, yet there seemed to be hectic activity behind their windows. More businesses were shut tight with CLOSED signs out front.

"I wouldn't suggest we spend the night here, if that's what you mean. Not without more lethal weapons on us. Like a rocket launcher. Body armor or an invisible protection shield. A concrete bunker to hide in."

"Where are all the news media trucks? The reporters?" Steven posed. "You'd think they'd be all over this story. Dinosaurs destroy Klamath Falls!"

Justin actually laughed. "Well, would you believe someone if they called you and told you that story?"

"Well, probably not. It is sort of unbelievable."

"Yep."

After another minute or so, Steven asked, "While we're here in civilization, so to speak, how about we stop at Freddy's and grab some burgers to eat on the way? I don't know about you but I'm starved. Dinosaur researching does that to me."

"That's not a bad idea. If they're open. And as long as we make it quick and don't stick around. I wouldn't put it past our prehistoric friends to do a repeat performance. Freddy's is right over there," he cocked his head at the restaurant ahead of them on their right, "and it does appear to be open. We'll run in, grab bags of cheeseburgers and fries and take them to Henry and his men. They've had a hell of a few days. He's worried sick about his two missing rangers and what's been happening. And I know how Henry and Ann love Freddy's cheeseburgers. It might cheer them up some." And who knew how long the luxuries like restaurants would remain open for business if the situation worsened as he expected it to do. Better take advantage of the opportunity while it was still offered.

"Well, that's thoughtful of you."

"Henry and Ann have always been good to me. Their rangers, too. Least I can do. Besides I could use something to eat myself. Didn't we skip breakfast?"

"We did."

Justin parked the car and they hurried into Freddy's and when they exited their arms were full of white bags. Enough to feed Henry and most of his rangers. Freddy hadn't seen the dinosaurs that had terrorized the town, didn't believe in them, and that's why he was still there. Justin felt sorry for the man. He wanted to tell him that, yes, dinosaurs were real, extremely dangerous, and he should leave town while he could. But the middle-aged bald man with the pot belly and the smell of grilled hamburgers about him was set in his ways and he didn't want to leave his business, his home or his town. Justin hadn't bothered trying to convince him. Like the police chief, the businessman would learn the truth soon enough if the dinosaurs returned. Besides that Justin was in a hurry. A real hurry. Not only was he uncomfortable within the town's limits but he knew Henry and Ann needed him at park headquarters. Steven and him had been gone long enough. More importantly, night was coming.

Justin drove away hoping the man and his business would still be there next time he came through town. He hoped the town would still be there.

They left Main Street and were turning onto the highway that would take them to the park when the cry bellowed through the air above and around them. A loud primitive shriek that echoed through the houses and streets. Justin knew that cry well.

"What is that?" Steven breathed once the sound had died away. His face ashen.

"What we've been searching for the last couple of days."

"Land dinosaur?" A hoarse whisper.

Another cry shook the silence, louder. Closer this time. More pissed off. The ground beneath their tires shook so much Justin could feel it through the car's undercarriage, even while they were moving. Peoples' faces in the cars around them reflected first confusion and then outright terror as they tilted and looked out their windows. Up. Up. Up.

Whatever was coming was really BIG, was advancing swiftly and headed their way. The Range Rover bounced on the road and Justin had to fight with the steering wheel to kept the car on it. He stole a quick glance out his rearview mirror. It was full of dinosaur mouth and teeth. That's how big the creature was–and the one beside it.

At first glimpse, Justin thought they looked somewhat like Utah's Cedar Mountain Formation species discovered in 2008 called *Siats meekerorum*, named after a cannibalistic man-eating monster from Native American tribal legend. His fellow paleontologists believed the *Siats* might have been one of the three largest carnivorous dinosaur genus ever found in North America; the biggest of that group being the T-Rex, which came along 30 million years after the *Siats* and probably weighed double what they did. They'd been a member of a group of gigantic meat-eaters called carcharodontosaurs, which lived during the Late Cretaceous period and included some of the largest predatory dinosaurs ever discovered. He looked again. They were a dark greenish hue, their scaly-appearing skin virtually iridescent. Eyes, much bigger than any he'd seen so far, recessed deeply into cavernous sockets. No, not looking exactly like the *Siats*. Mutants again. Though these two renegades had the T-Rex shaped heads, they were modified, rounder and full of triple-rowed teeth, and their bulky bodies were larger and the front legs longer and heavier. They could bring them up close to their chests and run on two legs–bouncing great distances really–or put all four to the ground and run…even faster. Hmmm, for their size they could sure move. Really *move*.

Oh, lord. They were gaining on them.

"*Dinosaurs*. Two of them. On our tail and closing in fast," Justin shouted and his foot slammed down on the accelerator pedal. "So we better get the hell out of here!"

Out of nowhere he had the weirdest thought: The dinosaurs had gotten the scent of the cheeseburgers in the rear seat and were after them? Nah. That was silly. More likely it was the human smell that had attracted the predators. The stream of metal bugs full of human tidbits entering and leaving the town. Bright colored little metal bugs luring them out like bait. Justin had little doubt as to where Police Chief Chapman's missing townspeople had gone. The dinosaurs were most likely coming back for seconds.

And he wasn't about to be an entrée.

"Oh my God, look at the size of those suckers! Big as a moving house on feet," Steven exclaimed, gaping out the windows at their pursuing shadows. "Seeing those Nessies back at the lake was bad enough, but they were distracted. Fighting among themselves. These are after *us*! Wow can they travel. Oh my God they're catching up to us...oh my...GO FASTER!"

The Range Rover rocketed forward, a space ship hitting warp drive. Justin took another hurried look over his shoulder. The dinosaurs were determinedly chasing them now. Had zeroed in on them as prey. Roaring and trumpeting their intent. Running with their powerful legs, their mouths were yawning, ready to scoop them up, teeth slobbering, and they were easily keeping up with the car. One as tall as a three story building and the other nearly the same size galloping along behind it. They'd begun bounding on two legs but had dropped to four to increase their speed. Were they similar to some of the ones Ann and Henry had come up against…just larger? Possibly the mature versions? Or just some new nightmare altogether? Justin didn't have the luxury of dwelling on it. Self-preservation kicked in.

"*Go faster! Faster!*" Steven yelped again, his eyes on the danger behind them.

"I'm pushing the car as hard as I can and remain on the road! Hold on! Going to start evasion tactics."

There were unlucky vehicles on the highway ahead of them and some coming towards them. Why they'd want to go to Klamath Falls when most of the inhabitants were leaving, was a mystery to Justin. At the moment, he didn't have time to think about it. He passed the first couple cars in front of them, beeping his horn wildly; Steven waving his arms out the windows, pointing behind them, as their car raced ahead of those around them.

One of the dinosaurs slowed down, came up on its hind haunches and with an ear-splitting screech reached out and swatted a blue SUV, with two occupants, in the opposite lane off the road. It left the highway, rose into the air, flew like a bird for a few seconds, and crashed into the trees. The dinosaur followed. Poor people.

One dinosaur down, one to go.

Steven groaned, swiped his eyes with the back of his hand. "Can we help them?"

"We can't! We still have one almost on our rear bumper." And it was true, the second dinosaur had moved up to take the first one's place. They had to keep driving, a metal dodge ball, staying ahead of the beast eager to catch them. Not travelling as fast as Justin wanted because there were sometimes cars in the lanes around them, or the highway kept sharply curving into the hills. The dinosaur was fixated on them. Wanted them. Wouldn't give up.

They weren't pulling away from the beast, barely keeping ahead of it. Skidding over the road now, their tires' traction were uneven. The second dinosaur stuck to them, ignoring the other cars on the highway. It kept coming.

"What are we going to do?" Steven was turned in his seat, staring at what was pursuing them. "Should we swerve off on a side road, try squeezing through some trees or something?" His voice touched with horror. The creature was swiping at them whenever it could, which slowed it down just enough to allow them to stay ahead by a heartbeat or two.

Justin knew the best chance they had was speed. Pure speed. For the first time since their flight had begun, there were no cars visible anywhere ahead of them in either lane; there was a straight stretch, no twists or turns, and he took his chance. "NO! We stay on the highway. Hold on. I'm going to push this pedal to the floor. Now!"

The Rover surged down the highway at a higher speed than Justin had ever driven it and they finally tugged away from their prehistoric nemesis. It roared in rage as they left it behind. The last thing Justin saw was it standing in the middle of the highway, completely halted and rearing up on its hind legs. Thrashing its arms around in frustration. They drove around a curve and left the scene.

"Yes!" Steven cheered, but his relief didn't last long. They passed a string of cars coming from the other direction and heading for what waited ahead of them, unseen, around the curve in the road.

"Warn them!" Steven yelled, his eyes on the cars as they sped by them and disappeared around the bend.

Too late. They'd been speeding and so had the other cars. Gone.

"I'm sorry," Justin voice was unsteady. He slowed the vehicle down. There were no bouncing dinosaurs anywhere he could see. "Not enough time."

"We should go back!"

"We can't. Before we took that last curve, I saw more of the creatures, a mess of them, emerging from the woods. All were converging on the place, the crashed car and those other cars we just passed. We can't go back. We're outnumbered.

"We have to get to headquarters. Henry and the army needs to know there's a pack of those over-sized nightmares sneaking towards Klamath Falls to join their buddies. Up to no good by the looks of it." Justin had resumed their journey and the car was again traveling at a normal speed down the road. Sixty miles an hour instead of a hundred.

Steven stared at him. "They'll decimate

what's left of the town. All those people still there...."

"That's what will happen. The town needs help. Protection. The National Guard or anyone else we can get to respond has to be dispatched there before it's too late." Taking his right hand off the wheel, he picked up his cell phone from the center tray beside him and pressed a button.

"Who you calling?" Steven's eyes still searching the expanse around them.

"Police Chief Chapman. He has to be warned what's headed his way."

"Yeah, like he's going to believe you now, when he never has before." Steven shrugged. "That man is an idiot."

"Exactly what Henry always says. But he still needs to be warned. The town needs to be warned."

"Good luck," sarcastically delivered.

Justin, phone to his ear, listened in silence for a minute or two, then disconnected, made another call, listened a while longer, disconnected again and put the cell back where he'd gotten it. "No answer. Not even an answering machine. What kind of policeman is he anyway?"

"You called his cell or called the police station?"

"Both. No answer either place."

"You tried."

"That I did. I'll try again when we get to headquarters. I need to be sure we get there in one piece and deliver the news."

"That sounds good to me." Steven slumped against the seat, rubbing his eyes with his shaky fingers. He let out a heavy sigh. "You know seeing those water Nessies was one thing, they hadn't seemed all that interested in eating us, but being actively chased by those land dinosaurs, who definitely wanted to eat us, was so much worse. Man, that was way too close. See my hands are still shaking." He put his hands up and sure enough, they were shaking.

Justin didn't say a word. His brain was furiously devising plans of what to do next.

When they arrived at the barricaded entrance of the park, Justin telephoned Henry. Told him what had happened and what was going on. Where they were.

"I'll take care of it, Justin. I have a direct line to the army base in Klamath Falls. I'll alert them to the dinosaurs amassing outside the town. I'll try contacting Chief Chapman again, too. I might have better luck than you. You say you're at the south entrance?"

"Yes."

"No one there on guard?"

"No one. The booth is empty. No rangers or soldiers anywhere."

"That's not good. There were three sentries stationed there this morning. They should be there."

"They're not." Justin didn't know what else to say. He didn't need to. Three more men were missing. Way too many missing people lately, he muttered to himself. Too many.

"You two sit tight until I can send an armed escort for you," Henry said. "The park is as bad as the surrounding areas or the town. Those damn dinosaurs are everywhere now. It's too dangerous for you to come through it without armed guards. But lift up the gate and move your car to the other side of the barricade, here's the code to let yourself in. Key in 4-8-9-5-5-. Tuck your vehicle next to the booth so my men can find you and wait for them."

"We made it this far," Justin protested. "we can make it just fine to headquarters. What, that's only about fifteen miles?"

"Don't fool yourself, you made it this far out of pure luck. My daughter would be really mad at me if something happened to you, especially now with the new baby coming."

"All right, all right. We'll sit tight and wait for reinforcements. But hurry, those giant primordial mutants aren't that far behind us. Some of them could have split off from the rest and be coming this way, hunting for us even now. One of them really seemed to be determined to catch us for some reason. Could be he liked or hated the paint color on my car. Who knows?" Justin glanced behind them as he spoke. "I wouldn't put it past it to not have continued the pursuit."

"It won't be long. I'm sending soldiers out for you now. Stay down. Stay quiet."

"Stay invisible, you mean?" Justin supplied.

"If you can do that, too, that would be great."

Justin could almost see his father-in-law

Dinosaur Lake III: Infestation

smiling on the other end of the line. "I'll try." Then he hung up.

"We wait here?" Steven's eyes were seeking any movement in the woods around them, his face still drained of color.

"We wait. Henry says he's sending soldiers out to get us through the dinosaur infested jungle. Supposedly, the creatures are everywhere and multiplying." He snorted. But his eyes, too, were on the dense forest. The shadows of evening were filtering the woods into a mist of faded green. There were odd noises coming from among the leaves that made Justin jumpy.

"So, have you seen enough live dinosaurs to populate your book?" Justin quipped. "Have enough hair-raising adventures to make a riveting story?"

"More than enough." Steven met Justin's gaze. "Too many. I think I'm on dinosaur-overload."

"I have the feeling you're about to see more."

"I feel like…bait suddenly," Steven's voice was low as his eyes went to the windows.

For a while they sat quietly in the car, as if by doing that they wouldn't alert any passing predators, until Steven, most likely out of nervousness, began softly humming a song Justin didn't recognize. The melody was haunting. It'd make a fitting soundtrack for a horror flick and under the circumstances not inappropriate.

Because it didn't take long before the bait was taken.

"Don't look now, friend," Steven hissed out

of the side of his mouth, slowly sliding down further into the seat, "but, as they say in all the scary movies, we have company."

Justin saw it as well. Them, really. Three dinosaurs, ranging in size from about three feet tall to around five, were emerging from the trees and inching closer. Delicate heads held high, with glittering stygian eyes, noses sniffing the air. Tiny arms with wicked looking claws on the end hanging before them. They reminded Justin of reddish kangaroos, but with scales instead of fur, no big ears, and not nearly so cute. Were these the same ones that had attacked Ann and Henry a while back? By her and Henry's descriptions, they could be.

One of the things hopped up to Justin's side of the car and Justin, as Steven was doing, slithered down so he wouldn't be so visible. The car doors were locked. Check. Windows closed tight. Check. Rifles were close at hand. Check. Help was coming. Check.

All they had to do was hang tight and…stay alive.

The dinosaur at the window hesitated about five feet away. Studying the humans hiding in the car. Justin had slowly retrieved his rifle, held it ready in his lap, lowered his head and after a minute or two, being curious, peeked over the door frame.

The creature was still glaring in at him, its head slanted slightly, licking its lips, or what passed for lips. It watched for a bit and then, Justin could have sworn, it smiled. Big wide grin revealing rows and rows of tiny needle teeth. Then, again he almost couldn't believe what his eyes were seeing, it seemed to gesture *come on out* at its friends behind it. No way. It couldn't be that intelligent, could it? Organizing an ambush? Cognizant of what it was doing? Could it?

The dinosaur's two accomplices slunk closer. Canted their heads, eyes intent on the humans in the shiny hard container; probably trying to figure out how to pry them out of it.

Squinting at the woods, Justin saw more of the creatures coming. A lot more. A dinosaur army. Creeping in and around the car. Silent and deadly. He slid back down below their sight.

"Those soldiers better get here quick," Steven grumbled under his breath. "I got a bad feeling about this. This ain't no welcoming committee."

"Sure isn't." Justin stealthily retrieved his cell phone and clicked in a number. "Henry, we have a real situation here," he kept his voice right around a loud whisper. There were hungry eyes on him so he tried not to make any sudden movements as he talked. "No. They haven't arrived yet." A pause. "Okay." He ended the conversation.

"They should have been here by now, Henry said. Should be here any second. We're supposed to wait, but we're not. If we don't move, we'll be overrun. The troop escort is coming down the main road so we'll meet them along it at some point."

"I'm with you, friend. Let's go." Steven spoke from lower down in the seat. It didn't help. Suddenly the creatures were crowding around the vehicle, peeking in at them like naughty children. Making clicking noises and tapping on the car with curved claws. One of them, an over-sized beast with a bloody slice of his hide going up his chest and neck gone, wound gaping and ugly, hit the window with such force it cracked. The creature struck it again and the glass shattered like a cracked egg. It raised its head and screamed to the sky.

Oh, oh, he's calling more of his buddies to come join the fun.

The dinosaurs around them heaved against the Rover, some jumping onto its hood and roof. The car rocked and bounced.

"Time to go!" Justin cried as he bolted up, wrenched the key to the on position and accelerated the car into overdrive. Down the road towards headquarters. Faster than a speeding bullet. "Hold on, we're in for another hell of a ride!"

And Steven held on.

Some of the more tenacious dinosaurs clung on to the vehicle but most fell off on the wayside. Others threw themselves at them and bounced off.

"Holy cow! Look at that mother!" Steven yelled suddenly. "It must be at least thirty feet tall!"

In the middle of the road highlighted by the waning sun a behemoth waited for them. It resembled the ones that had chased them out of town. Whoa, so they were in the park as well? Or was this one of those same ones? Had they beat them here? Justin didn't have time to think long on that.

"Get the Steyr SPP from the back seat," he shouted. "You know how to use it. Remember I showed you on the boat that day on the lake? So start shooting."

"Are we stopping?"

"Hell no. We're doing a drive-by! Hit where and what you can. Going to go off road for a while and circle around the mother. It'll be bumpy, but it's the only way we can go."

Justin drove towards the howling dinosaur blocking their path and at the last moment swerved to the left and circumvented the creature by going through the tall grass and bushes as Steven hung out the window and shot at it with the Steyr. His rounds must have hit flesh because the creature screamed over and over, pivoted around and grabbed at them. Almost got them. Though swift for its size, it hadn't moved quite fast enough. The car slipped through its claws.

They reconnected to the road on the other side and raced deeper into the park with the creature sticking close on their tail.

They'd been unbelievably lucky. Again.

"It still coming?" Justin was hunched over the steering wheel, his face pale.

"No...wait...yes! It's tracking us. It just completely annihilated that tree. Smacked it down with one blow. Big tree, too. Oops, it's seen us. Here it comes again."

Justin concentrated on his driving, pulling ahead of the monster, and almost didn't see the M1A2 Abrams Main Battle Tank coming straight for them down the park's main thoroughfare.

"Help has arrived," Steven exclaimed. "And just in time. But a tank? Really? A *tank?*"

"Looks like the perfect ride to me. An armored tank should keep us safe from those smaller dinosaurs and maybe the big beast behind us. Get ready. I'm stopping and we're getting out. Trading rides. Don't forget your weapon. Here we go!"

Someone in the military vehicle must have seen them coming because the machine wheeled over into the grass to wait. The Abrams, a monster itself, though metal, was a strong mobile land weapon platform low and sleek; mounting a large caliber cannon in a rotating gun turret capped with a secondary weapon, a general-purpose machine gun set coaxially with the main gun, and a heavier anti-aircraft machine gun on the turret roof. The one before them was a drab army green ideal for blending into the trees.

Justin banged on the brakes and the Rover, throwing dirt and rocks everywhere, slid in beside the army tank. He could hear the large dinosaur roaring beyond the trees behind them somewhere. Close.

The two men scrambled out of the car.

The tank hatch opened and Ranger Gillian's helmeted head popped out. "Need a ride, Dr. Maltin? Mr. James? We've come looking for you. Found you, too."

It took Justin a second to recognize the ranger and when he did, he cried, "And are we glad to see you, Ranger! Sure, we'll hitch a ride. But we better hurry because there's a particularly large and irate dinosaur on our tail. The tank might not even be enough to stop the beast. Hear it?"

Ear shattering cries echoed on the warm air around them. Closer now.

"Let's get out of here."

Justin and Steven clambered up onto the machine and Ranger Gillian made way for them to lower themselves into it.

The ranger handed them intercom helmets so they could communicate with him and the crew and the two new arrivals put them on. Justin was reminded of the last time he'd been wearing a helmet, on the Black Hawk helicopter with McDowell, her soldiers, and Henry when they were looking for the gargoyles' nest. Had that only been four months ago? It felt like yesterday. They'd lost two soldiers that day. Even now the painful memories were still too vivid for him.

"I'm flattered," Justin mouthed loudly at Ranger Gillian over the headset so he could be heard over the machine's rumble, "that you came for us in a tank."

"Don't be. The army brought in five of these babies for this assignment. We use them in the park all the time now. We find it's safer than a park service vehicle or a truck. Especially now that the dinosaur population has exploded since you've been gone. You have no idea, Dr. Maltin. They're everywhere now."

"Great, I return to a park you can't travel in without steel armor enshrining you."

"You got it, Doc. Chief Ranger says we're truly a Jurassic Park now." A nervous laugh. No one else laughed with him.

They weren't in the belly of the tank for more than a minute, giving Justin and Steven barely enough time to be introduced to the two other soldier crewmen, a middle-aged and serious faced Sergeant Cassons and a younger man, Lieutenant Becker, before the lieutenant, as the tank's commander, gave the order to his driver, the sergeant, to move out.

Not soon enough.

The tank rocked back and forth violently. Sniffing, pushing, and playing with them like a toy, the dinosaur must be curious. Had it seen Justin and Steven slip into it? Could have. Could it be chasing its supper? Probably.

"Lieutenant Becker, our overgrown monster friend has found us," Justin informed the commander. "I'd strongly suggest we immediately flee the premises. Before his buddies find and join him. They're all around us in the woods and if they congregate here we could be trapped. I'm grateful for the rescue, but I'm not sure even this modern weapon of destruction can protect us from the giant creature that's stalking us now."

"Oh, I believe this vehicle can handle it. We're leaving, Dr. Maltin, but first we're going to turn our main gun on our assailant and shoot the hell out of it. A parting gift. We've learned since we've arrived that forcefully dealing with these creatures is the best way. Kill them whenever we get the chance. Otherwise they just keep on coming. Somehow they respect lethal force. It keeps them at bay and under control. Somewhat.

"Then we'll flee." A stiff smile.

Justin nodded. He was no soldier. This man was. He knew what he was doing, or Justin hoped he did.

The tank was battered again. This time it was shoved further into the trees. Their attacker was no longer playing with them, it wanted the sweetmeats inside the metal shell.

"Ooh, I'd say our friend outside is really mad at us for taking its supper away," Ranger Gillian stated, dropping down into a seat and locking himself in. Justin had already done the same.

"Too bad. But I wasn't ready to be a dinosaur eggroll." Steven had collapsed into one of the tank's uncomfortable seats as well. He was soaking in the crisis and was possibly making mental notes for his memoirs. But he did look scared.

The commander gave orders to his subordinate, who was also the gunner, and the tank's main cannon began booming. Inside the noise was deafening. So were the cries of a wounded dinosaur as it hastily retreated. They must have gotten it good. Yes! Maybe it'd go off somewhere and die and there'll be one less monster in the park.

Again Justin was reminded of how clever the dinosaurs were. They knew when they were outgunned and didn't stay around. A shiver crawled along his skin. Smart. Too smart.

This time the commander's smile was a real one. "Now we get the hell out of here."

There was a clamorous racket outside the tank. Sounds of something, many somethings, scrambling over and across the exterior. Scratching and clawing to get in. Screeching and hissing like little demons from hell. The commander swiveled his head and checked the monitors. "We have company," he said dryly. "Again.

"Looks like the indigenous pack inhabitants of the park, except for the larger one we just wounded and frightened off, and so far they seem to be the most dominant species. The smaller, bouncing ones that like to throw objects and eat cats." He winked at Justin. "Or so your chief park ranger tells me."

Justin peeked at the monitors and saw the crowd around them. "Yikes, there must be dozens of them coming out of the woods." And there were. And all different sizes. Had the large one called them? They couldn't be that symbiotic, could they? It was a truly bad sign if they were.

"I think it's time we get out of here," he said to the commander.

"Sergeant," Lieutenant Becker growled, "fire the smoke grenades from the launcher; deploy a blanket smoke screen to hide us as we leave. It'll confuse the creatures and give us time to get back to headquarters, hopefully without any more creature encounters."

"Yes, Sir!" Sergeant Cassons spoke up.

The commander fixed his eyes on Justin. "Since my basic orders were to get you and your musician friend here back to headquarters safe and sound, Dr. Maltin, I'll refrain from going after any more dinosaurs. This wasn't an expedition to deplete the dinosaur population. So I aim to do exactly as I was told as much as I'd like to continue the fight. That's for another time."

"That's fine with me. All we want is to get to headquarters. I have urgent news for the Chief Ranger. I need to talk to him. Sooner than later."

Ranger Gillian gave him a curious look but didn't ask him what the news was and Justin didn't offer. He'd tell them all at one time when they got to headquarters.

"Lieutenant Becker," Justin inquired, "I imagine you have direct radio contact with your home base at Kingsley Field in Klamath Falls?"

"I do."

"Is there any way you can immediately alert them there's an emergency in Klamath Falls? A gang of those large dinosaurs like what was just hunting us have converged on the town, or will soon, and I believe troops should be sent there without delay. Peoples' lives are at stake. There was an attack earlier in the week but it was nothing compared to what's approaching the town now."

"I'll do that, Dr. Maltin." The soldier spoke over his headset and let his superiors at Kingsley Field Air Base know what was going on.

After his conversation, he glanced at Justin and nodded. "It's done. Troops are heading to Klamath Falls. I am surprised none were sent before this if, as you say, the town was already infected. Didn't the local authorities call in support?"

"Ha! The local authorities as you put it, in this case Police Chief Chapman, doesn't believe in dinosaurs."

The commander released a dry laugh. "He ought to visit this park then. He'd have no doubt then, especially when one sidles up next to him and tries to eat his face."

Ranger Gillian agreed. "You can't go anywhere in this place without hearing or seeing some sort of dinosaur. Or a mob of them. Chief Ranger Shore is beside himself. It's happened so quickly."

"Dr. Maltin, tell me about your experiences today in Klamath Falls and those since you entered the park," the lieutenant pressed. "The more we know about the dinosaur, er, invasion the better prepared we can be to fight them."

And Justin did.

The tank was lurching through the forest along the roadway in the direction of headquarters. It was making good time. For a tank. But then it was one of those fancy fast-moving ones with streamline tracks and immense power. It could travel. Watching their progress on the inside monitors, Justin felt exhaustion seeping in. It'd been a hard week or two. Too many frightening truths learned and too many dinosaurs to evade. He was extremely grateful to be within the sanctuary of the tank and to be rejoining a group of men where he knew he'd be as protected and safe as he could be under the circumstances in a park of deep woods full of cunning ancient predators.

"You know," Steven said, more to Justin than the others listening, "except for all the heart-stopping danger and gut wrenching terror of the last week, on the boat as the leviathans fought below us in the water, as we ran from those dinosaurs outside the town and here inside the park...this has been the most alive I've felt since Julie died."

"You are kidding, aren't you?" Yet Justin couldn't stop a grin from emerging. "You mean with man-hungry monsters chasing you, trying to maim or eat you...you liked it?"

"No, not liked. In fact it often scared the spit out of me. But, for the first time in years I didn't wish I was dead, like Julie, every second of the day. I felt invigorated. Heck, I even looked forward to each day we were on our fact-finding mission." His eyes were shining, his face flushed. "Thanks Justin. Thanks for giving me my life back."

"You're more than welcome, my friend. But your euphoria, believe me, won't last long. I've been at this game longer than you and, yes, you will get sick and tired of looking for, romping after, and running from dinosaurs. If you can stay alive, that is."

"It doesn't matter." Steven leaned back, rubbed his neck, though his smile reflected his weariness. "It's made me a new man. I'll let tomorrow bring what it may. Because for today I'm just so happy to be alive."

Justin let out a sigh and returned to studying the monitors. Outside the light was going, but they were getting near headquarters, and he was relieved.

He had so much to tell Henry.

And he knew, now that he and Steven were safe, he had to call Laura and tell her what he'd learned, too; what he'd seen and what he suspected. He had to warn her to start preparing and their lives were about to change. Perhaps unimaginably. She wasn't going to like that much. With the baby coming so soon, all his wife wanted was to feather her nest and have her life, their lives, be as they'd always been. He felt nearly as sorry for her as he felt for himself because that was not going to happen. Not now.

Because if what he suspected came to pass, nothing for them would be normal ever again.

Chapter 11
Henry

Henry was exhausted, but had to check on Ann before he stole a short rest. She'd been sleeping on his office couch since they'd made it to headquarters early that morning and he wanted to see how she was doing. He had much to tell her. Justin was okay, his friend, too, and they were even now being escorted by tank, no less, to headquarters. Ann would be so relieved to hear that.

But there was still no sign of Ranger Kiley and Stanton. Henry was worried and had requested the army send out another tank with a crew of soldiers and young Ranger Williamson to search for the two. The tank hadn't come back into base so he assumed Kiley and Stanton hadn't been found. Yet. Now the day was all but gone and the evening's shadows were drifting in. Soon it'd be night and the monsters would rule the park again.

He'd had a productive meeting with his rangers and McDowell's soldiers and had made certain important decisions. He only wished he felt better about them, but he didn't. He couldn't help but feel as if things were swirling out of control and he had no idea how to rein them in anymore. There were way too many dinosaurs, of way too many species, and all behaving badly, slithering around, attacking and devouring any living thing that moved. They were rapidly depleting the park's resources. What next?

King Kong and aliens? Better not think about that, they might materialize.

And where in God's name were his missing rangers? They should have made it back to the station long before now.

He entered his office. The lights had been lowered along with the blinds and it was a room full of elusive shadows. Apparitions–lost friends–from the last dinosaur wars played in them, tormenting him. The pools of gray and ebony transformed into silhouettes that could have been humans. Once.

He thought he heard a familiar voice whispering, *Hang in there, my friend, you'll get through this as you did the last times. Don't lose hope. You might not see me, but I'll be there by your side. I'll protect you. The gods of the land and water will protect you.* Henry could have sworn it was George Redcrow's voice. One of his rangers and his old friend dead from the first dinosaur attack years ago. George had given his life to save Ann's and Henry owed him more than he could ever say.

To his right another voice haunted him. *I wish I was there with you to fight at your side, Chief Ranger. We'd show them. Be ready for the war. It's coming. It's coming. Don't turn your back. Be prepared. You need to build a wall...a wooden wall around you if you want to survive.* This time the voice was FBI Agent Dylan Greer's. He'd recognize that gruffness anywhere. A man who'd gone down into the cold waters of

Dinosaur Lake III: Infestation

Crater Lake in the Big Rover submersible with him and Justin, had helped him defeat the first dinosaur, Godzilla, and who'd also given his life to save him and others. A truly brave man. Another friend. Dead. A long time now. And these were only two of the many who'd died fighting the dinosaurs.

You need to build a wall...now what had Greer meant by that?

Henry sighed. He missed them both. Missed them all. All the good people taken by the dinosaurs in the park. He felt as if he'd been fighting the monsters forever.

He switched on his desk light and turned to see Ann, not sleeping as he'd thought she'd be, but sitting up on the couch, her head hung in her hands.

"Ann, have you gotten any rest at all?"

"A little. I can't stop thinking of what we went through getting here. And I've been worrying about Ellie and Matthew."

"But are *you* all right?" He walked over and sat down beside her, pulling her into his arms. She was trembling, shivering, and it was hot in the office. "What is it, sweetheart?"

She lifted her head. He could see she'd been crying. Her face was streaked with tears. There were purplish circles around her eyes. "Everything."

Before he could ask her what she meant, she probed, "Any word from Ranger Stanton and Kiley? Have they gotten here yet?" For a brief second her eyes were excited, hopeful.

God, he hated to tell her, but it'd do no good to lie. "No, no sign of either of them. Not yet. I'm sorry. We have people out searching everywhere. But nothing. Don't worry, honey, we'll find them."

Ann reclined against the sofa and wiped the wetness from her face with her fingers. Henry thought she looked not only tired but unwell. She shook her head. "We never should have taken two cars from town. We should have stayed together. I knew that but never said anything. I should have."

"It isn't your fault, Ann."

She exhaled a tremulous breath. "Oh, I know." Her eyes were frozen on the dimming windows above them and she looked so sad he hugged her tighter. He couldn't stand it when she was like this. Despairing.

"But here's some good news for you. Justin and that friend of his, Steven, are on their way here right now. Captain McDowell sent out a tank to bring them in from the south entrance. They should arrive any minute."

"Oh, thank God, they're okay. Laura was so concerned. So was I. They've been gone far longer than Justin had originally planned. He was supposed to have been back five days ago. I'll have to call her and let her know as soon they get here."

"We'll do that. Though I'm sure if he has called me he's called her."

"Maybe. But as of last night when I last spoke to her, he hadn't." Then, sitting up a little straighter and brushing the hair away from her face, she asked, "Are we going home soon?"

He moved away from her and looked into her eyes. "Well, I was going to talk to you about that. I think it's best if we hole up here for a bit. Until we know how bad things are in the park. Larger, fiercer dinosaurs have begun to show themselves I've been informed from our military sources in town and they chased Justin and Steven all the way here. Let's face it, our cabin is smaller and easier to destroy than this structure. This building is brick, stone and concrete. We have all the outlying buildings, too. We're safer here. For now."

Ann saw right through his little cover up. She knew what his 'hole up here for a bit' really meant. "You mean we're going to live here?" She looked around. "What, move into headquarters, this office, and live here?"

Henry placed a kiss on the top of her head, rocked her gently in his arms. He never could fool her. "For a while, yes. In fact I'm requesting my rangers to remain here within these walls, too, when they're not out hunting dinosaurs. As we've already learned it's too dangerous for any of us to be separated. There's safety in numbers. That and we have the full protection of the National Guard's soldiers, tanks and artillery. It makes sense to set up base here. Fortify and hunker down."

"All right. I see the sense in that. But what are we going to do about beds? Other items we'll need for a long stay?"

"I can let you visit the cabin with a soldier escort and retrieve whatever necessities and comforts you think we might need for as long as this crisis lasts."

"You really think things will ever reset to normal? Will we ever beat these monsters once and for all? Will we ever get to go home?" She whispered, "I'm beginning to doubt it. They just keep on coming, proliferating and growing smarter with every new generation."

Henry didn't say anything because he was beginning to doubt things would go back to normal any time soon. No need to make her feel worse than she was already feeling.

Taking his silence as his answers, she continued to speak against his chest. "There's something I need to tell you. I've been putting it off because of the dinosaur complications and everything else you've had on your shoulders. But I guess this is as good a time as any."

He looked down at her and for a moment wanted to freeze time. Because he'd recognized that serious tone of hers and knew something else was weighing on her mind besides the mess they were in.

If he didn't hear what was wrong, then it couldn't hurt him. It couldn't change things. He didn't want to hear it.

But there was no going back. Only forward. Always forward. That was life. "Oh, now you have me worried. What is it?"

Another sigh full of deep-seated weariness. "After this dinosaur thing is over–once we have them beat, I mean, and the park and our lives are ours again," she smiled weakly, "I want to sell the newspaper and take early retirement."

That was all? Just that? He felt instant relief.

But he was stunned anyway. "But Ann, you love your job, running the newspaper, dealing with the public and mentoring your reporters. Writing. It's been your life for as long as I can recall. Why in the world would you want to sell?"

She hesitated, as if she were drawing her thoughts together, as he waited. "Remember I went through that last round of radiation and chemotherapy while I continued to work?"

He nodded.

"It wasn't easy. You know what I went through. But having cancer made me realize something. Life isn't infinite. We don't know how long we have. No one does. That's one reason.

"But mostly, I want to begin enjoying life, really enjoying it, Henry, instead of running back and forth to town to put out personnel and financial fires…just to make money. There's more to life than a job. I want to spend more time working on those stories I've wanted to write; spending time doing my crafts. Playing with Sasha. Reading. Baking. I want to give more of it to you, Laura, Phoebe and the new baby coming. Be a real grandma. Have the grandchildren come and spend the weekend with us so we can take them to the local museums and movies. Get to really know them. I want to live in the moment, sit on the deck of our cabin–when the dinosaurs are gone, of course–and, if I feel like it, just breathe in the sweetness of the day and daydream for as long as I want; bathe my face in the coolness of the breeze. Stare at the sky, trees and grass and just relish being *alive*."

"Oh Ann, what's really wrong? I know something is, so you better just tell me."

In a calm voice she announced, "I went to my doctor's last week. I had tests. Dr. Williams says the cancer has returned. She wants me to start treatment again. From the beginning. All of it, all over. I don't want to have to balance work and medical treatments again, especially since there might be surgery this time after the radiation and chemotherapy." There was a catch in her voice and Henry knew she was close to tears.

Oh no, the cancer was back. His worse fear had become real.

All he could do was hold her in his arms and murmur, "It will be all right, sweet heart. We'll face this together like last time and you will beat it. You'll see. We'll beat it."

"We will, won't we?" She wiped her eyes and gave him a weak smile. "We will!"

"And, sure, if you want to sell the newspaper and retire now, more power to you. We'll make it happen. I'm behind you one hundred percent. I always wanted my woman home barefoot in the kitchen baking me pot roasts and apple pies."

"I do that now." A bigger smile.

Dinosaur Lake III: Infestation

"I know. I was teasing. You'll never be just a barefoot housewife tied to the stove or cleaning the house."

"I don't know what we'll do for money, though. I don't expect to get much for the newspaper. Small town and all. The day of the printed page is swiftly coming to an end. People can get the news they want on the TV or the Internet in neat little packages. Condensed, abbreviated life. Simple. And I know we don't have near enough saved for retirement. You know we should–"

"Hush, hush," a gentle admonishment. "Don't bother about that now, about anything. We'll make it. We do have savings. I do still have my job and the medical insurance you're going to need. So far anyway. Besides, I expect you to write a bang-up best-selling saga about this new dinosaur plague and we'll make a bundle off of it. I'll put you on You Tube with incredible photos, first-hand accounts and live video of some of our new residents. We'll become Internet successes. With millions of downloads."

She giggled at that, knowing he was kidding her. He hated those homemade You Tube videos. "Whew. So you don't mind me retiring? Selling the newspaper?"

"Not at all. In fact, knowing what I know about your health, I would have insisted on it. Remember, we'd decided if the cancer ever returned you would stop working anyway?"

"I remember. I just never thought I'd be put

in that position. I just never thought...." And her voice died away as if she couldn't bring herself to say what she was going to say.

But Henry knew. *I just never thought the cancer would return.*

They grew quiet and sat there, embracing each other, together. And in tentative voices they began to plan for their new future. Or what they thought it would be.

Both knowing that unless they could stop the dinosaur infiltration there might not be a future for any of them. They kept their hopes and wishful thinking simple and Henry was struck by the mantle of sadness that had already settled over him. Nothing must happen to his Ann. Whatever it took, even if it bankrupted them, she would have the best care, the most compassionate attention, he could get for her or give her. Nothing was too good for her.

A short time afterwards someone rapped on the door, Ann dried her eyes, exhaled, and Henry stood up. "Come in."

It was Ranger Cutters. "Sir, Dr. Maltin and his friend have arrived. They're coming in now. I thought you'd like to know."

"Thanks Cutters."

Ann was up from the couch with a genuine smile on her lips and out the door even before Henry could pass through.

When he walked into the main room Justin and Steven were coming in the front door and Ann ran over to their son-in-law and threw her arms around him.

"I'm so relieved you're okay, Justin!" Ann's voice was so much happier than it had been in his office. "Have you called Laura? She and Phoebe have been so worried."

"I'll call them as soon as I speak with Henry. That can't wait."

Henry would have liked to hug his son-in-law as well, but couldn't bring himself to do it in front of the soldiers and his rangers. Being the boss and all. So instead he shook the scientist's hand warmly and offered both men a large grin of welcome. "Glad you made it, kiddo. We have enough people to fret over and you being here, unscathed, eases our minds a bucket load. You, too, Steven."

"Heck, you're not any happier than we are to be here. And have we got stories for you!" Steven bobbed his head and then aimed his body in the direction of the conference table which had an array of snacks set out in the middle. Sandwiches, finger-food and chips. Soda and bottled water. "Great, sustenance! Being chased by man-eating dinosaurs and almost dying–many times–does make you hungry."

"Go ahead help yourself, music man," Henry offered as he and Justin followed him to the table. Ann still had her arm around her son-in-law. Her tears were gone.

Chief Ranger," Steven confessed as he hovered over the selection and began digging in, "we did have a mess of Freddy's cheeseburgers and fries for you all, but in our hasty retreat from the rapacious primevals we abandoned them in the car. They're most likely in the monsters' stomachs now...along with the car." He grinned and started munching on a bag of potato chips, a ham sandwich in his other hand. He grabbed a warm can of soda and popped the tab.

Henry almost smiled at the way the musician was shoving down the food as if he was really starving. No wonder he and Justin were such good friends. They had so much in common, like always being famished.

He turned to his son-in-law, who'd also snatched a sandwich and a bottle of water. "Come on in my office and spill your guts. I know you want to."

"Sure, Chief Ranger." And Justin's staid expression already told him more than he'd wanted to know. This wasn't going to be good news.

The two of them, with Ann straggling after, went into Henry's office and shut the door. Henry knew better than to ask his wife not to stay. She wouldn't listen to him anyway. Besides since she'd confided in him about the cancer he craved her being as near to him as he could manage to have her. Soon enough the problems of their new life would separate them. Right now he wanted her at his side. He wanted to touch her, hold her hand.

"So, what's so delicate you can't say it in front of my men? What can't wait?"

Justin collapsed in a chair in front of the desk, Henry claimed the chair behind it, while Ann propped herself on the edge and let her legs dangle. Her eyes, now bright and alert, were on Justin's face. Waiting. He could almost see her mind tumbling over and over the possibilities of what was about to be exposed. Her reporter instinct on high alert.

Stealing looks at her he couldn't believe she was sick again. How cruel was life.

Henry's hand crept over and took hers. He had to comfort her. Now that he knew.

Justin didn't seem to notice. He was stuffing the rest of the sandwich down his throat.

There was a knock on the door and it was Ranger Cutters again. He had a cup of coffee and more sandwiches on a plate in his hands. "Sorry to disturb you, Chief, but I thought Dr. Maltin might like something warm to drink and something more to eat after what he went through. His friend outside is being taken care of as well."

"That was kind of you, Ranger Cutters. Thank you." Justin reached up and took the coffee and sandwiches from him.

"Just made a fresh pot of coffee for anyone interested." And the young ranger politely excused himself. The door shut quietly after he exited.

Henry was anxious to hear what Justin had to say. "Okay? What is it? Tell me now before I have a heart attack from the suspense. What did your little adventure in California glean you?"

"We didn't just visit one park in California, but a few, and some in Nevada." Justin appeared tired, older. Disturbed. The paleontologist began his story. He left nothing out. When he was done Henry felt the earth slipping out from beneath him. Inch by inch.

So the dinosaurs weren't just in Crater Lake Park and Klamath Falls.

By the end of Justin's story Ann had left the desk and was huddled in the corner of the sofa, her eyes closed, the back of her head against the cushions. Another person would have thought she was asleep, but Henry knew better. She was deep in worry land. Trying to solve all their problems in her head. Fix things. Typical Ann.

"Are you sure of this, Justin?" Henry had picked up a pencil and was writing something on a notepad. Things he wanted to remember.

"That there are dinosaurs hatching all over the west coast and most likely up into Canada? And more will be showing up here real soon? Pretty much."

Henry frowned. "Besides reproducing like big-toothed lemmings in the park, they're already outside of it, in Klamath Falls, and California, Nevada and possibly other states? They're all around us?"

"That's about it."

"And the close call I told you about that Ann and Zeke had in town isn't anything to take lightly, either," Henry said. "They're lucky to be alive. There was so much damage."

Here Justin grunted. "I know. Steven and I drove through Klamath Falls before we came here today and I saw the destruction with my own eyes. Buildings flattened. Utter pandemonium. The populace fleeing and the police department in disarrayed denial. But that's nothing compared to what it probably looks like now. On our flight out of town, after we picked up the doomed cheeseburgers, we were stalked by three more dinosaurs, but of a heftier breed; possibly some of the same ones which had originally smashed up the town.

"And here's the clincher for you...not only did those three behemoths hound us out past the city limits and practically up to the park's entrance, there was a herd of them corralling cars and converging on the fringe of town. They could be there now stomping it to smithereens. From what I glimpsed, there were so many of the brutes I lost count.

"Good thing Zeke and his gal pal are both out of there."

"Good thing." But Henry's attention was suddenly divided, listening to some noise outside his office walls he couldn't identify. What was it?

"So, here's where we stand," Justin was still talking, "the dinosaur problem isn't just our problem any longer. It's spreading. I've even sent messages to many of my paleontologist friends as far away as Missouri and they are sending me cryptic emails and leaving me voice messages about further unidentified creature sightings in *their* wildernesses.

"They don't know what to make of any of it. I do, though. It's only a matter of time, and short by the way I measure it, before a lot more people will be witnesses to what we already know. We have dinosaurs birthing all across the United States. They're here. To stay. And, if we—and the human race—want to survive we're going to have to learn how to fight and conquer them. We can't waste any more time, either.

"But what's also shocked me is how many of the beasts I've seen since we've returned. Hundreds. *When* did that happen?"

"It's been happening for months," Henry divulged, "feasibly even years, but we're just now seeing the tipping point. That and the creatures have been clever enough to stay in partial hiding until now...until their numbers reached a level where they're no longer afraid of us. That'd be my guess."

"And they're emerging as a new species on our planet," Justin concluded. "Staking out their territory. And their territory is America."

"Yeah, they're out to get us," Henry said. "They want to rule America."

He stared out the windows. The darkness was coming. His thoughts were spinning around like dried leaves in a storm. What were they going to do now?

That noise again and it sounded nearer. Louder. What was it?

He swung his head around to look at Justin. "I've decided it's safer if we all bunk down here at headquarters for a while. Civilians, soldiers, rangers. I had emergency cots and bedding, food and supplies, stashed in the rear buildings months ago during the last dinosaur outbreak. In case we ever needed them. We don't separate. The army, the tanks and larger weaponry are here. Protection is here. This structure is strong. We rough it until we can decide what our next move will be. Or until we know how many dinosaurs are out there."

Justin glanced at Ann, who still had her eyes closed; seemed to be sleeping. Maybe she was.

"Laura's not going to like me camping out here," he groaned. "She's been having a little trouble lately, she told me on the phone earlier today, with the pregnancy. Nothing really serious, but I have to go home and make sure she's okay. Help her if she needs it."

"Son, I can't force you to remain and if your wife needs you, you have to go." His eyes slid to his own wife. "If you have to travel I can send you with an army escort past Klamath Falls and even lend you two rangers to ride with you beyond that or until you think you're in the clear."

"I would appreciate the escort out of the park, but I think Steven will be traveling back with me so I won't need the loan of the rangers. Under the circumstances, he's canceled his next couple gigs. Most were in Klamath Falls anyway. He's not even sure the venues are still there."

He shrugged and stretched in the chair. "I'll telephone Laura and see what she thinks I should do. I've been gone over a week and that's too long at this time of her pregnancy." He took another sandwich from the plate and bit into it.

Henry was familiar with that look on his son-in-law's face. He was thinking deep thoughts, trying to decide what to do.

That's when the mysterious noises outside exploded in volume and became undeniably recognizable. It was the howling of dinosaurs, two, then more, dozens...coming nearer. Growing louder until it filled the world.

"Ah, now what?" Henry jumped up and grabbed his MP7 from the gun rack.

"The natives are restless, it sounds like." Justin snorted, shaking his head as he came to his feet as well.

"They're not natives of this land or time."

"Then they're just restless."

"I'll say. That seems to be their natural state."

"I guess I'll be staying here with all of you then until we see what this means," Justin said. "Laura will just have to understand."

"There's no way you and Steven can leave now. Maybe tomorrow."

"Maybe."

There was shouting beyond the door and the stomping of booted feet. The reverberations of rangers and soldiers preparing for battle.

Henry and Justin departed the office at the same time. Ann was asleep on the couch, but Henry knew if the god-awful racket continued she wouldn't be for long.

He nearly collided with Ranger Gillian.

"Chief, there's an angry congregation of those beasties gathering outside our perimeters and as you can hear, they're getting worked up something fierce over something."

Yeah, they want supper. Us.

Standing next to Gillian, Ranger Cutters tossed in, "The soldiers have pulled the tanks in closer around the building and have brought out the cannons. They're waiting for further orders from their Commanding Officer. McDowell."

"Where is she?" Henry asked.

"Outside with the troops."

Henry brushed past his rangers and, with Justin sticking close, he walked through the front door and outside.

The day was dim as evening with its gloom settled in. It was that time, twilight, where you could still see everything...but as if through a gray filter. Everything blurry. It was cooling down, a breeze fanning his face. Sweat still broke out on his skin, though. He saw McDowell talking to one of her soldiers, a private, and walked over to them.

"What's going on?" Henry's eyes swept the nearby area. No dinosaurs in sight. Yet. But now outside somewhere in the shadowed woods he heard even more so the hubbub the creatures were making. Cries and shrieking communications bouncing back and forth between their enemy and all of it getting closer. The creatures were hiding in plain sight somewhere. Waiting for...what? Riled up about...what?

"Nothing but commotion so far," McDowell answered. "But something's happening to our scaly friends out there and they're scheming between each other, preparing, but for what I don't know. I'm leaning on the side of caution and having my men tighten ranks around the building; keeping their eyes open for an advance force of intruders. We'll fight them if we have to."

Henry peered up at the sky. "It'll be dark soon. If they wait to attack until it is full night, it'll be difficult to repel them."

"Don't I know it, Chief Ranger. Let's hope they're only sounding off, chattering, albeit loudly, among the trees. But it doesn't come across like that to me. Sounds like war drums."

As if to punctuation what McDowell had just said, a piercing series of dinosaur howls ripped through the air above them, followed by a hellish chorus of echoing replies coming from all across the park.

"How *many* are out there, you think?" Justin was listening intently. "Sounds like hundreds."

"Heaven help us," Steven, who'd slipped out to join them, whispered.

Henry's stare included the people around him. Some of them were frightened. Their faces, their twitchy movements, showed it. Even McDowell appeared edgy. The dinosaur's trumpeting could do that to a person. In the gloom of the dense forest around them the cries seemed unearthly. The danger surreal. But it wasn't. Oh, it wasn't.

"What do you suppose they're up to?" Steven wanted to know. "Why are they making so much noise?"

"They're communicating," Justin supplied thoughtfully during a lull in the cacophony. "And whatever they're squawking about we'll learn of here before long."

The soldiers hurried to take positions, weapons clutched in their hands. The tanks were in place, circled around the building, their turrets unmoving and pointed towards the sounds. The machine guns silent. Waiting. Like the people.

The world fell quiet.

Minutes went by. Henry held his breath. Everyone around him held theirs. The last of the light pulsed out. The dark had come.

"What, is that all? They serenade us until our heads hurt and then just stop?" Steven griped. "Some sort of psychological torture? They smart enough to do that?"

Justin said, "Smart enough and more–."

"*Ssssh!*" Henry's hands rose and dropped in a curt gesture. "Listen. Something's coming."

And it was true. Something–an army of somethings–was advancing on ranger headquarters. A stampede of invisible enemies in the dark. Branches were snapping. Trees were breaking. The ground was shaking. The dinosaurs began to cry out again. Closer now.

We're sitting ducks out here, Henry thought. Nothing between us and an attacking force except a couple of outbuildings and the walls of headquarters. Something has to be done about that and soon.

A rock hit him hard in the cheek under his

left eye. *"Ouch! Damn! What the–"* His hand went up and touched a trickle of blood. Then another larger rock or clump of dirt hit his right shoulder, spun him around, and nearly knocked him to his knees.

And around him there was a rain of stones, sticks and compressed dirt clods. Dinosaur bombs.

Steven and Justin both yelled, raising their arms as protection against the natural missiles.

The crazy dinosaurs were throwing things at them! Henry thought, shocked. Again. What was it with these smaller dinos that they barraged them with pieces of earth?

Wow, he'd have to be sure to warn the men not to leave any rifles laying around. What would happen if the red dinosaurs could use them, too? He could almost imagine little dinosaur claws grasped around the gun stocks and pulling on the triggers. *Bang. Bang. Bang.* Beady dinosaur eyes squinting and lining up the shots. *Got another human! Dead center. Yeah!* Yikes.

For a time, with his rangers fighting beside him, Henry lifted his MP7 and shot at as many attacking beasts as he could. Killed some. But the creatures were fast and it was hard to hit them in the dark, especially the small ones as they infiltrated the grounds, some getting as close as the sidewalks in front of the building or sneaking around the corners.

While the tanks' cannons were doing much more damage against the dinosaurs. The soldiers snuggled inside the metal vehicles were protected far better than Henry and his men. And the soldiers fighting outside the tanks had body armor and helmets on. His men didn't.

So after two of his rangers were clawed and bitten, and one knocked unconscious by a huge rock, he lifted his arm and shouted, "Rangers, get in the building! Now!" Henry turned and ran through the door. His men with him, except for McDowell, who joined her soldiers behind the tanks.

Once inside the bombardment grew worse. Rocks and pieces of trees were hurled at the outside stone walls. Boulders. The sound of the hits ricocheted through the building. It was like being in a bomb shelter as the bombs fell.

Outside the gun and cannon fire became a groundswell. The soldiers were shooting furiously at something. The tanks' big guns thundered into the darkness. The ground jumped.

Beyond the window Henry saw what he hadn't wanted to see. There were dinosaurs, of all sizes and species, charging from every direction. Lobbing earth shrapnel at the building, the machines, and the humans stationed or fighting around them.

The tanks' cannons and machine guns were firing into the scaly melee but it was hard to tell if it was doing any good. There were so many of the creatures jumping, hopping and bouncing about; some throwing themselves at the outside walls of headquarters itself. Dinosaur projectiles. *Splat, splat, splat!*

He'd seen so much since the dinosaur epic had begun–Godzillas, swimming leviathans, flying gargoyles and herds of raptor-like rock-tossing creatures...but this beat all. A synchronized and organized direct assault from a dinosaur army. Who or what, Henry speculated, was giving the orders? Hmmm.

Henry told the rangers inside to guard the entrances, the windows and the doors in case any of the dinosaurs found a way in. "Have your weapons, your rifles ready. And let's further secure the windows by nailing iron bars across them." He was glad he'd ordered the iron grills, though he hadn't had them installed yet, for the windows when the structure had been rebuilt. Just in case. Good thing he had. "The bars are in the rear storage room. The glass in our windows are triple-paned, extra strength but they won't hold up if a large enough dinosaur tries to smash through one of them."

As Henry uttered the words a dinosaur visage, hissing, jaws wide open, teeth gleaming, filled a window near him. It wasn't one of the largest monsters, thank goodness, but it was large enough. It stood so tall it had to stoop to stare in at him. Glaring in hungrily, it snarled and scraped massive claws along the glass, then beat them violently against it. The window cracked but didn't break. Even in the dark it was an ugly sucker. Oversized head, tiny eyes. Big sharp fangs.

It'd be the first window to be covered.

He felt like a fish in a bowl. Big hungry

monster eying him. Licking its lips, uh, incisors. Wanting to devour him. Dinosaurs! They were all alike. No arguing with any one of them, all they wanted to do was maim you or have a piece of you for supper.

He wanted so badly to lift his MP7 and blow its hideous head off. But couldn't. The creature hadn't broken through the window and there was no way he was going to make it easy for it. Instead he slunk up against the wall, so the thing could no longer see him, and dropped the blinds down. He could hear it screeching, banging atced glass but after a minute or so it stopped. Moving on, he suspected, to another square of glass where it could see its potential meal.

The other rangers, taking his lead, started taking down the blinds and curtains and hammering up the iron grills across the windows. For a while the pounding sound of hammers accompanied the bedlam of the attacking force.

"Henry, what's going on?" Ann was standing behind him when he turned. Her hair mussed up from her nap. Her pale face lined with anxiety and her hands fidgeting at her side. She did that when she was upset or frightened. "Henry?"

He told her. Then he gently placed his hand on her shoulder and guided her back to his office. It was safer there. More walls between her and the monsters trying to break in.

"So we're under siege, huh?"

"I'm afraid so."

"Tenacious bastards aren't they?" She settled down on the couch. Her eyes on the windows as

Henry closed the curtains over the dark glass. It was only a matter of time before the beasts found their way to the rear of the building and began their onslaught there as well. The good thing about that section of the structure was it was fortified by towering trees lined up behind it. A natural fence.

But Henry knew sooner or later the dinosaurs would find a way to slither in between the trees there as well.

"Very."

Another round of gunfire came and went. Henry hoped they were killing a bunch of the creatures. Only good dinosaur was a dead one.

Ann was staring at the curtained window. "Who's winning?"

"So far? We are. We have soldiers, tanks and cannons." He grinned and sat down beside her, put his arm around her. He couldn't leave his men alone too long, there were things he had to do, a war going on, but he could spare a minute for his scared wife. His scared sick wife.

"Have you heard or seen anything of Ellie or Ranger Kiley yet?" That frown of hers had returned.

"No, honey. I'm sorry. No sign of them yet. And," he added, "it'd be really difficult for them to slide into home now, what with the war going on outside."

"No phone call, nothing?"

He shook his head. "But I'm sure they're probably holed up somewhere like we are; waiting for the coast to be clear. Kiley and

Stanton can take care of themselves. I know they're okay. We will see them again. You'll see."

Her lack-luster reaction let him know she didn't believe what he said. Her face swung away from him and the air seemed to go out of her.

The shrieking of the dinosaurs rose to a feverish pitch and subsided as weapon fire matched its volume. The cannons, MP7's, M4 Carbines, AK-47's and rifles boomed into the night. The dinosaurs boomed back. Bigger rocks. More aggressive claw-to-hand raids.

"I'm scared," Ann mouthed against Henry's chest after he'd drawn her to him. "Are we going to get through this alive this time, or is this the end?"

"We will get through it. I have no doubt whatsoever. We are smarter than those ugly bastards outside, and we're safe behind these strong walls." And well they should be. Years ago when the first dinosaur destroyed headquarters, even though no one would have ever thought they'd have to face another prehistoric rampage again, Henry had made sure the new building had been as monster proof as he could arrange. He'd insisted on double or triple strength everything. He had made sure the foundation was fortified with concrete, steel and rock. Because deep in his mind he'd reasoned: *If the dinosaurs ever return they won't get in here. They won't demolish this headquarters like they did the last one.*

Thank goodness for his foresight.

"Can I still go home and get the things we'll need if we have to stay here for a while?" Ann looked at him, waiting for an answer. "If I have to make this office our home?" She looked around the sparse room, a flicker of distaste in her eyes.

"Ann, I don't know. If we can fend off this attack, kill enough of them, I'll ask McDowell if we can go for a ride tomorrow in the daylight to fetch what we need in one of the tanks. We'll just have to see."

She nodded, accepting what he said without argument. Which was unlike Ann. But then the unusual and perilous situation warranted no debate. Ann was an intelligent woman. It was what it was and she knew that. Their safety came first.

Henry rose. "I have to get out there with my men."

"I know. Go on." She got up, too. "I'm coming. I want to be in the thick of the action."

"Taking notes, huh, so you can write about this when it's over?"

"You might say that." She started to smile but the sound of the guns cut it off.

A humongous thump reverberated across the room followed by an ear-shattering roar.

"That must have been a big rock," she said. "Man, they're resourceful, aren't they?"

"Next thing we know," Henry bellyached, "they'll be digging tunnels under the ground to get to us."

"Ech, don't say that. Don't even think it." Ann visibly shuddered. "And not out loud." Her finger pointed towards the window. "They might hear you." She flashed him a mischievous smirk.

Henry walked across to the gun rack and handed her a Bushmaster semi-automatic. "In case."

"In case," she repeated and cradled the rifle in her arms as if she'd been born with it there. As always, it occurred to him, looking at the fragile, slender woman with the short blond gray-streaked hair and the soft gray eyes that seemed to see everything, she was nothing if not a courageous woman. A brave woman, his wife.

And for that he had to give her credit.

*****

The battle against the horde dinosaurs lasted most of the night, on and off. Just when Henry and his men believed it was over, more of the animals would arrive and the massacre would continue. All on the dinosaur side. The soldiers and his rangers killed so many of them when Henry looked out the windows in the dawn's eerie light all he could see was a blanket of lumpy red or brownish dead things. Surely, they had depleted the population enough to have made the park safer? Surely?

"Ranger Gillian and Cutters come with me," Henry said when full daylight arrived and it sounded like the clash, at least for now, was over. "We're going out among the carnage to see what we have.

"Justin, you should come, too. I'll need your expertise to take stock, perhaps explain, what we find. Grab your MP7. I can't promise all of the monsters are dead. In fact, I don't believe they are all dead. So best to be prepared."

"I'm right behind you, Chief. And I have my weapon."

The men walked out into the new morning. It was going to be another hot day, the waves of heat were already dancing low to the ground. The humidity inching up. There were soldiers everywhere checking the fallen to see if any were still alive. Captain McDowell was nowhere to be seen, but Henry assumed she was out there somewhere among her men directing the cleanup.

"Geez, look at all of these dead carnivores," Ranger Gillian huffed. "There must be hundreds of carcasses out here. A lumpy carpet of dead dinosaurs."

"But we won the battle." Ranger Cutters had knelt down and was examining one of the smaller creatures. Like one of the breed Henry had saved his cat from and like those mob demons that had attacked Ann in the park the week before.

"But not the war." Justin was working his way through the corpses with Henry beside him. "Look at this one. It's the same species as the ones from town that chased us all the way into the park. This one is a young fellow, though. Not nearly as mature or as huge as those that followed us from Klamath Falls. I'd guess this one is, oh, only about fifteen feet tall. The others were closer to thirty, if I had to guess."

Henry examined the body. Part of the head was blown off. He had to be careful where he planted his boots. There was dinosaur blood, bones and slabs of flesh everywhere.

"And this one. Strange looking thing." Justin had moved on to another dead creature and knelt down next to it. Not too close. Henry had never seen one like it. It was an enormous specimen with scaly crocodile-textured crimson skin. Small spikes along its spine and head, heavy ridges over its eyes and a head that also resembled a croc's. Long of snout and rows and rows of fang-like teeth.

"Oh my God," Justin was muttering, "this is another genus we've never seen before. Look at its body." He pointed a finger along it. "Thicker through the torso but the legs are heavier. I'd guess it was also related, perhaps distantly, to the *carcharodontosaurs*."

"Which were gigantic Cretaceous meat-eaters, right?" Henry stared down at the thing.

"Ah, you remember. Yes. Cretaceous meat-eaters."

"And this one," Justin came to his feet and looked over his shoulder at another dead creature, "looks like a mutated version of that apex predator Tyrannosaur Rex we all know and hate. Except it's different in some ways. It's got a more compact body. Shorter tail. Spots."

"Great, now we have mutated Tyrannosaur Rexes and crocodile dinosaurs sprinkled in among all the other nutty varieties. What's next? Wolf or moose dinos?"

"The number of Tyrannosaurs represented here are bad for us. Tyrannosaurs had larger brains than most of their contemporaries. A lot larger. Could be these are some of the ring leaders in the uprising."

"Then pray we killed them all."

Justin cocked his head to the side. "And did you get a load of that pile over there? They look more akin to the earliest *velociraptors*. They appear to be the same sort, of different sizes and colors, but with variable distinctions which leads me to believe they're still mutating. Basically smaller of bodies than the others here, front legs ending in claws tucked up close to their chests–and covered in feathers. Feathers! Heck, there's even undeveloped feathered wings behind those front legs. Astonishing.

"Crater lake has, as you said earlier, transformed into a real Jurassic Park and the big question is how? And why so many species? And how and why are they so…smart? Why are they behaving so aggressively?"

"Now that last question is what I'm wondering about. That and how many of the things have hatched and are still out there waiting to ambush us." Henry looked out over the battlefield. Nothing moved. But remembering the time one had pretended to be dead, but hadn't been, he was being cautious. His weapon was at his side as he made his way through the remains.

It was going to be a hell of a cleanup. But they couldn't let the corpses lie out in the hot sun too long or the smell would soon be overpowering and it'd draw other wildlife to the smorgasbord. That's all they needed, bears, cougars and vultures coming in for the buffet. *If* there were any of the natural animals left in the park. The dinosaurs had been eating something. Could be there were none of the native inhabitants left. It was a sobering and sad thought.

He shaded his eyes with his hand and searched the area. The soldiers and their weapons had done their jobs. Nothing but dead dinosaurs to be seen and not a sign of live ones anywhere. Not the sounds of any, either. "You think we killed all of them?"

Justin's laugh was caustic. "I wouldn't bet on it. The rest of them are probably off somewhere, hiding, licking their wounds and plotting the next assault. Just a gut feeling."

"You know what I don't get?" Henry was once more staring out into the distance, the sun strong on his face which only served to highlight the exhaustion on it. He wiped sweat from his forehead and peered down at a creature that reminded him of the gargoyles which had once afflicted the park. This one had wings, too, but more like a bat's. All leathery.

"What?" Justin was inspecting an expired dinosaur beneath a tree. Its hide was riddled with bullet holes. It had a lengthy neck and tiny razor teeth. No tail. Had a funny shaped head, elongated with a bump on top. Ugly as hell. It stunk, too, like spoiled eggs. Ha, a skunk dinosaur.

"How are these different species getting along with each other well enough to fight as one host? Shouldn't they be squabbling, killing and eating each other...instead of us? How are they doing this?"

Justin had been kneeling, but came to his feet. "Now that's a true mystery. From what scientists believe, most dinosaurs didn't get along with other species, especially the herbivores and carnivores. The meat-eaters ate the plant-eaters. The meat-eaters ate the meat-eaters."

"See any plant-eaters here?" Henry shoved a smaller dinosaur's tail aside with his boot so he could get past its owner.

"No. Just flesh-eaters. And most of them the apex predators of their times. Also, I can't be a hundred percent sure but I think most of these beasts aren't even from the same time periods. Or, at least, the creatures I recognize, which aren't many. Another bizarre incongruity."

"You're telling me." Henry took off his cap, scratched the side of his face, and replaced the cap on his head. The heat was roiling in and sweat trickled down his back under his shirt. He wasn't used to this kind of heat in the park. It was never this hot. A sudden thought occurred to him: *Perhaps the magma deep beneath the park was stirring again; heating up, moving and baking the land above it?* There was a river of molten lava turning the park into an oven. Wiping more sweat from his brow, he prayed it wasn't true. He hated living in an oven.

He pivoted around, he'd seen enough dead dinosaurs, and led his team back to headquarters. The soldiers had begun clearing away the carcasses, hauling and dragging them by hand, truck or tank to an area, a deep pit further away, where they could decay and not stink up the compound. He assigned some of his rangers to help. They were all in this together now. Soldiers and rangers. Even representatives–not many, the first signs of dinosaur trouble and most of them had scurried back to their home bases–that the Park and Forest Services had sent out to monitor the problem, see what was going on, had to help.

Inside again, he called Captain McDowell on her cell, and requested a meeting. When the proper players were in place around the conference table he told them what he thought they should do now. He'd remembered what a ghost memory had told him.

"We should fortify this place better. I say we build a fence all around headquarters. A big fence. Any other suggestions or thoughts?" he politely asked of the men and women, mostly in uniform, around him. Ann had snuck in and was sitting beside him. Under the table she took his hand for a moment and squeezed. At least now she looked more rested, less in shock. But she still acted exhausted.

Captain McDowell spoke up. "I agree. We

build a stockade around headquarters and include the outlying storage buildings and sheds. There's enough wood and though I know it's radical taking the park's trees for such a use, it is necessary if we're going to remain safe and fight the enemy from a secure location. This is it. The dinosaurs could attack us again at nightfall and this time we might not be so fortunate–they could get into the building or destroy it. We can't let them. So a strong barrier is necessary as a first defense."

"Except with those big suckers," Steven grumbled, "like the ones that chased us yesterday coming here. Some of them were thirty feet tall. How's a stockade fence going to help keep those creeps out? They'll just knock it down."

"We make it as strong and as tall as we can," McDowell said. "Further strengthen it by propping poles along the inside deep into the ground."

It'd been dark pretty soon after the attack of the night before had begun, but Henry had seen a couple of those big boys outside. Not many, but some. "The biggest dinosaurs? They make good targets because of their size. We just make sure we shoot them before they can do the damage."

"We'll target the larger ones first then," McDowell concurred.

They briefly discussed other things and afterwards Henry broke the meeting up. They all had work to do. The day would go by swiftly and they had to be better prepared for the next assault than they'd been the night before.

One of the search teams looking for Stanton and Kiley he'd sent out the day before had returned and Henry needed to talk to them. Ranger Collins, who he'd put in charge, had strode into the meeting half-way through, standing against the wall until it was over, and by the solemn look on his face Henry knew it wasn't good.

"You have news?" Henry asked the ranger after the meeting ended.

"I do." Collins waited for Henry to disperse the gathering. The man had been a ranger his whole career, but in different parks. He'd worked for Henry for nine years and hoped to retire from Crater Lake's park service. In his mid-fifties, he had three grown children and a wife who'd never worked. Henry trusted him implicitly because he dealt with difficulties straight on and never evaded his responsibilities. He also played a mean hand of poker.

He ushered Ranger Collins into his office. Ann wouldn't be deterred and followed.

"Okay," Henry sighed after they'd sat down, "what do you have?"

"We found Stanton and Kiley. Both of them." And by the way he said it Henry knew it was the worst news. Ranger Collins stole a glance at Ann and spoke, "I'm sorry, Ranger Stanton and Kiley are dead. There's a rental cabin about four miles away that's been totally destroyed. Looks like dinosaurs, big ones, found them, where they must have taken shelter, and attacked. Flattened it like a table top. The bodies were found inside it."

"Ranger Stanton and Kiley are dead?" Henry repeated, letting it soak in though he didn't want to believe it. It seemed impossible. Not after all both rangers had been through.

Ann had lowered her head into her hands to cover her grief. She rarely cried, but he could hear her muffled sobs. He got up and put his arms around her. He of all people knew how hard it was to lose a dear friend. Now they'd both lost another two.

"I'm afraid they are. Most likely it was quick, though. Their deaths." Collins continued, "And they went together. We found them in each other's arms."

Henry bowed his head and shoved the sorrow away. He had too many lives depending on him to lose it now. He'd have to call Ellie Stanton's sons and give them the bad news. It'd be awful and he dreaded it. But he'd do it. There was no one to call about Ranger Kiley's death. His wife and daughter had passed away long ago. The deaths had devastated Kiley, each in their own way, but meeting and falling in love with Stanton had saved him. Or so he had always maintained. Lord, but he'd miss them. Ranger Kiley had worked with him and been his friend for over thirteen years and at his side during and through all the dinosaur escapades. Stanton hadn't only been a great ranger but a beautiful human being who'd loved life so much. Both of them had.

"We brought the bodies back for burial," the

ranger said. "They're in the blue storage shed."

"I don't know what we will do about the funerals. No telling how long this crisis will last so I don't know when we'd be able to get them to town, much less have funerals. If the town's still there, that is. Under these circumstances we might have to bury them here in the park. I'll ask permission of Stanton's sons, though, before we do it." He was sure they'd approve of it if there was no other way.

Ann was taking the deaths hard. Still crying, her head bowed, she didn't ask Ranger Collins any questions. She didn't look up.

It was only when Collins left them that she opened her eyes and spoke. "Ellie's cat is all alone at her house. We can't leave her there. Miss Kitty Cat will starve."

Henry sat down by his wife. "When I send someone to get the things you want from the cabin, I'll have them pick the cat up, too, and bring her here, along with ours. Hope they get along." He smiled tenderly, taking her hand. There was no way he was going to let his wife out among the dinosaurs after Stanton and Kiley's death. They'd been trained rangers with weapons and hadn't made it.

"When you send someone to our cabin? Aren't we going?"

"After last night, I don't think it's wise for you to be out in the park, even with a guarded escort. I don't think the war's over. I fear it's only beginning and so does Justin."

"But there's so many items we're going to

need if we have to stay here for any extended amount of time. I need to be the one to collect them," she protested. "Won't being in the belly of a tank be safe enough?"

"Not in my mind. There's some large Godzillas out there and even a tank might not be invincible enough to fend them off."

Ann's stare was petulant. "I'm not afraid of no dinosaur," she sing-songed and then let a small smile escape. She wasn't actually angry; she understood.

"I know, sweetheart. But I am. I think it's going to get worse. Here. Everywhere. At least here you're protected. Better safe than sorry. So...make a list. A detailed one. I'll send Ranger Gillian along with the soldiers to gather what we'll need. He knows our house well and he's good with cats. He and his escort will also go by Ellie's place and collect Miss Kitty Cat."

She merely nodded her head. "All right. I do see your point about the danger out there." Her gaze wandered to the now barred-up window. Outside the cutting, sawing and hammering noises filled the day. The stockade fence was going up. "I don't suppose the army will finish the enclosure anytime soon?"

"McDowell estimates it might take a few days."

"Do we have a few days?"

"Probably not. But you have to start something to finish it. In the meantime, McDowell also has her men planting sharpened wooden stakes around the perimeter of the compound. Optimistically they'll give us some defense until the barricade's completed."

"If any of that will help us." She looked directly at him. "So you expect another onslaught tonight?"

"Justin and McDowell do. So do I."

She seemed to remember something. "Have you heard anything about Klamath Falls? Was it overrun by those monsters Justin and Steven escaped from?"

"I don't know. There's been no communications between us and the town now since yesterday. I can't get Chief Chapman on the phone. No one's answering their switchboard, either. So I have no idea what's going on there." It occurred to him in that moment the hospital Ann was supposed to be having her next treatments at was in town. The doctor that was taking care of her was in town. Now how would his wife get the medical care she needed? Just another glitch to nag at him. Dinosaurs were to blame...again.

"Thank goodness Zeke and Wilma are safe in Idaho with her friend. Heaven knows what's happening in town. If it's as bad as it is here...." She was watching the windows. The grinding of chain saws, construction, and men shouting was so loud it was hard to hear each other over it.

"Let's hope it's not as bad. That the National Guard is there taking care of things. Defending the townsfolk."

Ann said nothing.

Ranger Gillian came into the office and

Henry gave instructions on what he needed him to retrieve from their cabin. Collecting Ellie's cat and theirs. Ann made her list.

And Ranger Gillian left.

A short while later, outside, amid the construction noise, they could hear a tank moving out. The engine a loud growl.

"Give me something to do, Henry. I'll go crazy sitting here twiddling my thumbs."

"All right. You can help my rangers in any way you can. Just don't overextend yourself, you hear?"

She flashed him a look he knew all too well. "I know, I know," she carped. "Take it easy. Don't forget I'm sick. How can I?"

The cries of a dinosaur shattered the morning and both sprinted for the door and whatever awaited them beyond it. More chaos probably.

The dinosaurs apparently weren't waiting for sundown to attack again. So much for that theory.

Chapter 12
Henry

The skirmish was a brief one. Dinosaurs shrieked, lobbed lumps of stones and sticks and themselves against the outside of the building, desperate to get to the humans. Soldiers shot them dead. After a bloodbath, what was left of their numbers retreated into the forest and harassed the humans from a distance, unseen but constantly heard. It was as if a boisterous zoo had moved into the park and it wasn't far away.

When the remainder of the dinosaurs escaped into the forest the work on the stockade recommenced, but this time with more fervor among the men, soldiers and rangers building it. Everyone who could saw wood, swing a hammer or hold up a post was outside doing it. Even Ann helped as much as she could, fetching things for the builders or bringing them water. Henry kept an eye on her to be sure she didn't overdo it, which she did anyway and by mid-afternoon he had to shoo her inside.

Night was approaching and everyone feared what it would bring. The previous assault had been a modest one, but by the sound of it there were *so many more* of the denizens riling themselves up in the zoo. Waiting to begin the next wave. Perhaps awaiting the night.

Henry was in the scorching sunshine with his rangers, supervising and doing the work when McDowell stepped up to him. A train of dark-rimmed clouds glided across the sun and shadows enveloped everything but it didn't help dampen the heat. It was miserable for everyone working so strenuously out in it. But the stockade was coming along nicely if a little too slow for his liking. It was half done. He wanted it completed, up, shielding his wife and his people sooner than later. So he was working like a demon alongside his men to get the job done. The heat sucked the energy out of his body and the T-shirt he wore was soaked in perspiration. He was worn out, but if his men could continue frantically working hour after hour in the searing sun, so could he.

"We should take the initiative, now, and send tank crews out to track the dinosaurs down and exterminate any they come across. Thin the herd some," Captain McDowell recommended. "That's how you win a war. Go on the offensive, not wait around for them to thin *our* herd. The tanks will guarantee my soldiers' safety."

She didn't need his permission, but was in his jurisdiction, his park, and she respected that reality. That and she counted him as a friend and had since the fight they'd shared in the helicopter against the gargoyle dinosaurs.

"That's an excellent idea, Captain. I and my men will be doing the same thing as soon as headquarters is more secure. I'm planning for it now."

"I can also tell you the army is sending me more soldiers, more weapons. They'll be here within a hour."

That caught Henry's attention and he stopped working to face her. "Why? I thought you said your superiors weren't bulking up your presence here? That what men and hardware you brought were all they could spare?"

She hesitated then confessed, "There's been a new...development. I shouldn't be telling you this but you'll learn about it soon enough–if you don't already know." She smiled that soldier's smile of hers. Enigmatic. Concealing secrets she had to conceal.

"I won't tell anyone I heard it from you. What is it?"

Still wavering, her grave eyes were on him. "Klamath Falls has been overrun with the same monsters we're fighting here. The large ones. A nest of them. An army of them. The military moved into the town late last night and the fighting has been brutal. There's been many casualties because the soldiers were ambushed coming into town; before they were ready."

"I'm sorry." And Henry was, but he could sense there was something else she wasn't disclosing. "And?"

She shifted from one foot to another, her stance the usual military one she preferred, standing straight, hands hovering near the gun belt around her waist.

"Klamath Falls isn't the only location being affected. Dinosaurs have been sighted in other nearby towns. Ashland. Medford. Phoenix. All of them have reported strange, aggressive prehistoric-like creatures infiltrating their borders, destroying property and attacking their citizens.

"The government is trying to keep this quiet but it's only a matter of time before the information is out. Only a matter of time before it's splattered across the evening news and Internet. Too many people have cameras in their cell phones. Have blogs. Facebook. They tweet. So far the powers that be have the hysteria contained, but not for long. There's been a lot of human disappearances and deaths."

So Justin had been right. The infection was spreading. But this, this was too much. Rampaging dinosaurs in Ashland, Medford and Phoenix. So close? And how many more townships and villages by tomorrow or next week? Next month? Next year? Good God.

Henry felt very old and very tired. He'd been preparing himself for this reality for months, years really, but now that it was here, he felt lost. Unready. Lacking. The world was swiftly evolving into something he didn't recognize and wasn't prepared for. Was this, then, to be their future…combating monster-like anachronisms from another age on an everyday basis? How terrified the people in the targeted towns must be. Poor humans.

"What's being done about this?"

"Orders have been given. Troops have been dispatched. Experts have been called in to brainstorm about what's to be done. How best to defeat the creatures. There's just so many of them in so many places. I've been notified the army has advanced into all three towns and are dealing with the influx.

"The war has begun."

"Yes," he agreed, "it surely has."

Henry's eyes traveled over the men laboring on the barricade. Rangers and soldiers. Cutting trees and swinging hammers. Worried faces. Courageous men. Sweating out in the sun and trying to beat the clock. Was this what the rest of their lives were to be...building defenses and battling dinosaurs? The previous six years had just been a long slow warm-up? Justin believed it had been.

Early that morning before the latest clash with their enemy his son-in-law had sat across from him at the conference table as they were gulping down their cold breakfast. "It's getting away from us, Henry. Now we need to step up our game. Find a way to get more people into the fight. It's no longer a Crater Lake problem. It's America's. We need more help."

"I guess we didn't get rid of every last one of those dinosaur eggs in the gargoyles' nest last spring," Henry had retorted.

"Or we didn't destroy all Godzilla's eggs years ago in that cave."

"Hmmm, that, too. We missed a whole mess of them somewhere. Somehow."

"Well, our bad and now we're going to pay for it." Justin had been busy scribbling entries in his notebook. Keeping track of everything as he always did. Always the scientist.

"How's Laura doing?" Henry had finished

his instant coffee, because they were getting low on the real stuff and saving it for suppertimes, and had stood up to go join his men building the fence. What with the attacks, Justin hadn't been able to go home as he'd wanted and the way things were he wouldn't be able to for a while longer. Or at least until they had the dinosaur population leaned down. Even a tank could be stopped if it was land locked by the great numbers of dinosaurs they'd been dealing with.

Justin missed his wife and child. Understandable. But Henry was relieved his daughter and granddaughter where somewhere safer than where they were. They were miles and miles away from Crater Lake, Klamath Falls, Medford and Ashland. He prayed they'd stay safe as well and the dinosaur pestilence hadn't reached as far away as they were.

"I just talked to her on the phone. She's fine. Phoebe's fine. The unborn baby's fine. The little medical problem she was having seems to have resolved itself, thank goodness. But she misses me. It's been over a week since we've seen each other."

Henry had patted his son-in-law on the back. "You'll see them soon. Have faith."

"I do. I'm just glad they're not anywhere around here. But I sure miss them."

"I know, I know." And Henry had felt sorry for him. Ann had been in the next room but Justin was apart from the people he loved the most. With a new baby coming it couldn't be easy for his wife or for him.

Dinosaur Lake III: Infestation

The two men headed outside to continue building the fence.

*****

Henry worked through the whole day and when he checked in on Ann in the evening, she was up and about again busy helping get food out on the tables for the men. Nothing could make her sit still when so much needed to be done. That was his Ann.

"How you feeling, honey?"

"Not bad under the circumstances. A little weary. I miss our home and all the comforts of it. I miss my cat."

"So do I. To all of that."

"After the festivities last night," she said sarcastically, "I hope it's still there."

"As I do. We'll find out soon enough when Ranger Gillian returns from his errands. Should be any time now. The tank and its crew left early this morning. McDowell mentioned her men were going to do some scouting before they returned here. Going to see what's out there."

"Going to check out the zoo you mean?"

Henry had told Ann about the noises beyond the compound.

"Yep, the zoo. They're gonna sneak up on where they think it is and see what we're up against. How many of the creatures are nesting out there and exactly where. Come back with the info."

"That should be interesting." Ann gifted him

with one of her lop-sided grins. "I hope Gillian brings the cats and all the stuff I had on the list back with him. I'm having him bring out our air mattresses, the good ones? Along with our bed clothes. I'm going to put them in your office so we'll have a cozy place to sleep."

"You're turning my office into our very own little sleeping refuge, huh? Our boudoir. Complete with plush accessories and tiny furry companions?"

"Or as close as I can get it to be a cozy sanctuary. I'm also going to manage the newspaper from here. Vanessa and Jacob are going to help. I've already telephoned both of them and told them what was going on. I don't think Jacob believed me...about the dinosaur invasion and all. He hasn't seen any yet. He lives on the other side of town more out in the country. But Vanessa, apparently, who lives in town, was in the middle of that last dinosaur intrusion and saw them. She believes. Though she told me she might be leaving her rental house and going to a friend's place further out if things get any worse. So I'll work from your office for now. Since all I need is my laptop and the Internet."

"Good. We could be here for a while." He didn't tell her that *sure, Jacob and Vanessa might help you run the newspaper...if the newspaper is still even there...if Jacob and Vanessa can stay unharmed and alive. And keep working.* Since McDowell told him what she'd told him, he wasn't sure any part of Klamath

Falls would be safe for very much longer or any of the surrounding townships. Though he couldn't bring himself to say any of that to Ann. Not now. Not yet. He'd have to find a good time to tell her. Later.

"I know we could be here a while. It's all right, as long as we are together. I'll make do." Ann started to leave the room and Henry stopped her, snagging her arm.

"I wanted to let you know I'm joining the tank expedition tomorrow–if they locate where the zoo is today. The stockade is coming along, it's almost completed, and McDowell asked me if I'd like to go on the first dinosaur hunt."

Ann's eyes clouded. "Do you have to go?"

"Ann–"

"I know, I know." She shook her head and gave him an apologetic look and patted his arm comfortingly. "It was only a momentary lapse. I know you have to go. It's your job to protect the park and the people in it and get rid of this threat."

"I'll be careful, you know I will. I'll be absolutely safe in the tank's belly with a cannon and a machine gun above me; oodles of weapons inside. Surrounded by the army's finest. It'd take a more formidable foe to waylay us than what we've seen so far."

She met his eyes and hers were dead serious. "And that foe could be out there waiting for you. An even bigger and badder version of what we've already seen. A version that even a tank can't fight against."

A strange sensation, the hint of a premonition, crawled across Henry's skin but he shrugged it off. "I have to go. The park needs to be rid of these invaders sooner the better and outside of Justin I have the most experience fighting them. Besides, there is no creature, no matter how mean and how big, that one of those Abrams can't blow to hell."

"Or so you hope."

"Or so I hope," he repeated with sincerity.

Before the sun set the tank with Gillian rolled back into headquarters filled with everything Ann had put on her list and two meowing, yowling fur balls in cat carriers.

Aside, Captain McDowell reported to Henry they'd discovered where the dinosaurs, most of them anyway, had their lair. "They're gathering around the lake, in the lake, which makes complete sense. It's a source of water. We're going tomorrow, three tanks and a complement of soldiers to kill as many of them as we can find–you still want to ride along?"

"Damn straight I do."

"See you at dawn then. I'll be out by the tanks with my men. You can bring one other person along if you like. There's room."

"I'll be there. With Justin. If anyone can make sense out of whatever we find, he can. Moreover, he's turned into a formidable dinosaur hunter."

"I agree. Good choice. We can always use another sharpshooter."

"He's become that too. He's better than me

these days and, as we all know," and here he had canted his head at her, "nearly as good as you."

McDowell had left to see to preparations for deterring the possible night assault and Henry had helped Ann unload and bring in their personal items. And the homeless felines.

It made Henry feel good to see Ann smiling as she snuggled the cats, though cuddling Miss Kitty Cat also made her cry again for what had happened to Stanton and Kiley. Their loss was just beginning to settle in for her, and Henry.

But it was nice when later that night they got to sleep on comfy air beds on their own sheets and amidst their blankets; two cats curled up between them and other comforts from their home scattered around. They had their own pillows, coffee mugs, alarm clock, Ann's laptop, Kindle and all her work papers. Ranger Gillian, quick thinking as he always was, had also grabbed every goodie, every can of coffee and a container of tea Ann had had in the kitchen and brought them along as well. Nice touch.

He felt somewhat guilty Justin and Steven were sleeping on cots in the main conference room, his men were bunking out in the other rooms on cots or in sleeping bags and the soldiers were tenting it out in the yard. But because it was warm none of them seemed to care, so in the end, he was fine with it, too. Hardships under the circumstances were to be expected. The soldiers and rangers on duty accepted the conditions without complaint.

At least Ann was comfortable, or as

comfortable as she could be. That meant a lot to Henry.

In the end, none of them got much sleep that night anyway because the dinosaurs hit the compound at around midnight and, as the night before, the fighting was brutal. This time though it didn't last as long. The soldiers and the rangers fought them off and the creatures evaporated into the dark woods and, also unlike the night before, there was no repeat performance. The dinosaurs didn't mount another attack.

Later, in their makeshift office bedroom, Ann remarked on what had already occurred to him, "Now that was odd. Them coming at us so late. I thought most of them didn't like the dark? And, did you notice, there weren't as many of them tonight...you think you've killed more of them than you thought?"

"I don't know. I hope so. It was peculiar, so few of them. But I don't trust them for one minute. I have the sneaking suspicion they're up to something."

"Aren't they always? Devious little monsters–and big monsters." Ann muffled a snort, snuggling into him on their pushed together air mattresses. There was only the desk lamp for light so the room was dim. The windows were squares of ink. It was after three in the morning and he needed to get some sleep before the tanks rumbled out of the compound at sunrise.

Ann was soon gently snoring and the cats,

too, were asleep but sleep evaded him. Restless, he slipped from bed and checked the weapons he'd be taking that morning for the dinosaur hunt. His MP7 and a high-powered rifle. The tank was equipped with more aggressive firepower to tackle the big brutes they'd run into, but he knew at some point their feet would be on the ground and their weapons in their hands to flush out the stragglers or the smaller varieties. He had to be sure his weapons were in good working order. When he was sure they were, he snuck a few hours of uneasy sleep.

*****

When the sun's rays brightened the windows and the room, he was already dressed and, after laying a gentle kiss on his sleeping wife's cheek, he exited the building and walked out into the humid morning. The day was going to be another real hot one, he thought. All the dinosaurs were going to be down by the watering hole.

Captain McDowell was lounging in the sunshine against one of her MIA2 Abrams battle tanks, speaking with two other soldiers. Probably part of the tank crew. As Henry strode up to them, Justin appeared and joined them.

"Morning, Chief Ranger Shore. Dr. Maltin." McDowell tipped her head at both him and Justin. "Are you ready for the hunt?"

"Ready," Henry replied.

"Ready." Justin pushed his gold-rimmed glasses higher up on his nose. The sweat was already shining on his face and his glasses kept slipping. His hair was tied in a ponytail. Cooler that way.

"Where's your sidekick?" Henry smiled at Justin, looking around.

"Steven? Oh, he's riding with another tank crew. McDowell said there wasn't room in this one but placed him in the tank that'll be behind us. We'll meet up with him if and when we move out onto the ground. And that way he gets to interview this one soldier who has an interesting dinosaur story to tell him."

"He still trying to soak in the full dinosaur experience for his book, huh?"

"Trying. Myself, I think we've turned him into a dinosaur addict. He's hooked. I don't believe he's ever going back to the musical gigs. He wants to be a dinosaur hunter now. Claims we're going to need more of them."

Oh great, another tag-along. Henry liked the musician well enough but the man was a troubadour, a writer of songs and a scribe, not a hunter. He had no business being out in the woods looking for man-eating monsters. But it was *his* life. "Well, as long as he knows the dangers involved. This ain't no picnic we are going on," Henry tossed back.

"He knows. If you ask me he's simply hooked on the excitement of it all."

"That'll change the first time he's face to face with one of these creatures and it takes a bite out of him," McDowell interrupted with a straight face, the hot sun glinting off her fair skin which already had the flush of a sunburn from being outside the day before building the fence.

"Possibly, but he's already been chased by an angry rabble of them. Saw and faced the danger they represented up close; yet, I have to admit, he kept his head. Fired my MP7 adequately, kept the dinosaurs from eating us, and everything. He's not a bad shot, either. He won't be a hindrance at all from what I can see."

"All right then. He can join our team on the ground." Gesturing at the two Oregon National Guard soldiers McDowell introduced them. "This is Sergeant Gilbert and Private Harmon. They're two of our crew. Sergeant Gilbert will be driving the tank and Harmon is going to be the ammo loader–when we need the guns. I'll be the commander, of course, up in the turret." Gilbert was a small wiry man probably somewhere in his thirties with close cropped black hair and a pock-marked face, probably from a bad case of early acne. But his eyes, a flat blue color, were alert; his manner open and friendly. The Private was a young guy maybe in his twenties with an innocent looking face, a crew cut and intense eyes. He kept tapping the fingers of his right hand on the hull of the tank he was leaning on. Nervous, but trying hard to hide it. It wasn't often, Henry surmised, he went out into the woods hunting for dinosaurs.

"You know how to work this baby?" Justin asked McDowell, gazing up at the tank in all its metal glory. It looked like it could protect them from anything. Well almost anything.

"I've been trained on every role: commander, gunner, driver and ammo loader. Today I sit up in the turret and command. Our gunner will be at my feet. We'll squeeze you and the chief ranger in with me somehow. A tight fit but we'll do it." There was confidence in her voice. She was in army fatigues, gun at her hip and rifle hanging from her shoulder, as were the other men with her. She was a true soldier and played the part.

"We're going out to the rim, then, huh?" The rim that Ellie Stanton had once been snatched from on a snowy night. And for a moment images of Ranger Stanton and Kiley flickered in Henry's mind and sadness washed over him again. He still couldn't believe they were dead. He'd phoned Stanton's sons, asking permission to bury her in the park, a place she'd loved, and they'd given it, because he didn't have a clue how long they'd be holed up at headquarters, and that phone call had been difficult.

Kiley had been put into the ground beside her in a grassy spot underneath a large maple tree behind headquarters. A lovely spot Henry knew they would both have approved of.

A somber group of them, rangers and soldiers, had attended and Henry had spoken heartfelt words over the graves; Ann had cried silently through the whole service. Many of the rangers, him included, had damp eyes as well. The official memorial services still had to be arranged and he had no idea when that would be.

"Yes, our destination today is the rim. That's the place my men saw tracks yesterday of where they're gathering. They followed the signs and located a herd of them as far as Cleetwood Cove. Some, the amphibious species, must be tucked away in those caves along the shoreline or in the woods around and below the crater's rim. They spotted some of the larger creatures hunkering up on Garfield Peak and not far from the lodge. But, truthfully, they're hiding all over and throughout the woods. They're sprinkled out there like hidden Easter eggs."

Henry had a sudden image in his mind of Easter egg colored dinosaurs, with pink and blue stripes or purple polka-dots and shiny ribbons tied around their necks nestled in the tall grass around the lake, ready to be found. But when a person found one they didn't get to stash it in a pretty little Easter basket to be eaten later with a dash of salt...instead it hopped up and ate them. Surprise!

"I'm ready whenever you are," Henry said. He wanted to get it over with. The sooner the interlopers were dealt with the sooner he'd get his park, his life, back.

"Gonna be another sultry day, huh? In the nineties I've heard. Maybe even hit a hundred or above again." McDowell continued the conversation, shading her eyes with her hand and looking up. As if she had all the time in the world. "It's nothing like our last adventure together. Remember Ranger Shore? On Mount Scott in the freezing cold and snow. Brrr. Doesn't this place have moderate seasons and temperatures? Like anything between sixty and eighty degrees? Not hot as the sun or cold as the North Pole?"

"It does, but they're extremely brief ones." Henry wanted to hurry her along. *Let's go. Let's go.*

"Yeah, so brief if you blink you can miss them, right?"

"You got it."

Henry decided it was as good a time as any to query, "So our men and the tanks can take care of any land dinosaurs we come across, but what about the population of the lake? There's some formidable leviathans in the water. I've seen them. These tanks can't go underwater, can they?" Of course they couldn't. He knew that.

McDowell shook her head negatively. "They can't Ranger Shore. But my superiors are tackling the problem of the water dwellers and I'll leave it up to them to handle it. It is in the works. There has been talk about dropping a sonar grid of buoys across the lake by Apache helicopter and when the sonar shows anything dinosaur-like moving below the water, the Apaches or the F15s from Kingsley ANG Base in Klamath Falls will return and bomb them. There's nothing in the lake those explosives can't blow out of the water, no matter how deep they try to hide. Home base will let me know if and when they're successful. My orders are to take care of the land intruders and the Apaches and F15s will take care of the aquatic ones."

Well, Henry thought dolefully, there goes the lake's delicate eco system. Boom!

"It's a shame we can't use the helicopters to rid ourselves of all the park's dinosaurs. Drop bombs on their heads and explode them back to the stone age, or whatever age they came from."

"But, as you are well aware, Captain, from our last thrilling adventure together," Henry interjected, "it's hard to lower a helicopter into deep forest growth, much less find and shoot at the smaller dinosaurs bopping around beneath the forest canopy. They move too fast. Dropping explosives into the woods would also decimate substantial sections of the park. And with this heat wave we've had the parched conditions could be a catalyst for massive forest fires. Far too hazardous. A match in a tinder box. As if the dinosaur trouble isn't enough try adding a forest fire to the mix."

"As you say, I'm well aware of those complications. No bombing in the tinder box. Though," she added, "barbequed dinosaurs would do the trick, too."

Henry wrinkled his nose at the idea of burnt to a crisp stinking dinosaurs. But the last thing they needed were forest fires. There'd already been enough destructive upheaval in the park and more was coming. He tried not to think about the harm they were doing to the wild lands, yet they were past that signpost. He tried not to think about the F15s dropping bombs in the lake and blowing the leviathans to pieces. Remembering the water monsters' battle in the lake that day still gave him the willies. He and his companions so easily could have become fatalities.

As he gazed into the forest, from somewhere among the ravines a dinosaur's deep-throated bellow broke loose and crowded into the air. After it faded another echoed after it and then another. Soon the zoo was at full volume. The dinosaurs were waking up. And he wondered if he would be alive and in Ann's arms tonight or would he be dead? It was a scary thought, so he stopped thinking about it. They had work to do.

"We're going now, Chief Ranger. The other two tanks accompanying us are loaded and ready to roll out. So you and Dr. Maltin climb in. But first put these on." McDowell handed them their intercom helmets so they could communicate with the crew and the other tanks; showed Henry how to use them, Justin already knowing how from his last ride, then slid another one on her own head.

The crewmen had scrambled up and into the tank's hatch and the turret when the discordance had begun and McDowell, Justin and Henry followed into the interior.

Henry hadn't been in an armored fighting vehicle before, other than the flying one, the Black Hawk, months earlier. So it was a first. But the helicopter had had windows and the tank didn't. He thought he'd feel claustrophobic in the tiny space. He usually did in tight places and it had become worse the older he'd gotten. And he wasn't disappointed. As soon as he lowered himself through the cupola and wiggled down into the compartment he fought off a growing panic of wanting to escape. Every inch of him ached to get out of that shrinking metal canister. He knew he couldn't. He was safer in that canister, armed with deadly weaponry, than skulking around in the woods without it. Still, he wasn't totally a happy camper.

The tank trundled along the twisty roads through the woods. It was a bumpy ride. The vehicle's motor whining and the tracks circling. Henry spoke with his tank mates via the intercom and learned more about the Abrams they were riding in. They talked about how they were going to slay any dinosaurs they came across. Talked to cover their nervousness. Sometimes it even worked.

Henry had the eerie feeling they were heading into a trap of some kind. That the dinosaurs were clever enough to have laid one for them. He couldn't shake it. But Justin was the only other one who shared his trepidation. The soldiers thought they were merely ridding the park of dangerous animals, some larger than others. Shoot them, kill them, move on. Clean out the park. Mission accomplished. Easy.

It was never that easy.

The first segment of the journey was uneventful. No sign of their quarry, of any species, anywhere. Everything looked and felt like any other day in the park. It almost made Henry believe it was already purged of the ancient marauders. Wouldn't that be great? Ha.

As their tank convoy sluggishly made its way up Rim Drive towards the lodge a herd of the small kangaroo-like critters were suddenly rushing out of the woods at them. First hint they were being pounced on were the thumping sounds on the outside of the armored vehicle.

"It's some of those rock-tossing critters," the driver observed through his small window, "the ones with the red skin. There's a flood of the snapping, snarling and hissing little monsters, though some aren't so little. They're throwing rocks and other objects at us. Oh, and their bodies. Dinosaur grenades." But everyone inside could hear the banging against the metal. The creatures must have been drawn by the Abram's loud vibrations as the tank rumbled by, the profuse heat or the pungent smell of diesel fuel it emitted.

"We have contact," Justin groused over the headset. "It's our old friends. And just as hyper as ever."

"They're swarming over the tank," Sergeant Gilbert spoke again, "boxing and scratching at it and wanting in. Ugh, they give me the heebie-jeebies. They're so ugly."

The other tanks reported the same situation. Dinosaurs crawling all over them.

Henry had no notion how the creatures knew there were humans inside, but somehow they did. Couldn't fool those critters.

Henry and Justin hovered over the screens and watched the mayhem.

"Yep, those are some of the same kind that ganged up on me and Steven coming here. Wow, though, have some of them grown." Staring at the monitors, Justin expelled a low whistle.

"After the slaughter yesterday, I can't believe there's still so many of them. Where are they coming from?"

"Eggs, I'd imagine." Henry's tone ironic. "Too many of them."

Justin chuckled. "It's far worse than I expected. We have so many to exterminate."

"Then we need to start. No time like now." Henry was jolted in his seat as the tank hit and climbed over something on the ground beneath them. Nearly straight up and then straight down. Plop! The tank's engine grinding as the ground below it became increasingly bumpier.

Still rolling, the tank bounced and bucked. They were squishing dinosaur bodies left and right beneath their spinning tracks. A lumpy layer of them made for a rough ride.

The tank came to a full stop. Too many dinosaur bodies. A wall of them fluxing and rising before them.

"Good Lord...would you look at that!" McDowell exclaimed. "There are hundreds of them. We're too close to the other tanks to use our cannons, but, gunner, you have my permission to use the machine guns. Anytime you're ready. *Fire!*"

"If we can't grind them into mush we'll shoot them into bloody bits and pieces."

The turret swung around and the machine gun fired continuous bursts in a circular pattern. The tank kept moving. Crunch, crunch, splat. The guns kept firing.

The other two Abrams had fallen behind

them a ways so they could use their guns as well. But being in the line of fire, sometimes the other tanks' shots hit their vehicle and ricocheted off the metal hull, going every which way into the forest around them. If they were lucky the stray bullets would down a few dinosaurs. Good thing machine gun bullets couldn't pierce the tank's metal skin or else all the humans inside would be Swiss cheese.

Inside Henry heard the shrieks and cries of agonized rage as the ammunitions cut through the dinosaurs' ranks; cries cut off as the bodies slid beneath the tanks or flew apart. Or fled. The wall dissolved. The sounds of live entities pelting the tank ceased. Only the whiz and clank of bullets hitting soft or hard surfaces remained.

"They're retreating," the driver's excited voice updated them over the intercom. "We have the little shits on the run."

"Should we go out there and finish them up?" Steven, breaking onto their com line from inside one of the other tanks, pressed in a tentative voice. Henry was surprised he hadn't heard from the man before this.

"Nah, there's too many of them and they're fleeing off into the forest anyway," McDowell answered him. "Don't worry Mr. James, you'll have you chance to shoot them up close before the day is over. We're still not at the gathering hole yet. Be patient. Leastways we have thinned the pack some. It's a good start."

Henry sent Justin a conspiratorial look, pushed the microphone away from his mouth so no one else could hear and whispered to his son-in-law, "You're right, son. The man has the fever. He has become a hunter and I don't believe it is only fodder for his book." Justin merely grinned at him. Henry scowled back. "Crazy musician."

The tanks resumed their advancement. They were trolling up the steep hills overlooking the lake and not far from the lodge when the next flank of dinosaurs rose up before and around them. This time they faced the big ones. The species Justin claimed reminded him most of the earliest T-Rexes, but larger. Mutants all. They most likely moved faster than a T-Rex might have. They had stronger front arms, sharper claws and bigger teeth. Their gleaming eyes followed the tanks like a snake's would a juicy rabbit.

Henry watched over the screens as the group of them stomped through the trees and encircled them. Their upper bodies, perched near the brink of the drop off to the lake far below, were outlined by the sky. The convoy was that high up on the rim and the realization of how far up they were made Henry uneasy. Heat waves drifted from the tanks and mingled with those swirling around the beasts. Strange thing was, the dinosaurs weren't making a ruckus. They were virtually silent, stealthy in their encroachment. Only the sound of their huge bodies crashing through the foliage gave them away. And that they were easy to see on the monitors.

What were they up to? Hell if he knew. No

good probably.

For about the hundredth time since the dinosaur wars had begun, Henry couldn't fathom how these modern dinosaurs could be anything like the ancient ones that had once roamed the earth. These new strains were so clever, so resistant to any forms of control or annihilation. He couldn't imagine them becoming extinct.

Of course, Justin had told him many times, that when the world shattering incident happened millions of years ago–the one created by a civilization killing asteroid or something comparable to it–it wouldn't have made any difference how smart the dinosaurs had been. It wouldn't have mattered. The food chain had been utterly destroyed. Plant life and the plant-eaters. The dinosaurs couldn't have planted fresh crops to feed the animals they needed to survive, even if they'd known how to. Even if there would have been sunshine to grow those crops, which there hadn't been for decades. Total global winter.

So, perhaps dinosaurs had *always* been highly intelligent and paleontologists had gotten it totally wrong. Their intelligence wouldn't have saved them back then…but unfortunately for mankind, their existence's repeat performance had no planet destroying space junk to cull them and humans would now be faced with the job. Or at least that was what Justin believed.

The new world dinosaurs, lined up like colossal trolls with very big teeth, glared hungrily down at the three tanks. Henry counted six, nine...and more lumbering in to block their way.

"Gunner, now you can use the cannons," commanded Captain McDowell. "Aim for the heads, if you can hit them. Knock their brains out."

The tanks rumbled to a halt below the edge of the rim, abreast of each other so the cannons could be used without blowing each other up, and the main guns began to blast away.

What happened next was swift, and later, Henry would have ample time to replay their mistakes. But as they began cutting down the beasts, the cannons firing and hitting their targets, other dinosaurs moved in around them. Even larger ones. The real giants. By the time they realized they'd been caught in a trap, it was too late.

The mutant Rexes were wounded, died, and fell and their comrades closed in tighter behind them. And using their huge bodies the dinosaurs began shoving the tanks and the humans inside them forward. Towards the rim and the lake so far below it.

Damn! We've been played. The SOBs lured us up here to topple us over into the water. They can't get to us inside these tin cans, but they can sure as hell push us into the lake.

"Tell the drivers to turn and pull back!" Henry shouted. "Pull back! They're pushing us. We're too near to the edge! We're going to go over!"

And like McDowell said, these babies don't

swim.

Their Abrams pivoted its turret and began firing at the creatures shoving them from behind. And as they fell back, the tank did a severe U-turn and headed away from the abyss, the guns still firing at anything around them as the other two tanks tried to do the same. They'd come close. Henry released the breath he'd been holding and exchanged a horrified look with his son-in-law. *God, that was close.*

But one of the tanks hadn't swung around fast enough.

"Two of us are safe," McDowell whispered hoarsely. "But one is still being propelled towards the precipice. It didn't react quickly enough. *Oh no!*"

Henry couldn't see where the other tanks were, but McDowell claimed only one was beside them. One was still on the rim. Now he stared over at the screens in time to see that tank being pushed over the edge into the water below. A gigantic dinosaur going with it, roaring and flailing its claws, its jaws open and gnashing on air. Both went over the brink and, though the people in the tank couldn't see it, all the way down to the water. There was nowhere else to go.

Oh, God, no! Not again! Not–

It was like watching the terrible trolley catastrophe all over again. Watching and not being able to do anything but feel the horror as a vehicle full of trapped humans plunged into oblivion and certain death by drowning for all inside.

Henry thought he and Justin might have shouted out at the same time. But it was hard to tell because his headset suddenly filled with screams and cries from the doomed tank. Bedlam. Nearly blew his ears out. The soldiers in it going into a panic as they felt the falling sensations and knew what was occurring. Knew what their fate would be. Some sent hurried messages to their loved ones, others just yelled.

Then silence.

"Sergeant Brinker? Are you there?" McDowell reacted, trying to discover which tank had been taken.

"Yes, Captain."

"Good. Sergeant Brinker get out of here. Get away from the rim!"

"Yes, Ma'am. Going now."

"Lieutenant Lansing?" she beseeched. "Lieutenant Lansing?"

There came back a garbled reply Henry had a hard time understanding. Then the series of words that sent chills through his body and he'd never forget.

"Going down...dear God! Hitting the water! Something has us...something in the water has us! Must be huge as a whale...help!...help...aaaagh–" And then the terrified voice, all the voices, were gone.

The bedlam quieted into an eerie tomblike silence. Henry had never heard the tank hit the water. Too far away. But, sickeningly, he knew it had. There was only one thing below the rim.

Water. Very deep water.

"Steven!" Justin demanded. "Steven...are you still there?"

"I am still here," a voice from the other tank was uncharacteristically subdued.

Henry caught the look of relief as it washed over Justin's face, practically in the same instant as the guilt. Sure he was happy his friend was alive, his tank hadn't been the one to plunge into the lake, but others were gone. Soldiers, good men, with families. Dead. Henry's stomach lurched. And it was about to get worse.

They didn't have time to mourn the dead. They were busy fighting off the new wave of dinosaurs coming at them. Another giant, as big as the one that had toppled over with the tank; emerald of skin with a rapacious snarling mouth of fangs, was now targeting McDowell's Abrams, coming behind it and ramming it towards the cliff.

The tank slowly, inch by inch began to move in the opposite direction they wanted to go.

"Driver, reverse this machine! Get us out of here!" McDowell ordered the soldier steering their tank, her voice somehow calm. She'd learned a lesson. Stay away from the rim of Crater Lake when dinosaurs were attacking.

After a grinding halt, the tank shuddered in its tracks and held its ground for too brief a moment and then slowly began to be thrust towards the rim again.

Henry's gut was screaming. *Get out! Get out! GET. OUT.*

The tank was nudging closer to the ledge foot by foot. Outside the dinosaur roared and continued to push.

"Should we abandon ship, er, tank?" Justin squeaked, swaying in his seat as the vehicle jerked over and over.

"Where would we go? We're surrounded...and by some of the big brutes." Henry was studying the video screens, yet all he could see was a misty sky. They must be near the rim's brink. Tilted upwards. Next stop the lake. Would they end up in a waiting leviathan's stomach like the tank that had already gone over? He fought to remain composed, though fear had dried his mouth and frozen his blood. He needed to remain calm to face whatever was coming next.

The Abrams dragged across the ground, shifted a little, stopped, jerked again and tipped over further. The machine gun was still firing, finding targets, and so was the cannon, but the tank had continued to move towards the rim, even though the driver was valiantly trying to maneuver away from it.

They were balanced precariously on the cliff. Seconds until space launch.

"We get out of here or we go into the lake! That's our only choices," McDowell cried. "Everyone grab your weapons and abandon tank! Sergeant Brinker has escaped, is in the clear, and is waiting a short distance away to pick us up. We won't have to be on the ground long."

Henry and Justin didn't need to be told twice.

They grabbed their MP7s, flipped up the hatch, and seeing their flight path basically unobstructed and how precariously near they were to the rim's edge–feet away–the five humans scrambled out, slid along the tank's surface, and dropped to the ground.

Swinging around when his boots hit the dirt, Henry saw there was only one direction to run. Forward. "This way!" he shouted and sprinted away from the rim, firing the MP7 as he went and dispersing a bunch of smaller herd dinosaurs that had seen them exit and had closed in on them. The big mutant pummeling the Abrams had also seen them but could do nothing about it...as it went over into the lake with its empty prize clutched in its arms.

They'd gotten out just in time. Henry muttered a quick *thank you God!* and kept shooting as he and the others escaped at a dead run into the copse of trees in front of them.

There were monsters crowding around and their guns fired as they stumbled and wove through the line of them, sometimes barely avoiding injury or capture, and slid in among the trees.

They were free.

And they ran in the direction McDowell led them. "The other tank is waiting for us. This way," she'd yelled.

And after endless, or that's what it felt like, minutes of violent fighting, swearing and sweating, Henry spied Sergeant Brinker's tank in a thicket, hidden among the trees, and they made a final dash for it.

The hatch slammed open and they dived into the hole like mad rabbits with slavering wolves on their tails. *Safe!*

Henry had never been so happy to see an army vehicle. There were too many humans jammed into it, but McDowell swore, tight as it was, they'd make it back to headquarters. At least they were away from the slavering horde. Justin was relieved to see Steven alive, as Steven was to see Justin and Henry okay.

"Hold your breath, men, squeeze in and think skinny," the Captain told them. "We'll make it." And they did, running the tank at its top speed. Fighting dinosaurs with cannon and machine gun the whole way. As they traveled dinosaurs died, littering the blood soaked ground behind them.

At one point, during a break, they'd wheeled up over a hill and McDowell gestured Henry to glance at the screens. "Take a look behind us." Her voice grave, the look in her eyes dark as she wiped her face with a trembling hand. Losing two tanks, one full of her soldiers, had shaken her. There was sadness mingled with the determination to survive on her face and rage at the creatures that had killed her men.

There behind them, moving and shifting, was a sea of dinosaurs. Endless numbers of them. Again of all species, except there weren't any of the flying gargoyles that had tormented them in the spring. They'd seen none of them. Not so far anyway. It reminded Henry of a mass migration or of one of those history channel documentaries that animated the process. A migration from hell was what it most looked like.

They were in a race for headquarters. One they couldn't lose. There were times Henry thought they were done for. Out maneuvered or outnumbered. Blocked in by lone enemies or facing a multitude. They cut through them with their weapons and tediously surged onward.

Finally, as the sun was setting, the headquarters compound loomed ahead and McDowell confessed to Henry, "There weren't that many of the creatures yesterday when my men exploded those areas. Where could they have been hiding? Why are there so many now? I underestimated their numbers and the danger. I won't do that again. We need even more soldiers, weapons and tanks. When we return to headquarters, we'll have to rethink our tactics. Take a fresh look at things. I'll contact my superiors. Even the extra troops they sent this morning aren't going to be enough. This operation has gotten out of hand."

Henry spoke what he supposed she was thinking. "If there are these many in the park, if they've proliferated this rapidly, to save surrounding homes and towns you might yet have to bring in the air power." It was difficult to say and he regretted it as soon as it came out of his mouth. The collateral damage of bombing the lake, park or surrounding areas would be terrible.

"That would be a last resort, Ranger Shore, I promise you. The last resort."

He prayed she was right. But he kept seeing

that sea of dinosaurs swarming below the hill. He remembered the terror he'd experienced barely escaping the tank in time before it plummeted into the lake. He kept seeing the T-Rex mutants pushing the first tank over the rim. Heard in his tortured mind those poor souls trapped in the lost vehicle crying out... *"Going down...dear God! Hitting the water! Something has us...something in the water has us! Must be huge as a whale...help!...help....* Then blood-curdling screams which dwindled away until there was nothing but the absence of sound interspersed with static.

Now there would be more night terrors to add to his growing list of night terrors.

He no longer had to dream of dinosaurs...they'd come and taken over his real life. No waking up any more.

*****

The army sent out more men and tanks. Henry and McDowell spent the remainder of the week going out and thinning the herd, as they'd taken to calling their daily incursions into the forest. Using all the army's deadliest machines, weaponry and man power they could muster from the ranks of soldiers and rangers. They dispatched hundreds of the beasts. Yet more kept appearing. Like magic, Justin was wont to say. Yeah, black evil magic, Henry would retort.

They stayed away from the lake's rim or any place like it where they could be shoved over or locked in. They'd learned their lesson well.

*****

Over the following weeks, using the forest for cover as much as they could, they fought and killed dinosaurs. Endlessly.

Most days Henry could hear the explosives going off inside the crater, exploding the lake and the monsters living in it. The F15s were busy as they swooped in and targeted the leviathans and destroyed them. After a while the lake appeared empty; sanitized.

After a while the land appeared clear or mostly clear of unwanted predators.

Key word being *appeared*.

"Maybe they're hiding again?" Justin said one night to Henry.

"Maybe."

"But we have killed a considerable amount."

"Perhaps the dinosaurs," Henry couldn't believe it was over, "have migrated to the outlying villages and towns?"

"Could be we've gotten all of them this time."

"Could be." But Henry wasn't sure. The park had become too quiet. The weather had cooled and with the lower temperatures, after the heat, the woods filled with a creeping fog. It covered the land and the water, crept around the boulders and buildings. It hid the world around them. It made Henry extremely uneasy.

The attacks on headquarters had completely

stopped. Not a sign anywhere of dinosaurs. For days and days. But they kept going on the hunting raids because Henry didn't trust the false peace, not for a second.

He still had this really bad feeling.

One night, weeks later, Captain McDowell told them Klamath Falls was essentially deserted. The townsfolk had fled, frightened by continued attacks. The businesses were shuttered or were piles of debris. The dinosaurs had slithered in and taken full residency. McDowell alluded to the town as Dinosaur Falls.

"According to reports I've had recently, the place is in shambles," McDowell confided. "The National Guard has vainly attempted to evict the creatures, but they keep sneaking in; nesting in the ruins and ferociously defending their turf. Multiplying like rabbits."

"Yeah, giants rabbits with razor sharp teeth. What is the army doing about it?"

"Just what we're doing. They're hunting down and exterminating any dinosaurs they find. Using strategically placed bombs and tanks. From what I hear they're not having much luck, though. There's so many of the creatures."

Henry was shocked but not surprised. He'd feared as much. He felt sorry for the townsfolk. For the town. For all of them. For Ann. How was she ever going to get the medical care she needed if the town had been taken over permanently by dinosaurs? Was Ann's doctor still there? Alive? Was the hospital still there?

He'd telephoned the doctor's office and the

hospital's switchboard but no one answered. His wife was losing weight, was pale, and always exhausted and he was worried about her. For him a growing frustration had set in. He didn't like being helpless and there was nothing he could do under the circumstances, other than to love and care for her as best he could.

But returning from the latest hunt everyone was cautiously optimistic. They hadn't come across any dinosaurs. And after many targeted bombings Captain McDowell had confidence the lake might be dinosaur free as well.

It was something to celebrate. And after what they'd gone through the last weeks, how they wanted to be able to relax. Henry understood that. Declare their freedom, pick up their normal lives and start rebuilding what had been destroyed. Ann, especially, was anxious to return home and begin her chemo treatments, even if she had to travel to another town to get them. And he was just as eager as she was. He, too, was sick of living in his office and being trapped behind the stockade in the prison compound that headquarters had become.

Thing was, he didn't trust the dinosaurs. They were sly devious devils. They seemed to know when they had to lay low and keep out of sight. That's how they'd evaded extermination so far. But...they always came back.

So now...where were they hiding and what were they waiting for?

Dinosaur Lake III: Infestation

Chapter 13
Henry

A month after the first attacks, Henry came trudging into headquarters after yet another raid which hadn't netted even one dinosaur. The weather had slipped from the suffocating heat of summer into a cool September. The fog had taken firm residence and a couple of mornings frost laced the gold or pale orange leaves. A cold wind whistled through the trees. And he knew the Oregon winter wasn't far behind.

Ann met him at headquarter's front door, her expression distraught and the lines around her mouth more pronounced than usual. Her clothes hung on her thin frame.

"How was today, Henry? How many of our unwanted monsters did you and your tank crew dispatch?"

"Not a one."

Ann gasped, her frown curving up into a fleeting smile before it resettled on her lips. "That's good news, right? Really good news?"

"I hope so."

"So…we might be able to go home soon, huh?" Eagerness in her voice.

He felt bad dashing her hopes. "Maybe, honey. We have to be positively sure the park is safe before we take that step."

"Any idea when that might be?" She shadowed him as he made his way to his office. The outer rooms of the building had over the last month grown very cluttered as any place would with as many people living in it. Noisy, too. Even at night. Rangers and soldiers coming and going.

"Soon I hope. We are working as hard as we can. We've made great progress. At least there isn't bands of dinosaurs roaming everywhere, causing trouble." He also didn't say there might be more dinosaurs staying out of sight somewhere, waiting to strike when the humans guard was down. He couldn't bear to see her frown reemerge.

Within his office he put his arms around her and took energy from holding her. After the month he'd had, he sorely needed it. They both did. "Enough of all that. I'm sick of dinosaurs, sick of fighting or running from them. How are you feeling?"

"All right, I guess. Tired, but I'm always tired lately. No biggie. I've spent the day surfing the Internet collecting stories about mysterious sightings of fantastical beasts and reports of missing people as far away as Washington State. Watching weird videos."

Her head shook slowly. "It sure is a strange time. You'd be shocked at how many people, police, local and state officials are in denial there are prehistoric creatures encroaching into their towns and states. Mauling and taking people. Smashing everything. People sometimes just don't want to accept what they see, what really is there. Nothing ever changes."

"Did you expect it to?"

"I guess not. Dinosaurs and the problems they bring are now normal fare for us but not so for everyone else. People would rather think they're nuts, or are hallucinating, than accept that live dinosaurs roam the earth. They want to be left alone in their ignorance so they can continue to watch their reality shows on cable, play with their smart phones, iPads or Facebook and Twitter each other. They want what they know. Their sane safe routines. I don't blame them," she whispered. "When it comes down to it, isn't it what all of us want? Normalcy?"

She snuggled against his chest and kept talking. "But things have gotten really crazy. I called Laura this morning and updated her on things here. She and Phoebe are fine but they're really missing Justin. You know she's only a month away from having that baby. It's getting so close. I want to see her and my granddaughter so badly."

She sighed. "But I can't reach anyone at the newspaper. My reporters are MIA. I can't contact anyone or any place in town. Not even the hospital. Where are all the people? Do you know what's going on there?"

"Captain McDowell says Klamath Falls has been, like us, under heavy attack for weeks. Everyone has vacated. It is a ghost town...except for our lizardry pals. They've taken over."

His wife released a deeper sigh. "It feels strange not going into the newspaper, working on stories or getting ready for the weekly edition. Working. I'm at loose ends. Going stir crazy. I've become one of those silly women who scroll through Facebook and other social sites as if I'm addicted to them. Looking for traces of dinosaur encounters. Strange news."

"You can work on your personal account of what's happening here. Pay our bills online. Keep searching the web for more information on sightings in different places. Play with the cats. Keep decorating our new bedroom."

"Yeah, that'll keep me busy." She grimaced. "I'm not used to doing so little, Henry. You know me. I guess I've got office fever."

"I know," he placated her. "Now what is really on your mind? I know that look on your face too well. You've got bad news for me, don't you?"

This time she moved away so she could turn and face him. This was it, he thought. This was the real news of the day and what she was really upset about.

She took a deep breath. "You know me too well. Okay. Today I also telephoned Wilma's friend in Idaho–her name is Rosie remember–you know, where Wilma and Zeke were supposed to be staying until the coast was clear in Klamath Falls? I called just to see how they were doing and if they'd heard anything about the town's quandary from their end. I've been doing that every week or so since this mess began. I usually talk to Zeke, sometimes Wilma. You know how I fret about Zeke. Anyway, when I called today you won't believe what I found out."

Oh, oh. Henry felt an uneasy twinge somewhere in his brain. His left eye twitched. "Okay, I'll play. What did you find out?"

"Zeke and Wilma aren't there any longer."

"What? Where are they?"

"Rosie said they left yesterday heading back to

Klamath Falls. She said Zeke has been wild to get back home, missing and vexing about his belongings and his house, as he put it, but was fine with it until a few days ago when *little boy* showed up missing one morning."

"Who the hell is *little boy*?"

"His baby pet squirrel, remember? The last surviving tree rat from his yard after the dinosaurs apparently devoured the others? The one he had saved? Little furry thing about this big," she measured off about six, seven inches with her fingers, "with a fluffy tail?"

"Oh, that rodent in the cat carrier Zeke and Wilma drove off with?"

She gave him a mean look. "His baby pet *squirrel*. Cute, friendly little critter. Zeke's really attached to him. He loves him."

"Okey-dokey. Pet squirrel. But it's still just a rodent with a poufy tail," Henry couldn't help throwing in. "So what's happened?"

"Well, *little boy* escaped his cage and he's disappeared. Zeke was frantic to find him. When he couldn't, he got it in his head somehow the squirrel would make his way back home. His home in Klamath Falls. And Zeke had to get back to his house to find him before the dinosaurs eat him. Wilma, of course, had to do the driving because Zeke can't."

"You're kidding, aren't you?"

She rocked her head back and forth. "No. Afraid not."

"So Zeke and Wilma are driving back to Klamath Falls?" Henry couldn't hide his dismay.

"To look for that rodent at his house?"

"By my calculations, they should already be there by now."

"That's lunacy. Idaho is hundreds of miles away so how could a silly baby squirrel find its way back to its home town across that many miles? Ridiculous. And, heck, the *town* is full of dinosaurs. What is Zeke thinking? You did tell him the town was full of dinosaurs, didn't you, and that it was too dangerous to come back?"

"Yep," was all she gave him. She was staring at Henry with another look he knew all too well. The *we have to do something...we have to help* look.

"What would possess Zeke to do such a crazy stunt? I know he was daft about that little critter, but, for heaven's sake...Klamath Falls is a hot bed of prehistoric monsters right now."

"We know that, but he doesn't care. He wanted to come home. And I don't recall if I told you before but Zeke's been really slipping the last few months. His health is extremely frail and his mind is, well, sometimes...confused. He forgets a lot and sometimes becomes fixated on things. Can't be talked out of them."

"Come on Ann, are you telling me that Zeke might not be in his right mind and that explains his premature return into a battle zone?"

"That's what I believe. I'd call it the beginning of dementia, but I'm not sure. I'm no doctor. I just know Zeke and he hasn't behaved like himself for a while. And I saw him with that squirrel. He loved that animal. Felt responsible for it when its family was eaten. He's just trying to retrieve some little thing of what he lost. And perhaps out of desperation the only thing he could think to do was travel home in hopes *little boy* is there.

"That and after a month away he's missing his home, his routine, the newspaper and the town. Us. All reasons to return. Even for a short visit."

"Then he and Wilma are in real danger. This morning McDowell told me as we began our hunt that Klamath Falls is a total loss. The National Guard continues to patrol and defend it but it's overrun with blood-thirsty predators and is uninhabitable. For humans anyway."

"Oh, God, I hope those two old people are okay." She wrung her hands, gazing at the dark windows. "Where are they now? What is happening to them? Why didn't Zeke call me and let me know he was coming home?"

"Because you would have tried to talk him out of it. He's no fool. Besides you know Zeke, he's such an independent cuss. He'll do what he wants to do. To be truthful I'm surprised he abandoned his home when he did and not surprised in the least he's coming back."

"Oh Henry, you know, we have to do something!" She'd turned to him, her white face tilted towards his, her eyes tinged with tears.

Just what he'd been afraid of. They had to do something. That something, the only course of action he could see, wasn't something he wanted to do. But then Zeke was like family. She felt responsible for him. And now, especially, even more so.

"Like what?" He waited for it.

"We have to go and get him—and Wilma. As soon as we can. Bring them here where it's safe. Klamath Falls is a death trap full of you-know-what. They could be fighting for their lives right now. We can't wait."

There it was. His mind ticked over any alternative solutions and, of course, found none. The old man had to be rescued and who else would do it but them?

He didn't answer quick enough and Ann plunged on. "We could take one of those army tanks and go into town with it. Go get them. I'm sure they're either at Zeke's house or Wilma's. But if Zeke is looking for *little boy* he's most likely at his place searching or waiting or whatever he feels he has to do."

"Getting the army to lend us a tank for an iffy rescue attempt might not be so easy."

"Ask Captain McDowell. I am sure she'll figure out something. She knows Zeke and she would want to help. Isn't that why they are here? To help?"

Henry knew better than to argue with his wife over such a life and death issue. Once she got something that important in her head it was hard to dislodge it. The second thought he'd had when she had made the request was now that the park was clear of dinosaurs, or seemed clear, they had a window of opportunity to do a rescue mission. If McDowell would go for it. "Have you tried calling Zeke lately? On that cell phone you sent him?" The first week Zeke and Wilma had been gone, Ann had ordered a cheap phone off the Internet for him and had had it delivered. She'd wanted to stay in touch with him.

"I have. Many times today. I only get the message machine. Either he is not answering or he's lost the cell phone again. He misplaces it all the time." Her eyes were boring into him. "Well? Can we go get them?"

There was nothing he could say but yes. "All right. I'll speak to Captain McDowell tonight. We're meeting later to strategize what we are doing next. I will put this on the agenda. But, Ann, we can't go this very minute. It'd be suicide to travel through the park and into town now in the dark, though we suspect most of the dinosaurs are gone between here and the highway. But the town is still swarming with them. The best we can do is leave at first light–if McDowell gives us permission to borrow a tank that is."

"And if she doesn't?"

"I am sure she will. She knows we can't go into an infested area without a tank's protection. Cars or trucks won't do it. Not if Klamath Falls is as bad as has been reported. Once in town we can meet up with the soldiers there and increase our force."

"Dawn, huh?" She sounded disappointed but resigned.

"Best case scenario."

"I sure hope they're okay. Gosh, I wish Zeke would answer his phone." Her eyes returned to the windows. Night had fallen completely. There was silence for once except for the soughing of the wind through the trees. No roaring or night calls. No war drums. No attacks.

It turned out Henry had no trouble convincing Captain McDowell to journey into Klamath Falls for a recon operation.

"With things calmer here, everything seemingly under control, I was thinking about going into town anyway, meeting up with the troops defending it and offering our assistance. I've been in touch with their commander and, frankly, he could use some help. He's lost a lot of men. You and a few of your rangers are welcome to hitch a ride if you would like. I can spare a couple of my soldiers to help you round up the two old folks that have escaped the asylum." She'd smiled.

Henry had been relieved it'd been that easy. Ann wouldn't have left him alone if it had gone any other way. But he was as concerned about the two old people as she was. He was fond of the old man, too. And someone had to go get them.

"We will roll out as soon as the sun peeks above the horizon," McDowell promised as the meeting was breaking up later that night. The soldier appeared frazzled, her steps slow. It'd been a hard month of defending and fighting and it was showing on all of them. Living in tight quarters day in and day out or sleeping outside, going out on daily killing sprees, had worn everyone down. But Henry knew McDowell was proud of the job they'd done in the park, proud of the kills they had made. More importantly they'd made the park safe for humans again. For now anyway.

"Dawn it is.

"By the way, have you heard anything from your friend Patterson lately?" he had to ask. Only a couple of people lingered, milling around the conference table, preparing to leave or speaking with others, and Henry knew Ann was waiting for him in their temporary bedroom. After being gone all day, he wanted to spend some quality time with her. He wanted to relax and prepare, at least mentally and physically, for what the next day would bring.

McDowell paused a few feet away from him and nodded. "I talked to him on the phone day before yesterday. There is something really bothering him, I can tell, but he won't or can't discuss it or where he is. Says he will spill everything he knows when he sees us next. But he has been so busy. Whatever consulting case he's on it is shrouded in miles of red tape and governmental secrets. And it is so important he wasn't able to come here and help us. I don't like it, but I trust him enough to know better than to nag him about it.

"He also said he would see us–and you–soon, Henry. He says he needs to talk to you."

"Hmm, and you have no idea what it's about?"

"No. You know Scott…a man of many mysteries." The shadow of a good-natured smirk came and went.

Henry flashed her a strange look and laughed. It was true, Patterson was good at keeping secrets. Working for the FBI so many years had taught him well. But it was good to know he'd be visiting soon. Henry could use his advice, his help. And it would be good to see his old friend again. It had been months since he'd seen him.

"Catch you in the morning. Better get some rest,

Chief Ranger," McDowell remarked, "you're going to need it."

"You, too, Captain. Now if the dinosaurs will leave us alone for the next eight hours we'll all have a full night's sleep."

"I believe they will. I think the park is rid of them, or most of them, and tomorrow we will go see how Klamath Falls is faring. Good night."

"Good night." Henry watched as the soldier left the room. The nights were becoming cooler but McDowell still insisted on bivouacking outside with her men. It wouldn't be long, though, before the Oregon winter would come blowing in and it'd be too cold for her or the soldiers to sleep outside. In the park chilling temperatures and snow could come any time after September.

He was outside his office, hand reaching for the doorknob, when Justin and Steven caught up with him.

Justin started off with, "Henry, I hear you're going on a journey into town tomorrow?"

"Where did you hear that from?" As if he didn't know.

"Ann. And Steven and I want to go along. Well, we need to go along."

"Really? You want to return to the new heart of monster land after what we've gone through here? I thought Laura was expecting you home now that our crisis is over?"

"She is and that is where we're heading, but with a detour through Klamath Falls first. Steven wants to see, for his book, what's happened to the town and so do I. His car is at the lodge where it was left and we'll take it because one of your rangers told me a while back they saw my car out in the woods all mashed up. Dinosaurs." He shrugged. "But we thought it would be safer to join your convoy tomorrow, at least through and past the town."

"Smart thought. You would be safer traveling with us. Even here in the park I can't guarantee you wouldn't run into a lone dinosaur or two. And the war continues in Klamath Falls."

"So we can tag along tomorrow at least as far as town?" Steven confirmed.

"I would insist." Henry looked directly at his son-in-law. "Can't let anything happen to my daughter's husband, not with the new baby coming. You two be ready at dawn and we'll take you to the lodge to pick up Steven's car. Now, good night. I'm beat. My air bed calls."

"See you in the morning." Then Justin and his friend went to find their cots.

*****

That night Henry dreamed for the first time in weeks. He was in Klamath Falls and he supposed it was present day, but the town was full of dinosaur…ghosts. Huge yellow, sapphire and plum colored ones. Some had spots and some were striped just like Easter eggs. Some could crawl straight up high rise buildings like spiders and some could fly. One was jumping from roof top to roof top. They had corkscrew claws and teeth and tried to attack the townsfolk ambling around. But because they were apparitions they roared and stomped up and down in fury, swiped at people, but couldn't touch or hurt anyone.

Well, that was different.

The townspeople were busy rebuilding the place. It was beginning to look like the town it had once been. But ghost dinosaurs prowled the streets and sauntered through solid buildings, trees and humans. They were so angry they were dead; so pissed they couldn't bite or eat anyone. It was a strange sight…that town he knew so well full of dinosaur phantoms visibly trying to interact with people and not being able to.

The people laughed at and taunted them, and went on their business as if nothing unusual was happening. Ann was there, coming out of the newspaper's building. Suddenly she morphed into a pink dinosaur and flew away. It was all so bizarre.

Henry woke up in the dark, disoriented. He reached out to touch his wife's sleeping shoulder. He was back at headquarters, but the dream didn't fade.

Ghost dinosaurs. Sheesh.

In the six years since the first dinosaur had shown itself at Crater Lake his dinosaur dreams had become full-length in-living-color features of weirdness. Serials. It wasn't enough the beasts plagued his waking hours, they also on and off had plagued his sleeping ones.

According to the clock on the desk it was five a.m. Sun rise would arrive in a half-hour so he crawled out of bed, shut off the alarm, and dressed. He packed a large duffel bag with essentials he'd need for the trip. He couldn't be sure he would return in a day or two, if they didn't find the two old people right off, and wanted to be prepared for a longer absence. He was as quiet as he could be so as not to wake Ann. She had tossed and turned most of the night and had finally settled down, so he didn't want to disturb her.

But as he was ready to leave the room and meet up with Justin and Steven he thought better of it and kneeling down gently shook his wife. She'd never forgive him if he ran off without saying goodbye. The last few years had taught them how precious their time, their life together was. They never forgot it and tried never to go anywhere without saying goodbye to each other.

"Honey," he spoke softly, "I'm leaving now. Just wanted to say goodbye." He swept the tousled hair off her forehead and pressed a tender kiss on her lips. She reached up and pulled him closer and the kiss's pressure increased. Finally their lips broke contact.

"Be careful," she urged. "Promise me you'll be careful."

"I'm always careful, you know that."

"Bring them back, you hear me?"

"I'll bring the old folks back," he said. "Just pray I can find them."

"I'm praying now." Her smile was a shadow.

"I have to go now."

After a final kiss he walked from the room but felt her eyes on him. For her sake, he hoped he could find Zeke and Wilma and bring them back quickly. Ann didn't need more to be upset over. None of them did.

The day was forecasted to be sunny but chilly. Good, no rain or snow. Nothing to hinder visibility when they rumbled into town in the tanks. Justin met him as he was leaving the building. His friend Steven was at his side.

"You ready for this, you two? It could get pretty hairy. The town's supposed to be dinosaur city."

"You mean as it was when Justin and I zipped through there weeks ago and as the park's been for the last month?" Steven was grinning, keen excitement in his eyes. As Justin he had on a jacket and his borrowed MP7 hung from his shoulder by a strap.

"Yeah, sort of like that."

"Then it is business as usual. The more exploits I go on, the more dinosaurs I battle, the more sensational my book will be. Nothing beats authentic experiences."

"And here I thought you were supposed to be a music man, not a big game hunter."

"I can be both. And an author. Though I do miss my guitar and my gigs. If I'm lucky my station wagon parked at the lodge will still be there, unscathed, with my guitar and musical equipment inside. Good thing I left it there when Justin and I made our little excursion to California. Otherwise it'd be out there in the woods crushed along with Justin's Range Rover. I've had that guitar since I was fifteen. Oh, the stories it could tell. I would miss it dearly if I lost it."

"Well, first stop then will be the lodge and your car. Where did you park it?"

"On the rear side of the building, tucked in

between two towering oak trees."

"I know the spot. It's fairly protected so chances are the car is probably still there waiting for you."

"I can only hope. As big a junk heap as it is, I've had that car, Old Lizzy, a long time, too. I am attached to it."

"Your car has a name?" Henry was amused as the three of them went out to catch a ride with a tank.

"Sure. Doesn't yours?"

"No. I just call it car."

Steven was lucky. His car was where he had left it, untouched, and the guitar was there as well.

While they were at the lodge, Henry checked in on the skeleton crew who'd elected to remain behind and care for the place. The owner, some of the maintenance people and a friend of the owner, Norma, an elderly waitress who had lived there for years and refused to leave no matter what. She hadn't left the last two times there had been dinosaur trouble, either. She was an obstinate old lady set in her ways and no prehistoric trespassers were forcing her to desert her home.

Norma was sitting at a window table nursing a cup of tea when Henry walked in. It seemed strange with the empty dining room and no visitors filling the tables and yakking over coffee or breakfast. It only reminded Henry of how different things were in the park now.

"Well, if it isn't the Chief Park Ranger, as I live and breathe," the elderly woman professed, mimicking a phrase Henry often used. Her short brunette hair looked as if it hadn't been dyed recently and the gray roots were showing. He'd never seen her wrinkled face look so haggard; her usually bright smile so passive. "It's great to see you're still alive and kicking. Jimmy, the owner, has kept us informed as to what has been happening at headquarters and around in the park. It has been a wild month or so, huh?"

"It is great to see you too, Norma." He stood above her. He had slipped in to see how she was doing while Steven collected his car and before they took off for Klamath Falls. "And yes it has been quite a month. How's the arthritis?"

"Hasn't been bad. Of course I've been off my feet mostly. That helps. How about I fetch you a cup of coffee, Chief Ranger? It's been so long since I have waited on a customer, could be I've forgotten how. Be good practice for me."

"No thank you. I'm in a hurry. Sorry I can't take the time to sit and chat; perhaps another time soon. I have men waiting for me. I just thought I would check up on you, be sure you are all right."

"I am. You know me, nothing fazes me, not even those pesky over-sized lizards." The old lady took a sip of her tea. Henry noticed the cup had a crack in it by the handle.

"Where is Jimmy? I also need to see how he's doing."

"He's in the storage room taking stock of how much food we have left. He will be a while. Since these difficulties have begun we haven't gotten fresh supplies in."

"None of us have. I can't wait, so tell Jimmy I will call him later."

"I will. Is it all clear yet out there?" She nodded her head at the outside framed by the windows. "Are the monsters gone?"

"They could be. We have been busy depleting their population, but I can't guarantee it. So keep your eyes and ears open and continue staying inside until we can be sure of it. I'll give you a heads up when that happens."

"Thanks Ranger Shore."

She offered him a seat but he refused it. "No thanks. Sorry, like I said, I can only stay a minute. A team of us are venturing into town to bring back some friends of ours and see how the town's doing."

She didn't ask and he didn't elaborate on what condition the town was in. Norma was like that. All she cared about was the park and the lodge. She rarely even went into town.

"We heard the fireworks and all at headquarters," she kept talking. "Sounded like you've had quite a war down there."

"We have. But we have come out on the other side victorious. The dinosaurs have mostly been routed from the area, or so we believe. How has it been here the last month? Any problems or run-ins with the dinosaurs? Any close calls?"

"Ah," she waved her hand around her lazily, "you know, no customers, just dinosaurs peeking in the windows and traipsing across the lawns. We have been really lucky, though, none of the big ones have bothered us and the smaller ones can't get in. We bolted the doors and windows on the lower floors when this latest incursion began. It's worked just peachy. You only were able to stroll in because I saw you coming and unlocked the main door. The lodge, so far, has been dinosaur free."

She grinned. "But I did see this one mammoth fellow, ugly as hell with prodigious fangs and all, pass by the window there," she nodded at the glass panorama she was seated in front of, "one morning. Pretty as you please. He peered in at me with his beady glowing eyes and looked as if he'd love to swallow me whole, but he kept moving, didn't try to get in. Good thing. Second story up we never thought to board up those windows. I hid behind the curtains and peeked out as it turned and dived into the lake. Must be a thousand feet to the water below. Let me tell you that was really terrifying.

"And, oh, I've had numerous close calls with some of those miniature monsters, too. Once a couple cornered me outside by the trash cans–they had been dumpster diving by the looks of it because what a mess they'd made…trash everywhere–and started throwing dirty cans and empty bottles at me. I showed them. I tossed 'em right back and hit this one square in the noggin. Knocked it flat to the ground. The others were hopping around and yowling like banshees. Funniest thing I ever saw." A gleeful chortle. "Then I high-tailed it for the lodge as fast as I could go. I could hear those ugly midgets bouncing against the door like hard balls after I slammed it shut. Whew." She chuckled wickedly and made an exaggerated gesture of wiping her brow. "I was a heck more careful going out to empty the trash after that, let me tell ya. But that was a couple weeks past."

"How about the last week or so? Seen any more prehistoric rejects out and about?"

She mulled that over a minute and replied, "Nope, come to think on it, not for over a week at least. It has been quiet. No monsters dumpster diving or parading past the windows up here at all. Thank the Lord."

"Good. Well, I have to go now Norma. It has been nice seeing you and I'm so glad you and Jimmy are okay. I'll come by for a longer visit as soon as I can. You take care now."

"Wait a minute Ranger Shore…you might not have time to sit and have a cup of coffee with me, but if you hold on for just another minute I'll hustle into the kitchen and pour you a thermos to go. I just made a fresh pot." She was up and hobbling towards the kitchen before he could protest.

"All right," he hollered behind her. "You know how I like it. Cream and sugar." The lodge made the best coffee.

When Norma handed him the thermos, he thanked her, and they said goodbye.

Henry was grateful the lodge and the people left taking care of it were all right. One less worry to carry.

Two tanks with a car sandwiched between them exited the park a half hour later–Henry sharing his thermos of coffee with his tank mates–and set off on the highway in the direction of Klamath Falls.

Henry dreaded what they'd find there.

*****

The Abrams could reach a dizzying top speed of forty-two miles an hour and they were pushing that number rolling into town. Still it meant it'd take them an unusually long time to reach their destination.

Not one dinosaur crossed their paths or was glimpsed in the bordering woods on the way, and with Justin and Steven virtually unprotected in the station wagon that was a good thing. It gave Henry hope things were getting better.

They were supposed to meet up with McDowell's in town soldier counterpart, Captain Alan Harvey, at the Klamath Falls Police Station where the National Guard had set up their headquarters.

"What does Captain Harvey have to report on the dinosaur problem there? Does he have it under control?" Henry questioned McDowell over his headset when they were on their way. They were sharing the same tank, the one leading the procession. Sergeant Gilbert was their driver again and Private Harmon was in charge of the guns. After weeks of hunting expeditions Henry had grown to know both men and respected their dedication and proficiency. He trusted their judgment and felt safe with them running the armored vehicle.

"He feels they might soon. They've been slaying the creatures as quickly as they come across them but there is still a rogue pack roaming the town, evading them, ensnaring the patrols and causing havoc. I've offered our help when we get there."

Henry didn't say anything. He had pretty well

accepted they'd have to fight once they arrived and he was prepared.

Like everyone, Henry's eyes were glued to the monitors as they entered the city. And the first thing that struck him was its desolate emptiness. It looked like one of those ghost towns seen in an apocalyptic horror film. All it was missing was the spooky musical score and a tumble weed bush bouncing down the empty street. There were no people anywhere, or that he could see. Perhaps they were locked behind sturdy doors and plywood covered windows, guns near at hand, alert for any dinosaur intruders.

Businesses were shut down, their windows shattered. He didn't see one still operating. Most buildings were piles of bricks and broken plaster. There was trash littering the yards and shards of glass glittering on the roads. No cars moving. There were no sounds of children or anyone human for that matter. No people milling on the sidewalks or visiting stores, chatting and passing the time of day. A lone fast food wrapper skittered down the unoccupied sidewalk. It gave Henry a case of the shivers.

It was so different than the town he'd always known and it made him unhappy to see its empty husk.

This is what the world will look like if dinosaurs proliferate past the tipping point and overrun humanity. This is the future. This is Armageddon. This is war.

The car and tanks shouldered their way down Main Street. Nothing blocked their route, nothing challenged them, but an eerie silence cloaked the collection of forlorn houses and deserted businesses. Even Freddy's restaurant was locked up and shuttered.

"Where are the people?" McDowell was the first one to express it.

"Hiding?" Sergeant Gilbert supplied.

"If they're lucky," Henry muttered. "My guess is most of them left long ago. Justin here and Steven did say that when they came through here last month there was a healthy exodus going on. People were fleeing like a tsunami was coming."

"By the looks of the town, or what's left of it," McDowell remarked, "that tsunami came through. I hope all the inhabitants did evacuate."

There was no signs yet of dinosaurs. It made Henry wonder if McDowell have been wrong about how dire the situation was. Could be the menace was over and Klamath Falls was now dinosaur free too. Wouldn't that be great?

They parked in front of the police station, climbed from the tank, and Justin, with Steven catching up once he exited his vehicle, trailed them into the building. Inside, Henry was introduced to Captain Harvey and his soldiers, but there was no Lester Chapman or police officers anywhere.

"Where's Police Chief Chapman and his men?" he asked Captain Harvey as the man put his hand out to shake Henry's.

"Now that's a conundrum, Chief Ranger." Captain Harvey thoughtfully rubbed the side of his chin. "When we got here four weeks ago this place was unoccupied. Not a cop in sight. And in the time we've been here Chief Chapman and his officers have yet to put in an appearance. No one's heard from them, either. We think they are just…gone. Like a lot of the citizens that used to live here. Vanished." He was a tall man, taller than Henry. Husky build. His grayish hair was a bit too shaggy for a soldier and his face was scruffy with a three day old beard. His uniform rumpled and well lived in. But his eyes, the color of blue ice, were friendly enough. They seemed to be laughing most of the time as if he knew this private joke and wasn't going to tell anyone what it was.

The news didn't surprise Henry. To him it was an old story. "About how many people have disappeared? Do you have a count?"

"Unfortunately no. We just know, besides the townsfolk who have fled, there are many unaccounted for. Many missing. But I think we have killed off most of the creatures and pretty much have the situation under control. Except for that rogue gang, I mean."

Henry sighed inwardly. He and Captain Harvey knew where all those missing people had ended up but neither one had to mention it. Instead he told the soldier why he was there. To find their friends.

Justin waited until they were done with their conversation. "Excuse me," he turned to Henry. "I'd like to go with you to find Zeke and Wilma before I head home. What's another hour or so. Can we come along?" He cocked his thumb at his friend Steven who was sitting on the edge of the missing police chief's desk.

Steven grinned and gave them a thumbs up. "I'm

in, too. Let's go find those old folks and get them somewhere where they will be safe."

"I wonder if Zeke's found his escaped little squirrel friend?" Justin directed the question to Henry with a touch of humor in his voice.

"Now that would be something. Lassie come home in squirrel form. Not much chance of that, I'd say. Idaho is so far away."

"Poor Zeke. He sure loved that little fellow. Shame he's lost him."

Captain Harvey was staring at them as if they'd lost their good sense. There was a slight smile on his face, though. Possibly he liked squirrels, too.

"Well, then, are we ready to go find those AWOL friends of yours? Day's a wasting. And it's best not to be out after dark around here," Captain Harvey spoke to Henry, "just to be on the safe side."

Henry made one final call to Zeke's home phone and then his cell phone. Still no answer. It had crossed his mind more than once that perhaps Zeke and Wilma had never made it home at all. Something had waylaid them somewhere along the journey. He didn't want to dwell on that possibility, though. He had to go on the assumption they were at Zeke's house waiting for *little boy* to return home.

"We're ready." Henry looked towards Justin and Steven and they nodded.

"We will use the tanks." Captain McDowell had been leaning against the wall, just listening to the conversation, but at that time came forward.

As the group of them left the building Captain

Harvey and McDowell conferred about what the previous month had brought. Soldier stuff. Future plans. Orders. What he'd seen and experienced since the Guard had been stationed in town. She did the same and filled him in on what had been going on in the park.

"You can't traverse this township without an armored vehicle's protection," Harvey told them. "The rogue beasts are of the large varieties. It's too dangerous. Even a Humvee doesn't do the job."

"Where is this house we are going to?"

Henry gave Harvey directions to Zeke's house and Wilma's. "We'll try Zeke's first. I believe they're there."

They took the two tanks and Harvey followed in one of his. Henry had been impressed to see that Harvey's troops had a fleet of the Abrams they used to patrol and protect the town. Apparently the tanks had come in handy.

Traveling down the same once safe roads to Zeke's house Henry had done so many times before was a melancholy trip. Even though it was midday and the sun was shining strongly around them, everything had changed so drastically it didn't look like the same town. There was so much damage. Trees split and broken, telephone lines down, houses leveled and the ground tore up everywhere as if a giant plow had been dragged through.

Klamath Falls was no longer Klamath Falls.

But so far not a trace of any ancient reptiles lurked anywhere. Strange. So okay, where were all the people and where were all the monsters? Unease rippled beneath Henry's nerves. It was as if he could feel the creatures out there somewhere. Were they smart enough to elude them…were they hiding…were there any left in town at all? Captain Harvey maintained there were. Hmmm.

What a picture it must make if there were anyone in Zeke's house, three tanks roaring up to the curb and a stream of soldiers, heavily armed, scrambling out and sprinting towards it. The house looked empty. The murky windows had nothing moving behind them. It was daytime so if lights were on in the house they wouldn't be visible. It was hard to tell if anyone was inside.

Henry led the men to the front door. He knocked loudly with the butt of his MP7. Knocked again and again. He was about to give up and kick the door in when it cracked open and Zeke's grizzled face peeped out at them. There was a bruise and bloody cuts on his left cheek. A nasty purple scrape on his lower face. At first, his expression was confused, frightened, and then the big grin came.

"Oh, my God, it's Henry! Am I glad to see you! Wilma, come out here. It's Henry!"

Then Wilma was peeking out as well. The door opened wider. She also had cuts and bruises on her face and she held her right arm carefully close to her side as if there were something wrong with it.

And out came the old man. He hugged Henry like a long lost son, so excited to see him. Henry had no choice but to hug him back.

"What are you doing here, Henry?" He looked behind the ranger and seeing Justin, Steven and McDowell, waved at them. Justin waved in return.

"What do you think? We've come searching for

you both. Ann found out you and Wilma had escaped from Rosie's and were coming back here. A really stupid move if you ask me. You actually believe we'd let you stay in a house surrounded by a town under siege by giant dinosaurs? A town evacuated because of the dangers? Not on your life. Ann's been a nervous wreck worrying over you two. And you know I can't let Ann worry more than she already does." *Not with the cancer back, she worries enough*, he almost said out loud, but didn't. Zeke didn't know Ann was sick again and no need to lay that on him now.

"I had to come home," Zeke, who looked as if he'd aged another twenty-years since Henry had last seen him, explained. "I had to find *little boy*. He can't survive without me. He needs me. He's just a baby." The old man's eyes were rheumy, his movements jittery. Easy to see he was distressed over something or he was ill.

"Well, has *little boy* shown up yet?"

Zeke's tone bereft, his voice fell to barely a whisper. "No, he hasn't. But it's not been long enough–"

"Zeke, you know he can't make it all the way back here. One itsy-bitsy squirrel. It is too far. I am sorry. Most likely he's joined up with other squirrels out in the forest somewhere in Idaho. He's safe with others of his kind. You know that, don't you?"

"I know. But I didn't just return for *little boy*," Zeke inserted. "I needed to see if my house was still standing. Collect my important papers I forgot to take with me. Memories of a lifetime. Everything I own in the world is here. I had to come back. That's what me and Wilma have been doing. Stashing our important papers and memories down in the basement in a safe I have."

"That's good then. Your memories are protected. But now you and Wilma have to go. It's still not safe. When did you get into town?"

"This morning." Zeke was trembling. He swayed and Henry steadied him.

Henry knew what was wrong then. "You and Wilma had trouble on the way in, didn't you?"

The older man's eyes shifted as he stared around. He seemed reluctant to answer, but did after a leaden pause, his eyes closing for a moment. "About five miles outside of town we were chased by some of the biggest dang monstrosities I've ever seen, bigger than the one that chased us here in town before we left. They nearly caught us but caused us to wreck the car. Thank goodness we weren't hurt that badly. Scratches, bumps and aches mainly. We barely escaped and had to hike in, sneaky-like. That hike was hard for me and Wilma. Old bones, you know. We had to hide from dinosaurs once or twice. Took us half the night to get here. We're pooped.

"Goodness gracious, are those damn creatures everywhere now? I...think I might even have seen some in the woods along the Idaho border. Not sure. We did not stick around to find out. Lordy, lordy, what has happened to the world?"

Henry didn't mince words after that. "You and Wilma are coming with us. Klamath Falls is a ghost town right now. Most of your neighbors are either dead, missing or have fled town. We have secured park headquarters where we're all living until the infestation is contained and there is room there for you and Wilma until things get better. Come on, I will escort you both to your ride."

Zeke looked towards the curb and his eyes grew wide.

"Tanks, huh? Never been in one of those big boys before."

"Well, now you will. You or Wilma need to bring anything with you?" He directed the question to both old people. "We don't have much room in the tanks but we can squeeze some necessities in for you if you want to bring them."

"Just clothes and personal items. We left what we brought from Rosie's in the wrecked car, but we have spares of everything we lost here. We'll go and pack them up in a jiffy and be right out."

"As long as it's quick." Henry pivoted around, his gun firm in his arms, and his eyes met Justin's before they swept over the neighborhood. He didn't trust the calmness. The lack of noise. His skin tingled. Something was out there. Something was watching and waiting. Coming.

The old folks reemerged with suitcases and a bag each and Justin and Henry ushered them to the second tank where they were pulled up and helped into the interior. Their suitcases and bags were divided between McDowell's two tanks and then all of them set off.

Henry had accomplished his mission and was anxious to return to headquarters and Ann. But there were other things he had to do before they left town.

Ann had asked him to check on something for her. Two somethings really.

He provided directions to his driver and the tanks rumbled through town and halted in front of the Klamath Falls Journal.

The building wasn't there. All that remained of it and the others around it were mounds of bricks, concrete chunks, glass and broken dreams. He hoped her insurance policy was up to date. Now Henry knew why Ann couldn't contact any of its phones. And the reporters? Heaven knew where they were. If they had been fortunate, they'd escaped town before the destruction. But sadly, Henry didn't think that was what had happened. Ann hadn't been able to reach them on their home or cell phones either and still couldn't. It was as if they'd just disappeared. This was really going to distress her. Her whole business was gone. And after all the money she'd spent redecorating, updating, and on new computers. This loss was going to hit her hard. But nothing compared to the loss she felt over her missing reporters. Ann still had hope they'd call or show up one day, but Henry didn't.

"One last stop before we return to home base," Henry informed McDowell.

Unless they bumped into dinosaurs on the way, then he'd be fighting them with her and Captain Harvey.

"Where this time, Chief Ranger?" McDowell inquired.

"Mercy Hospital on Third Street. We keep going

straight on Main and in about seven miles we make a left. The hospital is on the right at the top of the hill. My wife's doctor has an office there and since she hasn't been able to reach her, I told her I'd check on her as well."

The journey to the hospital mimicked the journey so far. Destruction and ruins everywhere. No people. Not even stray dogs and cats. No dinosaurs.

The absence of life anywhere of any kind and of threats were beginning to spook Henry. Captain Harvey swore the town was rife with prehistoric beasts but, so far, he hadn't seen one. Why?

The hospital was there, untouched. But empty. All the humans had left the premises. Henry, Justin and Steven walked briskly through the dim hallways and up to the door of Doctor William's' office. It was locked. No one was there. The building and offices all seemed vacant. Some doors were even unlocked. It looked as if everyone had left in a hurry.

More absent people.

They reassembled at the police station and Henry saw Justin and Steven off on their way. Since they were going in the opposite direction Zeke and Wilma had come from that morning they were fairly sure they'd be safe, or as safe as anyone could be anywhere these days.

And Justin was steadfast in his desire to get home and Henry, as unsure as he was about the young man going, also knew Laura and Phoebe needed him. He'd been gone too long already. But Henry did see to it that the two travelers had enough weapons to protect themselves if need be. It was the least he could do.

"Tell our daughter and granddaughter we miss them and we'll see them soon, I promise," Henry told his son-in-law.

"I will tell them," Justin said.

"And be careful out there, you two. Just because we haven't seen any monsters lately doesn't mean they aren't out there."

"How well we know that."

"Call me when you get there, Justin. So Ann and I don't worry."

"I will."

Justin and Steven said their goodbyes to everyone and got into the station wagon.

Henry watched as they drove off down the empty street through a desolate town.

Am I doing the right thing...letting them go unescorted into the reptilian wilderness? What if they run into some of those over-sized mutant T-Rexes? Well, they've been surprised by them once before and they did just fine. Escaped without a scratch. Of course, they were rescued by a tank....

He had to stop worrying about it. Justin wouldn't have been deterred from going home no matter what Henry had said. The young man was tenacious. He knew what he was doing and how to handle himself when dinosaurs attacked. He wanted to be with his wife and child in the worst way and Henry understood that well enough. He would have done the same thing if in Justin's place.

"Now what, Captain?" Henry, with McDowell, stood outside the police station by one of the Abrams after seeing Zeke and Wilma inside for something to eat and drink. Of course Zeke's house, as usual, had been foodless. Captain Harvey was in the station conferring with his soldiers. The sun was high in the sky but the air was cold. Freezing really. Henry was sure he smelled snow. Coming soon. Just what they needed, on top of an abnormally hot summer now they'd have an early winter.

"Captain Harvey and his men are going out to track that rogue dinosaur herd–he knows they're out there somewhere and he's resolved to rid the town of them–and he has requested I accompany him. You're welcome to join us." She gave him a smile. "We could use the help. And once we have made sure the town is empty of any unwanted predators we'll transport you and your friends back to park headquarters."

"Of course I'll ride along." Henry knew as soon as they handled that problem they could return to the park and the sooner the better. He didn't care for leaving his people and Ann alone too long, even though there were soldiers and rangers to protect them if the dinosaurs decided to make another appearance. But he'd still feel better once they were back there.

But the hunt did not turn up the results they'd anticipated. Though they took three tanks through town and searched the residential areas, the businesses and the bordering woods, there were no unusual creature sightings.

They did come across various residents who'd decided not to run away. An elderly married couple who had nowhere else to go. They were hiding in their basement and the husband came running out as the tanks went by. They were warned there could still be danger, but opted to stay. The man claimed his wife was sickly and he had to care for and stay with her. All the intricate medical equipment and supplies they needed were in the house. They couldn't leave.

They also discovered a few families that also wouldn't leave. Captain Harvey gave them all the same speech he had given the elderly couple but they, too, insisted on remaining. Since they had weapons and basements and had already gotten through the worst, they were allowed to stay in their homes. At least, as Henry had at first thought, Klamath Falls wasn't a complete ghost town.

But they didn't encounter any dinosaurs. And for that Henry was grateful. He wanted to go home to Ann.

The day was well along when the tanks wheeled into the police station's parking lot.

"You and your soldiers have done your jobs extremely well, Captain," McDowell spoke to Harvey when they got to the missing chief's office. "Looks like the town is liberated from its enemy."

"I wish it were so, Captain. But, like your Chief Ranger there," he'd nodded at Henry, "I don't believe they are really gone or done with this town. They are just laying low, plotting their next move. The fighting was so fierce here until three days ago. Then, suddenly, the intruders are gone? Not likely. I've been ordered to continue the daily patrols indefinitely and I will comply."

"Do you need us to stick around any longer?"

"No, you and Ranger Shore can take off to Crater

Lake. It'll be dark soon and I wouldn't want you to be on the road when it is. We're fine here."

Henry had been glad to hear that. Within minutes they had everyone in the tanks, a tight fit with the two old people and their things, and were on their way home. If they drove the Abrams at top speed McDowell projected they would make it by nightfall.

Everyone put their headsets back on and extras were given to Zeke and Wilma so they could all speak among themselves. The old people were especially chatty. Zeke asked a hundred questions and had Henry catch him up on what had been happening everywhere and with everyone. He was saddened to learn of Ranger Stanton and Kiley's death. Surprised that Ann and Henry, and all his rangers and McDowell's soldiers, were bunked down at headquarters and it now had a tall stockade fence around it.

But they were barely through town when their driver, Sergeant Gilbert, cried out, "Dinosaur! No, dinosaurs! On our left coming in from between the houses and, oh, my God, they're goliaths!

"And they've seen us. Here they come!"

"Evasive measures, Sergeant!" McDowell ordered. "Get far enough away and fire the cannons at them." The driver of the other tank had seen the beasts as well and was maneuvering away from them, raising and aiming their main gun. Henry's tank followed and the turret swung around so they could shoot at their pursuers.

The monitors only showed glimpses of the monsters coming after them. They were moving in fast and Henry could hear the roars and screeches over the rumble of the machine.

They must be giants, he thought, *I can feel the earth beneath us quaking*.

McDowell was radioing Captain Harvey for immediate assistance and describing the situation.

Wilma was scared and Zeke was comforting her, but Henry could see the fright as well in the old man's eyes.

"It's all right, Zeke," he told him over the racket of gunfire and dinosaur cries. "We've been fighting these brutes for weeks now and, believe me, they can't get to us in this tank. We're protected." He didn't tell him about the two tanks pushed over the rim into the lake. No need to tell him that.

"I believe you, Henry, but it's still scary."

"We will be fine, you'll see." Then the ride got crazier.

Their tank was bumping and bouncing down the road behind the first tank, weaving in and out among the houses and businesses, wherever they could find a conduit to get them away from the advancing creatures. The guns were blasting, McDowell shooting an AK 47 out of the open hatch, Private Harmon on the cannon, Gilbert driving; the dinosaurs were chomping up the ground. And Henry, unable to sit still and do nothing, with McDowell's permission, had taken control of the turret machine gun–he'd been shown how to use it often enough in the last month. And he had deadly aim with it.

The creatures on their tail were five of the largest dinosaurs Henry had seen so far and he'd seen many. Again of the species distantly related to the super predator Tyrannosaurus Rex. These must be the full grown fellas because they dwarfed the others. They had longer and stronger front arms, though, and their heads were smaller than a regular T-Rex, which allowed them to move quicker and more sure footed. Their teeth were as wicked as any T-Rex, yet bigger and sharper. They were like curved swords sticking out of their mouths. Weird thing was, the dinosaurs were also the strangest bluish-green color he had ever seen on any of the over-sized dinosaurs they'd encountered. Just great, big voracious Smurf monsters.

Where in the hell had they come from? Henry and the soldiers had driven through these streets a short while ago and there hadn't been a trace of any of them. How had they gotten to the heart of town so swiftly?

As the dinosaurs raced after them they tore up the town behind them. Smashing into and through houses and trees and leaving a wide path of wreckage in their wake. The town would never be the same, Henry mourned. It was a pile of rubble miles long. *I hope there aren't any townspeople in those houses.* With their immense size the creatures were leveling everything they stomped on.

Henry shot at them, aiming for the heads, but the monsters were so fleet on their feet, he missed more than he connected. And the creatures closed in around them as if they were a tag team circling in for the kill.

Captain McDowell had her hands full shooting at the monsters, directing her men, collaborating and strategizing with Captain Harvey on his way from the police station. The cannon fired over and over and everyone cheered when one of the T-Rexes cried out and collapsed in a heap to the ground, taking two houses with it. Its body writhed and its legs twitched at the skies.

"One down, four to go," Henry breathed as he continued to plug bullets into the tough hides. Of the four remaining attackers one was right in front of Henry's vehicle, closing the distance rapidly while the other three were blocking the other tank.

Henry shot at the one above them. The cannon following suit while McDowell fired at the one behind them. And a second and third beast fell thunderously to the earth, bleeding and clawing at the air.

More cheering. But the celebration didn't last. One of the surviving dinosaurs had caught up with the other tank and kicked it against a thick-trunked tree on the side of the road, while its scaly partner came in from another direction. The tree shook violently and snapped off half way up. The dinosaur rammed up against the armored vehicle and tried to bite it, its huge mouth enclosing the side of the turret the cannon wasn't on. It wrenched at the machine and dragged it a distance away from the tree; lifted it from the ground and shook it. Then the other dinosaur grabbed it, too, a tug-of-war, and tried to tip it over. Almost succeeded.

Henry aimed the machine gun at the two creatures and fired, targeting first the one assaulting the other tank. At the same time Private Harmon shelled them with the cannon. One of the monsters screamed and crumpled to the ground. The last dinosaur roared and turned on Henry's tank, its great long tail whipping out to jab against them. The vehicle bucked and slid across the grass, stopping at the edge of a deep creek. If the tank would have gone over it would have stuck in the crevice and been unable to move.

Wilma had cried out and hid her head against Zeke's shoulder. Zeke's frightened gaze found Henry's and Henry smiled bravely back. The old ones had gone through a lot since the dinosaur incidents had begun and Henry could tell they were tired and afraid. Henry only wanted to get them–all of them–back to the park safe and sound. He wanted out of Klamath Falls.

"It will be okay, you'll see. We are not beaten yet. Only one monster left to kill. Hold on, we will make it."

Zeke nodded, flashed Henry another smile and a thumbs up of encouragement.

The final dinosaur rammed into them and Henry felt the machine sliding…when the other tank, having maneuvered away from the tree and closer to them also began to shell the monster.

Suddenly they were surrounded by five of Captain Harvey's tanks, arriving to help.

"We thought we'd rescue your asses," Harvey's authoritative voice came over the intercom. "But I see by the carcasses spread around you really didn't need our help."

"We can always use your help, Captain," McDowell said loudly. "Ready whenever you are."

"Ready," Harvey replied and their cannons began

firing at the lone dinosaur.

But no one finished it off. One minute it was attacking and they were shooting at it and in the next, after posing to roar to the sky, probably because it realized it was outnumbered by the metal monsters tormenting it, it spun around and bounded away across the creek and thrashed into the woods on the other side. Then it was gone.

Henry suspected the reason it ran was because the other tanks had arrived. The creature was smart enough to know when it was beaten.

"Wow, can those things travel! Like quicksilver," Henry exclaimed. "Now I understand how they have hidden so well from Harvey's soldiers. I bet they're still all around in the woods. They have become proficient at hiding from the military. Clever bastards."

"Good," Zeke said over the intercom, "and they can just keep traveling. I want my town back, want my house back. I'm sick of being homeless."

Henry glanced at the old man. "Me and Ann, too. We all want to be able to go home." Someday. It hadn't escaped him that if these big monsters were concealing themselves so expertly in Klamath Falls that possibly they were still hiding out in the park's deep woods as well. Waiting for heaven knows what to resume their attacks or an organized full-fledged assault. And suddenly his optimism about his park being clear drained away. It couldn't be that easy now, could it?

"Should we turn around and return to the police station Ranger Shore," McDowell asked, "or do you want us to continue on to the park? Captain Harvey says we have the choice. He knows the town isn't free of dinosaurs but he says they can handle it. He is giving us a green light to leave."

"Yes, onward to the park. We need to be there because I don't believe the dinosaurs are done with us, either. They're hiding out somewhere and eventually they will resume their raids."

They said thank you and their goodbyes to Captain Harvey and his soldiers and the two tanks continued their passage to Crater Lake.

And Henry was relieved...for he could hear Ann calling him. Ann needed him. Something was terribly wrong. He could feel it in his heart.

"Let's move it," he said.

"You got it," McDowell responded. "We are on our way."

They couldn't get there fast enough for Henry. He had this really *bad* feeling. It'd hit him that Ann hadn't called him all day and that was unusual. He pulled out his cell phone and tried calling her, but he was only able to leave a message. It wasn't like Ann not to answer her phone.

Something *was* wrong.

*****

They rolled into headquarters as twilight's gray fingers crept in around them. They'd heard the gunfire, squawks and roars of dinosaurs, though, long before they got near the compound. Well, so much for the dinosaurs being gone from Crater Lake. That dream hadn't lasted long.

As they drew near Henry saw the dinosaur army,

of every species they'd met so far, surging against the stockade. The larger ones trying their best to tear down the fence and the smaller ones trying to jump over it. There were sections that were weakening. One was partially down. It wouldn't take much more to collapse it and let the monsters in. Bullets and shells were flying everywhere. The air was full of drifting gun powder and the cries of the combatants, human and reptile. It was like a scene out of Hades. Horrifyingly chaotic.

Henry had tried to contact someone inside but never reached anyone. It made sense now. They were busy fighting and trying to stay alive; couldn't hear the phones.

Captain McDowell, using military communications did contact the soldier she'd left in charge, Lieutenant Becker, and was informed the compound had been under heavy attack almost since the time they'd left that morning.

"How are we going to get in?" Henry was looking in all directions through the video screens, spying on the battle. "No way we're getting through that crowd of hissing mutants."

"Lieutenant Becker knows we are out here and I've asked him to send out backup to guide us in…as soon as there's a break in the fighting. In the meantime, we can do a surprise rear attack and help our inside people."

And that's what they did.

It was almost morning by the time the creatures were turned away from the stockade and chased off, or what was left of them anyway. The dinosaurs wouldn't give up and kept coming. The soldiers and rangers kept killing until they'd devastated the mass; scattered the remnants. The two tanks Henry and the others were in killed many of them and managed to evade their grasp by moving around the outside of the stockade at a high speed the whole time.

Henry and McDowell didn't receive their escort into headquarters. When there was a pause in the fighting Lieutenant Becker alerted them and told them to get to the gates in a hurry and they'd let them in. Which they did. The gates opened and both tanks drove through.

Ann was waiting for him as he climbed from the vehicle and after hugging and kissing each other, she hugged Zeke, who protested but allowed it, and then Wilma. She was so happy to see they were with him.

Together they walked into the building and Ann took Zeke and Wilma into Henry's office so they could rest on the air mattresses for a while. Then she joined him again as he stood talking to McDowell and a crowd of rangers and soldiers. He broke away immediately and put his arms around her as everyone smiled and watched. It was good to see there was more to life than just blood-thirsty creatures and one crisis after another. Two people in love filled that bill.

"Oh Henry, I am so glad you're back! I was so worried."

"And I was worried every second about you. How are you feeling?"

She smiled after kissing him. "I have been better but now that you are here, it's all okay. We're both all right and together again. Zeke and Wilma are here safe and sound. My prayers were answered."

"Mine, too. Have I got some tales for you." He shared her smile, still holding her near.

"I bet you have stories and so do I. Things went crazy after you left this morning."

"I saw." Henry hesitated. "I have a couple things to tell you about what we found in town."

"You don't need to. Zeke and Wilma have caught me up on things. Most things anyway. I know my business is gone. My doctor is MIA as are countless other people, including my employees. The town is a war zone and looks it."

"I am sorry, Ann."

She shook her head. "Don't be. I was going to sell the newspaper anyway. Now I'll just be collecting insurance for it. Whenever that'll be possible. I'm sure the insurance companies are overwhelmed right now with claims."

"I'm sure they are."

"But sooner or later I'll get that check and deposit it into our retirement account, end that chapter of my life and start a new one. It's what I was going to do anyway. I just feel sick about Vanessa and Jacob being missing. Dr. Williams. Sick about what's happened to the town. To us. Our park." Her eyes were sad.

"But thank God Zeke and Wilma are okay. That is one good thing. You saved them and I'm so happy they are here. I've been making a temporary bedroom for them out in one of the offices. Not done yet, but almost.

"I also told them if we ever get to reclaim our

cabin, they'll be welcome to stay with us as long as they need or want to. Zeke, of course, wants desperately to return to his own house but that might not be possible for a long time. Maybe never."

Henry met his wife's eyes. "You know, for that matter, we might not be going back to our home, either, for a long time. I thought we'd cleared the dinosaurs out of the park but now I am not so sure that's not true. I'm not going to lie to you, honey, I don't know when we'll be able to reclaim our cabin."

Ann lowered her head and said nothing.

*****

The rest of the day was quiet. The lull had turned into a retreat for what was left of the dinosaur army. The sun rose and they were faced with a massive cleanup of dead bodies again. No humans had been hurt. They had all been safe behind the walls.

"Patterson just telephoned," Ann related to Henry when he'd come in on a break from dead dinosaur disposal, "and he's on his way here now. One of the National Guard's helicopters is bringing him in. It will drop him down on a rope in front of our gates. We'll need to open them before a dinosaur gets him. He says he needs to talk to you and Justin. I told him Justin wasn't here, was heading home, and caught him up on what we have been through. As much as I could anyway. He couldn't talk long."

"So he will be here any minute, huh?"

"That's what he said."

"I'll get cleaned some up and wait."

"And I'll make you a sandwich. Not much to choose from these days. But I believe I can rustle up a stale cheese sandwich from somewhere."

"Thanks. That'd be sweet of you."

"Of course, I'm a sweet woman." And off she went to look for some cheese and bread.

Henry went to clean up and when he returned, he'd barely had time to gobble down his sandwich before he heard the helicopter outside come and go. It was strange to hear the rotors after so long an absence. They sounded good. Let him know they weren't alone in the world.

"Looks like our friend Patterson has arrived."

Then there was Patterson strolling in, arm in arm with McDowell. Henry was sure they'd hugged and kissed before entering headquarters because their flushed faces betrayed them. Being lovers he couldn't hold that against them.

"Hi old friend. Been a while. It's good to see you." Henry stood up and shook the man's hand. He couldn't help but notice Patterson somehow looked older, carrying a heavier burden, than the last time he'd seen him. There was a strange look in his eyes, too.

Oh, oh.

"You might not feel that way once I tell you what I have to tell you."

"Nah, it'll still be good to have you here whatever news–good or bad–you have for us. We've had our own disasters since you left. Nothing could surprise me anymore. Believe me."

Dinosaur Lake III: Infestation

Henry sent a knowing glance at Ann and she released a sigh. She too was studying Patterson and, intuitive woman that she was, probably guessed there was something even worse coming.

"Before you three start your little meeting," she turned to Patterson and McDowell, "can I get either or both of you some coffee? I just made a new pot."

"That sounds good. I've been running from airport to airport for weeks now and, let me tell you, their coffee sucks." Patterson moaned and lowered himself into a chair at the conference table where Henry had been eating his sandwich.

McDowell took a chair next to him. "Thank you, Ann. Coffee sounds great. After clean up duty all morning I need a short rest." The weariness as she sat down was apparent in the way she moved, in her face.

Ann went off to get the coffee.

"You talk to Justin yet?" Henry asked Patterson.

"I did. And with what I've learned, his news didn't make me feel any better."

"Oh, he blabbed about how the dinosaurs are spreading up the west coast down into California and up into Canada, huh? Not to mention we've had a real infestation of every sort of prehistoric nightmare here you can imagine…except, strangely enough, none of the flying gargoyles we dealt with here in the spring. Yet anyway. I've been continuously amazed at the mutants we've already seen and fought. All the varieties. How intelligent they are. I swear I'm beginning to think these dinosaurs have come in on space ships from other galaxies or something. They are such bizarre and alien creatures. Or sometimes I just fear I'm going insane.

"All right…what is *your* news? Does it trump mine?"

Ann returned with a plate of sandwiches and two cups of coffee. She must have run to the food area and run back to have made it so quickly. She hated to miss anything. He gave her *a take it easy now* look and she sat down.

"Ah, Ann's back. Excellent." Patterson acknowledged her with an inclusive gesture. "You're going to want to hear this, as well." He stopped speaking and glanced at the window then back to the people around him, a solemn expression on his face. A cry had come from outside. A dinosaur's cry.

"Yes?" Henry wanted to hear but didn't want to hear.

"You know I've been busy the last couple months on a secret international consulting case for the FBI?" The man had slipped his jacket off and draped it across the rear of his chair. "It's been real hush, hush and that's why I couldn't tell you or anyone else, not even my girlfriend here, anything about it. Until now. Now it doesn't matter because soon the whole world will be hearing about it and most places first hand."

Brushing his hair away from his forehead, it kept flopping down because he'd let it grow too long again, he was staring at Henry. His clothes, a white shirt and jeans, looked as if he'd slept in them. "They picked me for this particular job because of my earlier experiences with you. They knew I would believe whatever I discovered."

Henry waited. They all waited.

"Justin has it partly right. Dinosaurs are birthing along the west coast and up into Canada, fueled by the ever increasing volcano eruptions, the deep-ground earthquakes and the expanding reach of the underground lava flow. A heavy concentration especially in places with heavy forest wilderness and active volcanoes; places where they've been able to hide and not be seen as easily unless they wanted to be...until now. But I found it's far, far worse than that.

"Dinosaurs are showing up *all over the world* in many countries. Those countries are having unprecedentedly powerful earthquakes and volcanic eruptions too. What they're uncovering are unhatched dinosaur eggs that are now hatching. So the infestation isn't just in the Western hemisphere but in the Northern and Eastern as well. There has been sightings and sometimes even direct contact everywhere all over the planet. I know. I've been to Great Britain, Brazil, China, Africa, and other countries meeting with people who have found traces of, heard or seen live dinosaurs or have had experiences with them. I was shocked at how many have in the last six years.

"This year alone the number of encounters and sightings have exploded exponentially. It's simply a matter of time before everyone everywhere will know we've been *invaded*." Patterson's smirk wasn't a nice one. He leaned back in his chair and rubbed his eyes, clearly exhausted now that he'd delivered his bad news.

Henry was horrorstruck. Oh, he'd known the problem was worse this time; hell his park was ground zero, or so he'd thought, but *all over the world?* Oh, my God.

What was to become of the human race now that primeval predators were challenging their right to the planet? Predators that weren't only stronger, bigger and faster than their ancestors had been...but were capable of using weapons like rocks and sticks. Of organizing. What would come next? They'd learn to ride horses, swing swords and shoot guns? Make bombs? The image of dinosaurs on horses didn't make him smile. The idea of dinosaurs similar to the vicious ones they'd been warring with the previous weeks hatching out across the world scared the bejesus out of him. As bad as everything had been up until now–all the horrible experiences and deaths–nothing compared with what could come.

He looked over at Ann. Her eyes were shut, her face and lips whiter than skin should be. She looked so weak, so unwell he reached over and gently touched her arm. "Are you all right?" he whispered, fear a sharp sliver of pain in his chest.

"*All over the world*," she whispered. "Oh, my, my, my. It's worse than we ever dreamed. What is going to become of humanity now?" Her eyes glittered with fever and Henry was hit with guilt because he knew she should be getting medical care, not be trapped in a park building battling monsters. But how could he get her out of a dinosaur infested park, state and country and find her the help she needed? For the first time since the troubles had begun, he felt defeated. Tired beyond words.

He had Patterson's attention again. "What is our government going to do about this?" He didn't ask about the world because each country would have to deal with their own infestation. Right now he only cared about his country, his state, his park. His wife. It's all he could handle at the moment.

Patterson slightly lifted then dropped his shoulders. "Beats me. I turned in my reports and flew here. I'm sure the places I found evidence of the dinosaurs existence will discover soon what I did and once they have accepted the reality of it it's up to them to deal with it. Our country has their own dinosaurs to face."

Henry sat there with his friends speechless for a while. No one said anything. What was there to say? The worst had happened and their lives, their world would never be the same.

McDowell was the first one to speak again. "Henry, you know this changes things?"

"I know." He'd taken Ann's cold hand and held it tightly. He noticed Patterson was holding McDowell's hand opening now. Why not? This could be the beginning of the end of life as they had all known it their whole lives. He addressed his next question to Patterson again. "You said there have been sightings and encounters…how bad were they? Has the final war begun?"

"Oh, it's begun all right. What's been happening here the last month has been happening in many places. Take a look on the Internet. There are You Tube videos galore with dinosaurs in them. Most people watch them and think they're fake…but they are not. The first person accounts of what are occurring have grown, too. I'm sure some people are still snickering at the You Tube videos and reports but more are believing, accepting, because it's happening to them."

Henry knew about the videos on the Internet. Ann had kept him up to date every evening with what she'd seen on them. He'd known it would only be a matter of time.

"We can't do anything about the world's situation," Ann interjected, "but what are we going to do about ours? Here and now? Henry, does this mean we can't ever go home?"

It was hard for Henry to tell her the truth, yet he knew he had to do it. He and Ann never lied to each other, or tried not to anyway.

"I've done some soul searching about that, Ann, and I have to confess I feel it's not safe right now to live in the cabin. Or for any of us to go anywhere unattended by an armored vehicle and soldiers with weapons. We're going to have to stay here. I have no idea how long. I am so sorry." He squeezed her hand.

She merely bobbed her head. "I guess I knew that. We stay here." Acceptance in her words. She was a realist and always had been. It was one of the things he'd always loved about her.

They listened to everything Patterson had heard and seen on his world tour and then Henry caught him up on their events. Patterson was sad to hear about Ranger Stanton and Kiley's deaths. He'd known and liked both of them.

Dinosaur Lake III: Infestation

"I can't believe they didn't make it. They both seemed so…indestructible. S.O.B. dinosaurs," Patterson groused. "How many more of us will be gone by this time next year…or a couple of years from now because of this dinosaur epidemic?"

Henry stared at him. What a defeatist thing to say. Until he realized how true it was. How very true.

How many more of them would be dead before the dinosaur wars would be over?

He had no idea. And then he couldn't bear to think about it any longer. It was so much easier to sit and listen to Patterson weave stories about what he'd learned since he'd been gone. Over the years Henry had known him the man had evolved into quite the storyteller. But then any distraction from their recent realities was welcome.

They all sat and talked for a long time. It was good to have friends around, to share your fears with. It almost made them manageable.

*****

Late that night when everyone else was sleeping, Patterson and Henry sat up drinking the bottle of whiskey Patterson had brought and continued talking.

"What are you going to do now, Patterson?" Henry was bleary eyed. It'd been a long day in a longer month. But he had to have private words with his friend because the man was helicoptering out early the next morning.

"I'm expected at FBI headquarters to give them

a briefing. I should have left before now, but if I don't get some sleep and spend a little time with my girl I'm going to have a nervous breakdown. Not to mention I'm not going anywhere in the dark. I don't want to get eaten. Sounds like the natives are restless out there." He turned his head to look at the night reflected in the windows.

There was the near and distant roaring and snarling clamor of dinosaurs. They were out there. Gathering. Doing whatever the hell they did between assaults. Square dancing maybe or playing Tiddlywinks.

"And you?" Patterson looked around the room with the large table in the middle.

Beyond it there were people bunking down for the night. Growing quiet. A comfortable rhythm had developed in their everyday living. Friendships had been formed. Alliances made. Sleeping spaces staked out. They had become one large family with all the dysfunction and quirks as well.

"I guess we stay here, keep going out on patrols and fighting until we're sure the park is ours again. Safety in numbers, you know. After all that's occurred I understand things can't be as they were before. After what you and Justin have told me, I'm afraid this is a new age. And we must learn how to live in it."

"Yep, it's a new age. The new age of dinosaurs. The human race is going to have to fight for this planet now against a predator greater than we are. Survival of the fittest."

"Don't I know it. Survival of the fittest."

"Now Henry…about Ann…."

After their conversation they exchanged goodnights and in the morning Henry accompanied Patterson to an open space among the trees not too far from headquarters and watched as he flew away in a helicopter.

Then Henry returned to headquarters and their new life went on.

Chapter 14
Epilogue

It was late November and Henry and his people had been living at headquarters for months. They'd been difficult months. Life has slowly been adapted to. When supplies grew thin they sent out hunting parties for rabbits or deer, even bear at times, and rationed their food. Game was thin, though. The dinosaurs had eaten most of the wild animals. Thank goodness Henry had in some ways foreseen this exact emergency and had stocked the storage sheds with nonperishable foodstuffs and other necessary items in the spring when they'd had the gargoyle infestation. His foresight was a godsend because the outside world was slowly falling apart.

In the last couple weeks having supplies trucked or flown in was no longer an option. The new reality and all the dangers it created was sinking in. More each day the Internet was rampant with dinosaur tales. Battle scenes. Human death tolls. Now the evening news, which they viewed on their laptops, was taken over by dinosaur madness. And the planet had swiftly fallen into two opposing camps: one wanted to preserve the amazing creatures that were living dinosaurs resurrected and the other camp wanted to hunt the suckers down and savagely butcher every last one of them. The world was going crazy.

Heck, and there was money to be made. For a

thousand dollars you could go on a dinosaur safari in at least five countries. Biggest dinosaur bagged gave you a grand prize of twenty-thousand and bragging rights. The safaris were a great hit. The in thing. There was a damn waiting list. Hunters for sport and cash.

Insane human idiots, all of them, Henry fumed. It wasn't a game. The dinosaurs were dead serious about taking over the planet and shoving humankind into extinction. So humans had better take heed. Stop fooling around. Take it dead serious as well.

Henry and his friends were still fighting the creatures, not as a game but to survive.

Ann was no longer with them. Patterson sent a helicopter for her days after he had left and she'd been flown to Justin and Laura's home hours away. She'd needed to begin her chemotherapy treatments and needed nursing, more than Henry could give her locked in a building with soldiers and rangers and skirmishing with giant reptiles every day. While Henry remained to continue the fight with his men.

Ann understood. Laura and Justin would care for her and Ann was thrilled to be with her daughter who was preparing to have her second child. It was the best solution for Ann. For all of them.

Henry missed her terribly and spoke to her by phone every evening or by Skype if he could. Their forced separation made him work harder to clean the park up; not that it seemed to be helping any. The dinosaurs kept multiplying no matter how many they exterminated. Where were they all coming from?

But Henry and his people weren't alone, it seemed everyone everywhere was fending off prehistoric beasts.

Henry wanted his old life back. Wanted his family and Ann back. Desperately.

The world wasn't cooperating.

Ann called him late the night before Thanksgiving.

"Laura had her baby this morning, sweetheart. Nine pounds three ounces. She and the child, Timothy Logan, are doing fine. There will be no Thanksgiving dinner though. We'll be here at the hospital tomorrow, as well. They will let Laura come home the day after," she intoned in the whispery voice she'd acquired the last few weeks. Chemotherapy, which she'd recently finished under a new doctor's care, had changed her. Her illness was changing her. Laura had said she was weaker and had lost weight. Was a stick. Her skin tight across her bones and her eyes dull. Laura was worried about her.

Henry had wanted to catch a helicopter ride to Justin and Laura's house for a Thanksgiving visit and be with her, his family, for a short while at least but a round of especially virulent dinosaur attacks sunk that plan. Turns out not going for Thanksgiving then would be okay as he wouldn't miss anything because there was no Thanksgiving dinner to go to. He could deal with the new park emergency and see his family afterwards.

It worked for him. He hated hospitals anyway. Must have had something to do with getting shot when he'd been a cop sixteen years ago. He'd spent way too much time recuperating in that New York hospital. Hospitals and all they stood for reminded him of an awful time in his life. Almost dying. The small boy he'd accidently and tragically killed. Ann knew all about that, too. She'd done everything she could to keep him out of hospitals since.

"That's great, honey. We have a grandson." It was the first purely happy thing to happen to them in months and he was beyond grateful for it. God, he wanted to be there, see his wife, his daughter and his newborn grandson.

Soon.

"Hey, Justin wants to gab with you before we hang up," she finished after they were done conversing. The phone was given to his son-in-law.

"Congratulations, *dad*. You have a son. You must be so happy. And, hot dog! I have a grandson."

Justin's voice when he responded wasn't as elated as Henry would have thought it would be, which was an instant tip off.

"Oh, I'm thrilled to be a father and have a son. I'm over the moon actually." The young paleontologist's voice dropped in volume. Henry had to strain to hear his next rushed words. "I don't have much time Henry, Ann just stepped away for a moment and I don't want to scare her.

I have to tell you something important."

"What's wrong?"

"Henry, the dinosaurs are here. *Here in our town*. I left the hospital for a short time to collect clothes and toiletries for Laura from the house and as I was leaving, I saw *them*. In the woods behind the house. A herd of those scrappy looking smaller stone-throwing ones like those you have in the park, but larger. They were trapping cars of people down the street, tearing off the doors, breaking the windows, and yanking them out. It was horrible. And in the distance I saw a mutant T-Rex coming to join them—and then another and another. Monsters three stories tall. So I couldn't help those poor people. I felt so bad, but I only had my rifle with me and knew I had to return to my wife, Phoebe, Ann and Laura at the hospital. I had to protect them if it got worse.

"Then I get to the hospital and there's more creatures swarming outside the parking lot in that wooded area that surrounds the building. An oversized variety of those feathered velociraptors. Thank God they didn't see me. I barely escaped. But the town is overrun with dinosaurs and the police, army and their gunfire are suddenly everywhere. It's a mad house. We have to get out of here. And we can't go back to the house."

There was no hesitation on Henry's part. "Come here. As soon as you can. We've spent more time further fortifying the compound and it's safer now than any other place I can think of.

Dinosaur Lake III: Infestation

We have rangers, soldiers, guns and tanks. We are a fortress."

"Do you have room for us? Steven will be with us. He showed up two days ago when his neighborhood became infected. He didn't know where else to go."

"He's welcome. Another hunter always is. We will make room. I'd been thinking of taking three of our outside supply sheds and converting them into extra shelters for our people. We've been here longer than I thought we would be and we could use the extra living spaces. You and your family can have any one of the three you want. It'll be primitive, small, but I'm sure Ann and Laura will make it a home for all of you."

Justin didn't hesitate either. "Okay. We're coming. As soon as Laura's well enough to leave the hospital we will be on the road. Thank you Henry."

"Don't thank me. I want my family to be safe as much as you do and being here now seems to be the safest place. Just be careful driving down. We have snow on the ground and they're forecasting more any time. There has been reports of dinosaur sightings between there and here, too. Call me when you get near Klamath Falls and I'll have Captain Harvey come out in tanks to meet you, get you here."

"Okay. See you soon."

"Be careful Justin. Take care of my family. Get them and you all here alive."

Henry held the cell phone in his hands for a long time after he'd rung off, his mind heavy with his thoughts. Oh, the world was changing…had changed. Nothing would ever be the same. He got up and walked to the window. Night time.

A strange animal's primitive cry rang out and echoed on the winds. Then another and another. Communicating with each other. No doubt chattering about how to kill the humans.

It had begun to snow. A soft swirling of white flakes.

Please God, he prayed, *let my family get here safely.*

*****

His prayers were answered two days after that when his wife, Steven, Justin and his family arrived at their front gates at twilight as the snow began to fall in earnest. They couldn't have timed it better. Extremely heavy snowfall was predicted that evening.

Henry was so happy they were all okay and back with him, his infant grandson, too, that for a short time he nearly forgot the mess they were all in.

Ann was happy to be with Zeke and Wilma again. The old people had adjusted exceptionally well to living in the compound and had made themselves useful. Both Wilma and Zeke had taken to cooking for everyone and Zeke, when his energy allowed, helped patrol along the fence when he was needed. Funny thing was, Zeke seemed to enjoy being there with everyone. He had thrived. Wilma, too. They had become one of them.

Henry had one of the heated storage units cleaned out and it was waiting for Justin's family, Steve included. Drained and needing rest, they were settled in by evening and he and Ann retired to their bedroom. Everything else could wait until the following day.

Later, he held his frail wife gently in his arms and listened as she told him about her life the last few months, the cancer treatments and how frightening the journey coming there had been. How they'd spied dinosaurs along the way and had to either outrun them or evade them.

"They are everywhere now," she'd muttered. "We also saw a flock of those gargoyles in the sky, but they were flying in the opposite direction, thank God. So now they're back, too.

"How have the dinosaurs spread so far so quickly?" she moaned.

"Justin believes they've been breeding clandestinely since the first one we fought so many years ago…perhaps even for the last decade or longer in the wildest and most primitive places. But hiding. Waiting until their numbers were great enough to actually challenge us. Now they have the numbers."

"That would mean they're extremely organized and cunning to plan that far ahead."

"I know. But it is the only thing that makes sense. Now they're coming out to face us, a united front."

"Good God, tell me this is just some

nightmare?"

"Wish I could, honey, but it's not. Sorry."

"You and me both. What a world our children and grandchildren have inherited," she said, shaking her head. She'd lost weight and was thinner than he'd ever seen her. Yet her smile and her spirit were still strong. She was still his Ann. No cancer was going to defeat her. She had completed chemo, had the MRI results which showed the tumors had somewhat shrunk and she had medicine to take daily, but would need follow up and more tests within six months.

That concerned Henry...what state would the world be in by then? Would they be able to get her to a hospital and doctors? Would there be hospitals and doctors? It worried him how she'd get the care she'd need when the time came. But for now, Ann was with him; she'd had her treatments and what could be done for her had been done. She had a six month supply of medicines. His family was with him, safe and sound and together. It was the best he could hope for in their crazy new existence, whatever the future would bring.

*****

Hours after that, as Ann lay lightly sleeping behind him, he stood at the window as he had so many nights before. He wasn't able to sleep. Not yet. Too much to be done. Too much on his mind. Contentment mingling with dread.

Outside the blizzard had come with below

freezing temperatures. Visibility was almost nil. Ice laced the glass in front of him. At least the Arctic cold and the snow would keep the dinosaurs away and in their lairs and they'd all have a blessed respite from battling them, a sort of peace for a while. Thank God.

His earlier happiness at being a new grandfather had been diminished by the danger his family, the world, was in. The circumstances they found themselves in. He was tired of this compound life and he wondered how much longer they'd have to live behind tall fences like prisoners, with guns slung over their shoulders, surrounded by soldiers and tanks, waiting for the next offensive.

Forever?

He stared at the cascading white stuff a little longer. He was bone tired, brooding over how his life had changed so much in the last year. At times he felt as if he were living in a never ending horror novel or one of those cheap Sci-Fi movies–*Dinosaur Commandos*–and he kept praying he'd just wake up. His whole life now had become one of fighting, killing monsters– and simple survival.

Justin had spoken to him earlier about how unreliable the telephones, cell phones and Internet were becoming. Sometimes he couldn't log in at all.

"Lots of crazies are saying the world is ending and the dinosaurs are just the beginning. They're disrupting the Internet with viruses or Trojans. It's all going to get worse before it gets better," he'd predicted gloomily. "And one of the last articles I read on the web was about how many police forces were being militarized and deployed in almost every state along with the National Guards to fight the creatures. Marshall Law. I believe soon that will be worldwide as well, but recently information isn't coming as freely from the rest of the world on that subject. Tonight I couldn't raise the Internet at all. It was just...down. No explanation, nothing."

Henry hadn't had much to say about it. He'd been expecting those eventualities for a while. And Justin was right, it wasn't going to get any better.

On the other side of the glass the snow kept falling, as large as white leaves. He shivered.

And what would the spring bring? He couldn't bear to think of it. He would tomorrow.

He sighed, turned from the window, switched off the light and, with draggy steps, went to his bed that now, thankfully, had his wife in it.

Sleep was his only escape these days...unless he had more of those crazy dinosaur dreams. He'd begun having them again lately. Weird vignettes where dinosaurs were the main characters and had all the power. Dinosaurs hiding everywhere ready to attack and devour him, his men, friends and family. Dinosaurs running the world, sitting in the United Nations around shiny mahogany tables planning what to do with the last of the doomed human race they had imprisoned in concentration camps. Dinosaurs throwing rocks, firing guns, eating hamburgers made of human meat; dinosaurs in suits with murder in their creepy reptilian eyes. Multiplying faster than anyone could have foreseen. Dinosaurs ruling the earth. No room or place for men anymore.

A dinosaur world.

It seemed they stalked him everywhere now, awake and asleep, and had for a long time. He could barely remember when his life had been anything else but running from, chasing or fighting the bastards. He could barely recall his old mundane life but missed it terribly.

Heaven help him. Heaven help the world.

But he would keep fighting, never give up. They all would. Their world had changed, was changing more now...but it was *their* world, not the dinosaur's, and they'd win it back. No matter how hard they would have to fight or how long.

Of course, they'd win it back.

What other choice did they have?

*If this is the first of my dinosaur books you've read, be sure to check out its two prequels Dinosaur Lake (which was a 2014 Epic EBook Awards *Finalist* in their Suspense/Thriller Category) and Dinosaur Lake II: Dinosaurs Arising. Both, as well as my twenty-two audio books are also available. Dinosaur Lake IV: Dinosaur Wars will be for sale in early 2017.*

About **Kathryn Meyer Griffith**...

Since childhood I've been an artist and worked as a graphic designer in the corporate world and for newspapers for twenty-three years before I quit to write full time. But I'd already begun writing novels at 21, over forty-four years ago now, and have had twenty-one (eleven romantic horror, two horror novels, two romantic SF horror, one romantic suspense, one romantic time travel, one historical romance and four murder mysteries) previous novels, two novellas and twelve short stories originally published from Leisure Books, Zebra Books, Avalon Books, The Wild Rose Press, Damnation Books/Eternal Press. These days I self-publish exclusively. My Dinosaur Lake novels and my Spookie Town Murder Mysteries are my best-sellers.

I've been married to Russell for thirty-seven years; have a son, James, and two grandchildren, Joshua and Caitlyn, and I live in a small quaint town in Illinois, which is right across the JB Bridge from St. Louis, Mo. We have a quirky cat, Sasha, and the three of us live happily in an old house in the heart of town. Though I've been an artist, and a folk singer in my youth with my brother Jim, writing has always been my greatest passion, my butterfly stage, and I'll probably write stories until the day I die...or until my memory goes.

2012 EPIC EBOOK AWARDS *Finalist* for my

horror novel **The Last Vampire**-*Revised Author's Edition* ~ 2014 EPIC EBOOK AWARDS * Finalist * for her thriller novel **Dinosaur Lake.**

<u>**Novels and short stories from Kathryn Meyer Griffith:**</u>
Evil Stalks the Night, The Heart of the Rose, Blood Forged, Vampire Blood, The Last Vampire, Witches, The Nameless One short story, The Calling, Egyptian Heart, Winter's Journey, The Ice Bridge, Don't Look Back, Agnes, A Time of Demons and Angels, The Woman in Crimson, Human No Longer, Four Spooky Short Stories Collection, Forever and Always Romantic Short, Night Carnival Short Story, Scraps of Paper, All Things Slip Away, Ghosts Beneath Us, Dinosaur Lake, Dinosaur Lake II: Dinosaurs Arising and Dinosaur Lake III: Infestation.

*All Kathryn Meyer Griffith's Amazon books can be found here:
http://tinyurl.com/oqctw7k

*All her Audible.com audio books here:
http://tinyurl.com/oz7c4or

My Websites:
Twitter: https://twitter.com/KathrynG64
My Blog: https://kathrynmeyergriffith.wordpress.com/
https://www.facebook.com/pages/Kathryn-Meyer-Griffith/579206748758534
http://www.authorsden.com/kathrynmeyergriffith
https://www.goodreads.com/author/show/889499.Kathryn_Meyer_Griffith
https://www.amazon.com/author/kgriffith
http://en.gravatar.com/kathrynmeyergriffith
http://www.amazon.com/-/e/B001KHIXNS

CPSIA information can be obtained
at www.ICGtesting.com
Printed in the USA
BVOW03s1929220617
487620BV00001B/2/P